Praise for Mason Cross

'Terrific stuff!' Ian Rankin

'Mason Cross is a thriller writer for the future who produces the kind of fast-paced, high octane thrillers that I love to read' Simon Kernick

'So pacy, I'm exhausted! Definitely one to read if you like your thrillers thrilling' Emma Kavanagh

'On of the most interesting 'loner' heroes to have arrived in rece t years . . . Told with pace and vigour by a writer who seer s to have a natural aptitude for thrillers, it is not to be miss d' *Daily Mail*

'If y u're a thriller fan who packs a summer blockbuster as a h day read – then don't leave home without this'
Peterborough Evening Telegraph

'P -pounding. Mason Cross launches into *The Killing Sea n* with no-holds barred . . . Prepare to read all night'
Lisa Gardner

'Mason Cross has created an enigmatic character in Carter Blake . . . The writing is taut, intelligent, oozes suspense'
Matt Hilton, author of the Joe Hunter thrillers

'Ac fans rejoice, there's a new name on the Scottish thriller squad. He plays fast, he plays dirty and, with this calibre of high octane action, he'll definitely be taking prisoners' *Daily Record*

Mason Cross is a British novelist whose debut novel *The Killing Season* was longlisted for the Theakstons Old Peculier Crime Book of the Year 2015. His second novel, *The Samaritan*, also featuring his inimitable lead character Carter Blake, was selected as a Richard & Judy Book Club pick. Mason has written a number of short stories, including *A Living*, which was shortlisted for the Quick Reads 'Get Britain Reading' Awards, and *Expiry Date*, published in Ellery Queen. He lives near Glasgow with his wife and three children.

To find out more, visit his website or follow him on Twitter or Facebook.

www.masoncross.net
🐦 @MasonCrossBooks
📘 /MrMasonCross/

By Mason Cross

The Killing Season
The Samaritan
The Time to Kill
Don't Look for Me

DON'T LOOK FOR ME

MASON CROSS

ORION

An Orion paperback

First published in Great Britain in 2017 by Orion Books,
This paperback edition published in 2018 by Orion Books,
an imprint of The Orion Publishing Group Ltd,
Carmelite House, 50 Victoria Embankment,
London EC4Y 0DZ

An Hachette UK Company

10 9 8 7 6 5 4 3 2 1

A CIP catalogue record for this book
is available from the British Library.

ISBN 978 1 4091 5969 8

Typeset by Deltatype Ltd, Birkenhead, Merseyside

Printed and bound in Great Britain by Clays Ltd, St Ives plc

MIX
Paper from
responsible sources
FSC   FSC® C104740
www.fsc.org

www.orionbooks.co.uk

To Ava – keep writing

PROLOGUE

You have to disappear.

Carol Langford took one last look around the small apartment. It had been four days since she had last spoken to its owner. Four days since the phone call, after Senator John Carlson and his wife had been murdered.

She remembered the terrible quality of the line. Not surprising, when she discovered that he was calling her from seven thousand miles away. She remembered how the static couldn't mask the pain in his voice: physical, as well as the other kind. He was hurting. Trying and failing to hide it.

She thought about how he hadn't really answered any of her questions. But that was standard, of course. What was he doing over there? What did he have to do with the death ... no, the *assassination* of her boss? Who exactly was it that she had to fear so much?

Who the hell was he, really?

No. The conversation had been one-way, as usual. Don't go near the office. Go to this address. Lose your phone.

You have to disappear.

Four days. She had left the apartment only once in that time, to buy bottles of water and some toiletries from the CVS two blocks away. After hours of watching rolling news coverage of the assassination, going outside had been a terrifying experience. She was constantly on edge, flinching when she caught the eye of someone smoking in a doorway, or when one of the other pedestrians veered a little too close to her on the sidewalk. On reaching the store, she immediately averted her eyes from the rack of newspapers, but not before she saw the senator's face smiling back from every one of the front pages. Almost as an afterthought, she had picked up a pack of Revlon black hair dye.

Four days of confinement to this tiny apartment, with its window looking out on a brick wall. Four days of ordering takeout with the cheap cell phone he had left, paying with cash from the bundle in the closet. There were so many other preparations: IDs in three different names, cash in different currencies, a set of car keys. The gun.

Who did that? What kind of person maintains an apartment ready for when they need to disappear? She had had four days to ponder that question now, and she kept coming back to one conclusion: she didn't know what kind of person did that. And that meant she really didn't know him, period. All she really knew was that he was involved, somehow. He had called to warn her, so perhaps that meant he hadn't known exactly what was going to happen to the senator. But he was a part of it—that much was certain.

Too late, she had realized how far her focus on career had taken her from a normal life, even before the man with inquisitive green eyes had walked into the foyer of Carlson's building all those weeks ago. Her parents were both gone. There had never been any siblings. Friends and acquaintances had gradually melted away since college, until the only people she ever talked to were work people. She wished there was somebody she could call. But then, even if there was, could she be sure she wouldn't be putting them in mortal danger?

She had avoided coming to the decision at first. She had forced herself to try to think rationally, to wait for the anger to burn off. But it hadn't; it had only intensified. It was only in the last hour that she had made up her mind. That last time they talked would be the last time they would ever talk. She had thought she loved him. Now? She wasn't sure what she thought. But it didn't matter anymore.

She took the last two bottles of water from the refrigerator and walked over to the coffee table where the canvas backpack was sitting. The pack was almost full. She put the bottles of water on top of the bundled-up shirts, which were stuffed on top of the nearly five thousand dollars in cash from the closet. One last time she wondered about taking the gun, and one last time she decided that it would be more of a burden than a benefit, given she had no firearms permit and no real idea of how to use it. She wondered if that would have to change. She zipped the pack closed and lifted it to the ground.

In two strides, she crossed the floor to the breakfast counter that marked the boundary between the living room and the galley kitchen, and sat down on the wooden stool. There were only three items on the counter: a pen, a sheet of notepaper, and an envelope.

Over the last four days, Carol had written a hundred letters to him in her mind. The message changed each time she went over it. Sometimes it was a few lines, sometimes several pages. There was so much she wanted to say. But now, sitting in front of the paper with pen in hand for the first time, her very last act in this apartment, it all seemed to become very simple.

She took a breath and wrote the message. Four words. She breathed out.

She folded the notepaper in half and placed it in the

3

envelope. She put on her coat and hat, slung the pack over her shoulders, and walked out of the door, closing it behind her without looking back. She walked down the six flights of stairs and through the lobby and out onto the sidewalk. She glanced quickly up and down the street, uneasy after four days of confinement. The people rushed past in each direction, paying her no heed.

It was as though she wasn't there.

PRESENT DAY

1

Over a hundred degrees today, easy. The noon sun beat down relentlessly and radiated back up from the pitted concrete beneath his feet. It felt like being slowly microwaved. Trenton Gage peered into the darkness in front of him and decided that Laurence Farnam had unwittingly done him a favor when he picked this place to hide from what was coming.

He forced himself to linger outside of the mouth of the tunnel for a little longer, surveying the road and ensuring that there were no prying eyes watching where he was going. Without thinking about it, he touched a finger to the thin, crescent-shaped scar on his cheek. The scar, a souvenir of the last time he had gotten careless, always itched in the heat. When he had satisfied himself that there were no onlookers, Gage took his sunglasses off, narrowing his eyes against the glare as he approached the entrance. Although the storm drain was more than wide and tall enough for him, he paused a little before he went fully inside. A big man's natural caution on approaching a confined space.

As he stepped across the shade line, the temperature plummeted blissfully. It grew cooler still with every step, as the tunnel grew darker. The respite from the heat was so welcome that he almost didn't mind the smell. A heady

7

mixture of damp and decay, with an undertone of excrement.

The main tunnel was a large rectangle, slightly curved at the corners: ten feet wide by eight feet high; the walls were molded concrete. He knew that this stretch was a mere fraction of the whole system: a network of tunnels that branched and spread beneath the city above like the roots of a great oak. In an ideal world, he would have a map, but that resource would have been difficult to procure at short notice. People weren't supposed to be down here. He supposed he was probably violating some trespassing laws, but he knew he was far from the only one. Tourists are sometimes surprised that Las Vegas seems to have fewer rough sleepers in evidence on the streets when compared to other major American or European cities. They're there, of course, probably in greater numbers, if anything. But during the long daylight hours of unremitting heat, they go underground.

A map would have been an asset, certainly, but he had something better: a guide. Or at least, he did if Meyer had been on the level. Gage would be very disappointed if Meyer failed to deliver. He would be sure to make that disappointment clear.

He paused and surveyed the dank surroundings. The last target he had hunted had been a hedge fund manager, tracked across four states and eventually cornered in a plush hotel room in Dallas. Aside from the obvious differences between that job and this, Gage's usual maxim held true: the best way to find someone was to let someone else show you the way.

There was a small trickle of water along the dead center of the tunnel. In one of Vegas's occasional flash floods, it would be a lot wetter down here, but the system was big enough to cope with the worst. As Gage got farther from the entrance, the darkness gradually exceeded his eyes' ability to compensate, and he switched on the Maglite in his left hand, illuminating the stretch ahead. He heard a squeal from up ahead, beyond the field of the beam, and saw two tiny pinpoints of reflected light which vanished immediately as the rodent turned tail and fled deeper into the darkness.

Gage shined the beam of the flashlight around and immediately saw some graffiti on the wall, sprayed in red. *Ever Been Unlucky*, the graffiti asked. At least, Gage assumed it was a question, despite the absence of a question mark. Gage didn't believe in luck. It was another point to add to the long list of reasons he didn't belong in Sin City. He turned the flashlight beam back to the ground and illuminated some man-made tumbleweed: sheets of newspaper, porno flyers, an empty bottle of Seagram's, a single sneaker.

Gage kept walking, listening to the echo of his footsteps and the muted hum of the traffic above him. In five minutes, he estimated he had covered around a quarter-mile. He was probably beneath the Beltway. Sure enough, just as Meyer had said, he found a triangle sprayed on the wall in yellow. His contact would be nearby.

"Hey, Stretch," the voice came from the shadows ahead, as if in response to Gage's thought.

Gage turned his flashlight in the direction of the sound and saw a black man in his mid-twenties approaching. He was thin and wiry. His clothes were too big, and they looked as though they had been on him for a decade.

"Kevin, right?" Gage responded. "Meyer sent me."

Kevin nodded after a moment's hesitation, and looked him over appraisingly. "You got a name?"

Gage shook his head and fixed him with a stare. "Nope."

Kevin's lips broke into a wide grin. "Shi-it," he elongated

the word over a second or two. "Well, I know you ain't a cop. The cops don't come in this far. You know what they say, right?"

"What's that, Kevin?"

"What goes on under Vegas, stays under Vegas." Kevin broke into a cackle that bounced off the concrete walls and echoed into the dark. Gage wondered how many times he had shoehorned that line into conversation.

Tiring of the exchange, he produced the hundred-dollar bill, holding it between his middle and index fingers. Kevin's laughter cut out abruptly and his eyes widened. His hand reached out for the bill and Gage pulled it back.

"Show me, first."

Kevin looked momentarily disappointed, and then shrugged. "Whatever you say, Stretch."

Kevin led him deeper into the tunnel until they came upon the opening of one of the smaller tunnels that branched off. He paused at the mouth of the tunnel, his expression serious.

"I'm gonna bring him out. Can't take you in among the community, if you know what I mean."

Gage knew exactly what he meant. Kevin wasn't in any way conflicted about selling out one of his neighbors, but he didn't want anybody else to see him do it. His eyes moved to Gage's hand, where he held the hundred, and Gage could see him think better of asking for an advance ahead of delivery.

"White dude. Nice clothes. Doesn't belong down here. That's who I'm bringing. Okay?"

Gage didn't suppose there could be too many people down here who would fit Farnam's description. "Bring him out here, and you get paid."

Kevin nodded and disappeared into the tunnel. Gage moved back from the edge so that he could not be seen by anyone approaching from within. A minute passed. Five. He was patient. He didn't doubt for a second that Kevin would be back. The look in his eyes when he saw the hundred had been a guarantee of sorts. Eventually, he heard the low murmur of voices. Kevin's voice, and that of another male. They were getting closer.

Kevin emerged first, locked eyes with Gage and stepped out of the way. He was followed by a slightly pudgy white guy with dark blond hair. Gage recognized Larry Farnam from his DMV picture. Farnam wore a gray athletic t-shirt, expensive-looking jeans, and maroon Chuck Taylors. All were the worse for wear, but everything fit him and together seemed to form a considered sartorial choice. He had pulled these clothes from a drawer or a suitcase at the same time, not from a selection of Dumpsters over several months. Gage could see what Kevin had meant. Relative to the other residents of Down Here, the newness and expensiveness of Farnam's clothes stuck out a mile.

The guy stopped when he saw Gage, glanced at Kevin, confusion on his face.

"What—"

Gage was already on him, gripping his hands on his shoulders and pulling him out of the opening with the ease of a parent whisking a toddler away from a busy road. Gage slammed him against the tunnel wall.

"Yo, Stretch . . ."

Gage turned around to Kevin. Kevin flinched back at his stare, but Gage took one hand from Farnam, easily restraining him with the other, and dug in his pocket for Kevin's hundred. He didn't have to tell him to beat it. Kevin snatched the bill from his hand and vanished into the smaller tunnel.

Farnam was already begging before Gage had turned back to him. "Look, man, tell Granger he doesn't have anything to worry about."

Gage was unmoved. He was here to do a job, and that job did not entail negotiation.

"I can't help you," he said.

Farnam evidently saw a premonition of his future in Gage's eyes, because he started hyperventilating. "Come on, man, we can talk about this. I'll do anything, I'll give you anything."

Gage looked him up and down, from his stained t-shirt to his mud-streaked sneakers.

"What have you got?"

Farnam started to speak a couple of times, realized he had nothing to give, and ended up just blinking stupidly.

Out of force of habit, Gage looked around, though he knew there was no human being within a hundred yards, and no one who would care within a mile. Ordinarily, he would have used a gun. He wouldn't even need a silencer down here. But Granger's instructions had been very specific.

He braced his left hand against Farnam's throat, increasing the pressure so he couldn't talk, and his squeals became almost inaudible. Then he reached for the knife, pulled it free of its sheath, drew his arm back, and drove it into Farnam's sternum with force.

Farnam bucked and struggled. Gage pulled the knife back and stuck him another three times in succession. Then he released his arm and Farnam dropped to the floor of the tunnel like a sack of wet sand.

Gage stood back and surveyed his work. Farnam's body shuddered for a few moments, and then went still. Gage wiped the blade down on the back of his shirt and replaced it in the sheath. He kicked the body over so that the stab wounds were facing up. The blood was nice and obvious against the light gray of the t-shirt. He took his cell phone out and snapped three quick pictures.

As soon as he got clear of the tunnels and picked up a signal again, he would email the pictures to Granger, and the money would be in his account within twenty minutes.

Not bad for a morning's work.

2

GRAND ISLE, LOUISIANA

It was the longest I had stayed in one place for years.

After spending the spring and summer drifting between different towns on the East Coast, I had decided to head south when the snow came in. Grand Isle fit the bill perfectly: a small town on a barrier island in the Gulf of Mexico, and about as far south as I could get without having to swim. I had planned to stay for a few weeks when I had arrived in early November, but the temperate climate had been hard to resist, so I decided to stay put until the New Year. While I was still within the technical limits of that decision, it was now early June and I had yet to make a move. The problem was, the Gulf Coast just kept getting more pleasant as the year advanced. I kept expecting to get tired of waking up to blue skies and beaches, and peace and quiet, but it never happened. I read books, I went for long runs, I ate good food in a different place every night. I did everything I could to not go looking for trouble, and for the most part, I was doing a good job. Right up until the moment I pulled my used Ford into Vansen's Auto Shop.

A tall man wearing blue coveralls came out to greet me, waving me forwards into the bay. I parked in the allocated position and turned my attention to the guy in the coveralls. He was in his mid-thirties, gym toned, thick eyebrows. There was a nametag on the left breast pocket labeling him as "Chris." If only everyone was as easy to identify.

"What can I do you for?" Chris asked with a professional smile. I turned off the engine and got out, patting my hand on the sill in mild concern.

"She's running a little rough," I said. "I wondered if you could take a look under the hood?"

"You're in luck, mister. Quiet morning, and one of my jobs just canceled."

"My lucky day," I agreed.

He gestured at the hood and I obliged, reaching through the window and popping the lever. Chris took a second to survey the outside of the car. The Ford Fusion was only three years old, under forty thousand miles on the clock. Ideally I would have picked a more plausible car to be having car trouble in. But then again, isn't it the newer cars that always give you trouble?

"I've been doing this for twenty years," Chris said, as though reading my mind, "and there's always something. You'd think they would have figured everything out by now, but there's always a design flaw in every car. Exhaust, transmission, ventilation ... always some damn thing ready to go at the wrong moment."

"What is it that goes wrong on these?" I asked.

"I'll tell you in a couple of minutes."

He bent down and started examining the engine, his brow furrowed as he investigated connections and valves. Then it was like a lightbulb went on and he nodded approvingly.

"It's your drive belt," he said, pointing at the drive shaft, where the belt was indeed snapped.

"Simple explanation's always the way, huh?" I said.

"I think we can deal with this right now," he said. "You okay to wait ten minutes?"

"I have all day," I said.

"Day off, huh?"

I nodded, although in truth every day had been a day off lately, and this was the closest I had gotten to working in quite some time.

Chris disappeared for a couple of minutes and came back with a new belt. The packaging told me it was a cheaper make than the one I had in the trunk.

"Haven't seen you around before," he said as he reached into the engine and pulled the old belt out. "New in town, or on vacation?"

"A little of both," I said. He looked confused by that, but before he could question me, I carried on. "One of your customers recommended you, actually."

"Oh yeah?"

"Yeah. Her name's Emily," I said.

His expression faltered for a second and he looked back down at the engine.

"Emily huh?" He said it in the manner of one trying out the pronunciation of an exotic new name for the first time.

"Yeah, you know. She lives down at the beach. Has a little dog."

He pretended to think about it. Snapped his fingers. "BMW 2 Series, right?"

"That's right."

"Man, you want to talk about trouble, that thing takes the cake. She should be signed up for frequent flyer miles. Or garage miles or whatever."

"Sure," I agreed, watching him carefully.

He avoided my eyes and took the new belt out of its packaging.

"So I think we'll be able to fix you up here, Mr ..."

"Blake."

"Mr Blake."

"She's had some problems lately, you know," I said. "Not car trouble."

Chris was wiping his hands with a rag and stopped. He met my eyes and shrugged. "Okay."

"Somebody following her around. Watching her when she goes for a run. Sending nasty letters talking about stuff he'd like to do to her."

Chris stared me out. I didn't blink.

"You know what, Mr Blake?"

"What?"

He stuffed the replacement belt firmly back in its packaging. "I think I was mistaken. I don't think I have your part in stock after all."

"No?"

He shook his head slowly. "There's a garage up in Galliano. Kelly's. Reckon they'd be able to help you."

"And what about my friend's problem? Do you know how I can make that go away?"

He looked at me for a moment and then turned without another word, walking back to the office. I removed my jacket and tossed it on the passenger seat of the Ford. I closed the door and waited. I had known this would go one of two ways. It looked like Chris was going for the hard way.

A minute later, he reappeared, as I had known he would. He had a friend with him, as I had known he would. The friend was even taller and wider. He had a mustache and wore a denim baseball cap. The two of them approached me purposefully, the big one in the lead, Chris following in tow, now carrying a heavy wrench. All trace of good humor was gone from Chris's face, but it looked positively welcoming in contrast to his colleague's raspberry-toned visage.

"Who the fuck are you?"

I glanced behind me, to check if he was addressing someone else and then looked back at him.

"Excuse me?"

"You heard me."

"I think I'd like to speak to the manager."

The guy jutted a thumb at his chest. "I am the fuckin' manager. And I don't like faggots harassing my employees."

My eyes moved from him to Chris. "Seems to me it's your employee who's been doing the harassment."

Chris swung at me with the wrench. It was an awkward, stupid move, because he had to twist his body in order to make sure his boss was well out of the danger zone. I sidestepped easily and the wrench arced through the space I had been standing. The ice broken, the manager put his head down and charged for my midsection, aiming to bring me down. I caught his shoulders and brought my knee up into his face, hearing his nose break. He tripped over his feet and I let him fall past me onto the concrete floor of the workshop.

I looked up to see Chris trying for second time lucky, swinging the wrench diagonally down toward my head. There was red mist in his eyes. He had forgotten all about giving me a scare to persuade me to back off. This guy was trying to kill me now. It was a good thing he was as inept in a fight as he was covering his tracks as a stalker.

I caught the wrench with my left hand an inch before it caved in the driver's side window, and then drove my fist into Chris's gut. As he doubled over I twisted the wrench free of his hand, grabbed him by the shoulders and slammed him into a pile of tires. He tried to brace himself and tripped as the pile toppled and loose tires bounced across the garage.

The manager was slowly getting to his feet again. He took a step back, preparing to rush me and then his eyes darted to the wrench in my hand, giving him pause.

I waited a second and then dropped the wrench, beckoning to him. He took a step back.

I walked over to where Chris was sprawled and knelt down. I took a handful of the front of his coveralls, turning him around. His nose was bleeding and he had a dazed look on his face.

"The police are going to receive a file detailing all of your activities, along with evidence. They'll be in touch with you soon. Hopefully that will convince you to stay away from Emily. But just in case it doesn't, I want you to bear something in mind. If I hear about you going within a mile of her, her car or her house, I'm going to be upset."

Chris gritted his teeth. "Go fu—"

I cut him off with a hard kick in the stomach. He folded over and gasped. I gripped the lapels of his coveralls and hauled him back up into a sitting position, keeping my voice calm.

"Just so you know, that wasn't me upset. You want to keep going?"

Chris blinked and averted his gaze. He shook his head.

I dropped him and looked back up at the manager, who had backed even farther away.

"Thanks for your help. I'll try the other place."

3

SUMMERLIN, NEVADA

The new couple had moved in next door to Sarah Blackwell on an overcast day in January. They arrived quietly, without any commotion: one day the house was empty, the next they were there. When they left three months later, it was just as suddenly.

Sarah lived at 34 West Pine Avenue. Number 32 was owned by a lawyer who, like many others around Vegas, had seen the value of his property plummet far below the balance of his mortgage after 2008. Rather than try to sell, he had moved to California and rented the place out. The previous occupants had been a noisy family of six. While Sarah had nothing against kids, she was relieved when she looked up from her computer screen on that January morning to see the new neighbors pull into the driveway in a compact sedan. No baby seats in the back. It would be nice to sit in the yard minus the screams of unruly kids, not to have to clear trikes and space hoppers off her lawn every other day. In contrast, the new couple next door seemed quiet, like they would be no trouble.

In fact, it became clear after a few days that her new neighbors were very quiet indeed. Your classic keep-themselves-to-themselves type.

That was fine by Sarah. And if it had not been for Sarah's job, she might never have given the matter a second thought. Back when she had been a staff reporter at the *Tribune*, working long hours and eating on the run, she could have gone months without realizing she even had new neighbors.

But the latest round of layoffs at the paper, combined with a fortuitously timed book deal, had meant she now found herself spending a great deal of her day at home. She spent a significant portion of that facing the neighbors' house, due to the fact that the window on her study looked out onto the side of number 32. She couldn't help notice the comings and goings of the couple next door as she worked.

Every writer has a routine, and Sarah was no different: working in the morning, from seven to eleven, then taking a walk around the neighborhood. She would eat lunch and attend to light chores in the afternoon to let things settle a little, before editing the day's work in the evening, eight until ten. The routine was pleasant; the contrast with her old job was like night and day. If she was honest, it was a little too comfortable.

She noticed that neither of her new neighbors seemed to have a job. That was odd. West Pine Avenue was an expensive street, even after the round of foreclosures. Sarah could only afford to live there because her ex-husband had been well off and generous in the divorce settlement. Many of the households had two cars in the drive, both of which went out every morning and didn't return until late, working to service those colossal pre-crash mortgages. A fortunate few had bought their homes in the past few years, but most of the people on the street were holdouts: defiantly refusing to cut their losses and sell their dream homes for less than they paid for them. Early mornings, grinding commutes and lots of overtime would be immutable facts of life long into the distant future for most of Sarah's neighbors.

In her more honest moments, Sarah admitted to herself that this was part of the attraction of her morning routine. It was nice to sit in the warm with a cup of coffee, watching as the wage slaves set off for work. She had done her time at that, and she didn't miss those days at all. It made her all the more grateful for the way she now earned her living.

Sarah barely came into contact with the worker bees, and she was fine with that. The bigger problem was the stay-at-home moms who continually tried to involve Sarah in their bake sales and community events. During the day, the neighborhood felt like one of those historical revival shows, only dedicated to the 1950s rather than Elizabethan England or the Pilgrims. They meant well, for the most part. She could tell some of them felt sorry for her, being as she was divorced and on the shelf. She smiled away the pitying glances with amusement.

But the couple at number 32 didn't fit either of those profiles. The man never seemed to go out in the morning, and the woman had somehow resisted being involved in the bake sales. Occasionally, she would see the woman—in her thirties, slim, red shoulder-length hair, serious-looking— walk out to the car in the mid-morning and driving away, returning an hour later with groceries. The man—a little older than the woman, broad shoulders, blond hair thinning on top—would venture out in the car occasionally too, though his excursions tended to be in the evenings.

Sarah rarely saw them leave together, and when she did, the vibe she got from their body language was tension all the way. A relationship on the rocks, she guessed. They moved around each other like they had been very used to spending time with one another, being intimate, but no longer. They weren't demonstrative about it, particularly, but it was plain as day to Sarah. Maybe her reporter's instinct. Or maybe just her divorcee's instinct, if there was such a thing. Aside from that, there was no overt hint that there was trouble in paradise until the night the vase broke.

It was around the beginning of March. Sarah heard a crash

from across the way, like somebody had dropped a plate, or a lamp. It was warm for the time of year, and both her study window and the window of the bedroom in 32 were open. She looked away from the screen of her computer and toward the window. There was a light on in the bedroom. She could hear a voice. Too quiet to make out words, but the voice was deliberate and angry-sounding. A male voice. And then she heard a female voice, again, too quiet to make out, but the ascending tone was a question. A low murmur from the man and then the woman spoke again. And this time, Sarah thought it would have been loud enough to hear without the windows being open.

"Why the hell do I even bother, Dom? This is a bad idea, a bad fucking idea."

"Keep your *voice* down."

"I think I'm entitled to be a little pissed off here, you know?"

"It's too late now. I could end up ..." here, the man lowered his voice.

End up what? In trouble? In jail?

Sarah couldn't help herself. She switched off the lamp on her desk and stood up, leaning closer toward the window to hear more. Inwardly she chastised herself. She wasn't turning into one of *those* people, was she? A nosy neighbor eavesdropping on every conversation. But then again, they weren't exactly whispering.

The woman spoke again. "When this is over, we need to talk, okay?"

When what's over? As Sarah was pondering that, the woman appeared at the bedroom window, holding the base of a broken vase in her left hand, her right already extending to slam the window shut. But she stopped halfway, looking right at Sarah.

Shit. She had switched the lamp off, but had completely forgotten about the glow from the screen, which was lighting her up like the specter at the feast.

Hurriedly, Sarah ducked out of the way and backed against the wall, wincing in embarrassment. She heard the window slam shut, and there were no more raised voices that evening.

The next morning, the words were stubbornly refusing to appear on the page as Sarah looked up at the sound of a knock at the door. Grateful for the distraction, she got up from her chair and padded barefoot down the stairs to the hallway. She stopped in her tracks when, through the glazed front door, she saw the woman with red hair from 32 waiting, holding a paper bag with something inside it. This was the first time Sarah had seen her neighbor up close. She was a little younger than she had guessed, pretty too. She wore shorts and a white blouse, and her red hair was tied back in a ponytail. There was a nervousness in her blue eyes as she peered through the glass. When she saw Sarah, she smiled awkwardly and raised the paper bag in greeting.

"Hi, I'm Rebecca," the woman said as Sarah opened the door. "From next door?"

"Of course," Sarah said, trying to widen her smile enough to make up for the awkwardness. "I'm Sarah."

There was a pause.

"I, uh ... here," Rebecca said, drawing a bottle of Sauvignon Blanc from the brown bag and presenting it to Sarah. "I just wanted to apologize about last night. If we disturbed you, I mean, with the ..."

Sarah took the bottle and thanked her. "Oh, don't be silly. Everybody has fights occasionally. The last few months with my husband ... well, believe me, we would have made you

23

look like amateur night." This wasn't true. There had been no dramatic fights between Sarah and Edward, no broken vases. Just a gradual realization that the marriage wasn't working.

Rebecca seemed to relax a little. "Well, I appreciate that, and it's nice to meet you."

She was turning to go when Sarah called after her. "Why don't you come in?"

Rebecca glanced over in the direction of her house. From the doorway, Sarah could see the car was still in the driveway, which meant her husband was probably still home. Besides, if he had gone out on foot, she would have seen it from her window.

"Come on in," she repeated. "It's me who should be apologizing, I should have come over to meet you when you moved in. You know, welcome you to the neighborhood."

Rebecca looked back at her. "Really? I didn't think neighbors did that anymore."

"Let's bring it back."

Sarah knew they were going to like each other ten minutes in, when Sarah had asked how she was finding the neighborhood, and Rebecca had responded with a question of her own, asking how Sarah got on with the Stepfords. Rebecca had put a hand over her mouth immediately and then relaxed as Sarah burst into laughter.

"You call them that too, huh?"

They had talked about Sarah's writing, about the neighborhood, about the city, about a whole lot of things. But only occasionally did they touch on Rebecca or her husband, Dominic. Rebecca was between jobs, and Dominic was a consultant who worked from home. They didn't know how long they would be around.

Over the next few weeks, coffee at Sarah's house became

a regular thing, every couple of days. For her part, Sarah was pleased to have a break from the routine and someone normal to talk to. She had never gotten along with the immaculately dressed businesswomen or the soccer moms who populated the rest of the street, and she suspected that even if she had made an effort, it would have been unwelcome after the divorce. Rebecca seemed to get something out of the chats too, even though she never opened up much about herself beyond the sparse details she had furnished Sarah with on that first morning. When she mentioned Dominic, it was with a very mild undercurrent of resentment that Sarah recognized from the last months of her own marriage. When Sarah asked, Rebecca admitted as much. They had met two years ago, married in haste. "But hey, no such thing as a perfect marriage, huh?" She changed the subject quickly, obviously a little uncomfortable talking about her husband.

Initially, because of Rebecca's reticence and the fight she had overheard, Sarah had been concerned. As she got to know Rebecca—at least as far as it was possible to get to know someone who played her cards so close to her chest—she decided she didn't have to worry about domestic abuse. Unless Rebecca was hiding it very well indeed, that wasn't what was at the root of her reluctance to open up. No, if Sarah had to guess, she would say that Rebecca was just lonely. Occasionally she would mention a big project that Dominic was working on, and how she couldn't wait for this one to be out of the way. Maybe, Sarah thought, she was just catching them in the midst of a bad patch. Maybe it really would be okay once the big project was out of the way.

Eventually, they branched out beyond coffee at Sarah's and started to go into the city for lunch once a week, the occasional trip to the stores. Rebecca never offered to relocate the coffee and talks to her own house, and Sarah never asked.

Sarah never really spoke to the other half of the couple in all those months. She would see Dominic in passing, in the street or on the way out to her car, and they would nod politely to one another, but they never got into what you might term a conversation. If she had to guess, she would say they exchanged no more than a dozen words, until Liz Bowman's baby shower.

Liz lived in the big house at the end of the street. She and the other Stepfords had invited Sarah, and she begged Rebecca to come along for moral support. She had been hesitant at first, but had eventually given in to Sarah's pleas. They had expected to form their own little clique, subtly rolling their eyes at one another the whole time, but to their surprise, they had actually had a fun afternoon in Liz's gargantuan backyard. There was a barbecue, a pool, cold beer for the grownups and enough food and activities and games to keep the half-dozen or so kids occupied. Sarah started to feel a little guilty about her feelings of superiority over her impeccably turned-out neighbors. They were nice people, for the most part. Just ... a little beige. There were worse crimes.

The atmosphere changed when Dominic showed up. Rebecca saw him first, standing by the side gate and surveying the expansive backyard, clearly searching for her. When his eyes alighted on them, he made a beeline for his wife. He didn't acknowledge Sarah.

Dominic had always seemed serious, preoccupied, every time Sarah had seen him. He looked much more so now. The brow below his sandy-colored hair was knitted into a deep frown, his gray-blue eyes not seeming to register anyone but his wife. He didn't waste time getting to the point. His voice was quiet, but the tone was abrupt.

"We have to go."

Rebecca's demeanor seemed to become more relaxed in inverse proportion to her husband's. She held up her half-full bottle of Coors, signifying she wasn't quite ready to go on one second's notice. "In a minute, darling."

Sarah didn't think she was imagining that the "darling" had been infused with a slightly mocking tone. Rebecca bent her head forward a little and looked at her husband over the top of her sunglasses.

"We talked about this."

Dominic looked like he was fighting back the urge to snap at her, perhaps even to grab her arm and try to drag her out of there. Sarah was on her third beer, which was two more than she was used to in one sitting, so perhaps she had felt a little wicked, a little like provoking him.

"Come on, Dominic, lighten up." She reached into the cool box and her hand came out with another Coors.

She held it out to him. Dominic looked at the bottle as though it was some sort of primitive sacrificial offering, before dismissing her and turning his attention back to Rebecca. He gently moved her to one side by putting a hand on her shoulder, and moved his lips close to her right ear and started to whisper something. Sarah pretended not to pay attention while straining to hear, but the whisper was lost beneath the sound of the tinny speakers of the boom box on the other side of the pool blasting out a Taylor Swift song.

Instead, she took another drink and watched the couple out of the corner of her eye. She saw Rebecca's shoulders tense and a serious expression cross her face. Whatever it was, it wasn't good news. Dominic had pulled back from her ear now, though his hand was still resting proprietorially on Rebecca's shoulder.

Sarah took a step forward. "Everything okay?"

Rebecca looked around at her, like she had forgotten that Sarah, or anyone else, was there. After a second, she nodded.

The three of them turned at the click of a camera shutter. Their host was standing there. Liz Bowman was a slight, dark-haired woman with piercing green eyes. Liz was at least eight months gone, and every time she looked at her, Sarah wondered how she was able to keep her balance well enough to stand up. The woman looked as though she was about to give birth to a Sherman tank. She was holding the new Nikon DSLR she had been given by the McCains from number 20, the strap around her neck, the camera resting lightly on top of her bump.

"Just thought I would get a snap of our new neighbors. And you, of course, Sarah."

Sarah glanced at Dominic and saw the same expression she had seen on his face a few minutes before, like he was trying to decide whether to grab the camera and rip out the memory card. But again, he held back.

"Come on," he said, taking Rebecca's hand.

This time, she didn't resist, placing the beer down on the table and shooting an apologetic look at Liz and Sarah.

"I'm sorry, we have to go," she said. "I just found out my sister's in hospital."

Had Rebecca ever mentioned a sister? Sarah didn't think so, but then again, had Rebecca mentioned any family?

"Oh I'm sorry to hear that," Liz was saying. "I certainly hope it's nothing serious." The tone of her voice suggested that she certainly hoped Rebecca would tell her all the details.

"Thanks," Rebecca said. She touched Sarah on the arm. "I'll call you later, okay?"

Sarah opened her mouth to say something, but before she could think of anything, Rebecca and Dominic had turned and were leaving the barbecue. A hush fell over the party as two dozen suburbanites pretended not to watch and speculate about the new couple who were leaving so abruptly.

"I don't like that guy." Sarah turned from watching Rebecca and Dominic leave to see Liz Bowman had moved closer to her, still clutching her camera. For the first time, Sarah was entirely in agreement with her.

Sarah expected Rebecca to call or drop in that night, but she never appeared. She didn't get much of anything done during her editing session. She just kept thinking about how Rebecca's expression had changed when she heard whatever her husband had whispered. She didn't buy for a minute that her sister was in hospital. He had said something else that had convinced Rebecca to leave. Something she hadn't been expecting.

The next morning, Sarah woke just before six a.m.—an hour before her alarm. She couldn't get back to sleep, and decided to make an early start on her writing. She went through her usual routine: making coffee and toast, then taking it back up to the study. She switched her computer on and pulled the blinds up as she waited for it to come to life.

Rebecca and Dominic's car was gone.

Her eyes moved from the empty driveway to the house itself. It was in darkness, but the drapes were open.

She took her phone out and sent a text to Rebecca.

Everything okay? x

Despite it all, she managed to get a solid two hours of writing on the new book done before she saw the mailman stroll briskly around the corner. He ignored Rebecca's house, as he usually did, and put a single letter in Sarah's mailbox. Deciding she deserved a break, Sarah went downstairs, slipped her shoes on and walked to the bottom of the path to where the mailbox was. The letter the mailman had just placed there was a bank statement, from the savings account which for some reason didn't yet offer paperless billing, but she was more interested in the fact that it wasn't the only thing in the box.

There was a sheet of paper, folded in half, that must have been there since before the mailman came by. Since before six a.m., in fact, since she would have seen somebody else putting something in there.

It was a typed note.

We have to go away for a couple of weeks, sorry I didn't get a chance to say goodbye.

R

Sarah looked up from the note and back at 32. Where the hell had they gone?

She waited a couple of days and sent another text. When that received no reply, she tried calling, but it went straight to voicemail. She left a few messages over the next couple of days, saying she hoped Rebecca was all right and it would be great to hear from her, before giving up.

A couple of weeks passed quickly. And then a third, and then a fourth. Liz Bowman gave birth to a nine-pound girl. More time passed. Sarah kept to her routine: writing in the morning, editing in the evening. Every day she looked out at number 32 and wondered where Rebecca had gone, why she hadn't heard from her.

On the night Sarah was woken at three a.m. by Barney, it had been almost two months since Rebecca had gone. Barney was a black Labrador who belonged to her neighbors on the other side. The urgent barking wasn't like him. She lay there for a minute and decided to get up and have a look. From her bedroom window, she saw a man outside on the driveway, looking at the house, shrinking back from the barking. He was dressed in dark clothes, a beanie hat on his head. If he was a burglar, Barney was giving him second thoughts. As she watched, another man, also in dark clothes, appeared in her field of vision and pointed in the opposite direction down the street. It was as though he was saying "wrong house."

The two men disappeared out of view, heading in her direction. She backed away from the window, out onto the landing and through to the front bedroom. She watched the two men walk past her own driveway, one of them glancing at the ground floor of her house, and continue along the sidewalk. She saw they were headed for 32. She stepped out of the bedroom and crossed the landing to the study. The blind was down here, as usual. She crouched and raised the bottom of it with her hand, just enough to see out.

Number 32 was in darkness, as it had been every night for weeks.

She watched as the two men approached the front door, glancing in the windows. One of them stood on the porch and looked out at the street while the other walked around the back. Two minutes later, the one at the front turned around and the door opened from the inside. Whoever these men were, they didn't have permission to be there. If they knew Rebecca or Dominic, or if they were there on behalf of the landlord, they wouldn't show up at three a.m. and post a lookout while they went in the back door. Sarah decided her initial suspicion had been on the money.

Reluctant to move from her vantage point, Sarah dropped the blind and ran back across the landing to her bedroom, where she had left her phone on the bedside table. She dialed 911 as she ran back through and lifted the blind again.

The ringtone sounded twice as she looked out at the house. On the second floor, she could see dim light moving around. Somebody was moving from room to room with a flashlight kept low.

"Nine-one-one, how may I direct your call?"

Sarah had almost forgotten she was holding the phone. Quickly, she gathered herself. "Police, please."

A click, then dead air, then, "Las Vegas Metropolitan Police Department, how can I help you."

"I'm calling to report a burglary. 32 West Pine Avenue."

"Could I have your name please?"

"It's Sarah Blackwell."

"Are they on your property right now, ma'am?"

"No, it's next door. I'm the neighbor."

"I see. Is there anybody home next door, Ms. Blackwell?"

Sarah didn't say anything for a minute and the dispatcher had to say her name again to remind her to speak.

"No. Nobody's home. I don't know where they've gone."

As she watched, the man out front had stepped out from the cover of the porch. Something in his hand glinted in the moonlight. A gun.

4

The dispatcher confirmed a car was on its way and reminded Sarah to stay put before ending the call. Sarah clutched the phone and watched as the light moved around the ground floor. Her exasperation grew as the minutes passed. Where the hell were they? She took her eyes off the house to compare the time of the call to the clock on her phone. It had been almost ten minutes. She thumbed through the directory and called Rebecca's cell phone. Perhaps a call this late at night would not be ignored.

She cursed as a recording informed her that this number was out of service. And then she felt a surge of relief as she heard the sound of an engine approaching from the east, out of her field of view. She backed out of the study and hurried through to the front bedroom.

It wasn't a police car. A black SUV rolled by the front of her house before stopping outside 32. As she watched, the man who had gone inside emerged via the front door and closed it behind him. He was carrying a flat, magazine-sized object. A laptop, perhaps? He exchanged words with the one with the gun as they hurried down the path to the SUV, then shook his head.

"No!" she said aloud as she watched them get into the car—one in the passenger seat, one in the back—and close the doors. The car pulled swiftly away from the curb, and Sarah only just had the presence of mind to look at the license plate. She ran back through to the study and grabbed the notepad and pen from her desk, scrawling the plate number down before it went out of her head.

When she got back to the front bedroom, the patrol car was outside 32, its lights flashing silently away as the two cops got out and started to approach the house, guns drawn.

Ten minutes later, one of them, a bald guy of around fifty, was in her living room. The other one was checking the exterior of the house, looking for evidence of where the two men had gotten in. The cop was taking notes as Sarah spoke.

"They went in, they spent ten minutes looking around, and then they left with something. A laptop maybe. They didn't have it when they went in. If you had been two minutes earlier . . ."

"We got here as quick as we could, ma'am," the cop said, not looking up from his notes. His tone was bored rather than defensive. He probably had thirty years' experience of people telling him he hadn't gotten here soon enough. "Do you know the names of the homeowners?"

"They were renting," Sarah said. "*Are* renting, I mean." She groped through her memory for a name, and remembered seeing it on a utility bill that had been delivered to her house by mistake. As soon as she had it, she realized why it had been so easy to forget.

"Smith. Dominic and Rebecca Smith. They left in a hurry a few weeks ago. Actually, I've been—"

"You got the name of the owner?"

Sarah shook her head. He had lived there before her time. "No. I've been worried about her. About Rebecca. The thing is . . ."

The cop held up his hand impatiently. "We'll have to contact the owner. Maybe he sent a friend around to get something."

"At three in the morning? Through the back door?"

The younger cop appeared at the door, scuffing his feet on the doormat before stepping into the hall.

"No sign of forced entry. Everything looks secure, all the doors are locked."

The pair of them exchanged a glance and the older one looked back at Sarah questioningly. The look was a nonverbal way of asking if she was sure she didn't dream this whole thing. She wanted to punch him for that look.

"Did you check inside?" Sarah asked, to fill the silence.

"I took a look through the windows. Everything seems fine. No evidence of any disturbance."

The younger one's radio buzzed and he turned away from them, giving his badge number and telling whoever was on the other end of the line to go ahead. Sarah heard some codes and static as the older one examined her like a plumber surveying a routine but time-intensive job.

The younger one signed off and looked at Sarah. "No hit on that plate. Are you sure you got it down right?"

"Yes I'm sure. I wrote it down right away. Maybe it was fake."

"Maybe. And you're not sure what type of vehicle it was."

"No, I told you—it was an SUV, dark-colored."

The two cops exchanged another glance.

The next morning, Sarah felt a strong sense of déjà vu as she went over the story once again, with a similar reaction. In most ways, Officer Stansfield from Missing Persons was a contrast to the two cops who had come in the night. She was female, a little younger, and wore a smart gray suit with a white blouse. But she had the same tired expression on her face as she listened to Sarah's story.

"We contacted the owner ..." she consulted her notepad. "A Jeffrey Walters, lives in San Diego. He didn't know anything about people coming over in the night. He suggested maybe it was somebody the Smiths knew. To be frank, I got the impression Mr. Walters doesn't pay the property much mind, as long as the rent's getting paid."

That was a point. "And is it?"

Officer Stansfield looked down at her notes again. "They paid in advance. One year's rent, takes them up until January."

Sarah's brow furrowed. They had paid a whole year in advance? In that case, why had they disappeared with so long left on the lease?

"Is that normal?"

35

Stansfield shrugged mildly. "No such thing as normal, Ms. Blackwell."

She sighed. "Well what do you think?"

Stansfield looked down at her notepad again. She had been scribbling away as Sarah laid out the whole story, but Sarah suspected that was purely an exercise in projecting diligence. She was pretty sure that Officer Stansfield would never look at these notes again once she turned the page. After a moment, she picked up the piece of paper on which Sarah had printed the picture of Dominic and Rebecca at the barbecue, grabbed from Liz Bowman's unsecured Facebook page. She gazed at the faces for a moment and shook her head regretfully.

"I'm sorry, but I really don't think there's a case here." She looked up, her brown eyes calmly waiting for Sarah to object.

"What do you mean? I'm telling you that a woman I was concerned about disappeared saying she would call me and she never did. She hasn't been heard from in weeks, and her house is deserted. Her phone is out of service. And the note was typed—why would you type a note instead of handwrite it?"

"A note?"

Sarah realized she had forgotten to mention the note. She felt a triumphant rush. "Wait a second, I'll go and get it." Sarah walked through to the kitchen and took the note from the drawer where she kept mail. It was still there, just a couple of lines typed and printed out. She walked back through to the living room and handed the note to Officer Stansfield.

"It was in my mailbox, the morning after they left."

Stansfield gazed at the note for at least three times as long as it would take to read the message. When she had stared at the page for long enough, she looked back at Sarah. "You said you'd had no contact with her."

"Well that's right. Nothing since then, and how do we know this is from her? Why would she go to the trouble of typing and printing a note like that?"

"Perhaps she didn't have a pen. Some people like using computers for everything these days."

"Do you want to take it with you? Fingerprint it or something?"

Stansfield considered. "If you like, I could take it with me."

Sarah felt a flush of anger. She was being managed, humored. "You don't think this looks a little suspicious? Two people move into a neighborhood, they pay a year's rent in advance, and then they just disappear in the night. And then a few weeks later some people come by and search the place in the middle of the night? People with guns?"

Stansfield was looking around the living room, as though she had only just noticed it was a nice house in a nice neighborhood. "Do you live alone, Ms. Blackwell?"

She bit her tongue. "Yes I do."

"And what do you do for a living? If you don't mind me asking."

"I'm a writer."

"What kind of writer?"

"I used to work at the *Tribune*, now I write novels. The Farrah Fairchild series."

The corner of Stansfield's mouth twitched almost imperceptibly, as though she had found the answer to the riddle, and Sarah realized she had said too much. "Must take a lot of imagination."

"If you're suggesting ..."

"Oh I didn't mean it that way at all. It's just ... there was no evidence of forced entry at the property."

And no evidence you saw anybody at all, was the unspoken addition supplied by the way Stansfield was looking at her. Sarah sensed she had gone from being a minor waste of time to someone who was starting to make Officer Stansfield suspicious. Maybe she had faked the burglary report just to get somebody to pay attention. Maybe she had faked the note too.

Stansfield asked a few more questions and then left, taking the note. Sarah knew that most likely she would never see the note, or Officer Stansfield, again.

Maybe Stansfield was right to be dismissive. Subjected to cold logic, there wasn't a whole lot to go on. Maybe the men who had gone into the house had nothing to do with Rebecca or Dominic. Maybe the two of them really had gone to visit a sick relative, and decided to stay wherever they had gone to.

But there was one thing that Sarah could not produce as evidence: the look on Rebecca's face when her husband had whispered in her ear. In the course of her career, Sarah had had the opportunity to see people react to a wide range of shocks. She had delivered more than a few of those shocks herself.

Her instincts told her that Rebecca's reaction hadn't been that of someone concerned for a relative. It had been fear.

5

GRAND ISLE

How long is long enough?

A simple question. Or maybe a complicated one. Two o'clock in the morning brings out the philosopher in me, I guess. I had spent two hours lying awake on top of the sheets pondering the question, before giving up on a bad job and going out onto the deck of my rented beach house. All of the beach houses here had quirky names, like "Tax Dodge" or "Daddy's Escape." The one I had taken was called "Stormy Weather." I wasn't sure if the owner was a Billie Holliday fan, or if it just referred to a fact of life on a barrier island.

"Storms roll in fast," the man who had rented me the house had warned. A taciturn old guy who looked roughly a hundred, it had been the only piece of advice he had imparted, other than telling me you had to switch the shower on and off once to get it to work.

No storms tonight. I leaned on the guardrail and looked out at the Gulf. Ahead of me was a wall of black: it was impossible to tell where the water ended and the sky began. Along the shore to the southwest, the lights on the main road glinted back at me. I closed my eyes and let the still-warm breeze caress my face. I heard a light flutter from above me as a bat ran a flyby.

The dull ache in the knuckles of my right hand seemed to be throbbing with greater intensity. There would be bruising in the morning. I knew I should have put it on ice after the incident at Vansen's Auto Shop, but I had been too preoccupied. After I left, I had parked up to replace the drive belt myself, and then I had driven around for a while, thinking.

It had been a long sabbatical. The task of tracking down Chris and issuing a rather physical cease-and-desist notice had been unexpectedly stimulating. But now it was as though I had flipped a switch on, and I was having difficulty finding the off position.

I wasn't entirely sad about that, At the back of my mind, I had been starting to worry about getting rusty, about my physical and mental skills atrophying as I sat on the beach and watched the world go by. On the evidence of today, my concerns were unfounded. So what had been holding me back?

I ticked off the practical arguments. For one thing, I didn't have anybody finding me work. A very well-connected man named Coop had been the source of most of my jobs for the past few years, but he had been killed by the people who had come after me. I felt some guilt about his death, but I knew it had been an occupational hazard that Coop fully understood. If one of my enemies hadn't taken him out, it could have been a long list of other people.

Then, of course, there was the fallout from what had happened in a snowy corner of upstate New York two winters ago.

For several years I had worked for a US government initiative that technically had no name, but which was known to initiates as Winterlong. We had roamed across hotspots on four continents, operating with impunity and carrying out the jobs no one else could do. Unknown to me, several members of the unit had crossed a lot more lines than I had known about at the time. Torture, unauthorized hits, the indiscriminate murder of civilians. I had been approached by a US Senator named John Carlson. Carlson had shown me evidence of the kind of activities some of my teammates were indulging in, and recruited me with the idea of getting him the evidence he needed to shut Winterlong down.

It had not gone smoothly.

Winterlong had gotten wise to our plan. They came very close to killing me in Afghanistan, while simultaneously carrying out the assassination of Senator Carlson. It had been a meticulously planned job, and they had covered up well. Reluctantly, I had concluded that Winterlong was too big to take on alone, and so I had cut my losses: offered them a deal in return for staying away from me or anybody close to me.

Anybody close to me. That made me think about Carol for the first time in a while. I looked out at the inky void of Barataria Bay at night, thinking about the four simple words that comprised the last message I had ever received from her.

The deal with Winterlong had lasted for five years. Right up until I received an email with a picture of one of my former colleagues, dead in the Siberian snow. It was a very clear message: Winterlong had decided to take me off the board for good. But this time I was prepared, and it hadn't gone so smoothly for them.

I had lost a friend, and my home, but Winterlong was finished. It had seemed like an opportune time to take a break.

So. How long was long enough? Maybe the exhilaration I had felt tracking down Emily's tormentor was a signal. Maybe it was time to get back to work, find more challenging problems to solve.

I turned and looked back into the beach house. The empty, unmade bed wasn't calling to me yet. I laced on my sneakers and vaulted the waist-high guardrail, landing on the sand below. I jogged down to the edge of the water, where the sand was hard-packed, and started to run. I got all the way up to the pier at the state park on the eastern point of the island, turned and doubled my pace for the return journey. Five miles, give or take. I felt the burning in my lungs and pushed myself harder. I got back to the beach house as the sky was beginning to lighten on the eastern horizon. My limbs were on fire, my throat parched, my heart thumping as though it was trying to break through my ribcage.

I staggered into the beach house, drank some water and lay down on the bed, wondering why I still didn't feel tired. And that was my last thought before sleep claimed me.

6

SUMMERLIN
MONDAY, 00:15

The night after Sarah had spoken to the cop from Missing Persons, she made up her mind to cross a line. She had been considering this course of action for a few weeks, but it had taken Officer Stansfield's visit to convince her that no one else was ever going to take an interest in Rebecca's disappearance. If she wanted anything to happen, it was up to her. She waited until well after midnight, then slipped her bare feet into sneakers and walked out of her front door, across the front lawn and onto the lawn of number 32. She cast a wary glance at the windows of the houses across the street, but no one was looking out at her. Anyway, what would be the problem? She was just a neighbor, checking out the property in her friend's absence. It was kind of true, in a way.

A few weeks after her new neighbors had moved in, Sarah had been working when Dominic—although she hadn't yet known that was his name—arrived home one afternoon. She saw him pat the pockets of his pants, then knock on the front door. Locked out, obviously. After waiting a minute, he walked around the back and dug in one of the plant pots for a spare key. Sarah had forgotten all about it until she had seen the men go into the house. Of course, Rebecca and Dominic had probably taken the spare with them when they left.

She knelt down and examined the pot nearest the door. The plant itself had died weeks ago, with no one around to water it. She dug her fingers into the hardened soil and smiled as she felt something thin and metal. She drew the key out and dusted it off. She couldn't decide whether the fact it was still there was a good sign. Maybe it meant Rebecca really was planning to come back; or maybe they had just forgotten about it in their hasty departure.

She examined the lock on the back door using the illuminated screen of her phone. There was no sign of damage, just as the police had said. Had the men last night known where to look for the key as well? Or did they just know how to pick a lock without leaving a trace?

The lock clicked at the turn of the key and she pushed the door open, pausing in the threshold and listening.

"Hello?"

This was stupid. She knew there was no one in the house. Rebecca and Dominic hadn't been home in weeks. And yet it still felt transgressive, coming uninvited into someone's home. Technically, she supposed, it was breaking and entering, even though she had used a key. There was no answer to her call, just a deep silence from the house.

"It's Sarah. From next door."

Nothing.

She had never been inside the house before, so she didn't know what it had looked like when they lived here, beyond what she could see from her study. But when she had looked around the living room and the kitchen, she got the sense that there was nothing here that had not been provided by the landlord. The kitchen was stocked with all of the basic utensils you would need: not too expensive, but not bargain basement stuff. The refrigerator was almost empty: just some leftover Chinese, some celery sticks and a quart of milk gradually turning solid in the cold.

The living room was neat and clean, but again, Sarah thought that everything that was there had been in place before the current tenants. She moved through the rest of the rooms on the ground floor, her initial trepidation wearing off as she opened drawers and peeked in cupboards with a new confidence. The footprint of the house was identical to Sarah's own, so she knew she wasn't missing any nooks or crannies.

Something was wrong: the place felt almost as though it was ready for viewing by the next tenants, the ones who would come to view the place in December, or sooner if the landlord wanted to take advantage of the situation and temporarily double his rental income. But Rebecca and Dominic had left in a hurry. There had been no loading of a van or a truck on the night they left; Sarah would have heard it. So where was all their *stuff*? Even renting furnished accommodation, they should have had things they wanted to take with them. If they hadn't had time, then those things should still be here, like the milk and the takeout and the celery sticks.

An uneasy feeling came over Sarah as she moved back into

the hallway and stood at the foot of the stairs. She wasn't sure what she had been hoping to find, but it wasn't this. So far, there was very little to show that anyone had been living here for the past few months. It was almost as though she had imagined the whole thing.

She remembered the skeptical look on the faces of the two cops. The same look on the face of Officer Stansfield from Missing Persons. She banished the images. Rebecca had been here, all right. There was the photograph from the barbecue.

But that very thought, which should have reassured her, had the opposite effect. She remembered how uneasy Rebecca and Dominic had been when they realized they had been photographed. They had been leaving the barbecue already, of course, but that seemed to have spurred them on. And thinking about it, that photograph now looked like the single piece of evidence that Rebecca had existed. No worldly goods left in the house, a phone number that had gone out of service, a last name that was anonymous as could be.

The main bathroom at least showed signs of habitation. But only in the way a used hotel room will. Disposable razors in the trash, an unfinished shampoo bottle, aspirin in the cabinet. A nearly empty tube of toothpaste, but no toothbrushes.

The bed in the master bedroom was unmade, but there were no clothes in the closet and nothing in the chest of drawers. The closet had a shelf at head height, and Sarah could see a rectangular space in the dust where something wide and flat had lain until recently. A suitcase. They had packed everything away and gone. There was a desk beside the bed, nothing in the drawers but a phone charger and a spiral-bound notebook missing most of its pages.

There was even less to see in the other two bedrooms. Sarah doubted they had been used. The final room, the one Sarah used as a study in her version of the house, was entirely empty, not even a desk. She groaned out loud. A waste of time. They had left nothing, or at least nothing that had been overlooked by the men who had come in the night.

Frustrated, she went back through to the bedroom, the only room which showed some evidence that it had been occupied by humans, and went through the drawers and the closet again. Empty. She sat down on the edge of the bed, telling herself that she had done all she could. Rebecca hadn't called, the police weren't interested, there was nothing here that might help. And then she remembered there was one obvious place left to check.

She got off the bed and got down on her hands and knees. There was a pair of worn men's sneakers under the bed, but nothing else. Then she saw something stuck behind one of the rear legs of the bed, as though it had fallen down the back. She crawled under and stretched until her fingers contacted it. It was a small, rectangular object. It felt like a paperback novel.

She pulled it out and shuffled back out from under the bed, looking down at what she held in her hands. Not a novel; a square-bound notebook. It was thick, the pages distorted with use. Some kind of journal, or diary? She opened it and, at first, she was disappointed. The book was two-thirds full of handwriting. A neat, feminine cursive. But these weren't journal entries. There were doodles, and scraps of poetry, and thoughts. There were pencil sketches and cartoons. It was like an idea book, Sarah knew people who kept notebooks like this for therapy. Most of the pages had a few written lines or a sketch. One was entirely covered with what looked like the same signature repeated, only each time the name itself was different.

Rebecca Smith, Sam Kelly, Jane Hawkins, Carol Langford ...

Sarah felt a chill as her eyes ran over the names. Who the hell was she?

She leafed through more pages. A pencil sketch of an old building; quite good actually, like she had spent a lot of time on it. A cartoonish sketch of a man's profile that she thought was supposed to be Dominic. One of the last used pages had a series of numbers in it: 12, 14, 15, 16. The 15 was circled and underlined. Dates, perhaps? Sarah thought back. Rebecca had left town on April 14th. On the page after that, there was a single, cryptic line in the middle of the page:

Quarter by June

A quarter of what by June? What did that mean? Maybe nothing. It was like a line of poetry, or a fragment of a riddle.

The last thirty pages or so of the notebook were blank. In her rush to leave, Rebecca had obviously forgotten this just like she had forgotten to take the spare key. Sarah leafed through the blank pages just to be thorough, and found that the very last page in the notebook had been used. It was one of the doodles. At first glance, this one was a picture of a picture: some kind of frame with words inside. As she looked at it, she realized it wasn't a framed picture at all. It was a glass-fronted box, like the kind fire alarm buttons are shielded behind. There was a neatly lettered sign above the box.

BREAK GLASS IN CASE OF EMERGENCY.

Inside the rectangular frame was a word, each letter printed carefully. Actually, it wasn't a word at all.

It was an email address.

7

GRAND ISLE
MONDAY, 12:05

The feeling in my gut that had kept sleep at bay for so long the previous night had solidified by the time I woke up. It was the unshakeable conviction that something had changed. It was as though I had woken up with an unscratchable itch. Like somebody had pushed a button, and the uncomplicated contentment of the past few months had melted away. It wasn't a hangover, and it wasn't money worries, I still had more than enough in my bank account to pay for this extended sabbatical.

Sabbatical. That's what I had been calling it. Just a break, not a career change. Lately, the word had started to sound hollow. What had started as a sabbatical was starting to feel a little too much like early retirement. I had enjoyed the past few months of idling my time away, beholden to no one and nothing. But the slight diversion of the last couple of days had felt good. I wondered if that was what had begun to knock things off kilter. Solving Emily Button's problem had been just that, an enjoyable diversion, but it had rekindled something in me. An urge.

I got out of bed and walked across the small living room of the beach house to the galley kitchen, flicking the switch on the coffee maker. While it did its thing, I pulled on a t-shirt and joggers and went out onto the deck barefoot. The sun was already midway up in a blue sky. The bay, so dark and unknowable a few hours before, had transformed into a collage of shades of blue. On the horizon I could see the oil rigs and a scattering of small boats. I closed my eyes and let the warmth of the sun bathe my face. After the Winterlong thing, I didn't think I would ever take warmth for granted again. Not in six months on the Gulf Coast, not in six hundred years.

"Morning, Blake."

I opened my eyes and pointed them in the direction of the voice with the light southern accent.

Emily Button was approaching from the west, walking along the strip of sandy beach with her Yorkshire terrier Otis scampering along beside her. She was tall, with a lithe, athletic build. She jogged along that strip of beach twice a day, as well as the dog-walking. She wore red shorts and a dark gray vest top. Her curly auburn hair was pulled back in a ponytail which fed through the back of her LSU baseball cap.

I waved a hello. "Is it still morning?"

She glanced at the phone in her hand. "Ten after noon. Close enough."

That sounded about right. Early mornings were one thing I didn't miss from my days acting like a person who has a job. An electronic noise pinged softly from inside. "Coffee's ready, if you want some?"

We sat on opposite couches and drank coffee while Otis sniffed around the kitchen cupboards.

"I can't thank you enough. The police say he won't be bothering me again."

I waved it away. "I told you it was no problem."

"It would've been a big problem for me, if you hadn't worked out who was sending me those ... those letters. God, I had barely noticed the guy at the garage. You wouldn't think ..." She sighed and crossed her arms. "Anyway, thank you."

"What are neighbors for?"

She smiled. "Usually, they're for ignoring you. Or paying you way too much attention."

I guessed that was probably true. I wouldn't know. Having neighbors, however temporary, was a new experience for me.

"The Olbertsons, for example," she continued after I hadn't spoken for a minute. "They pay you a lot of attention."

"They do, huh?"

I had noticed. Sidelong glances in the store. Net curtains twitching as I passed by their beachfront house on one of my walks. Once, I had caught Mrs. Olbertson at my mailbox, examining the meager contents. I assumed she would have been disappointed by the personalized label on the Domino's menu addressed to "Pizza Lover."

"Mmmhmm," she agreed. "They think you're quite the mystery man. They're not alone."

I opened my arms and gestured at the small confines of the beach house. "What's the mystery? I'm a very basic guy."

She took a sip of her coffee. "This is good. Italian?"

"Colombian."

"So yeah, there's a little mystery here. You showed up out of nowhere, you don't seem to do anything for a living. You're too young to be retired."

"I'm on a sabbatical."

She grinned. "That's exactly it, Blake. Every time I talk to you about yourself, you deflect. A sabbatical from what?"

My phone bleeped quietly on the coffee table and I glanced

at the screen. A new email. That was unusual, things had been very quiet. Whatever it was, it could wait until later. I was finding that was the case with more and more things lately. Nothing was urgent. I looked up and remembered Emily was still awaiting an answer to her question.

I shrugged. "It's really very boring."

"Try me."

"I already told you, I'm a consultant. Freelance. Last year was a good one for me, so I'm taking some time off."

Her eyes narrowed. "What kind of consultant?"

"Logistics, problem solving. Like what I did for you, I guess."

She watched me over the rim of her cup as she drank. "The police mentioned Chris O'Brien had a black eye. Seemed to have hurt his ribs, too."

"Doesn't surprise me. A guy like that makes enemies."

"The Olbertsons have a theory. They think you're a reclusive dot com millionaire who's retired already."

"Do I look like a dot com millionaire?"

She considered that for a moment. "You look young, and you don't go to work. They think anyone who can order from Amazon is a tech genius, so with the other stuff, you can see how they'd reach that conclusion."

"I'm definitely not a dot com millionaire."

She sighed. "I think you do this on purpose. I think you're deliberately cultivating an air of mystery."

That was the last thing I wanted to do. I attempted to turn the conversation around. "So what's your day job?"

"I'm a realtor."

"Do you like talking to people about what you do?"

She sighed. "Sure. If they ask interesting questions."

"But what most people ask is, 'How's business?' right?"

She smiled in recognition. "Right."

I spread my hands to say: there you go. "I just think what a person does is usually the least interesting thing about them. I'd rather talk about music, or books, or sports or ... even coffee."

She drank the last of the cup and ran her tongue along her top lip. "Good coffee," she repeated.

"Another?"

She shook her head. "I have to be in the office in an hour." She got up and took her mug through to the kitchen and put it in the dishwasher. "Your sabbatical, it's ending soon, isn't it?"

"What makes you say that?"

She thought about it for a minute. "We never really had a real conversation until last week, did we? I mean, you were always pleasant, always said hi when I ran by, always held the door for me when we were at the store at the same time. I used to wonder about you. You just seemed so laid-back, so ... content. I envied that. I envied you being able to sit around all day and be happy. I guess I thought you were one of those shallow rich guys, not a care in the world. Not a dot com millionaire, but maybe an overgrown trust fund kid. But the other day I realized I had you all wrong."

"How so?"

"When I saw you doing what you do. Looking at those letters, asking me questions. Working it all out." She paused and recalled the phrase I'd used. "Solving problems. You seemed different. You seemed more like a human being. Engaged, you know?"

"Is that a good thing?"

She nodded. "I don't think you're the beach bum type, Blake. Sorry."

She turned her head and clicked her tongue at Otis, who had managed to open one of the cupboards with his snout.

"Come on, boy, we're running late." She turned back to me and smiled. "Thanks for the coffee."

When Emily and Otis had departed via the steps down from the deck, I poured myself another cup and sat back down. The display on my phone was blinking intermittently, reminding me about the unread email. I unlocked the screen and realized the message had come into my combined inbox via one of the old addresses. As in, very old. As in 2010. In fact, thinking about it, I hadn't sent or received anything from that particular address since . . .

I opened the inbox. It was completely clean but for the new arrival from ten minutes before. The sender was someone named Sarah Blackwell. The subject line was, *Wondering if you can help.*

That vague, teasing subject made it look like spam; a phishing email. The kind that makes you curious enough to open. Then hopefully you're dumb enough to download the virus or type in your online banking codes or whatever. Only you have to give your email address out to get spam, and this one hadn't been given to anyone for years.

I tapped into the email. Just by glancing at the layout, I knew it was wordier and better-formatted than your usual spam message. Three paragraphs. From the look of the grammar and syntax, it had been composed by a real person whose first language was English. There was an attached file as well, a jpeg. I ignored that for the moment and started to read the message.

Hi
You don't know me, and this is probably going to sound a little odd, but like the subject says, I'm wondering if you could help me. I'm looking for someone, and your email address is basically my last hope.

Definitely not spam. Looking for people is what I do, or did until recently. So this would be a strange coincidence. But who had given this person my email? I read on. Before I got to the end of the second paragraph, I was beginning to have my suspicions.

Sarah Blackwell, whoever she was, had managed to fit a lot of information into her three paragraphs. She wrote clearly and concisely, no words wasted.

She lived in Nevada. Summerlin, a suburb west of Las Vegas. She was concerned about her neighbor, who had vanished overnight several weeks before, along with her husband, and hadn't been seen since. There had been a note left in her mailbox, ostensibly from the neighbor, saying they would be out of town for a while. Sarah thought that was a little strange, because it had been typed and printed, not handwritten.

That wasn't the only thing that gave her cause for concern. Ever since the neighbors had moved in, she had gotten the impression the husband could be a shady character. Little things, she said, without elaborating further. And then one night she had seen two men arrive in the small hours and break into the house. She had contacted the police and they saw nothing to investigate. The neighbors were grownups and, hey, they had even left a note. Sarah had used a spare key to get into the house. She had done some poking around, and found an old notebook, with my email address in it.

So, long story short, that's why I'm contacting you. This is my message in a bottle, and if nothing comes of this, I don't know what else to do. But I know it's going to drive me crazy, not knowing where Rebecca is, or if she's safe.

Rebecca? I didn't think I knew anyone by that name. But then, names can change, as I knew better than most.

My thumb hovered over the jpeg attachment. The last time I had opened an image on an unexpected email it had triggered a world of trouble. I had the feeling this picture was going to do the same thing. *Storms roll in fast*.

I tapped to open the image. The status circle whirled for a tantalizing few seconds and then a photograph appeared. It showed three people—two women and a man—outside somewhere in the sun. It looked like a party. I didn't recognize one of the women or the man. The other woman I might not have recognized either, had I not been prepared. She was wearing sunglasses, and she wasn't looking right at the camera. Her hair was red, instead of the blonde I remembered. But there was no doubting it. Her name was not Rebecca. It was Carol Langford.

I hadn't heard from Carol since 2010, and the last message from her had been very clear cut; no room whatsoever for ambiguity.

Don't look for me.

8

LAS VEGAS

Gage only noticed the blood because his appointment was running four minutes late.

He finished the last of his lemonade and checked his watch. Officially late. Gage forgot about that for a second, though, when he noticed the dot of rusty brown-red on the cuff of his shirt. He had only found out about this meeting yesterday afternoon, and hadn't been expecting to stay over. He wasn't in a position to turn down work, so he had found a modestly priced hotel, soaked his shirt in the sink, and hung it over the shower rail overnight to dry it out. Somehow, the small bloodstain had survived the dousing.

He remembered Farnam's face, staring back at him, his beady little eyes moist and pleading.

I'll do anything, I'll give you anything.

It wasn't the first such offer Gage had heard in that exact kind of situation, and it wouldn't be the last. When a man realizes the remainder of his life can be counted in seconds, he'll say pretty much anything to try and extricate himself from the situation. The problem is, by that time it's almost always too late. What Gage had done to Farnam didn't bother him. He had done a lot worse in the past, and would again.

He raised his eyes from his sleeve and looked over the interior of the bar again. It was an authentic dive: torn linoleum flooring, mismatched stools lined up in front of the bar. Behind the bar was an elaborate mural of various celebrities playing poker: JFK and Lady Gaga and Muhammad Ali and many more. It was a crime against art. The place was way off the beaten track, and even more empty than you would expect on a weekday afternoon. Just two hardened alcoholics sitting separately at the bar and staring at the poker-playing stars. It was the kind of place someone asked to meet you if they didn't want anybody to know about it. In the eight years Gage had been in this line of work, he had seen the inside of a lot of places like this.

He angled his glass so he could dip a finger in the melting ice at the bottom and rubbed at the little rusty brown-red dot until it was almost invisible. Six minutes past two now. He looked up and saw three men approaching his table.

They made an interesting trio. If you lined the three of

them up at a bus stop, you would assume they had nothing to do with one another.

The middle one, the one closest to him, was a tall man in his fifties: bald, with horn-rimmed glasses. He wore a gray suit. Well cut, expensive-looking.

The one on the right was younger: late twenties, maybe. Short and stocky, with dark hair and eyes, wearing black jeans and an olive-green t-shirt. The black ink of a tattoo protruded from the sleeve on his left arm.

Gage lingered slightly longer in his appraisal of the man on the left. This one was late fifties, around six feet, wearing a blue shirt under a gray sport coat and with a short buzz cut that was graying a little around the temples. The look in his eyes was shifty, as though he expected someone to point him out at any time. A cop. Either current, or recently retired. Gage knew one when he saw one, of course, but he also sensed that this was not the kind of cop he needed to be worried about.

The three of them stopped a couple of paces in front of Gage's booth and stared at him, waiting for him to speak. Gage didn't say anything, just sat back on the upholstered bench and crossed his arms loosely.

After an uncomfortable twenty seconds, the man in the middle, the tall one with glasses, spoke.

"Are you here to meet us?"

Gage looked back at him. "That depends."

"On what?"

"On whether you were supposed to be here six minutes ago." He consulted his watch. "Seven."

"Are you serious?" the one on the left, the one who looked like a cop, asked.

Gage's eyes flicked to him. "I take timekeeping very seriously. Is there something wrong with that?"

"It's not even ten after two yet," the short one said, an edge of defensiveness in his voice. He was the driver, then.

"Traffic was bad," the guy in the middle said, extending a hand. "I'm Walter."

The name sounded odd in his mouth, like he was trying it on for size. *The hell you are,* Gage thought as he shook Walter's hand.

"This is Grant, this is David," he said, gesturing to introduce the cop and the driver. The two of them said nothing, neither one acknowledging the names that could be first names or last names, if they had been real. Gage saw Grant's eyes scan the room again. He doubted Grant had anything to worry about in this dump. Even if one of the two other customers happened to know him, they had probably stopped forming memories three rounds ago.

"Apology accepted," Gage said, giving a look that dared one of them to object. None came, which suggested they needed something in a hurry and had no time to waste on posturing. He picked his glass up and rattled the ice, staring at Walter, since he seemed to be the official spokesman of the group. "I'll have another while we talk."

David—the short one—shook his head slowly. He turned, as if to leave, but Walter grabbed his arm.

"That's fine," Walter said, a little louder than he needed. "You two sit down, I'll get us all something to drink."

David eyeballed his compatriot for a moment before relaxing. He and the cop going by the name Grant sat down across from Gage, while Walter walked across to the bar and returned a couple of moments later with four glasses on a tray. Three bottles of water, a glass with ice in it, and a bottle of lemonade. The same brand as the empty on the table. He hadn't bothered to ask the other two what they wanted, this was just table rent. He waited patiently until

Gage moved over to make room, and then sat down next to him.

Gage poured the lemonade over the ice and took a drink. "Thank you. Now, what can I do for you?"

Walter's eyes surveyed the room, to make sure nobody was within earshot. The barmaid was watching the wall-mounted television, the two soaks at the bar paid no attention to them.

"We're attempting to find somebody," he said. "Despite our best efforts, we haven't gotten very far."

"Find?" Gage repeated.

"That's correct." He lowered his voice. "This is not a hit, okay?"

Gage affected a look of surprise. "What makes you think that's the sort of work I do?"

Walter didn't answer. He reached into the pocket of his jacket and took out a sheet of paper, folded in half. He opened it up, flattened it on the table with his palm, and slid it across the table top to Gage.

Gage took the sheet and flipped it around. It was a police wanted sheet. It showed a mug shot—straight ahead and profile. The name was Dominic Freel. Approximately five-nine, a hundred and eighty pounds, blond hair, blue eyes, no visible scars or tattoos. The date showed the sheet was five years old, for a bail violation.

"You got anything more recent?"

The tall man reached into his jacket again and brought out another sheet of paper. This one was a color printout of a picture. It showed three people in what looked like a backyard. Gage guessed it was some kind of party. There were two women in the picture flanking a man who looked like the same guy from the wanted sheet, a few years older. One of the women was short, early forties, with dark hair tied back in a ponytail. She was holding a bottle of Coors and smiling at the camera. The other woman was a little taller, had red hair and wore sunglasses. She had one hand on her hip, and was talking to the man, their faces angled toward one another, maybe unaware of the fact they were being photographed.

"Who is he?"

It was Grant's turn to speak. "He's a guy we need to talk to."

"What did he do?"

Grant looked at Walter, as though checking for permission, before continuing. "He worked for my friend here. He left abruptly, and we'd like to talk to him about that. We need to talk to him before the police do."

Gage guessed he meant the *other* police.

"He knows something you don't want anyone else to know."

No reply.

"It must be important," Gage continued. "It would have to be."

David caught the implication right away: no dummy, when it came to financial matters. "How much are you going to charge?"

"Just finding him? You want him brought to you?"

Walter shook his head. "Just find him. We hear you're good at that. Find him, pick up the phone, and wait until we get there."

They were definitely keen, which suggested this could be a worthwhile meeting. The money in his account from the Farnam job was only there temporarily. Once he had settled his debts, there would be enough left to get back home, and maybe eat for a couple of weeks once he got there. He thought about his usual figure for a job of this kind and added fifty per cent. "Thirty grand. Half up front."

David's eyes narrowed, but he didn't make any theatrical moves toward the exit this time. He exchanged a glance with Walter, who looked back at Gage and gave a nod. "That's acceptable. This is a matter of principle."

Gage tried not to betray his surprise that his fee had been agreed to so readily. This was supposed to be an extra job while he was in the area. If this panned out, it would double the payday for killing Farnam. After a few very lean months, it appeared this trip had been more than worth his while.

Gage took a drink, pretending to think it over. Inwardly, he cursed himself for not upping the fee a little more. If they agreed to thirty without blinking, they would have agreed to forty. Perhaps he could bulk things out on expenses a little. In any case, he was intrigued now. Who were the three men who didn't seem to go together? Why did they want this Freel guy bad enough to go down this route? Thirty thousand dollars was a lot of money on a point of principle. It meant that either Freel had something they wanted, or he had seen something he shouldn't have.

"You have a deal," he said after a minute. "Now tell me where you want me to start."

9

GRAND ISLE—SUMMERLIN

The used Ford Fusion I had bought three months ago had done less than a thousand miles in that time. I was about to give it a workout.

In an ideal world, I would have traveled to Vegas by air. Sarah Blackwell had responded quickly to my suggestion that I come and see her, providing an address. She lived west of the city, less than twenty miles from McCarran International. But I hadn't attempted to get on a plane in eighteen months, ever since Winterlong had upgraded me to the No Fly list. I wasn't certain I was still on the list, but I did know that satisfying my curiosity would be a risky endeavor. It's much easier to get on the list than to get off it. A great deal of the broad strokes of counterterrorism rests on the maxim *Better safe than sorry*. Understandable, when you think about it. Nobody wants to be the guy who downgraded a terrorist to low risk right before he carries out his mission. If civil rights get a little bruised in the process, that, unofficially of course, is a price worth paying.

So ever since my name had been flagged on the system at Seattle Tacoma Airport, I had avoided air travel. It hadn't been any great hardship, for most of that time. For the last year and a half, I had had no pressing need to be anywhere in any kind of rush.

But that had changed with one email and one picture.

Within an hour of receiving Sarah Blackwell's message, I had cleared out the few belongings I wanted to take with me and packed them into the trunk of the Ford. I put the spare key in an envelope and dropped it through the door of the rental place with a note saying I was going to be out of town on business for a while. I spent another five minutes plotting the journey. Eighteen hundred miles. I was going to have to split the trip over two days, minimum.

As I put the keys in the ignition, I allowed myself a few seconds to take one last look at the Gulf of Mexico, thinking about another old saying: *Be careful what you wish for.*

I headed north and west, following the 90 past Lafayette and Alexandria, heading back inland. The drive gave me a lot of time to think. I thought about the last time I had seen Carol, at the little hotel out on Long Island. Drinking cold beers and listening to Sam Cooke. The look on her face when I told her I had to leave. Perplexed and pissed off in equal measure.

And then I thought about the last time I had spoken to her, weeks later, over the phone. The men I was working with had come very close to killing me, and had succeeded in killing her boss, Senator John Carlson. I thought we had been careful. We hadn't been careful enough.

I still felt the pain as I remembered the accusation in her voice. I knew she had put the pieces together and decided I had gotten her boss killed, and I had put her in danger. And the worst thing was, she wasn't entirely wrong.

I had told Carol to lay low for a while, directed her to an off-the-grid apartment I had set up for the purpose of evading pursuers if it became necessary. By the time I got back stateside and made arrangements to keep Winterlong off our backs—temporary arrangements, as it turned out—she was gone. She left nothing behind but a note: *Don't look for me.*

I wondered if she knew how ironic the message was. She couldn't know that it was a big part of what I did for a living: looking for people. She had tied my hands with four words. She knew I wouldn't go against her final request to me.

Until now.

Maybe everyone has someone like Carol Langford. The one who got away. The person you meet, fall in love with, and lose. And then think about for the rest of your life. Carol and I had been together for a matter of weeks, but somehow it had felt a lot longer. I had never given any thought to settling down before I met her, but if things had taken their natural course, I believed deep down that somehow we would be together now. Life had other plans.

I crossed the Texas state line a little after six o'clock in the evening. I was tired, but I was less than halfway to my destination. I pushed on past Dallas and made it as far as Amarillo by two a.m. I took a room in a motel and found myself wide awake now I was away from the road. I went for a walk around the neighborhood to stretch my legs, then ate a solitary dinner at a pizza joint that was the only place still open. I went back to my room and fell into a deep sleep as soon as my head hit the pillow. At seven a.m. I was up, showered and back behind the wheel for the second leg.

I tried to think about what I was going to do when I got to Vegas. Sarah Blackwell had my email address, which meant that there had been at least one tie that Carol had not cut. I wondered what that meant; if it meant anything. There was every chance there was a benign explanation for her disappearance, and that Carol would not welcome my intrusion. But I owed it to her, and myself, to find out more. Speaking to the neighbor was a precaution, nothing more. Chances were that Sarah Blackwell had an overactive imagination, and there was nothing to worry about. If I could find a simple explanation for Carol and her husband disappearing, there would be no need to take it any further.

Or maybe there was more to it than that. Even supposing there was, perhaps I would be able to find Carol without her knowing. Put her friend's mind at rest—and mine—without her ever realizing I had gone against her wishes. I wondered if I would be able to get that close to her and walk away.

I didn't like to dwell on that thought, and so I busied myself with logistics; potential courses of action depending on what I learned in Summerlin. I tried not to think about the way Carol's voice had sounded the last time we talked. But underneath all of that was a quite different impulse, a feeling I tried to deny was there. A feeling that didn't have a whole lot to do with the subject of the search: the excitement of starting out on a new case. A new puzzle to be unlocked. It had been too long.

I drove direct, stopping only for gas. I passed through New Mexico and Arizona and crossed the Nevada state line at the Colorado River just after seven o'clock in the evening.

The 95 freeway took me right through the heart of Vegas, not that you would know it. The famous welcome sign and the fountains at the Bellagio and the neon cowboy were all out there somewhere, but all I could see was miles of concrete channel and sound walls. The Spring Mountains rose ahead of me as I took the exit onto the Summerlin Parkway.

Summerlin was an affluent settlement by the looks of things. Big houses, generous yards, expensive automobiles parked outside. Sarah Blackwell's street was on the far western edge, just before civilization gave way to the Mojave Desert. I parked outside the house and turned off the engine. The house was a wide two-story structure with a generous yard. Two big ferns in terracotta pots flanked the glass doorway. The houses on either side were similar, and I guessed one of those had been Carol's. Perhaps the one on the left-hand side, since it was the one without a car in the driveway.

The warm Mojave breeze drifted through the open windows of my car. The evening was clear and quiet, the street deserted except for some kids playing hopscotch at the far end of the cul-de-sac. A nice place. I was glad Carol had wound up somewhere so pleasant. And then I remembered why I was here: to find out why she had left all this behind in such a hurry.

I heard a door open and turned my head to see a woman standing at the door of the house, her arms folded as she regarded the car parked outside and its occupant. I recognized Sarah Blackwell from the photograph: in her mid-forties, shoulder-length dark hair, a composed, inquisitive expression. She wore sandals, jeans and a white blouse. Her stance was wary, as though she didn't know whether what came next would be a good idea.

That made two of us.

10

LAS VEGAS

As was so often the case in Gage's experience, the trail to one man began with another.

Walter and his two compatriots had been somewhat successful in tracking Freel's movements, actually managing to find the place where he had been living. Unfortunately, they had found it several weeks after Freel had skipped out, along with his wife. That break had been down to blind luck. Someone had posted a picture on Facebook showing Freel at some neighborhood barbecue. They had narrowed it down to a particular neighborhood, and narrowed the house down by finding the one place that had been rented to a couple answering the description of Freel and his wife.

Gage had the address as a starting point. Walter told him they had already checked the place out a few nights before and had found nothing; just an old laptop with nothing of use on it. He wanted to give the place a once-over himself, but not until after dark. One of the neighbors had called the police last time, so he would have to exercise caution. In the meantime, Gage thought it would be worthwhile to look a little deeper into the other piece of information they had given him. The wanted sheet from five years ago.

Freel had not just been wanted, he had been got. He had served two years in High Desert State Prison for aggravated robbery, which meant he had committed the felony with one or more accomplices. Gage contacted a friend of a friend in the Nevada Department of Corrections and negotiated a copy of Freel's file. He was interested in known associates. He was disappointed when he discovered that Freel seemed to have kept out of trouble since his stretch inside. A guy named Logan McKinney had been Freel's collaborator on the job that had led to the jail time. McKinney had been released six months after Freel.

Gage returned to his hotel, a crumbling fifty-dollar-a-night dive just off the Strip. It looked worse in the daylight than it had the previous evening. He undressed and showered, and then he wrapped a towel on and lay on the mean single bed. The couple in the next room were having a full-on yelling match. Occasionally the wall would shake as one or other of them hurled an object or a fist at it. He tuned it out and made another couple of calls. Ten minutes later he had McKinney's record. This was more promising, because McKinney had either been busier, or just less careful than his friend. In contrast to Freel's relatively sparse criminal record, McKinney's was dotted with felonies and misdemeanors at regular intervals over the few years since his incarceration.

McKinney's last known address was a rooming house in Carson City. Gage found the number and dialed it.

"McKinney?" the weariness the man at the end of the line invested in that single word spoke volumes. "Not here anymore. And good riddance. He owe you money?"

"When did he leave?" Gage asked.

"I don't know, weeks ago."

"Any chance you could be more specific?"

The volume of the fight next door stepped up a couple of notches, the woman screaming an unintelligible curse at the man. It blocked out the voice on the other end. Gage switched the phone to the ear farthest from the wall and retreated to the far corner of the room.

"Sorry about that. Excuse the noise."

There was a pause, and when the man on the other end of the line spoke again his voice had gained a suspicious edge. "Who did you say you were again?"

"I'm sorry, I should have explained. Mr. McKinney doesn't owe me anything, but he did borrow some money from a friend of my mother's. She's kind of vulnerable, and ..."

"That sounds like the son of a bitch all right. Give me a second."

There was a rustle of papers and the voice came back on the line.

"I cleared out his room on April 16th."

That was interesting. Freel had last been seen a couple of days earlier.

"He left on the 16th?"

"No. Rent is a week in advance. If memory serves,

68

McKinney disappeared a couple days before. Fair's fair, so I gave him until the end of his week and not a minute longer."

Gage couldn't help but grin. He had no doubt that McKinney's belongings had been decorating the sidewalk at one minute after midnight.

"Any idea where he might have gone?"

"Sure, he went to Phoenix."

"How do you know that?"

"A guy down there called me for a reference. Some bar. I told him to run a mile. Just a second ..." more paper noises. He came back on the line with the name of a bar and a street. Gage scribbled the address down.

"Thank you, you've been very helpful."

He hung up and looked at the mugshot of McKinney, and then the one of Freel. Associates on one robbery, time in the same prison, probably keeping in touch afterwards, too. And they had both disappeared within days of one another. It might be a coincidence, but it didn't feel like one. The room had grown darker since Gage had started making the calls. The couple next door were still fighting, but not as loudly or intensely. They seemed to have peaked. He got up and looked out of the window, facing west where the sun was beginning to dip below the jagged outline of the mountain range. The suburb of Summerlin was somewhere in between. He had one more call to make first, though, and this one had nothing to do with Dominic Freel.

The phone rang four times before it was answered by a tired female voice, the effect of a pack of cigarettes a day making the voice sound older than its owner.

"Hello?"

"It's me."

There was a long pause. Gage was patient.

"What do you want?" Courtney finally asked.

"Is he there?"

"What makes you think he'll want to talk to you?"

"Go ask him."

Another sigh. Then a clunk as the phone was placed down on a surface. Gage pictured the old red plastic telephone lying on the table in the hall of the apartment on Exeter Street. Courtney hadn't given him her new cell number, but she hadn't bothered to change the land number either.

He heard footsteps approaching on the worn carpet, voices from off-mic.

"Who is it?"

"It's him."

The receiver was picked up.

"Hello? Jake Pelletier speaking."

The voice had changed a little in the two months since Gage had last heard it. More thoughtful, less babyish. He was going to be six soon, after all. A big boy.

"How's it going, champ?"

"Trenton! Where are you?"

Gage winced a little. The compromise. Courtney would allow him to see the kid every once in a while, plus the odd phone call, but she would never make it official. Never tell him who "Trenton" actually was.

"I'm out west," he said, keeping his voice light. "In a really big city called Las Vegas. Have you heard of it?"

"Sure, where they have all the signs that light up?"

"All the signs," he agreed. "How you been?"

"I'm going to be six in two weeks, did my mommy tell you?"

"She may have mentioned it."

"We're having a party, are you going to come?" There was a pause, and Gage could picture Courtney shaking her head vigorously. "What?"

"I don't know about that, Jake. But if you tell me what you want, I'll make sure Santa hears about it."

"Santa's only for Christmas."

"Oh really? Who handles birthdays then, the Easter Bunny?"

"You're silly."

"I'll tell you what, I'll make sure the Easter Bunny makes a special trip, out of season. What'll it be?"

There was a pause, and Gage could picture the furrowed brow, the calculations about what it was okay to ask for.

"A PS4?"

"Jake!" his mother's voice.

"I'll see what I can do."

The voice in the background again, telling him to say goodbye.

"I have to go now, Trenton."

"Well it was great talking to you. I'll see you soon, okay?"

"How soon?"

Gage hesitated. "Well, that's the sixty-four-thousand-dollar question, isn't it?"

"Oh. I don't have that much money."

Gage smiled. "Don't worry about it. Put your mom back on."

The kid said goodbye and Gage said the same. The smile faded as Courtney came on the line again, her voice low as she watched Jake retreat back to his room.

"Why do you keep calling, Gage?"

"He likes to speak to me."

"He's five, he doesn't know what the hell he likes. Why don't you do the both of us a favor and just forget we exist?"

"You get my last letter?"

Sigh. "Yeah I got it. This isn't about money, Gage. I'm not the same person I was. I can't be. He deserves better."

"Listen, I'm working on a job."

"I don't want to know about it."

"I have some money saved. In a year or two, maybe I can ..."

"No."

Gage said nothing. He had a hundred ways of forcing somebody to do what he wanted, but none of those ways would do him any good with Courtney Pelletier.

"Gage, we could be moving soon. There might be a job out of town."

"Where?"

"I think ... I think maybe it would be good if I didn't tell you where."

Gage gripped the phone and kept his voice even with an effort of will. "I'd like to come and see him before you go. The birthday party, okay?"

She didn't say anything for a long moment.

"Okay, but after that we need to talk."

"I'll see you in a couple of weeks."

Gage closed his eyes as the call ended. He pictured Jake and Courtney standing in the hall, probably talking over the call. He forced the image to the back of his mind, and brought back the face of the man he had been paid to look for. When he opened his eyes again, he saw the sun had set behind the mountains.

11

SUMMERLIN

The blue Ford had been on the road for some time, judging by the road-dirt streaked all over its sills. The man behind the wheel seemed to hesitate for a second before opening the door. And then he raised a hand in acknowledgment and got out.

In contrast to his vehicle, the man looked like he had weathered the journey well. He was six feet tall, wearing shoes and black suit pants and a white open-necked shirt with the sleeves rolled up. Like an executive on his way home after a day at work. As he approached the house in the fading light, Sarah realized for the first time that she didn't know the man's name. He had replied to her email an hour after she had sent it, suggesting they met in person and that he could be there the following evening. There had been no name at the sign-off. Up until this moment, he had been an anonymous email account. A last desperate try for information on Rebecca that had brought two perfect strangers together, for ... what exactly?

Break glass in case of emergency.

"Sarah, right?"

She nodded after a pause. "Rebecca's friend."

He was holding his hand out. She shook it carefully, wondering if he was going to even tell her his name. It seemed like he was hesitating a little on this, just like he had on getting out of the car.

"I'm Carter Blake," he said after a pause. "I knew Rebecca, years ago."

A very slight hesitation before he said the word "Rebecca," like he had been about to say another name. He made it sound like he hadn't seen her in a long time. And yet here he was. Sarah looked beyond him to the dirt-streaked car.

"I didn't know if you would actually come. Was it a long trip?"

"Louisiana." He said it matter-of-fact, like he was saying he'd come from two blocks away.

She looked back at him. She couldn't hear any Louisiana in his accent, so she doubted he was a native. It seemed like every word he spoke sparked off another series of questions in her mind. He might not have seen Rebecca in years, but something had compelled him to come all this way at a moment's notice. Who was he? Who was Rebecca?

She regarded him for another second. Up close, he looked tired. But there was something in his eyes that reassured her somehow. She couldn't put her finger on it. A second later it hit her. Though Blake was probably younger than her, the look in his eyes reminded her a little of her father: the way his concern had been hiding just behind the smiles and bravado. Her dad's concern had never been for himself; he simply worried about her worrying.

"Well, you must be tired," she said. "Come on in and we'll talk."

She showed Carter Blake into the same living room where Officer Stansfield had made her feel like a paranoid moron a day and a half before and told him to take a seat, offering to make coffee, tea, whatever he liked.

"I'm fine," he said, before reconsidering. "I'd love a glass of water if it's no trouble."

Sarah retrieved two cold bottles of water from the refrigerator and brought them back through to the living room.

Blake took one and thanked her, taking a long swallow. They sat down opposite each other.

"Where in Louisiana?" she asked.

"A little place called Grand Isle. It's on the Gulf. It's beautiful."

"You don't come from there, though."

He shook his head, and Sarah decided he wasn't going to volunteer where he was from. Besides, as his next utterance showed, he was curious about something himself.

"Do you still have the notebook, Ms. Blackwell?"

"Call me Sarah. I never got used to being Ms. Blackwell. I would change back to my maiden name, but who needs the hassle, right?"

Blake smiled politely and then realized that she was waiting for him to reciprocate. "Oh, you can call me ... actually, just call me Blake. Most people do."

She smiled, mentally adding "more comfortable with last names" to her list of observations. It might suggest a certain background, or type of occupation.

"Notebook," she said, bringing the conversation back around.

She reached for the notebook, which was lying on the table at one end of the couch she was sitting on. She leafed it open to the final page and turned it round so Blake could see it. "I don't think she meant to leave this behind. It was the only personal item in the house."

He made no move to touch it at first, just looked down at the doodle on the final page. The little frame with "*red21585@ gmail.com*" neatly lettered inside. Sarah had seen a lot of anonymous emails in her time, and in her experience this kind of thing worked best: simple and untraceable. A color followed by some numbers that were probably entirely random, or perhaps helped the owner identify when and where or to whom this particular address had been given.

Blake's mouth curled into a surprised smile as he read the sign above the frame.

"'Break glass in case of emergency,'" he read. He looked up. "You think that's what this is? An emergency?"

Sarah considered before answering. She didn't want to go through the same dead-end conversation she had had with the Missing Persons cop. "I don't know. All I do know is I haven't heard from Rebecca and I'm concerned about her."

"She didn't, though."

"Didn't what?"

"Didn't break the glass." Blake gulped the rest of the water—obviously he had been thirsty. He sat back on the couch. "I find people for a living. Sometimes those people don't want to be found. What if she just doesn't want to be found?"

Sarah sat back and folded her arms. "That's entirely possible, I suppose. Did you come all this way just to suggest that?"

He smiled and leafed through some of the earlier pages, stopping to examine some of them for a few seconds before flipping forward until he got to the page with the single strange line on it.

"Any idea what this means?"

"'Quarter by June?'" She shook her head. "Not a clue. It's June now. Maybe she was planning to have a quarter of some sort of task done by now."

"Or June could be a person." He stared at the three words a little longer and then closed the book and looked up at her. "Why don't you tell me it all from the beginning?"

Sarah couldn't remember everything she had said in the email. She had kept it reasonably brief, knowing that anyone being at the other end of the email address was a long shot. So she started from the beginning. How Rebecca and her husband Dominic had moved in the previous January. How they had kept themselves to themselves to begin with. How the position of her study had meant that she had been unintentionally surveilling them for hours each day. At that point, Blake interrupted for the first time to ask what her job was.

"I used to be a staffer at the *Tribune*. Now I'm a writer. I write novels."

"Have you written anything I might have read?"

"I don't know, are you a twelve- to sixteen-year-old girl?"

Blake considered this. "Do I need to be?"

Sarah smiled. "So my publisher tells me. That's my audience, apparently. YA. But you're right, I don't just write for your average teenage girl. That would be stupid, since there's no such thing. I get all kinds of people getting in touch. I write the Farrah Fairchild series. She's ... kind of a detective."

"Like Nancy Drew?"

"Or Veronica Mars."

"I'll check it out."

She didn't know if he was kidding or not. "Anyway, I'm at my desk upstairs for hours every day. It looks out onto number 32. I can see the front door, the backyard, the side windows. And that's how I first got curious about them."

"What did you see?"

"Not a lot. They didn't seem to go out much. Neither of them left in the morning and came home at night on a weekday, so I knew they didn't have regular jobs."

"Lots of people work from home these days," Blake said. "Maybe they're writers too."

He was questioning her, looking for clarifications. But it

didn't come across as though he was trying to poke holes in her story; or belittling her concerns the way Officer Stansfield had done.

"Maybe," she agreed. "But it was ... unusual. Unusual enough for me to wonder about."

She went on, told him about the patterns she had begun to notice over the weeks. How they never seemed to go out at the same time. Sometimes the man would go out, sometimes the woman. Often one of them would go out in the evening, or late at night. She didn't hear a peep from them until the night of the argument.

"It was a warm night, so the windows were open. Theirs and mine. I heard something breaking and then an argument. They were yelling about something." She shrugged sheepishly. "Curiosity got the better of me, I guess, and I was at the window trying to hear more when Rebecca saw me—caught me eavesdropping red-handed. She slammed the window closed and I basically wanted the earth to swallow me up."

Blake smiled. "Did they fight a lot?"

"That was the only time I heard anything," Sarah said.

"What's her husband like?"

Sarah shook her head. "I really never got to know him."

"Did your ex-husband ever speak to him?"

Sarah had noticed Blake scanning the room, probably concluding from the furniture and decor that she had lived alone for quite some time now, but polite enough to let her tell him that. "We've been divorced for almost three years— Edward was long gone before Rebecca and Dominic moved in, so he never spoke to him either."

Blake nodded. "Okay, what happened after the fight?"

"The next day, she showed up with a bottle of wine. Wanted to apologize if they'd disturbed me. I asked her in for a coffee and we got on pretty well. She started coming over every day or so."

"So you got to know her."

Sarah smiled. "Well that's just it, Blake. Yes and no."

He raised his eyebrows, but didn't say anything.

"We got on pretty well. It was nice to have somebody new in the neighborhood I could talk to. But she never really talked about herself. Only the occasional thing, and never anything really specific. Like she would tell me she wasn't in touch with her family, but not give me any reason. Or that she used to live in New York, but not what she did for a living. It wasn't like she was constantly stonewalling me; I don't mean like that. I thought she was one of those people who just don't talk that much about themselves. To tell you the truth, I didn't really think about it until after she disappeared."

"Tell me about that," Blake said. "About how she left."

She reached for the Samsung tablet that was lying on the coffee table and tapped her fingers across the surface until she brought up the picture she had emailed him. Her with the mystery couple.

"She didn't really socialize with the other neighbors. I didn't blame her, to be honest. But I asked her to come with me to a yard party and she did. Her husband showed up halfway through. I had spoken to him a couple of times in passing. Always brief, always a little awkward. That day he was different, though."

"Different how?"

She thought about it. "I guess what surprised me was I thought maybe he was shy, and that was why he kept himself to himself. But that day he was anything but. He showed up, found Rebecca and grabbed her arm. He said they had to go.

"Rebecca pulled away and told him to relax, that she would come in her own time. He got this look in his eye, like ... have you ever seen a mother who really wants to slap her kid in the supermarket, but can't because of everyone watching? Like that. For a second I actually thought he was going to grab her again and physically drag her out of there. But he didn't."

Blake's brow furrowed, and she knew what he was thinking. "What did he do?"

"He just leaned in and whispered something in her ear. I couldn't hear what he said, but her expression changed like that. And that's when the host took this picture."

Blake looked down at the picture again, his understanding deepened by the story behind this snatched moment. He didn't say anything for a while, lost in thought.

"She went with him right after that, and that was the last time I saw her."

Sarah continued, telling him about the typed note, about the men she had seen go into the house, about talking to the police. And then she told him about her decision to use the spare key and do a little investigation of her own, coming up with nothing. Or not quite nothing, as Blake's presence proved.

When she had finished speaking, Blake spoke after gathering his thoughts.

"It sounds like they always planned to leave in a hurry," he said.

"How do you figure?"

"They disappeared overnight without you noticing. That means they didn't spend time loading everything into a removal truck or a van, which means they can't have had that much stuff in the first place. Maybe they had no more than you could fit in a suitcase."

Sarah cast her mind back to the previous January and remembered that that held true for their arrival as well as their departure. Now that she thought about it, there had never been a truck when they moved in, either. They had arrived in a small car, and, so far as Sarah had considered it at all, she assumed their belongings had been delivered at another time. But what if they hadn't been? It would explain why Rebecca had pointedly never invited her over. An empty house would raise questions.

"Why would they do that, though? What would make them have to be ready to leave at a moment's notice?"

She could see that something she had said had struck a chord with Blake.

"What is it? You know, don't you? You know what they're running from."

He didn't say anything for a minute, the look in his eyes a million miles away. Then he seemed to snap out of it, re-membered where he was and shook his head. "No, I don't." He got up and walked across to the side window, the one that looked onto 32's front porch. "Everything you've said, it doesn't necessarily add up to something sinister."

Sarah felt a flush of frustration again, like the way she had felt talking to the police. "What the hell do you mean? They just disappeared like that, and then nothing—no phone calls, nada."

"She left a note."

She took a deep breath. "Why did you come, if you weren't going to listen to me?"

"I'm listening. Do you still have the note?"

She sighed. "The cop from Missing Persons took it. I have a picture, though."

She showed him on her phone. He stared at it for a long time, just like the Missing Persons cop had done. Trying to intuit meaning from the spare words on the page. He handed the phone back to her and she could see that hint of concern in his eyes again. Maybe he had just been playing devil's advocate, hoping he could find a nice, pleasant explanation for Rebecca's disappearance. His next words confirmed it.

"Is the spare key still there?"

12

It took Gage a while to find the place. The suburbs were a never-ending maze of closely packed cul-de-sacs and curving crescents that got his hackles up. He hated these little identi-kit communities. Everybody in their little boxes, just like the song. Gage had never understood the urge to invest so much of one's time and being into a trophy home. For him, it was enough to have somewhere to shelter, sleep and eat. It was much more interesting to do your living elsewhere.

He knew this was a product of his upbringing among the mountains and forests of British Columbia. His mother had died before he had been old enough to form a memory of her, and from the time he was old enough to walk, his father had never made him feel welcome around the house. This was fine by him. Gage had been only too happy to spend long summer days hiking and fishing, and then cold winter days hunting deer in the snowy forests. After dropping out of high school and joining the Royal Canadian Mounted Police, he had relished spending his days outside, patrolling the roads and the logging tracks in his jurisdiction. The RCMP acted as the provincial police force, covering a patch that was more than three hundred thousand square miles.

The sparse population and terrain made the region a favored destination for fugitives, from both sides of the border. He gradually built a reputation as one of the go-to guys for manhunts north of the 49th parallel. Over a five-year period, he helped track down a dozen prison escapees, several drug smugglers, and even one would-be domestic terrorist who fancied himself an outdoorsman. Gage knew the country, knew where experienced and inexperienced prey were likely to flee. Occasionally, the hunts would take him into more urban environments: Vancouver and Victoria. Some of the rules changed in the city, but he found the fundamental principles were adaptable.

He would have been content with that life, had matters not been taken out of his hands.

After his career in the police was brought to a premature end, Gage realized that his experiences so far had furnished him with talents that were of value on the open market. The money was better, much better, and he enjoyed the work. If the RCMP was squeamish about his methods, that was absolutely their loss.

He had been thinking about the three men in the bar as he drove back out to the western suburbs of Las Vegas. He knew they weren't telling him everything, but he was fairly certain they had given him all of the useful intelligence they had on Dominic Freel. A last known address and a known associate was a pretty good start—far more than he had to go on with some jobs.

Gage had a feeling there was more to this job than met the eye. A lot of clients expected a no-questions-asked service, and in most cases that was fine. He relished the small mystery, wondered how easy it would be to untangle.

After what felt like an eternity of driving through the streets, he found the one he was looking for: West Pine

Avenue. The sky was full dark now, the hints of stars showing through because the smog was lighter at this distance from the city. Gage slowed and made an initial pass of the address: 32. The driveway was empty, the windows in darkness. He passed the house without slowing, turned the corner, and parked at the curb out of sight of the house.

13

The backyard lay in the shelter of a pair of tall cypress trees. I stood by the back door while Sarah Blackwell knelt to retrieve the spare key from a plant pot. I was thinking about the question she had asked back in the living room. Not a question, really, more like an accusation: "You know what they're running from."

Sarah was quick on the uptake; she could see I was dwelling on something. But it had led her to the wrong conclusion. I had been thinking about another empty house, years ago in Manhattan. I had been telling Sarah the truth when I said I didn't know what they were running from. What happened in New York didn't explain why she had been living here, nearly three thousand miles across the country with this guy Freel. It didn't explain why they would move into a quiet suburban community, and then pull a disappearing act at a moment's notice. At first, at the back of my mind I had wondered if this could have something to do with Winterlong, but having spoken to Sarah, I was satisfied that it didn't. Whatever the explanation was, I had a gut instinct it was something to do with the husband.

I was surprised that it smarted a little to think of this guy in those terms. *The husband*. It was ridiculous to feel that way, of course. Those weeks in New York were a lifetime ago. We had both emphatically moved on. Or perhaps that was just wishful thinking.

Regardless, I hadn't expected ever to hear from Carol again. The only reason I was here was because her neighbor was concerned. And now I was concerned too.

"I never thought B&E would become one of my bad habits," Sarah commented as she slipped the key into the lock. "I'm a pretty boring person most of the time. Neglecting to sort my recycling is about as rebellious as I generally get."

I was grateful for the small talk. "It's a slippery slope. One day you're failing to recycle, the next it's burglary. You'll be dealing crack on the corner over there by Thursday."

As I glanced in the direction of the street to see if there was a corner, I heard the sound of an engine approaching. Slow. One of the neighbors returning home, or someone unfamiliar with the street looking for an address. Sarah had opened the door and was looking at me expectantly, as though she wanted me to make the incursion first.

"Wait a second," I said, lowering my voice.

She looked out at the street and we watched as a car approached. It slowed a little before it got to 32, but then passed by. In the couple of seconds it took to pass by our field of view down the side passage, I saw that it was a dark Jeep, impossible to tell the exact color in the streetlight. It picked up speed again after it passed.

I exchanged a glance with Sarah and we turned back toward the door. She pushed it open, and I could smell the stale air of a place that's been sealed up for weeks.

The house was exactly as Sarah had described it. It looked like the kind of property a prospective renter or buyer would be shown around, not a place that was actually in the process of being lived in. Taking the role of the realtor in that scenario, Sarah showed me from room to room. Only instead of demonstrating the floor-level lights in the kitchen and commenting on the roominess of the bedroom closets, she ticked off all of the places she had searched on her previous visit. I was impressed; she had done a good job for a civilian. I told her so, as she showed me into the final bedroom, where she had found the notebook.

"That's because I'm not quite a civilian. I was a reporter, remember? Sticking my nose into other people's business is a habit that dies hard, I guess."

"Tell me about it," I said.

"Talking of which, interesting use of the word 'civilian.' You were in the military, I take it?"

"Something like that," I said, making a note to be more careful of what I said to Sarah Blackwell. I played the beam of the flashlight on my phone over the interior of the bedroom closet. It was spick and span; like it had never been used. I switched the beam off again—I had kept the brightness on the lowest setting and made sure to stay away from windows, but it made sense not to draw attention from anyone who might happen to pass by the house.

"What do you think?"

I looked back at Sarah. Her face was lit by the glow of the sodium lights from the street outside. "I think you're right. They knew they weren't coming back."

We went back downstairs. I checked the drawers in the kitchen, finding all the usual cutlery and cooking implements, and the drawer everybody has that's filled with junk. I had been optimistic about that one: people leave all sorts of interesting things in the junk drawer. Things they don't want to carry around with them but don't want to throw away. But in this case, I was out of luck. All that was in the drawer was some utility bills and some AA batteries. The bills were addressed to D. Smith: no new information. I opened the cupboards and found the trash, glancing over at Sarah.

"I checked that too," she said.

I took a look inside anyway. The trash bag had been removed and there was nothing in the receptacle itself but dust and a lone popcorn kernel.

There was a small room leading to the back door. I opened the door and stepped in. A laundry room. Washer and dryer, a shelf holding a box of detergent. In the corner there was a wicker laundry basket, shaped into a right angle with a curve to fit into the corner. I opened the lid and saw that it was almost as empty as the trash. Almost, but not quite. There was a single sock and a pair of jeans at the bottom. They were flattened, like they had lain at the bottom of the pile for a while, and had been ignored when the rest of the laundry was removed. I reached in and pulled the jeans out, shaking them into shape.

"You're thorough," Sarah said approvingly.

They were men's jeans. A thirty-four waist. They were dusty and torn at the knees, and there was some kind of oil stain on one leg. I could see why they had been abandoned. Not expecting much, I started to go through the pockets. In the last one I checked, I found a balled-up piece of paper, which I took out and unfolded. It was a receipt. I like receipts: they contain a whole lot of information in a small space. This one was from a gas station, dated March 12th, 19:17. Thirteen gallons of unleaded, two cans of soda, two sandwiches, a Snickers bar. The name of the station was Grady's Rest Stop. There was no address, but there was a phone number. The area code wasn't one I was familiar with.

"520. Is that around here?"

Sarah shook her head. "Nope." She took out her phone and tapped it in, looking up from the screen a second later. "Arizona."

"Why were they in Arizona on March 12th? I thought they stayed close to home the whole time"

She thought about it. "I think they did go away somewhere for a couple days in March. Rebecca said something about a trip."

This was a break in the routine, and breaks in the routine are always worth investigating.

The sound of a car alarm going off a couple of streets away reminded us of where we were.

"We should probably go," Sarah said.

We retreated to the back door. We locked it behind us and replaced the spare key and headed back over to Sarah's house. A minute later, we were back in Sarah's kitchen looking at a pinpoint on a map on the screen of her tablet. The pin identified the location as Grady's Rest Stop, Navajo County, Arizona. There wasn't a lot to see on the screen: just the pinpoint and a line running vertically up the screen indicating the highway. Sarah pinched her fingers on the screen to widen the focus, having to repeat the action a couple of times before we zoomed out far enough to see anything else on the map.

"It's in the middle of nowhere," she said.

The rest stop was almost two hundred miles east of Phoenix. There were a few small towns dotted around, not much more than wide spaces in the road by the size of them. The nearest town that looked as though it might have a population over three figures in the area was called Iron City, ten miles from the rest stop. I asked Sarah if Carol had ever mentioned it.

She shook her head. "Never heard of it."

"She say anything about the days they were away in March?"

"I think she said they had been visiting friends for the weekend. I didn't exactly lose sleep wondering ..." I realized Sarah was staring at me with a look of concern.

"What?"

"I'm going to make some coffee."

I didn't argue. I wasn't feeling anywhere near as tired as I had an hour before, but maybe I looked it. While Sarah brewed a pot, I sat down at the kitchen table with the tablet. I switched to the satellite view and zoomed in on some of the smaller towns on the map, wondering if any of those had been Carol and Freel's destination on the mystery March road trip, rather than Iron City.

The closest place to the rest stop was a town called Corinth. When I zoomed in, I realized that something didn't look quite right. It took me a second to work out what it was: no cars. On closer inspection, I could see that the roofs of some of the buildings had collapsed in, and there were empty lots where buildings had been demolished, or fallen down. I zoomed out and saw the remains of an open cast mine southeast of the town.

"A ghost town," I said to myself.

"What?"

I turned the screen to show her. "This place Corinth: looks like an old mining town."

"Abandoned. Lot of them about," Sarah said. "Some of them are tourist attractions. I went to one once when I was a kid. They had a Wild West show, a theme restaurant. It was fun."

"This one doesn't look quite as touristy," I said. "And it's pretty far to go on a whim. Did they go away any other time, that you noticed?"

She shook her head. "Like I say, the reason it was noticeable in March was because they never went anywhere. The car was always in the driveway every day. When they went anywhere, they were back within an hour or two. That means this is important, somehow."

I had pulled up the Streetview now, mildly surprised that there even was one. Google hadn't attempted to map the whole town, but the camera car had passed through Main Street on its way back to the highway. I swiped along, looking at the boarded-up stores and the dilapidated single-story homes. Just from a glance, I could see why Corinth hadn't been renovated as a tourist attraction like the place Sarah had spoken about. From the looks of things, this place had been abandoned in the eighties. The remaining signs advertised pawn shops and Pepsi. No picturesque Wyatt Earp ambience here. An older building passed by on the screen, older than the rest, and something about it made me stop. I stared at it for a second while I worked out what it was that had caught my eye.

I reached for Carol's notebook and leafed through until I found what I was looking for. One of the sketches. An old building. I held it up against the screen. It was the same building.

I heard Sarah gasp next to my ear and realized she had circled around the table without me being aware. I definitely needed to get some sleep.

"That's it. This is where she was."

"It's not much to go on," I said, "but maybe it's a start."

"We can set off first thing in the morning," Sarah said.

I shook my head. "*We're* not going anywhere."

"What do you mean?"

"I told you, I do this for a living. And one of my rules is I work alone."

Sarah leaned back on the edge of the worktop and gave me a sardonic smile. "That's great. And I would be very interested to hear the rest of your rules. If I were employing you."

I adopted a suitably chastened expression. "I didn't mean to be a dick. But you contacted me because you were worried, right?"

She didn't say anything; nodded briefly after a second.

"And now I've spoken to you and seen the house, I'm worried too. I think your instincts are dead on. Something isn't right with this. Why would they just disappear like that, with no trace? Why wouldn't she call you? If it was a temporary thing, they'd be back already. If it was nothing to worry about, she would have returned your calls.

"But it's more than that. Somebody broke into the house the other night and searched the place. They weren't as thorough as you, otherwise they would have found the notebook. But maybe they didn't need to be."

"What do you mean?"

"Maybe they found what they were looking for. The point is, Ca ... *Rebecca* has disappeared and somebody's looking for her or her husband. I told you your instincts were right, but my instincts are usually pretty good too, and I don't like what they're telling me."

Her eyes had narrowed as I started to say "Carol," but she didn't pick me up on it. For the time being, she was more focused on the last thing I had said.

"You mean having to drag me along would cramp your style."

"It's not like that," I said. "But I don't like the idea of bringing you along when I don't know exactly what I'd be getting you into. Once I work out what's going on, I'll need your help."

She looked at me with skepticism, but I could see she was taking it on board. After all, she had been worried enough about the men who showed up the other night to call the cops.

"So you've said that a couple of times—you do this for a living. You're a bounty hunter or something?"

"Not exactly. I'm good at finding people. Yes, sometimes people pay me to go after bad guys ..."

"And sometimes you help to find people out of the goodness of your heart."

I smiled and gave her just enough time to feel bad about the sarcastic tone before I replied.

"I just want to make sure she's safe."

She considered it for a moment, holding my gaze. "You promise?" she said at last. "You'll call me as soon as you know more?"

"I'll call you even if I don't find out more. We're a team on this one."

"Even though you don't do teams."

"I'm fine with long-distance teamwork."

She sighed. "All right. She's in some kind of danger, isn't she? I wasn't just being paranoid."

"I don't think you were being paranoid."

We drank our coffee and Sarah told me I could take the notebook with me. She had already photographed each page—the journalist showing through again. She suggested that maybe my prior knowledge of our quarry might mean the notebook would tell me something she had missed. As I was leaving, I stood at the door for a second and surveyed the street. The kids who had been playing earlier were long gone, probably fast asleep in bed by now, and the night was quiet but for the sounds of cicadas and the far away traffic noise from the parkway. No sign of any pedestrians or cars.

"You'll call when you get there?" she asked again.

"Soon as I get there," I agreed. "Long-distance team."

She held her hand out again and I shook it. "Thanks again. For coming, I mean." She hesitated for a second, then said it. "Rebecca must have meant something to you, huh?"

"I'll call you tomorrow," I said as I turned and walked out to the car.

"Blake," she called after me. "What's her name? Her real name."

I hesitated, then answered without turning around. "Her name is Carol."

14

Gage was a cautious type. That was why he had parked around the corner from Freel's house. He locked the Jeep and walked briskly around the corner, not hurrying or skulking in the shadows, just looking like somebody out for an evening stroll. His eyes were constantly surveying the street, taking in the lighted windows in the other houses, checking the parked cars for anyone sitting in the darkness.

There were two cars outside the neighboring house to 32: one in the driveway, one at the curb, suggesting someone was visiting. Not a close friend, though, because there was more than enough room for two cars in the driveway. Perhaps the driver had not wanted to encroach on this personal space. He glanced at the blue Ford as he passed it to confirm there was no one inside and then looked at the house. The lights were on at the ground floor, but he saw no sign of anybody through the windows.

He slowed as he approached the six-foot wooden fence that marked the boundary with Freel's house, and calmly checked the surrounding street again before turning and walking up the path, headed for the side passage to the backyard. He reached into his pocket and withdrew the folding leather wallet that contained his pick set, and then stopped as he rounded the corner and saw the back door. It took him a few seconds to work out what was wrong. The yard was low-maintenance, and neatly kept. Just a rock garden and a paved section at the back door. Flanking the door were two rows of pot plants. On the right-hand side of the door, the second-farthest pot from the door had been moved, judging by the semicircle of dust protruding from underneath it. He looked closer and saw a small hollow in the soil, as though somebody had recently dug something out of there. Like a spare key.

Gage scanned the ground floor windows, and then the second floor. No signs of life, or light. He listened carefully, and then moved toward the door. There was a small catflap set into the door, just a few inches wide. He crouched down and nudged it open a crack, moving his ear to the gap. He listened for a few seconds, hearing at first only the sound of his own heartbeat. And then he heard something else, from within the house. The soft creak of floorboards, as though someone was ascending the stairs, and trying to be quiet about it. Somebody who didn't want anybody to know they were in the house.

Interesting.

Gage stood up and surveyed the yard. It was sheltered from the street by the bulk of the house, and the overhanging leaves of the thick trees at the far end blocked out a lot of the light from the sky. There was a small wooden storage shed at the far end of the yard. Casting another glance up at the windows, he moved quickly to the side of the shed and crouched down, watching the house. He saw nothing for long enough that he began to wonder if the creaking floorboards had been a trick of his imagination, or maybe a pet had been left in the house. No, Freel and his wife had left weeks ago. Any dog or cat unfortunate enough to have been left behind would be an ex-pet by now.

After five minutes, his patience was rewarded. He saw a brief glow of illumination in one of the second floor rooms. Someone had used a flashlight, but had been very careful not to shine it near the windows. Had he not been watching the windows so intently, it would not have been noticeable. The cautiousness went along with the creeping up the stairs. Somebody was searching the place. Somebody who had just as little right to be there as he did.

Five more minutes. The back door opened quietly and a man stepped out. He was mid-thirties, six feet tall, in good shape. He wore black pants and a shirt. He glanced from side to side, and then at the bottom of the yard. Gage resisted the urge to flinch as he looked directly at his position.

The man looked back at the door, and a woman came out. Shorter than the man, dark shoulder-length hair. They whispered something to each other, and the man glanced around the side passage to check the street.

Gage watched as the two of them headed back out to the street, and then listened as their footsteps faded ... and then got louder again. At first he thought they were coming back, and then he realized they were going into the house next door. The house with the blue Ford outside, where somebody was visiting. Again: interesting. Gage counted to a hundred after he heard the door open and close. Number 32 could wait until later. He was more interested in why the neighbor and a friend had been searching the house.

Gage examined the fence that separated the last known dwelling of the man he was looking for from that of the person he was now interested in. He satisfied himself that his next action was within the realm of acceptable risk before lifting himself up and over.

He dropped into the yard, immediately drawing back into the shadows at the fence as one of the rooms in the house was lit up.

He crouched motionless, watching as the man and the woman entered what looked like a kitchen and began talking.

He didn't need to risk getting closer to know what they were talking about. What else would they be discussing? He was satisfied that the man was the visitor. Their polite, slightly guarded body language confirmed that these two people had only just met. From the way she moved around the kitchen, he knew the woman was on home turf. This wasn't a romantic assignation though; this looked like business.

So she was talking to a stranger in her kitchen, right after the two of them had searched her neighbor's house under cover of darkness. Who was the man? Did he have a connection with Freel?

Gage watched for another few minutes. It didn't look like either of them were going anywhere.

He made his way back out onto the street and walked around to where his car was parked. He wound the windows down and let the cool night breeze drift across his face. He turned on the radio at a low volume and found a local talk radio station. He had no interest in what was being discussed, but it passed the time.

He waited ten minutes. Twenty. Almost half an hour. He was starting to wonder if the visitor was going to stay over after all when he heard the sounds he had been waiting for: the soft clunk of a car door closing, and then an engine starting up. Gage killed the radio, buzzed the windows up and hunched back in his seat.

He watched the blue Ford pass by. The man from the house was behind the wheel. His eyes were fixed on the road ahead. He didn't look in the direction of Gage's car.

Gage watched the taillights as the driver reached the intersection with the main through road. The Ford turned right, headed for the Summerlin Parkway. Gage buzzed the window down again and listened as the sound of the engine faded away into the susurrations of the night. That was one good thing about the suburbs, he had to admit. In the relative quiet, it was possible to isolate and keep track of a single engine noise or set of footsteps for quite a while.

He waited another couple of minutes. He opened the glove box and took out his Glock G43 pistol.

He walked back around the corner. Not hurrying, not skulking in the shadows.

The ground floor windows at Freel's neighbor's house were all now in darkness. The rooms at the front of the upper floor were too, though Gage could see slight illumination in one of them, telling him that a door was partially open and one of the interior rooms had a light still burning.

He continued past the house, his eyes reading the street, and he turned into 32 for the second time. He walked down the side passage into the backyard. Sure enough, there was one lit window in the house next door—on the upper floor, at the side. He stayed close to the fence, out of the line of sight from the window, and moved to the point where he had scaled the fence earlier. He glanced around again. Up and over once more. All of the rooms this side were in darkness. This time, he didn't wait by the fence.

The back door was locked. He reached for the leather case that held his picks. It wouldn't be locked for long.

15

Sarah was way too buzzed to sleep. After Blake left, she poured the remainder of her coffee into the sink and made herself a chamomile tea. After checking all the doors were locked, she turned the lights out and headed upstairs. She passed the bedroom and went into the study. She sat down at her desk and sipped the tea, looking at the big, dark house across the way.

Carter Blake seemed like he knew what he was doing. If anyone could find out where Rebecca ... where *Carol* had gone, maybe he was the guy. Blake's parting confirmation that the woman she thought she knew hadn't even used her real name should have come as a shock, but somehow Sarah had been expecting it.

What he had said made sense. If she accepted that she was right to be worried about what could have made her neighbors leave so abruptly, then it followed that tracking them down could be dangerous. But then again, she had never let a little risk get in her way in her old line of work. She turned on the computer. It made sense to look at the problem from a different angle. Up until now, she had focused more on where they could have gone. What Blake had said had her thinking about what could have motivated them to go.

A team, he had said. She didn't know Blake well enough yet to tell if that had just been a line, a way to placate her while he did things his own way. Her instinct was the offer had been genuine. But either way, a team was what he was going to get.

They were sure the woman she now knew was named Carol had been to this Corinth place, but since it was uninhabited, there was a limit to what Sarah could find out about it from a distance.

She looked at the computer again and referred to the map to remind herself of the name of the nearest inhabited town, noting it down on the pad she kept beside her keyboard. Despite the name, Iron City wasn't much of a city, with a population of only fifteen hundred or so. If Carol and Dominic had a reason to be in the vicinity of Corinth, whatever that reason might be, perhaps they had stayed the night in Iron City. Maybe that was where they were now.

She widened the zoom to see where else the couple might have gone. She scrolled north first, let her eye follow the highway through a series of small towns curving up and across until the road reached Flagstaff. And then she went the other way. Seen at this scale, the road seemed to meander aimlessly down toward the border, passing through Tucson and then a series of smaller towns with one-word names. She caught her breath when she saw the name of one of the last of these towns.

Quarter.

She stared at the dot on the map for a few seconds, hardly able to believe it. But it couldn't be a coincidence. She Googled the town of Quarter. Compared to Iron City, it was a bustling metropolis, with a population of several thousand. She wrote the name next to Iron City on the pad. All of a sudden, it felt like she was getting somewhere.

Sarah didn't have any direct contacts in that neck of the woods, but she thought she had something just as good: professional courtesy. A couple of minutes on Google told her that both towns still had some form of local media. Iron City's was all online: a blog and Facebook page, run by one or two people by the looks of things. She was heartened to see that Quarter actually still had a real-live newspaper: the Quarter *Observer*. Both organs were easily contactable by email. She sent off two quickly composed messages giving her credentials and asking with help tracking down an old friend. After consideration, she left her cell number at the bottom. She was sure Carter Blake would have his own ways of tracking people down, but it wouldn't hurt to put some feelers out.

She thought back to the barbecue. April 14th. A Friday.

What had happened then? She pulled up the websites of the *Tribune*, the *Las Vegas Review Journal*, a couple of the smaller local newspapers. Nothing much on the 14th, so far as she could see. One of the hidden disadvantages of online news: because newspaper websites are so fluid, they do not provide the time capsule of a printed newspaper. She could view all of the big news stories of that day easily enough, but she was missing the big picture. There was an online archive of front pages for the *Tribune* and she could try going through that in the morning, but that would only show the most newsworthy events. Besides, maybe nothing happened on the 14th. Maybe something happened before that, or something was about to happen.

She browsed for news stories in the weeks before and after, but she had no idea of what to look for, and nothing jumped out. She had tried looking for a trace of her neighbor online before, of course. She hadn't been surprised when she couldn't find one: no Facebook, Instagram, nothing. Rebecca Smith was far too common a name to be of any use by itself, and none of the pictures related to that name were of the Rebecca she knew. She would ask Blake for Carol's last name when he called tomorrow. She delivered herself a mental kick for missing the opportunity to do so earlier. Maybe she would have more luck finding a trace of Carol in her previous life.

That made her think of all the names in the notebook. She clicked into her cloud storage, where the photographs of the notebook had been backed up. She looked at the page with all the signatures. All the different names.

Previous life ... which previous life would that be?

Suddenly, she heard the low creak of the kitchen door from downstairs, as if it was being opened as slowly as possible.

Somebody was inside her house.

She took a sharp breath and felt a chill travel the length of her spine. She reached for her phone and realized she had left it in the kitchen. She didn't have a landline upstairs: the only wired-in phone in the house was downstairs in the hall, and she almost never used it.

She got up quietly and tiptoed across to the door and out onto the landing, taking care to maneuver around the floorboard that squeaked. The light was on in the living room, sure enough.

"Blake?" she called, putting a hand on the banister to steady herself.

She knew it would make no sense for it to be him. If he had forgotten something, he would simply have rung the doorbell. Whoever was down there, it wasn't Blake.

There was no response. Dammit, why had she left her phone downstairs? And then she realized that maybe she didn't need one. She stepped back into the study. She could email the police—that was a thing now, right? Emailing the police? Hell, she could tweet them if it ... her hand was inches from the keyboard when the screen and the lamp winked out. She turned around and saw that the light from downstairs had gone out. Whoever was down there had tripped the switch in the fuse box.

A paralyzing dread swamped her. She thought she had been terrified before, when the lights were on, but now ... she suppressed a whimper and hurried back to the bedroom door. She started to swing it shut, thinking she could drag the desk in front of it. And then what? Climb out of the window, she guessed. She paused and yelled out.

"Whoever you are, get the fuck out of my house. I already called the police and they have a car on the—"

"I don't think so, ma'am."

The voice came from right outside the door.

Sarah gasped and slammed the door the rest of the way shut. How could he have gotten up the stairs so quietly? The door stalled and she felt pressure pushing her back. She leaned her full body weight on the door, but it was no good. There was a grunt and the door smashed back into her face, knocking her on her back on the carpet.

Her eyes, still adjusting to the dark, made out a man in the doorway, silhouetted in the streetlight illumination shining up through the glass in the front door. The man didn't move, just stood there, filling the space. He was big, wide as well as tall, and his head was completely shaved. He was holding something in his left hand.

"I have two questions," he said, his tone calm and reasonable. "One: where is Dominic Freel?"

Freel? Was that their real name? It was clear who he was talking about. "I don't know," she said quickly. "Please get out. I won't tell anyone you—"

"I thought the police were on the way," he said, his tone mocking. He held a hand up and she saw that what he was holding was her cell phone. He knew she had been lying. There was nobody coming for her.

"We'll come back to question one. Question two: who is the man you were searching the house with?"

"Blake? I don't know him. I never met him before tonight."

"Why were you searching the house? What do you know about Freel?"

"Nothing!" she shouted. "If you're talking about the guy next door, I don't know him. His wife asked me to water their plants."

She started to get up off the floor, but the big man held out a hand to stop her. She noticed he was wearing leather gloves. He had come prepared to break in and leave no trace. He stepped forward and crouched in front of her. Her eyes, adjusted to the dark better, saw a face that looked as if it was carved out of granite, a terrifying blankness in his eyes. On the right side of his face was an old, white scar in the shape of a crescent.

"I'm disappointed in the quality of your answers so far."

16

I almost didn't go back.

By the time I left Sarah's house, I had forgotten all about the vehicle that had slowed as it passed by the house earlier on. There was nothing particularly suspicious about one particular car driving past on a suburban street, after all. But as I rounded the corner and saw the black Jeep parked at the curb a hundred yards away, I remembered that the car that had passed by earlier in the evening had been a Jeep too.

Even so, I might not have made the connection if Sarah and I hadn't had the conversation in the kitchen. If she hadn't wanted to come with me, perhaps I wouldn't have had to think so much about my concerns about why Carol had gone on the run.

But so what if the car was the same as the one I had seen earlier? So the owner of the car lived in a house around here. No reason to be suspicious. I glanced at the car as my headlights lit it up from behind. Force of habit, I read the license plate and filed it away just in case. There was someone in the driver's seat.

If this was the Jeep I had seen earlier, the driver must have been waiting for more than an hour. And if he lived in one of the homes on this street, or was visiting, why was he parked at the curb beside a stretch of fence, rather than directly outside one of the houses?

It wasn't much, but it was enough to ring an alarm bell.

I looked straight ahead as I passed the black Jeep, not giving any indication that I had even seen it. I turned the corner at the intersection and turned onto the main route back to the parkway. I drove a couple hundred yards and pulled to a stop beneath the ink-black shade of a cypress tree.

I opened the glove box and took out my Beretta 92 pistol. I started walking back the way I had come on the wide sidewalk, telling myself this was probably nothing. But it's always better to be safe than sorry. When I got to the first corner I saw that the black Jeep was in the same position, but it was too far away to tell if anybody was still in the driver's seat.

I took my phone out and called up a map of my current location. There wasn't a quick alternative route to the house. I decided just to go back the way I had come, on the opposite side of the road from the car. It could still be a coincidence, I reminded myself. Maybe he was waiting for somebody. Maybe he had pulled over for a nap. Maybe lots of things.

As I got closer, I still couldn't see anyone in the seat. A couple of seconds later, I was close enough to confirm there was no one behind the wheel. I crossed the road on the diagonal. The Jeep had Nevada plates. Spotless interior. No crumpled magazines, no baby seats, no fast-food garbage. The driver was a neat freak, or it was a rental. Again, that didn't necessarily mean anything. Nor did the fact the driver, who had apparently been waiting there the whole time I was in Sarah Blackwell's house, had then left the car right after I had driven by.

I quickened my pace. I heard footsteps approaching and saw an elongated shadow stretch out from the corner in the streetlights. A tall, skinny man in knee-length shorts and a white t-shirt appeared, holding a bunched-up lead in his hands. There was a patter of paws on the sidewalk and a golden retriever appeared in his wake. We nodded to each other and I rounded the corner. As soon as he was out of sight, I broke into a jog, starting to wonder if I had been too slow in coming back.

Sarah's house was in darkness. There was no outward sign of anything wrong. I glanced at the neighboring house. It was also in darkness, no sign of life. I made my way up to the door. I stopped and listened. At first there was nothing.

And then a sharp thump broke the silence, as though something heavy had been dropped.

A second later I heard a scream. It was Sarah.

The door was locked. I took a step back and picked up one of the big terracotta pots by the door. It was even heavier than it looked, which was good. I braced my feet and hurled the pot through the glass of the door. It shattered, and the pot smashed onto the tiled floor of the hall, breaking into big pieces.

I reached in, twisted the lock and shouldered the door open. I flattened my back against the doorframe for a second, then risked a glance upstairs. I could hear movement from the second level. I ducked inside and ran for the stairs, keeping my gun aimed up at the landing. The nearest door to the top of the stairs was open; the light was off but there was enough light from the windows to see the outline. And then a shape blotted out the light. Two shapes.

"Stop right there."

Sarah was there, and she wasn't alone. A man the size of a gorilla was in the doorway, his fingers clamped around her throat and bracing her against the doorframe. She was gagging. Her toes were raised an inch or so above the ground.

I aimed the gun at his head. "Let her go. Now."

The big man seemed to consider for a second, then moved like sheet lightning. He swung his arm around. Sarah stumbled forward and he used the momentum to throw her at me. I got my gun out of the way and caught her awkwardly with my left hand as her impact sent us both backwards down the stairs. I dropped the gun and flailed out, my hand finding the guardrail and gripping on as I took both our weights. As Sarah recovered her balance and sat down on the stairs, I heard a window open somewhere. Our eyes met. She was holding her throat but managed a thumbs-up with her other hand.

"Go," she said, her voice like an eighty-year-old smoker's.

I grabbed my gun and stumbled back up the stairs and into the bedroom the man had vanished into. The window was wide open, the curtains swaying a little in the night breeze. I looked out and saw the man scaling the fence at the back of the yard. From my vantage point, I could see how he could simply jump a couple of fences to come out on the street where the black Jeep was parked. It would be a much quicker trip across the yards. I turned around, launched myself over the windowsill, and dropped to the ground, rolling on impact. I raced to the fence and vaulted it, landing in the next yard, my eyes on the opposite fence. He wasn't there, which meant either he was a lot quicker than he looked, or ...

Stupid. As I turned my head toward the shadows at the side of the fence, I felt a fist like a sack of cement slam into me. As I staggered back, he kicked me square in the stomach. I doubled over and went down. I brought a hand up to protect my face, but he had already dismissed me. As I struggled to my feet, I saw the big man clamber over the next fence, the flimsy wood barely supporting his weight. I pulled myself to my feet and started to run, my speed cut in half by the fact I was still winded. I knew I was on to a loser. I tried to calculate how much of a head start he had as I reached the fence, feeling as though I was moving in slow motion. As if in answer, I heard the sound of an engine start up, the motor revving, wheels spinning as he took off in a hurry.

With difficulty, I climbed back over into Sarah's yard and went around the front. She was waiting at the door I had smashed through a couple of minutes before, one hand braced on the doorframe, the other massaging her throat.

"Is he gone?" Sarah was breathing hard; her voice sounded less throaty now, but like she was only just keeping hysteria at bay. Small wonder.

"I'm afraid so," I said. "Who the hell was he?"

Sarah turned around so her back was to the doorframe and slid down until she was sitting on the threshold. She drew her knees up to her chest and put her arms around them.

"I don't know," she said. "But he asked about somebody named Dominic Freel."

17

By the time she had directed Blake to the fuse box so he could get the power back on, Sarah guessed her heartbeat had decreased to only double its normal rate or so.

He seemed to be satisfied that the intruder was long gone, but he kept the gun in his hand while they went through the house, checking each room. Sarah found herself being as thorough as she had been when searching the house next door. She realized with a shudder that it would be a long time before she would come home and not have to do this: checking the closets, under the stairs, the basement, under all the beds.

After she called the police, she told Blake about what she had found before she had been interrupted by the noise of the door opening. Blake agreed with her, that it was too much to be a coincidence. They now had an idea of what *Quarter by June* meant.

While they waited for Las Vegas's finest, Blake did some investigation of his own. He worked out that the man had gotten in through the back door. The lock appeared fine to her, but he said it had been picked. He took a flashlight into the yard and found footprints in the loose gravel beside the fence bordering on number 32. Had the big man been there in the yard the whole time they were in the house?

It took Blake less than five minutes to come up with those details, but it was more police work than the cops who showed up almost an hour later did the whole time they were there. There were two of them, both male: an overweight old white cop and a slim, young black cop: Officers Derrick and Miller. They took a statement in the kitchen while Blake leaned against one of the kitchen counters, arms folded, speaking only when addressed. They weren't too interested in Blake once they had established he was just a friend who had happened by at the right time. Officer Derrick raised an eyebrow at the male friend dropping by in the middle of the night, but didn't comment on it. Blake seemed to subtly alter himself when the police arrived. He became ... not invisible, exactly, but certainly inconsequential. They asked for his details when they ascertained he wasn't a member of the household, and he had reeled off the name Pete Milligan and a California address like it was the unremarkable truth.

Sarah smiled at "Pete." Inwardly, she was screaming, *Are you kidding?* She wanted to excuse herself, go upstairs, and lock herself in the bedroom until she had a chance to work out exactly what the hell was going on. Now her mysterious visitor, who was friends with her mysterious neighbor with the fake name, suddenly had a fake name himself. What the hell had she gotten herself into?

The officers turned their attention back to her. She told them everything she could remember about the break-in, which turned out to be more than she would have liked. Every second of the encounter seemed as fresh as though it had just happened. She left out the fact they had searched Carol's house, of course, but she knew that had been the reason the man had taken an interest in her.

"Do you think the individual knew you were at home?" Derrick said.

Sarah sighed. They hadn't been listening to a word she

had said. She suspected Derrick had a well-worn list of questions to ask in the event of a home invasion, and he didn't like to deviate.

"That's why he broke in," she reminded him. "He wasn't trying to rob me, he wanted to know where my neighbor was, remember?"

They lingered a little longer, going through the motions of asking a few more questions before handing her a form they said she would need for her insurance claim. As they bid her goodnight, Sarah realized that she was actually grateful for the irritation she felt toward the two of them. It had taken her mind off the man who had entered her house, the way his muscular frame had filled the doorway of her study. Pissed off was better than afraid any day of the week.

She closed what was left of her front door, thinking she would have to call somebody about that, and went back through the kitchen. Blake was in the same position he had been all through the interview, leaning against the counter.

"I'm coming with you," she said, without preamble. "To Arizona."

Blake looked as though he had been expecting this. It wasn't as though he could continue to argue she was safer here after all. "Fair enough."

She was mildly surprised. She had been expecting him to put up more of a fight; suggest she go stay with a relative perhaps.

"Okay," she said, mentally shelving the rest of the planned argument and taking a second to figure out which part of the conversation they had skipped to. "First thing in the morning, then?"

"First thing in the morning."

"What was that about with the cops?" she asked, suddenly remembering the name he had given them. "Pete Milligan?"

Blake shrugged. "A bad habit, I guess. No reason."

"The bad habit seems to be catching."

18

Night traffic was light. Gage avoided the parkway, and was glad he had made that choice when he heard the siren heading west. On the way back to his hotel, he stopped in a deserted mall parking lot to remove the fake license plate. He didn't know whether anyone had gotten a look at it, but it was wise to take precautions.

He wondered who the man in the blue Ford had been. The man who had so inconveniently come to the rescue of Dominic Freel's curious neighbor. Still, he was almost certain she had known nothing useful. If she had, she would have started talking before her friend came back. More annoying was the knowledge he wouldn't get a chance to search Freel's house now. Too bad, but he already had another promising lead with Logan McKinney down in Phoenix. There was nothing else for him in Summerlin.

After he had changed the plate, he satisfied a hunch by taking out the picture of Freel at the party with the two women. He was right: the dark-haired woman on the right of Freel was the neighbor. He assumed the other one was the wife she had mentioned.

Looking at the carefree smile on her face in the picture made Gage think about the terrified expression he had personally put on her face tonight. He didn't revel in it, but interrogating her had been worth a try, to make sure she didn't know where Freel had gone. He wondered why she and the man were so interested in her neighbor's house, before putting it out of his mind.

He used the public access computer in the hotel's lobby to book a ticket on the first flight to Phoenix in the morning, leaving at seven-fifteen. He took out the pictures of his target. The two images the men in the bar had given him. If McKinney knew where Freel was, then Gage too would know very soon indeed.

He went back to his room, relieved to find the warring couple next door were silent. Either they were asleep, or they had done everyone a favor and killed each other. He lay back on the too-small bed, switched the light out and closed his eyes.

19

WEDNESDAY, 00:32

I made more coffee while Sarah looked up and called a twenty-four-hour glass repair company. A guy in dark blue coveralls appeared within an hour and quickly repaired the damage I had done to the door. The glass was replaced and the lock was secure, but we already knew the man who had broken in would not be dissuaded by locks. I talked Sarah into getting some sleep, because we had a long drive in the morning.

I knew I ought to take my own advice, but instead I spent a while leafing through Carol's notebook. It wasn't a journal or a diary, so there were no dates. In the first third of the book was a page with doodles and words. A few of them looked familiar: *Samaritan, Crozier, Carter Blake*. There was a question mark next to that last name. It wasn't the name she knew me as. It told me exactly when she had written on this page. I wondered if she had thought about contacting me when she saw my picture on the news during the Samaritan case back in 2015. Or when the Winterlong scandal blew up in the media the following January. I wondered if she had joined the dots to the killing of her boss, and my part in it all.

I looked back at the sketch of the old building from the mining town. After Sarah had gone to bed I had looked online for information on the place. There wasn't much to be had. Corinth had been abandoned decades ago, and it wasn't pretty enough or historically significant enough to be on the tourist trail. Something told me that the town's anonymity was important. I didn't think we would find her there. It was unlikely Carol and Freel would be camped out in the middle of nowhere with no running water, but I thought this would put us in the right area. On the face of it, they had no reason to drive hundreds of miles to visit an unremarkable ghost town in the desert. Nobody had any reason to go there. But that's what made it interesting enough to stick out. I didn't hold out much hope that we would find Carol in Corinth itself, but there was *something* there.

And then there was Quarter, a few hours farther south.

I opened the notebook again to one of the pages Sarah had highlighted: the one with all the different signatures.

The script was cursive, careful. I pictured Carol whiling away an hour in a coffee shop or a highway rest stop thinking about her different lives over the years since New York. The first name on the page was Carol Langford, the name I knew. The last was Rebecca Smith. In between were eight other names. Where had she been in that time? Did she ever think about when she was Carol Langford? Did she ever think about me?

I closed the notebook and put it down on the coffee table. I gave the ground floor of the house and the backyard another inspection and then walked out front, looking up and down the road and listening. Whoever the man in the black Jeep was, he was long gone.

Sarah had told me the spare bedroom was made up, but I elected to stay downstairs, just in case. I took a sheet and a pillow from upstairs and brought them down to the couch in the living room. I took my shoes off and unstrapped my shoulder holster and tucked my gun under the pillow, then I lay down. It was a comfortable couch. I had slept in beds that were far less comfortable. A short time later, I was asleep.

I awoke just after seven, with the rays of the sun streaming through the windows. I could smell coffee brewing. I stood up, put the gun back in the holster and walked through to the kitchen in my socks. Sarah Blackwell was either a naturally early riser, or she hadn't gotten much sleep. She had changed into jeans and a white t-shirt and brown leather sandals. She was standing at the island in the middle of the kitchen beating eggs in a mixing bowl.

"Scrambled eggs?"

I told her that sounded good. She motioned for me to sit down at the table. There was a big pile of paper stacked neatly. Printouts. I leafed through: they were front pages from the Las Vegas *Tribune*, all with dates around the time Carol had disappeared, as well as what looked like the property pages from the local newspaper in Quarter.

I leafed through some of them idly. Nothing jumped out. A moment later, Sarah joined me with two heaped plates of eggs, half a dozen slices of whole wheat toast, a big pot of coffee and a jug of orange juice with ice cubes floating in it. I guessed she was enjoying having somebody else to cook for other than herself. I ignored the juice and poured coffee for both of us.

"The guy from the Iron City news site got back to me," she said, after swallowing the first forkful.

"Already?" I took a drink of coffee. It was very hot and very strong.

"Don't get your hopes up, he wasn't a lot of help. He told me nobody new had moved into town and made clear that he would absolutely know if that was the case. I think he wanted me to apologize for bothering him."

"Quarter looks like a better bet anyway," I said. "Maybe he's done us a favor."

I had done some more research online last night. We could make a detour to take in Corinth on the way to Quarter, particularly since it would mean we could go to Iron City as well. Corinth was in the east of the state, a hundred and fifty miles or so north of the Mexican border as the crow flies, more by road. It had been a thriving copper mining town in the nineteenth and early twentieth centuries before going into a long, gradual decline. The mine had closed in the early 1980s, and the town itself had been entirely deserted for more than twenty years.

We still didn't know what Carol's husband was running from, or whether Carol even knew what it was, but last night's uninvited guest had confirmed it was something with potentially deadly consequences.

"It's a long way to go on a hunch," she said, her eyes studying me carefully.

"Yes, it is."

I thought about the trip. How long it would take to drive,

where we would take breaks, where we would sleep tonight. If things panned out, we would be away for more than one night.

"You sure you have time for this?" I asked again. "It could take us days to find her. Weeks, even."

She looked at me reprovingly. I got the message: stop trying to talk her out of it. "Beauty of my job," she said. "You can do it anywhere."

"You're not one of those artists who needs a room of one's own, then?"

She shook her head. "Twenty years of deadlines pretty much beats that out of you. Besides, I'm ahead of schedule on this one."

She piled the last of her eggs onto the last slice of toast and pushed it neatly and efficiently into her mouth. She picked up her phone and tapped on it, her eyes focused on the screen as she chewed and swallowed. "You know, there's a flight out of Vegas to Phoenix in a couple of hours. We could rent a car at the other end, save a few hours."

I pretended to consider that for a moment, then glanced back in the direction of the front of the house where my car was parked, like I didn't want the hassle of coming back here to retrieve my car.

"Let's stick with driving. Once you factor in getting to the airport, delays, security, baggage, we're not going to save any time."

She looked back up at me, her thumb still poised over the screen of her phone. She had that appraising look on her face again. Like she had a list of questions about me and I had just added another one.

20

An insect-like purr of metallic clicks echoed through the cabin as the plane rolled to a stop on the runway. Trenton Gage stayed in his seat as the other passengers stood up and started unloading their cabin baggage from the overhead lockers. He never understood why they did that. It always took ten minutes or so between the seatbelt lights switching off and the doors opening, but still people got up and unloaded and waited tensely like runners on the starting blocks, in the hope of getting off the plane thirty seconds earlier.

There was another reason for his habit of sitting out the initial rush, though he knew it was unlikely to be a concern on this occasion. It's easier to tell if you're being followed when you're the last one off the plane.

Ten minutes later, the doors opened and the lightly harassed passengers began to file out. Gage waited until the aisle had cleared and got up, taking his bag from the locker. He passed through security with no problems. That reminded him that the first order of business had to be securing a weapon.

He had never been to Phoenix before. It was hot, though not as hot as Vegas had been. He took the Valley Metro Rail system for the short trip from the airport into the city. He walked a few blocks east until the crowds became less dense. The expensive chain stores and restaurants started to disappear and he saw more liquor stores and pawn shops and small hardware stores. The right kind of neighborhood.

He passed by the first couple of pawnbrokers, disregarding them because the windows were too clean and the displays too well ordered. The third one looked more promising. It had a red and white sign that had probably been painted in the 90s, and was now faded and peeling. The sign advertised *Guns, Loans, Jewelry*. The window displayed a seemingly random assortment of junk: DVD players, a baby carriage, a cheap electric guitar. Some of the goods were obscured by faded flyers taped from the inside proclaiming the best deals in town. The door was glass, two-paneled. The bottom panel had been kicked in and boarded up. He pushed the door inward and a little bell chimed.

The display window had been an accurate advertisement for the interior. Items were piled up in almost every inch of floor space, leaving a passage from the door to the register that was barely a foot wide. Even narrower ancillary routes led off into the maze of the store. There was no air conditioning. Instead, a cheap plastic fan pointed at the guy sitting behind the register. He was in his fifties, wore a blue vest and had long, dirty hair that had started off brown but was now mostly gray. He looked up as Gage entered.

Gage stared at him, and then made a point of surveying the piles of junk with a suspicious look. He walked purposefully toward the register. The man behind it was already stiffening defensively as Gage reached a hand into his pocket. The initial look and the approach did most of the heavy lifting, he knew. The cop demeanor was something you had to actively suppress when necessary. It wasn't a problem to do the opposite and play it up.

He took out the leather wallet with the badge and ID and held it up. Not showing it too close or for too long, but not attempting to hide anything. It was an LAPD badge. Or at least, it was good enough to pass as one. But in Gage's experience, people who owned places like this usually weren't inclined to be picky about jurisdiction.

In any case, the guy with the long hair didn't take the time to read the details on the badge or the ID. His eyes were on Gage's.

"Help you with anything, Officer?"

Gage replaced the wallet in his pocket. "I'm looking for a weapon that may have been used in the commission of a felony. I'm checking local establishments like yours to see if I can find it."

The long-haired guy relaxed very slightly at the indication that this wasn't about him specifically.

"Weapon . . . You mean a gun?"

The guy was waiting for him to tell him what kind of gun. Gage played the odds. "A Colt .45."

Longhair shook his head, looking sorry not to be of help. "I'm sorry, Officer. I don't have any of those right now. Nobody's sold me a gun of any kind this week, or last."

Gage put his hands on the counter and leaned forward. "Well there's some ambiguity over the description of the weapon. Could have been a Glock. And it could have come in some time ago."

He looked a little unsure. A little more suspicious. He didn't move to get out of his swivel chair.

"When would this have been?"

Gage stood back and scanned the wall above the man, looking for his pawnbroker's license. He found it in a smeared, cracked frame, and started examining it. Longhair started getting nervous again.

"I mean, I could have a look for you," he said quickly.

He disappeared into the back and came out with a cardboard box with assorted firearms in it. Gage didn't think the storage method would pass muster with regulations. There were Glocks and Berettas. Mostly cheaper models; entry-level stuff. There was one nice piece: a Ruger LC9.

He picked it from the pile. Longhair tensed, but didn't move to stop him.

Gage examined the weapon. It was light, compact. He racked the slide, ejected the magazine. It was clean, in good condition. He hoped he hadn't picked one which actually had been used in the commission of a felony, but it wasn't like he would be holding on to it long. He could pick up ammunition elsewhere.

He nodded as though this was what he was looking for. "I'm going to need to take this with me."

"I thought you said you were looking for a Colt?"

Gage said nothing. Slowly and deliberately, he placed the gun in his bag, holding eye contact with Longhair, waiting for him to object.

"I'm going to need to take this with me," he repeated. "That won't be a problem, will it?"

Longhair looked as though he was working up the nerve to have a problem with it, but then he decided against it and shook his head.

"Not a problem, I guess. Can I get a receipt or something? I paid two hundred for that gun."

Bullshit, Gage thought. He had what he wanted now, he could turn around and walk out of here, and he was ninety-nine per cent sure that this guy would never trouble the Phoenix PD with a request for a receipt, or a description of the officer who had taken his gun. But it was worth being nice for a little peace of mind.

"I'm all out of receipts," he said. "How about I give you fifty bucks for your trouble? Save the paperwork, huh?" He smiled and put his hands back on the counter. Close enough that he could reach out and grab the guy in the blink of an eye.

Longhair considered the offer and nodded slowly. Smart guy.

21

We mapped out the journey. South and east on US-93, then west on I-40 through Flagstaff, and then straight on down toward Fort Apache. A little over four hundred miles. A reasonably long trip, although nothing compared to how far I had already come. Sarah decided she wanted to take the wheel for the first stretch. I was happy to sit in the passenger side. I had had my fill of driving the previous day.

As we cleared the stop-start traffic through Vegas, I went back over Carol's notebook, spending more time examining the doodles and drawings. It was a fascinating document, particularly for someone with knowledge of the person who had spent months or years writing and drawing in it.

"So you do this for a living," Sarah said after we had been driving in silence for a while. She was wearing sunglasses, her eyes focused on the road ahead.

I closed the notebook and rested it on my lap. "Used to. I've been taking it easy for a while."

"Freelance?"

"Yeah. Just like you."

The corner of her mouth twitched. "Maybe a *little* more interesting than my freelancing."

"Trust me, you can get too much 'interesting.'"

"So who do you work for? Who contracts you? When you're not working pro-bono, I mean."

The truthful answer to that question was nobody, not anymore. I used to have a guy who lined up work for me. A friend, in fact, although I never thought of him in that way until he was no longer around.

"It varies," I said. "Could be a situation like this: a missing person who somebody misses enough to look for. Sometimes I work with the police, if they're looking for someone who doesn't want to be found."

She took her eyes off the road for a second to glance at my upper body, and I could tell she was thinking of the gun she knew was strapped there.

"And you know how to handle yourself when you find them."

"Usually. So far, at least."

We drove on for while, neither of us speaking. I closed the notebook again and stowed it in the shelf above the glove box. We were well into Arizona now, the landscape flat and dotted with clumps of brush. The road ahead shimmered in the baking heat, but the air conditioning nullified the effect in our little bubble. The sky was a deep azure, only a few long wispy clouds and the contrail of a passenger jet forty thousand feet above us. I saw a series of mesas dotting the landscape ahead of us, their summits impossibly flat, as though somebody had shaped them with a paring knife. We passed a sign that told us the nearest town was fifty miles away.

"I suppose this is kind of a mixture of your usual type of work," Sarah said suddenly, and I realized she had been thinking about it the whole time. "I mean, we're looking for a missing person. But there could be trouble, if whoever's looking for Carol's husband finds him first."

"It's a good idea to assume that in any case," I said. "Always assume trouble."

Sarah smirked as she remembered something. "Somebody once bought me one of those embroidered, framed homilies. You know the kind of thing? It said, '*F.A.I.L. means First Attempt In Learning*,'" her voice took on a high, mocking tone as she recited it. "They said I should hang it on the wall above my desk. You should make one with that instead: '*Always assume trouble*.'"

I smiled at the thought. The three words carefully sewn into a framed piece of hessian sacking. Maybe some daisies or butterflies adorning the border. A glass frame. My only problem was, I didn't know where I would hang it.

Just before noon, Sarah's phone buzzed as we passed into an area of cell phone coverage. She pulled over at the side of the road, leaving the engine running, and examined the screen. I guessed preserving the signal was more on her mind than safe driving practice. It wasn't as though there was any traffic for a phone call to distract her from. She tapped the screen a couple of times and put it on speaker as she returned the call. As it rang, she told me she was calling the local journalist in Quarter she had mentioned. A woman named Diane Marshall.

The call was answered with a businesslike "hello," and I listened with admiration as Sarah gave her an edited version of our story. Diane asked a few questions in return, before agreeing to make some enquiries on Sarah's behalf. All things considered, I was starting to be very glad that circumstances had dictated Sarah come along.

When we were under way once more, Sarah started asking about me and Carol again. This time I turned it around and asked about her ex-husband.

She shrugged. "No mystery there, Blake. We were just

wrong for each other and it took us way too damn long to figure that out."

"What did he do?"

"He was a professional gambler."

"What happened? A big loss?"

"No. Never, in fact. I was always worried he would lose everything. He told me not to worry, and you know what? He was right. Every time."

"I see why you broke up."

She grinned. "Eventually I just realized that he wasn't going to give it up, and I wasn't going to stop worrying about it. And then I talked to him and we both realized we had been making ourselves unhappy, trying to make this work." She took her left hand off the wheel to show me her watch. I had noticed it earlier: a very nice Cartier. Probably three thousand dollars at least. "He got me this as a goodbye present. Engraved on the back: '*Time flies.*'"

"Sounds incredibly amicable."

"It's great. We still catch up for dinner every couple of months and we get on better than we ever did before. I can highly recommend divorce." She took her gaze from the road to stare at me pointedly over her sunglasses. "So much better than leaving things unresolved."

By one o'clock, enough time had elapsed since breakfast that we were both more than ready to eat again. We had been gaining elevation all day and the air was cooler, the landscape greener. Tall trees lined the wide divide between us and the westbound lanes of the highway. We pulled into a rest stop outside of Flagstaff. Sarah said she was fine to keep driving, and we were making good time, so we picked up cheeseburgers and sodas to consume on the go. Driving at the same time as eating didn't seem to cause Sarah any problems, the road was straight and quiet and she kept one hand on the wheel while she took bites out of her cheese-burger.

"That guy last night. Why do you think he wants to find Carol's husband so badly?"

My brow creased and immediately I realized I had fallen into a trap. Sarah was looking across at me, watching my reaction.

"I like how you pull a face every time I say the word 'husband.' How long were you together?"

I smiled. "I guess your new career must pay well. There's no way you quit journalism because you weren't good at it."

"People interest me. I like to find out about them. Better get used to it."

I said nothing. Turned my head to look out of the window.

"So how long?" she repeated, polite but insistent.

I sighed and looked back at her.

"Are you watching the road?"

"The road's fine. It's still there, look."

"Okay, we had a thing," I admitted.

"Back in New York?"

I hesitated, then nodded. I wasn't used to answering so many questions. Most people can be carefully maneuvered onto a different conversational track if necessary. Sarah Blackwell wasn't most people.

"Why did she break up with you?"

"Who said she did?"

"I do."

"I suppose it wasn't meant to be. Work got in the way, you know how it is."

She kept watching me for long enough that I started to get a little concerned I was getting more attention than the road. Eventually, she turned her eyes away from me.

I got the feeling it was going to be a long few days.

22

PHOENIX

Logan McKinney was proving more elusive than Gage had anticipated.

McKinney was still in Phoenix, as far as he could tell, and he had been working as a bouncer at a sports bar in Glendale. A visit to the establishment in question, however, had revealed that McKinney had already been fired, two days previously. Drinking on the job, lateness, unreliability. Gage was familiar with the type.

He finished speaking to McKinney's boss and turned his attention to the barmaid who had been hovering a little too close to the conversation, busying herself with arranging glasses. He had been watching her out of the corner of his eye. She was in her mid-thirties, he would guess. Five-five, slim with a nice rack. Dark hair tied up in a ponytail. White t-shirt, black jeans. Something about her eyes told him she was the type who made poor decisions on impulse. He sat down at the bar and ordered a Scotch, straight up. When she brought it back, he placed a fifty-dollar bill on the bar, pushing it toward her with his index finger.

She glanced at it and shook her head wearily. "Anything smaller?"

"I don't want change."

Her face brightened and she smiled, not quite believing it. "For real?" Not waiting for an answer, she reached out and tried to pull the bill toward herself. Gage kept his finger on it, right in the middle of Ulysses S. Grant's face. Her eyes moved from the fifty to him, the smile vanishing.

"What can you tell me about Logan McKinney?"

She shook her head. "How should I know?"

"I don't know," Gage replied. "All I have is a feeling you can help me. Can you help me?"

She bit her bottom lip and looked down at the fifty pinned to the bar by Gage's finger again.

"Come on, what's the harm? You're never going to see me again."

She looked back up at him, still unsure.

"Anything you tell me is between you and me. I won't mention it to McKinney."

She looked from side to side. Her boss had disappeared into the back. The only other two customers were on the other side of the bar, utterly absorbed in highlights of the previous night's Diamondbacks game on one of the big screens.

She reached under the bar and came out with a pen and a napkin branded with the name of the bar. She wrote a few words down on it. An address. She pushed the napkin across the bar to Gage. Simultaneously, he took his finger off the fifty-dollar bill.

"That's where he's staying. Least, that's where he was staying last week."

"Good enough," Gage said.

She took the fifty, folded it and put it in her pocket, and then took a few bills out of her pocket to put in the register for Gage's Scotch.

"He owe you money or something?"

Gage sipped the Scotch and said nothing. It was decent. Far better quality than he would have expected in a place like this. He kept his eyes on the barmaid until she grew uncomfortable and moved down to the other side of the bar to see if the two Diamondback fans needed a refill.

When he had finished the Scotch, he took his phone out and looked up the address. It was an apartment over in a part of the city called Arcadia. It was almost five miles across town, so he got the barmaid to call him a cab.

It took Gage twenty minutes to get to McKinney's address. The afternoon traffic was light, and Gage glanced at the neighborhoods he was passing through with interest. The city didn't seem to have traditionally defined wealthy and poor areas. It was a patchwork quilt: dilapidated public housing next to expensive-looking condo developments. McKinney's apartment building was on one of the rougher patches of the quilt.

It was a concrete three-story U-shaped complex that had seen better days. There was a Circle K next door with some dealers hanging around outside, and garbage was strewn in the street. There was a cheap-looking coffee shop across the street with a sheet of plywood over one of the windows. He examined the building. McKinney's apartment was number 35, which he thought would put it on the front-facing side of the third floor.

There were no security gates or buzzers or anything that might have delayed him in a more salubrious area, so he walked straight in and climbed the two flights of stairs. He found 35. The door had been badly painted using the wrong kind of paint. There was a peephole beneath the numbers. Gage knocked twice and then put his eye to the peephole. He could see only darkness and a pinpoint of light, no detail. That was enough. He heard someone approach, very quietly. The pinpoint of light disappeared, and he thought he heard a stifled gasp.

He stepped back, giving the occupant a clear view of him, if he was still looking, and knocked again.

After a second, a quiet voice.

"Who's there?"

"I'm looking for Logan McKinney."

A long pause. "Don't know him. Wrong door."

"Are you sure? Dominic Freel asked me to come and see you."

The voice took on an edge. Superficial irritation, fear underneath. "I said you got the wrong door."

After a couple of seconds, he heard the footsteps retreating.

Gage considered his options. He could be inside the apartment in seconds. But McKinney would be prepared now. He might have a gun. He was rattled—which was the intention, of course—but it meant that caution was advised.

Gage walked back down the stairs and out onto the sidewalk. He stopped and waited for a couple of minutes, watching the cars and the passers-by. He crossed over to the coffee shop across the street and took a seat in the window looking across to McKinney's building. He ordered a black coffee and watched.

Ten minutes later, the main door of the apartment complex opened and a tall, skinny guy wearing sweatpants and a faded purple hoodie stepped out. He paused at the door, surveying the street. Gage watched him out of the corner of his eye. McKinney paid him no attention if he saw him at all. Satisfied, he took off down the street, headed east. Gage watched him as he passed by the window of the coffee shop. It was definitely McKinney.

Gage counted to five, abandoned his coffee and started following him. The sidewalks weren't as busy as he would have liked: not enough other pedestrians to provide cover, so he kept his distance, keeping the distinctive purple hoodie in view at all times. McKinney was an exceptionally easy tail—not only the hoodie, but the lanky, up-and-down gait set him apart from everyone else.

McKinney moved quickly down the sidewalk, looking side to side and occasionally glancing behind him. Gage wasn't sure what McKinney thought he was looking for. Somebody conspicuously staring at him over a newspaper, perhaps.

They reached an intersection with a busier street. Less housing, more businesses. Convenience stores and phone stores and delis. More people here. The opposite problem to not having enough cover: it was too busy for a confrontation. Gage wanted to wait until McKinney went somewhere quieter. McKinney walked two blocks before entering a bar. Gage continued past it without breaking stride. A casual glance was enough to tell him that this place made the bar McKinney had been working in look like a classy joint. He turned into a narrow alley on the far side of the bar and quickly surveyed it. Dumpsters lined one wall, some of them overflowing and shedding their detritus on the ground. There was a steel fire door in the wall leading into the bar. The alley doglegged after the door, before terminating in a ten-foot-high chain link fence topped with barbed wire. It was secluded, out of sight of the street, and the air conditioning grill in the wall of the next building was loud enough to cover a reasonable amount of noise. Good enough.

Gage walked back around and entered the bar. It was dingy and dark inside; a jukebox playing "Take it Easy" by the Eagles. It was busy for a Wednesday afternoon. McKinney looked up from his phone as he entered, regarded him warily. Gage wondered if he recognized him from the street outside, from his many glances behind him. He didn't particularly care. McKinney had strayed into a dead end. He just didn't know it yet.

He stood at the bar and ordered a beer that he knew he wasn't going to drink. He watched McKinney play with his phone and look around nervously for a minute, and then he took the beer and walked straight across the room to where he was sitting. McKinney didn't make eye contact until he was five feet away, and it was obvious Gage was heading for him.

"Do I know you?" he asked.

Gage smiled and sat down. "Not yet. I'm a friend of a friend. I heard you could tell me about Dominic Freel."

McKinney flinched in his chair.

"I don't know what you're talking about. Were you—" he stopped before he finished. *Were you the guy who just buzzed my apartment?*

Gage sat back in his chair. It had the effect of emphasizing how big he was; how broad his shoulders were. "There doesn't need to be any trouble here. Tell me where Freel is, and I disappear."

"I don't know who you mean."

"Cut the bullshit, McKinney. Did you call him, after I buzzed you? If I look at your phone, it'll have his number in it, won't it?"

McKinney said nothing. Gage was pleased. It meant he had the information.

"Take It Easy" finished. "Tuesday's Gone" started up. Gage lowered his voice. "I'm walking out of here with the information I want. Do you want to be able to walk out of here too?"

McKinney's mouth stayed closed, but his eyes were working overtime. He looked at Gage. McKinney might be a physical match for him, in his dreams. He looked at the bar staff; no help there. He looked at the door. Too far, and Gage was in the way.

His throat worked as he swallowed and Gage noticed there was a slim beaded chain around his link, like the cord on a set of dog tags.

"Give me a second? I don't feel too good all of a sudden."

Gage stared at him for a few seconds before answering. "Okay."

He moved his chair to allow McKinney to get past him and head in the direction of the restrooms. The signage indicated that the fire exit was accessed via the same door. He waited until the door had swung shut and then got up and followed. He turned right where the corridor became a T-junction and saw McKinney pushing at the bar that opened the fire exit. He rushed him. McKinney turned, his arms outstretched in defense, and Gage slammed into him, mashing his back against the push bar and sending him flying out into the alley. Gage grabbed the front of his hoodie, bunched it up in his fist and slammed McKinney hard against the nearest dumpster, dislodging another avalanche of beer bottles and packaging and food waste.

"I'm sorry!" McKinney yelled, covering his face.

Gage said nothing. He shouldn't be sorry. He had gone exactly where Gage had wanted him to. He yanked him back, spun him around and grabbed a handful of the back of his hoodie now, marching him toward the dogleg at the back of the alley. McKinney was already talking.

"Quarter, he's in Quarter."

"What the hell does that mean?"

"Quarter," he repeated, louder this time. "It's a town."

"Keep going," Gage said, not pausing in his forward motion. They reached the dogleg and Gage yanked him into the dead end, walked him forward toward the chain link fence and pushed him into it.

McKinney looked up to see the barbed wire strung along the top of the fence, then spun around to face Gage.

"I called him, like you said. You can have his number. I don't have an address or—"

Gage stood in the middle of the space, blocking McKinney's exit. Without taking his eyes off him, Gage took his phone out and opened the internet browser by touch.

"Where is it?"

"Quarter, Arizona. It's down by the border."

Gage held the phone up so he could look at the screen without taking his eyes off McKinney. He tapped the two words into the search: Quarter, Arizona. It existed. It was where McKinney had said it was.

"What did you tell him?"

"That somebody had come by asking about him. I told him I didn't let you in."

"Anything else?"

"No, man, I fuckin' swear."

Gage looked past him through the chain link. The rest of the alley continued before cornering in the direction of the next street. Nobody around, no windows looking onto the alley. He put his phone back into his jacket pocket, then pulled out the Ruger from the opposite side.

He pointed it between McKinney's eyes.

"Wait!" McKinney yelled.

Gage didn't say anything, didn't move.

"I had to send something to him last week. He didn't give me his address, but he told me to mail it to him care of a diner down there."

"Name?"

His brow creased. Gage thought the expression looked promising, like he was desperately trying to remember a name, rather than making one up.

"You gotta give me a second."

"I'll give you two."

"N-something! Norman's? *Norrie's*. Norrie's Diner."

Keeping the gun trained on McKinney, he took his phone

133

out again. Norrie's, Quarter, Arizona. It checked out. Gage believed him, about all of it.

"Thank you." Gage lowered his gun. "Now, you wouldn't think of doing something silly, like calling Freel to warn him, would you?"

McKinney shook his head. His eyes were earnest. "No way, man."

Gage let the pause draw out. "That's good. Okay, we're done here."

McKinney gave a cautious smile and his fingers let go of the fence. He took a cautious step forward. He hesitated, and then moved past Gage, giving him a wide berth. Finally, he turned and started moving toward the dogleg that would take him into the wider part of the alley and then out on the street.

Gage took two light steps forward and grabbed the back of McKinney's hoodie with his left hand, yanking him backwards. McKinney started to yell, but the sound was cut off as Gage clamped his giant palm around the lower half of his face. Before McKinney could struggle, he braced his left hand on the shoulder and twisted McKinney's head sharply back, feeling the satisfying crack as his neck snapped.

23

After a spell heading east, the road curved around and they were heading south again, passing through the Apache-Sitgreaves National Forest when Sarah's phone rang. She didn't recognize the number on her caller ID. Blake, who had taken over the wheel when they stopped for gas in Winslow, looked over at her as it rang for the third time.

"Who is it?"

"I don't know."

She tapped to answer the call. As she raised the phone to her ear, an irrational fear gripped her. The illogical certainty that it would be the man from last night.

It wasn't. The voice was male, but belonged to someone older. Someone used to getting his way.

"Am I speaking to Sarah Blackwell?"

"Speaking."

"This is Detective Ray Costigane, Las Vegas Metropolitan PD."

She relaxed. A little. "If this is about last night, I'm not at home right now."

"I know that. I'm parked outside your house."

"Oh, sorry," Sarah said, before thinking there was no reason why she should be.

"This is partly about last night," Costigane confirmed.

"Partly?"

"I spoke with Officers Derrick and Miller. They said you got a good look at the intruder."

"That's right, even though it all happened so fast. He was big, and he had this . . ."

"Scar on his face, like a crescent," he finished, as though reading from something in front of him. Probably Officer Derrick's report. "I also spoke to Detective Stansfield from Missing Persons. Seems we've been visiting you a lot in the last couple of days."

"Okay," Sarah said. The inquisitive tone in her voice made Blake look around again.

He mouthed, "Who is it?"

Sarah mouthed back "It's a cop," as Costigane began speaking again.

"She mentioned you tried to report your neighbors

missing. Rebecca and Dominic, is that right?"

"Yes, I haven't seen them in weeks. They just left with no warning." A dark and unwelcome thought planted itself at the back of Sarah's mind. "Is this about them? Has there been any news?"

"No, ma'am. I'm investigating another case right now, and I think your neighbor may have some information I need."

"Rebecca?" The name already sounded artificial in her head. Sarah had had to make an effort not to say "Carol."

"No, I'm talking about her husband. I believe he was going by the name Smith, but we're aware of him as Dominic Freel."

"That's who the guy last night was looking for," Sarah said. "He said his name was Freel. Is he in some kind of trouble?"

"I don't want to go into details, certainly not over the phone. He's not in any trouble, but I think he saw something that could get him into it, if he's not careful."

"Are you saying he's a witness to a murder or something?"

Costigane continued without acknowledging what she had said. "I need to know if he said anything to you before going away. Anything about where he might have been headed."

Her eyes were drawn to the notebook lying on the dashboard. "No idea whatsoever, Detective. And to be honest, I didn't really know Dominic at all. I was friendly with ... with his wife, not him. Like I said: they were there one day, gone the next."

There was an uncomfortable pause. "That's interesting."

"What do you mean?"

"It's just, you must have had some cause to worry, to call Missing Persons."

She thought about the yard party, the hushed whispering

between the couple. The strong sense that something had been very wrong.

"Somebody broke into their house a few nights ago. Your colleagues thought it was probably somebody the landlord knows."

Costigane left a long pause. An old trick Sarah had used many times herself. "I would like to come to speak to you when you get back home," Costigane said at last. "Do you have an ETA?"

"I'm out of town for a few days. I didn't feel like staying in the house." She injected a sharpness into her tone, and Costigane's change of tone told her it had done its job.

"I'm sorry, ma'am, I appreciate last night was not a pleasant situation, and I'd be grateful for any help in locating your friend Mr. Freel. I think there's a chance what happened last night could be related."

Sarah thought there was a chance too. A better than even chance.

"Listen, I don't want to alarm you in any way, but I think we know who the man with the scar is. The description fits a guy named Trenton Gage. On our radar for a couple of murders in Vegas and California. He's a bounty hunter and a killer, and he's bad news. Links to some extremely shady people. If he's looking for Freel, you don't want to get in his way." Costigane paused. "Do you understand me, Sarah?"

"Of course," Sarah said. Was this a coded warning? Was he telling her not to go looking for Carol, to leave it to the experts?

"Anyway, when you get back to Vegas, I would appreciate it if you could give me a call on this number and arrange a time to come into the station. In the meantime ..."

"I'll call if I hear anything from them," Sarah said.

"I appreciate it."

"What department did you say you were from again?" He hadn't.

"VCB. Violent Crimes."

Sarah assured him she would call him if she heard anything and hung up.

She quickly gave Blake a summary of the conversation.

"It sounds like Freel's in some trouble," Blake agreed. "This Gage guy certainly knew what he was doing."

"Do you think he can track them down? I mean, he doesn't have the notebook, or ..."

"He struck out back in Summerlin, but there are always other ways around a problem," he said. "The cop said he was from Violent Crimes? That covers a lot of ground, none of it good."

"Drugs, murder, mob stuff ..." she agreed. "It sounds like maybe Freel saw something he shouldn't have. Like they want him silenced."

"Or was involved in something he shouldn't have been."

Sarah said nothing. Okay, Blake had a bias against Freel, but it was certainly something to consider. She ran over the conversation in her head again, remembering the detective's knowing tone.

"That guy Costigane. It sounded like he knew what I was thinking, like he knew I was holding information back. I have a friend pretty high up in the department, Greg Kubler. He was promoted away from the action a long time ago, but maybe I should give him a call, see if I can find out a little more about what Detective Costigane is looking into."

"That's a good idea, but tell him to keep it between the two of you."

"Kubler's okay; it won't go any further."

Blake said nothing for a few moments, his green eyes

staring ahead at the road. "Lot of people looking for your neighbors," he said at last.

"There sure are," Sarah agreed. "What do you think that means?"

"I think it means we should find them fast."

24

We still had a way to go to our first stop on the trail: Grady's Rest Stop. Sarah was waiting on a return call from the friend in the Las Vegas Metropolitan Police Department whom she could ask about Detective Costigane. She had heard back from Diane Marshall in Quarter—no news yet, but she would try a few more avenues and call later on, whatever happened. Sarah had her phone on speaker, and I could tell from Diane's voice that this was the most interesting thing she had had to do in a while.

After Diane's call, we talked a little more about Carol. We speculated about the man with the gun, and wondered how it all fit with whatever crime Costigane was investigating. The conversation moved on, and with no small amount of difficulty I made sure she talked more than I did. She talked a little more about her ex-husband. About writing her books. About her old job: big stories she had broken, celebrities and politicians and sports stars she had interviewed. She talked about her childhood, about her dad who had been a test pilot at Edwards in the '70s and '80s, flying F-15s and the new generation of stealths. I guessed that explained her relaxed attitude toward risk. Danger would have been a constant presence in her life, since she was old enough to understand that her dad's job meant he might not come home at the end of any given day.

We reached Grady's just after five o'clock. As we were pulling off the highway, Sarah received a text. It had been sent an hour before, but we had been out of range. I was surprised we were in range now. The text was from Diane Marshall. It was short and to the point, saying that if Sarah was still planning to be in Quarter tomorrow, it would be good to meet. Sarah replied and they arranged to meet at the newspaper office.

I parked and turned the engine off. We looked out at Grady's Rest Stop. As the culmination of a day's drive, it was underwhelming. It was a square of asphalt with four pumps outside, in front of a cluttered store with a small area with some tables and chairs. I topped the tank up and Sarah bought a foldout map of the county. Online maps are great, but given we were barely getting a phone signal now, we couldn't rely on internet access.

The guy behind the counter seemed to be cashier, waiter, cook and manager all rolled into one. He was a big man with curly red hair and a white shirt that was a little tight on him. He didn't wear a nametag. After we paid for the gas and the map I asked if he was serving food. He answered in the affirmative and indicated the seating area. We sat down ordered coffees and burgers. The coffee was a little stale. The burger wasn't going to win any culinary awards, either. I had forgotten how samey the diet can get when you're on the road. But we needed fuel, so we ate quickly. We needed something else, too, so I kept an eye on the guy in the white shirt to see if he was going to engage us in conversation. He seemed to be busy with paperwork. After we had finished eating, he looked up and came over.

"Would you like to see the dessert menu?"

"Just the check please."

"No problem," he said, starting to clear the plates. "You folks down here on vacation?"

"That obvious, huh?" Sarah said.

"We don't get a lot of people coming through here, these days. If it wasn't for the truckers, we'd be broke."

"That's a pity," Sarah said. "It's real pretty out here. In fact we only came to your place because our friends recommended it."

"For real?" The corners of the red-headed man's mouth shot upwards in a surprised grin.

Sarah nodded. "They were down here a couple months back." She turned to me, acting casual, as though she couldn't recall. "Back in February or March, maybe?"

"March, I think," I said. I looked up at the guy. "You might remember them. They told us the burgers here were good."

"They did?" He sounded skeptical. I didn't blame him.

Then he stopped to think, the plates balanced on his forearm. I took my phone out and got the picture of Carol and Freel up on the screen, hoping this place really was as dead as he said. His brow furrowed.

"Yeah, I guess I remember them." I could tell he wanted to be helpful, but his tone made me doubt it. For all the quietness if this place, a customer was a customer. I guessed he didn't spend time memorizing the faces of everyone who came in.

"They talk to you much?" Sarah asked.

"Sure. Nice folks."

I remembered the time stamp on the receipt. After seven o'clock in the evening. Unless they were driving through the night, they would probably have gotten a room somewhere.

I put the phone face down on the table, like I was moving

the conversation on. "Can you recommend a motel around here? We had a pretty early start, and we had planned to go farther south, but maybe we'll stop soon. No hurry."

"Well that's easy. Only town around here is Iron City, and it only has one hotel." A look came over his face like he had remembered where he left his car keys. He snapped his fingers. "Matter of fact I do remember your friends. I told them the same thing."

Sarah smiled. "That's perfect."

By the time we reached Iron City, the sky in the west was a furnace of orange and red and purple. The stars were already starting to come out in the east. The vast flatness of the landscape seemed to capture several times of day all at once. Corinth was another twenty miles distant, but we agreed to check out the hotel first. It was the first building off the highway, its red neon sign indicating vacancies. I pulled off the road and into the parking lot.

The Iron City Inn was a one-story brick building with a gray tile roof. There were only a couple of other cars in the lot, and most of the windows were in darkness.

The clerk at the desk, a morbidly obese man with a bushy beard and glasses, took a while to tear his attention away from the football game he was watching on the computer screen. He tapped on his keyboard, clicked his tongue while he considered where to put us, and finally handed Sarah two key cards for adjoining rooms. When she produced the photograph, he could not remember whether he had roomed the couple in it on March 12th, or even if he had been on duty that day. That was okay, though. We already knew the guy at Grady's had sent them here. Given the size of the town, it was telling that the clerk didn't recognize Carol or Freel. If they had been around this town for the past few weeks, he would have recognized them for sure. After unenthusiastically asking if they wanted anything else, the clerk sat back down on his rickety wooden chair and turned his attention back to the game.

"That guy was helpful," Sarah remarked as we walked back out into the gravel lot.

"It's fine. We can head for Quarter in the morning if we don't find anything here."

We got back into the car, and Sarah spread out the map we had bought at Grady's on her lap.

I looked up at the darkening sky. It would have been better to check out Corinth in the daylight, but Sarah wanted to get to Quarter as quickly as we could tomorrow.

"What do you think?"

Sarah ran a finger across the page, tracing the twenty miles from our current position to Corinth.

"The night is young."

25

CORINTH
WEDNESDAY, 19:41

Sarah noticed that Blake was quiet on the twenty-minute drive out to Corinth. Given that she wouldn't have described him as a chatterbox at normal times, that was saying something. It was fine; she didn't feel like conversing either. She was too preoccupied, thinking about what they might find in the old town. As the last embers of the sunset faded from the sky, her mind went to the image of Trenton Gage in her doorway again. She felt a sick feeling in her belly, and wondered if they should have waited until morning.

It was full dark by the time the headlights of Blake's Ford lit up a sign at the side of the road. The sign was old, pock-marked with shotgun pellets. The sign said *Corinth, 10m*, with an arrow indicating there was a turnoff ahead. Blake slowed and took the exit off the highway onto a narrower road. A triangular yellow highway sign warned, *Unimproved Road*. True enough. The road was rutted and decayed, prob-ably hadn't been resurfaced since the town died.

A few minutes later, they passed the massive crater left by the open-cast mine on their right-hand side. Were it not for the clear night and the full moon, they might not have noticed it at all. And then they were at the edge of town.

Corinth was, if anything, smaller than it had looked from satellite images: a few streets of houses arranged around a wide main street. Some of the buildings were still standing, others had collapsed in on themselves. Some were boarded up, others were left wide open, the doors missing and the glass long gone from the windows. Blake slowed down a little and both of them glanced from side to side, taking in the signs on the storefronts. Sarah saw a general store, a library, a barber's, a doctor's. Arranged at regular intervals at the side of the road were small craters where the street-lights had been ripped out and sold for scrap. She knew that if they were to look for plumbing or appliances in the stores and houses they would find the same thing. Anything the departing residents hadn't taken with them had long since been evaluated by salvagers and either removed or discarded, leaving a dark, empty shell. It was like the town itself had been mined.

It didn't take her long to pick out the old building from Carol's sketch. It was the tallest structure in town, sitting at the far end of Main Street. She guessed it had been the town hall. Blake parked in the middle of the road and the two of them got out. The chill in the air caught her by surprise. At this elevation, the temperature could really plummet after sundown. Almost as striking was the silence. There was no wind, no buzz of electrical wires, no traffic noise, no television chatter through an open window. It was like somebody had pressed pause on the world.

What had brought Carol and Freel here? It couldn't be idle curiosity, although seen in the moonlight, Sarah could see the attraction of that. The deserted town had a kind of compelling, wasted charm. But they wouldn't have come so far, just for that. Blake had Carol's notebook in his hand. He opened it to the page where she had sketched the old town hall, and held it up in front of the real-life building, using the Ford's headlights for illumination. Sarah's eyes flitted between the building and the sketch. Carol had a good eye, she had captured it perfectly.

She turned away and looked up and down the deserted main street. Nothing moved. From the highway, at least five miles away, she could hear the sound of a big rig's powerful engine.

"Creepy," she said in a library whisper. "But cool, though."

Blake's face was serious, composed. "Let's get started."

They had spoken at length about their plans on the drive down from Nevada. The first thing they wanted to make sure of was that Carol wasn't here. Blake suggested that would be pretty easy to confirm. Their secondary objective was more nebulous: they were looking for something, but they didn't know what. A reason for Carol and Dominic to come here, for Carol to sketch the building in her notebook.

Sarah opened the back door of the car and took her backpack from the back seat. She unzipped it and took out a flashlight and her tablet. She handed Blake the tablet while she swung the pack on her back. Blake pressed the button to wake the screen and a second later they were looking at their position from space. It wasn't a live feed, of course. They were at least twenty miles away from basic internet. When they had stopped for gas in Winslow, Sarah had zoomed in and taken a screenshot of the satellite view of the town, providing a reasonably up-to-date map.

Sarah watched Blake as he examined the map, the soft illumination from the screen bathing his features in a bluish glow. Her eyes went to the left side of his jacket. He looked up and seemed to read her mind. He patted the spot where his gun was holstered.

"Always assume trouble."

They started with the town hall. It wasn't hard to gain access. Just as in Carol's sketch, there was a gap ten feet high and six wide in the middle of the ground floor where Sarah assumed the doors had once hung. Blake stepped inside first and she followed. She was conscious of a large, open space. Blake directed the beam of his flashlight upwards and they heard shuffles and scrapes as the light disturbed the peaceful night for some hidden winged animals. Birds or bats, or both. In the beam of the light, Sarah could now see that the interior was a big open space, taking up the full three-story height of the building. The roof was arched, with rafters spanning the space between the two walls. There was a stage on the far side, and behind that, a spiral staircase leading up to a short platform about fifteen feet long. There was a door at the far end of the platform. The hall was mostly empty, the broken remains of wooden chairs and boxes scattered here and there.

The floorboards creaked as they made their way inside. As they got closer to the platform, Sarah noticed that there was also a door in the wall beneath it. It was unlocked, and gave into a kitchen and then a corridor that led to bathrooms. The fittings and many of the tiles had disappeared long ago.

They emerged back into the main hall and Blake shone the beam of the flashlight on the spiral staircase. It was iron, badly rusted in places. Blake exchanged a glance with her as he sized up the condition of the steps. She estimated Blake had at least fifty pounds on her.

"I'll go up first," she said.

Blake looked at her slim frame, compared it with his own, and concurred. "Watch your step."

The staircase creaked and the central column shook visibly as she stepped onto it. She stopped on the third step and examined the fourth. It looked almost rusted through. She stepped over it and onto the next one. She continued up the stairs. There were twenty of them, and she counted every one while holding her breath. After what seemed like an eternity, she made the platform. That, at least, felt a little more solid than the staircase.

Blake walked underneath the platform and directed the beam up through the iron grate as Sarah walked carefully along the length of the platform, stopping when she got to the door. It was chained shut and padlocked.

"I'll come up," Blake said as she examined it.

"Don't bother," she said. "Unless you have a blow torch. The padlock's rusted shut."

Sarah took even more care descending the staircase, feeling it tremble as she put her weight on each step. She sighed with relief when her feet were back on solid footing.

Then she heard a sudden noise from above them, and let out an involuntary scream.

They looked up to see shapes move across the ceiling in a flutter of wings that echoed in the space. A couple of pigeons had chosen that moment to shed their perches and fly up to the rafters. Sarah and Blake were probably the first humans they had seen in some time; no wonder they were getting tetchy. She let out a relieved breath, and Blake gave her a reassuring smile. He had been startled too. Neither of them had really noticed how on edge they were. There was something very disturbing about the weird, in-between state of a town that had once hosted a couple of thousand souls, now in the slow process of returning to nothing.

Blake cast the beam over the platform and the door one more time as Sarah started moving back toward the main door. Blake was in the middle of saying something when she heard a soft creak beneath her.

The next second, the world caved in.

26

Sarah's scream was a high, piercing sound in the darkness. I spun around, reaching for my gun. Sarah had been no more than twenty feet from me, but she had vanished.

I rushed forward in the direction Sarah had gone, calling her name. I stopped when she yelled again.

"Stop!"

There was a moment of disconnect. Somehow, it sounded as though her voice had come from below me. I heard another flutter of wings from above me in response to the cry. I looked down and saw my foot was inches away from a set of fingers. It took my mind a second to process what had happened, and then I dropped to my knees and grabbed Sarah's hand with mine, feeling the ragged edge of a hole in the floorboards, about six feet long by two wide. Had she not yelled, I would have followed her into the hole. It was virtually invisible unless you directed a light straight at it. We had been lucky not to fall through it on our way in.

Sarah was gripping on with one hand, but her fingers were starting to slip. I gripped her wrist with both hands and took a second to balance myself.

"You okay?"

She nodded quickly. "Just get me out of here."

I braced my heels against the floorboards, hearing them creak in protest, and started to pull her up. She grabbed the edge with her other hand and then steadied herself on her forearms as I helped drag her the rest of the way out.

Sarah let out a long breath and wiped her brow.

"That was close."

I got as near to the edge as I was comfortable with, trying to ignore the creaking, and shined the beam of the flashlight around. The cellar was clear aside from some broken packing crates. I examined the edge of the hole and saw the traces of dry rot in the struts holding the floor up. We were fortunate the floor hadn't caved in anywhere else yet.

I straightened up. Sarah was rubbing a graze on her arm and looking down into the hole.

"Daylight would definitely have been better," she said.

Carefully, we picked our way back to the entrance, the creaks of the floorboards sounding far more alarming than they had on the way in. I kept my eyes on the ground and the flashlight beam in front of us. It felt like walking across the surface of a frozen lake. We found another place where the floor had caved in closer to the door, but the gap was smaller.

We reached the exit and both of us breathed a sigh of relief as we stepped out onto the firm concrete of the steps outside.

"Let's not do that again."

"We still have the rest of the town to enjoy," I reminded her.

We stuck together, moving from area to area in an efficient, methodical pattern. We searched Main Street first. The buildings that were open or partially fallen down, we went into. The ones that looked particularly dangerous, we stayed outside and examined through windows and doorways. The few that were secured and boarded we checked for signs of entry. Had the town been less remote, I would have expected to find homeless people using it for shelter. But Corinth was too far off the beaten path for that. Living here without access to a car would require a twenty-mile hike across the wilderness every time you needed supplies.

Once we had cleared Main Street, we moved on to the southwest corner of town. Sarah brought out her tablet and we split the town into quadrants, using Main Street as the center. We started in the southwest and moved clockwise. It would have been faster to split up and cover twice the ground in the same time, but neither of us suggested that. Anyway, there really wasn't that much town to cover. Even at its peak, Corinth had been one of the smaller mining communities of its kind.

The houses were of a uniform design: one-story dwellings with three or four rooms. A square of yard out front and one at the back: usually surfaced with cracked paving or weed-invaded gravel, occasionally brown patches of dirt that might once have been a lawn. We searched from house to house, taking the same approach: going inside the open ones, checking the secured ones.

Like the stores, the houses had been cleared out and picked clean. In a couple, we found the remains of fires and empty beer cans: the residue of adventurous college kids seeking out an off-the-beaten-path party venue.

It took us just over an hour to cover the town with reasonable thoroughness. We found nothing. The whole time, the silence enveloped us like a blanket. It almost felt like a transgression when one of us spoke. We found ourselves back at the car just after ten o'clock.

Sarah opened the back door of the Ford and tossed her backpack inside, breathing out a heavy sigh. "So what now?"

She was disappointed. I was too, but this wasn't the end of the road.

From somewhere out in the desert, we heard the howl of a coyote. It could have been miles away; it was difficult to gauge distance. It was the first sound that hadn't been made by either of us in over an hour, and it was a little unsettling.

"Now," I replied, "we've crossed something off the list. So let's think again. Why would she come here?"

"Not for the club scene."

I didn't reply, looking back up at the hulk of the town hall. I knew I was probably imbuing the building with more significance than it warranted, just because it had been what led us here via Carol's sketch. I thought about the door on the platform inside. We had encountered more than a few secured doors in the old town, but something about this one bothered me.

"You want to take another look?"

I shook my head. It was time to call it a night. "If things don't work out in Quarter, we can come back in the daylight. We're not going to find anything tonight."

27

We didn't talk much on the drive back to Iron City. I wound my window down and let the night air blow through the car. It was cold now, but it was a refreshing cool after the heat of the day and the stale interiors of Corinth. We were in view of the lights of town when Sarah's phone buzzed.

"Looks like we're officially out of the wilderness," she said, looking down at the screen. She examined whatever the message was, and then tapped a couple of times and held the phone to her ear. I listened to her side of the conversation again.

"Hello, Greg? Sarah Blackwell, how you doing?"

Greg Kubler, I was guessing. Sarah's contact at the Las Vegas PD. I kept my eyes on the road as Sarah navigated the pleasantries and got down to business. What did her friend know about Detective Costigane and his interest in Dominic Freel?

Kubler was doing most of the talking. Sarah listened intently, chipping in with an occasional comment. "Yeah ... interesting ... naturally ..." and then something that surprised her. "Oh? Okay."

I glanced over at her. She was looking straight ahead at the road, her mind obviously miles away. She bit the corner of her bottom lip as she listened.

"No that's really great, thank you. One last thing, does the name Trenton Gage sound familiar to you? No? Just wondering."

There was a pause and I guessed Greg had said his piece and was now asking her a question.

"Oh, you know me. Idle curiosity." Another pause and

then a smile. "You'll be the first to know."

She thanked Kubler and hung up. We had reached the parking lot of the Iron City Inn. I pulled off the road, parked, and turned the engine off before I gave in and asked.

"Well?"

Sarah shook herself out of her thoughts.

"He says he doesn't know Costigane well, but he has a reputation for being kind of a hardass. He's been with the department thirty years. The dependable type."

"But he doesn't know anything about Gage."

"Didn't ring a bell, but like I said, Greg's not exactly front-of-house anymore."

"So what about Costigane? What's he been working on lately?"

Sarah paused. "Does the word 'Ellison' mean anything to you?"

The word did sound familiar. I repeated it, testing it out on my tongue. Someone in the news, recently, I thought. Not someone, something. A company name, not a person. I snapped my fingers as soon as it came to me.

"The big heist in Vegas over New Year's." I had read about it. It had been national news for a day or two.

"Bingo. Made the front pages out here for a week. Holiday weekend, perfect crime."

"But they got someone for it, right?"

"Right. But there was no way he was acting alone. And they still haven't accounted for some of the take."

"And this is the case Costigane is working?"

Sarah nodded. "Mmhmm."

"Refresh my memory."

"It was a professional job," Sarah said. "But the funny thing was, it didn't seem like the work of any of the usual operators. Vegas is fairly clean now, not like the old days.

I wonder about that sometimes. When you clear up a problem, it always pops up somewhere else."

"That's right," I agreed. "You want gangsters running casinos these days, try Macau. You won't be disappointed."

"So the police did a pretty good job. There were four or five men involved, but they tracked one down after an anonymous tip-off and he had most of the take."

"Most?"

"They got all of the high value jewelry. Some of the loose diamonds were unaccounted for. Not a trivial sum—definitely a couple of million, as I remember."

"And the easiest merchandise to sell," Blake said. "I don't think it was a coincidence that the loose stones were the part they didn't recover."

"So what do you think? Freel knows something about it? Maybe he has evidence on the people who did it? Or maybe he was the anonymous tip-off, and somebody wants revenge."

"Or maybe it's something simpler than that," I said.

All of a sudden, I began to see recent events in a new light. Freel lying low in a Vegas suburb. Telling Carol they needed to leave right away. The men who'd come in the night. Costigane's interest in finding him.

She shook her head. "I don't know Blake ... What are you thinking?"

The pieces were starting to form a picture. And I didn't like the look of it one bit.

"Same thing I've been thinking all day. We need to talk to Dominic Freel."

28

PHOENIX

Trenton Gage booked a room in a hotel on the south side of Phoenix, after first stopping by a branch of Hertz to pick up a car for the onward journey. They rented him a silver Chrysler 300 with an open-ended return date. It was more expensive than he would have liked, but the next best option would have been hitchhiking to Quarter. The room was as basic as the one in Vegas had been, but at least it didn't have the noisy neighbors.

He charged his phone, which had gone dead a little while after he had dealt with Logan McKinney. Just after eleven, he called the number the leader of the three men in Vegas had given him; the one who said his name was Walter. Walter answered immediately, and expressed polite surprise that he hadn't heard from Gage until now.

"How are things proceeding?"

"Things are proceeding well. I spoke to an associate of Freel's this afternoon."

"An associate?"

"That's right, his name was McKinney. Sound familiar?"

There was a pause of perhaps half a second too long.

"I'm not familiar with that name, no. And was this Mr. McKinney able to help you?"

Gage reached into his pocket and took a small metal object from it. Until a couple of hours before, the object had hung on a chain around Logan McKinney's neck, like a charm. It hadn't brought him any luck, or at least, not enough.

The object was a key. About three inches long, made of

brass, and with a small engraved logo: two Cs intertwined, and the number 2 in a smaller font. Gage had had a hunch of what it was almost immediately, but he had confirmed his suspicions by looking up the company represented by the logo. Centrum Co. A company that specialized in the manufacture of safes. As the number suggested, the key was part of a set: a dual system meaning two people had to be there to open it up. He had a good idea of who the owner of the key's twin was.

"I believe so," Gage answered. "I think we're definitely getting somewhere."

29

We rose early, and were on the road by seven. The sun was already full in the sky. The traffic was nonexistent as we headed south, and we were in good time for Sarah to keep her one o'clock appointment with Diane Marshall. I drove, and Sarah bunched up her hoodie against the window and snoozed for a little longer. As we lost altitude, the landscape flattened out and the greenery ceded to sweeping desert. The only features to break up the road were the telegraph poles. Distant mountain ranges rose ahead, but never seemed to get any closer. By eight a.m. I had to switch the air conditioning on. I thought about how different an environment this was from the one in which I had last seen Carol. A different world, almost. I thought about that rainy November night in a guest house out on Long Island. I had been called away in the early hours of the morning. I had said goodbye, and we had never seen each other again.

I had almost forgotten there was somebody else in the car with me when Sarah startled me with a question.

"If we find her, how do you think she'll react?"

I glanced over at Sarah. "Hmm?" I responded, pretending I didn't know exactly who she was talking about.

"Carol. I mean, it's been a few years, right?"

"I don't know how she'll react," I said. Which was the truth.

"What will you say to her?"

"I don't know."

Sarah yawned and stretched as best she could within the confines of the passenger seat. She stared ahead at the straight road that stretched to the horizon and smiled. "Of course you don't. I mean, it's not like you've had a long time to think about it."

I turned the question around. "What about you? What are you going to say to her?"

She bit her bottom lip, thinking. "I think I might try to wring her neck."

"Maybe I should speak to her first."

We saw our first car in nearly an hour twenty miles north of Quarter. It was a dark blue pickup driven by a big, tanned guy wearing mirrored shades and a Stetson. A minute after that, we saw another pickup, a green one this time. And then a yellow Toyota, and then the sight of other cars ceased to be a novelty and we were in light traffic. Ten minutes after that, we hit the Quarter town limits. The sign welcomed us and told us the population was a little under six thousand.

On Main Street, there was a line of stores, all open and doing business in stark contrast to the other town we had seen last night. There was a gravel parking lot next to a place called Norrie's that advertised COFFEE in type larger than the name of the establishment. I pulled into a space and went inside to take them up on the suggestion, while Sarah pulled up a map on her phone.

Norrie's was decked out like a '50s-style diner—red leather upholstered booths, black and white checkerboard tiled flooring, an old-fashioned jukebox in the corner. It was also just about deserted. I decided this would be as good a place as any to wait while Sarah went to see Diane Marshall. When I got back out to the car with two coffees in go cups, she had already worked out our itinerary. The meeting with Diane first, and then we would work through our list of potential locations until we either found Carol, or struck out completely.

At a quarter to one, Sarah gulped the last of her coffee and held her hand out for the keys.

"Sure you don't want me to come?" I asked.

"Better I go alone. You can put the finishing touches to the list, but if we're in luck, we won't need it." She inclined her head in the direction of the back seat, where her pack had lain since last night. "Paperwork's all there, enjoy."

I grabbed the backpack and got out of the car. Sarah took my place behind the wheel.

"I'll call you as soon as I get done," she said, starting up the engine.

I watched her back out of the space, turn and head back out onto Main Street, going in the opposite direction from where we'd come. I didn't know how long Sarah would be gone, but I had enough to keep me busy. I carried the pack into Norrie's and took a seat in one of the booths next to the front window. A waitress came over and offered me a menu. I declined and ordered another black coffee, to stay this time.

I looked out of the window at the street. There was a line

of stores and a Mexican restaurant and a library opposite. A weekday lunchtime, so the sidewalks weren't exactly busy, but not deserted either. Just a typical small town. I watched the passers-by. Mostly retired folks and moms with young children; everyone else probably being accounted for by work or school.

Quarter, population 5,827 according to the sign. I wondered how often they updated those signs. I assumed they didn't send someone out to the town limits with correction fluid and a Sharpie every time someone left town, so maybe they tied it in with the census. Or maybe they only bothered to update it when the signs were replaced. Either way, 5,827 wasn't a lot of people, considering. I hoped it wouldn't be too difficult to track down just two people out of that population.

Before I got to work on that, I hooked Sarah's tablet up to the diner's free wifi and looked up some news articles on the robbery of the Ellison Jewelry Company on New Year's Eve. I had scanned a few the previous night in the hotel at Iron City. I remembered the basic details from reading about it in January, but it was useful to find a summary of the case a few weeks later, after the first—and to date only—breakthrough. An anonymous tip-off had led the police to one of the men responsible for the heist. The suspect, a security guard at the company named Rayner Deakins, had been killed in an exchange of gunfire with the police. They had recovered eighty per cent of the yield, but that still left approximately two million dollars' worth of premium diamonds unaccounted for. The whereabouts of the stones was one of two important questions, from where I stood. The other was the identity and whereabouts of the person who had called in the tip. I was betting a lot of people would be keen to find that person, and not just the police.

My coffee arrived and I took paperwork out of the bag. The pages of archived newspapers Sarah had printed out at her house. I hoped Sarah's contact would come through, but this was the backup. The previous two months of the real estate section from the local weekly newspaper. I planned to go through and cross off everything that had come off the market in the time since Carol had left Summerlin. That would give us a list of addresses, and we could start knocking on doors.

It didn't take long. Quarter wasn't exactly a property hotspot, and I was barely halfway through my coffee and two-thirds of the way through the sheaf of pages when something caught my eye. It wasn't one of the rental or sales notices, though. It was from the April 19th edition, and there hadn't been quite enough property ads to take up the whole of the page. No such thing as blank space in a newspaper, so a couple of job ads had been snuck in at the side to fill the void. One was for a teaching assistant in a local school, the other was for a temporary librarian post. Fifteen hours a week, experience desirable, flexibility important.

I looked up from the printout and across at the library, wondering why that ad had set off some kind of synaptic spark. It could have been the coincidence that I was sitting right across the road from the library, but I didn't think that was it.

And then I had it.

Lying in bed next to Carol, that last night. She had been talking about college. How she had worked in the library to subsidize living costs. A good gig: she had always been a big reader, and she liked the orderly nature of the job: a stark contrast to what she ended up doing for a living, managing the chaos of a senator's day-to-day life.

I put the printout down on the table and took the time to

really look at the library building. It wasn't anything grand or ornate, just another single-story unit like the others along Main Street. It had big picture windows at the front, but you couldn't really see inside because bookshelves were lined in front of them.

Sarah and I had considered various ways of picking up Carol's trail, but I couldn't recall us thinking about job ads. Carol and Freel had left Summerlin in a hurry, before they had expected to. Maybe they were unprepared. Maybe it would be useful for one or both of them to find a low-key job to bring in some ready cash. It would help with blending in, too. I could picture Carol scanning the newspaper, seeing this ad, remembering how she liked the order. Different from how her career had turned out six and a half years ago, and in all probability very different from the way her life was today.

The papers and the coffee and everything else were forgotten. I kept my eyes on the library as I thought about all this. I could see someone moving around inside, behind the books.

It couldn't be this easy, could it? But then, the library was just across the road. It wouldn't take long to check it out.

I gathered up the printouts and stuffed them back into the bag. I left money for the coffee and exited the diner. I waited for a gap in the traffic and crossed the road.

I pushed open the glass door of the library and stepped inside. It was an open-plan space with a green carpet and a dozen or so freestanding bookcases arranged across the floor, as well as along the walls. Neat signs advertising the content of each section: mystery, children's, audiobooks, non-fiction, romance. The back wall was lined with shelves, but at the far end there was gap for a noticeboard and a door marked "Private." An elderly woman with rounded glasses was sitting behind a desk in the center of the room, tapping away at a computer. She looked up when I had made no move away from the door.

"Can I help you?"

I didn't have anything planned to say, but before I knew it I was speaking as though I had been given a script. My voice sounded a little far away as I spoke. "Is Rebecca here today?"

She stared at me for a moment and suddenly I was certain that I was mistaken, or that Carol had picked another new name. But then she smiled and pointed toward the back of the room. "Oh, you mean Becky? She's in the office, just about to finish up. You can go on back there if you like?"

With an effort, I kept my voice casual, nonchalant. "Thanks."

The woman looked back at her screen as I started walking toward the door in the back wall, passing war and horror and history. As I reached it, I could hear somebody moving about inside, moving papers around. I took a deep breath and knocked.

"Come in."

I turned the handle and the door swung open. She was there, leaning over a desk and scribbling something in a log book of some kind. She had changed a lot in some ways: the shoulder-length blonde hair I had known was long gone, replaced with the red color from the photograph, but cut again since then into a short bob. She wore blue jeans and a gray sleeveless shirt. She was just close enough so I could see the tiny scar on her upper left arm. I remembered tracing my finger over it, asking where she had gotten it. Crashing her bike in seventh grade. Wet leaves on the road. Eight stitches.

I didn't say anything, just stood in the doorway and waited for her to look up. She flinched and took a sharp

breath when she saw me. It took her a second to process
what she was seeing, and then her shoulders relaxed a little,
and her eyes narrowed.

"Hi," I said.

30

QUARTER, ARIZONA
THURSDAY, 12:58

Sarah parked Blake's Ford in the small lot outside the office
of the Quarter *Observer*. It was just a small unit in a two-story
stucco-fronted office building. A minuscule space compared
to the giant big-city newsrooms Sarah had seen over her
career. But then, most of those newsrooms had downsized,
some of them had closed down entirely, and this little local
was still going.

There was a woman in a pink t-shirt and rimless glasses
standing outside the door smoking a cigarette. Sarah recognized Diane Marshall from her LinkedIn picture, although
her frizzy blonde hair was a little less tidy and she had
gained a few pounds. Diane's eyes regarded her as she
parked, taking a moment to note the out-of-state license
plate. As Sarah got out of the car, the woman dropped her
half-smoked cigarette, ground the butt out with a heel and
extended her hand.

"Sarah?" she asked, blowing the last of the smoke through
her nostrils. "I'm Diane."

Sarah smiled and took her hand. "Thanks for taking the
time to meet me."

Diane waved it away. "Time is not a problem. Lot of it about, not much interesting to do with it."

She beckoned Sarah inside the door. It opened onto a narrow corridor. Diane made for the third door on the left and held it open for Sarah. There was about a square yard of floor space at the entrance, in front of an unmanned reception desk that joined with a low wooden partition to divide the room in two. Diane opened the little gate in the partition and held it open for Sarah to walk into the back area. There was another desk and a photocopier. Every wall was lined with shelves stacked with ring binders and books and document wallets and magazine folders crammed with folded copies of the Quarter *Observer*. A wastebasket beside the desk was overflowing with balled-up printouts and junk mail. Sarah smiled. Over the years she had trained herself to keep a tidy workspace, but there was still a part of her that felt you weren't doing it right if there weren't a hundred projects on the go. The chaos of the small-town newsroom felt a little like coming home.

"Okay, where were we," Diane was saying to herself. She stared at her overflowing desk. She lifted a couple of items before remembering something and opening the bottom drawer and closing it again.

"So you were at the *Tribune*, huh?" she said, without looking up.

"For thirteen years," Sarah confirmed.

"You miss it?"

"Sometimes," she said truthfully.

Diane abandoned the desk and looked purposefully across the room at one of the steel shelving units, crammed full of box files.

"Yeah, I looked up your books on Amazon. That's going pretty well?"

"Pretty well."

Diane had done her research, as Sarah had known she would. It was the main reason she and Blake had decided that she should come alone. If she had shown up with Blake, Diane would have known in a heartbeat that there was more to this than Sarah's cover story of trying to locate a missing school friend. Blake doing his tall dark and mysterious thing would introduce a whole raft of new questions for a person who was curious by profession.

Sarah knew that if Diane thought for a second she might be helping a questionable ex-boyfriend or some kind of debt collector track down an unsuspecting woman, she would be less forthcoming.

But calling as one journalist to another and asking for a favor? That stood a much better chance. Diane could look her up and ascertain that she was on the level about her background. Just as importantly, she would know a comrade-in-arms when she met one. So she would trust Sarah, go a little above and beyond for someone who was not only a former bigshot reporter, but an honest-to-God published author. Sarah thought about what Diane had said a minute ago: "Lot of time about," and realized with mild embarrassment that she was basically what would pass for a celebrity around here.

"Got it." Diane pulled a well-used spiral-bound notebook out from where it was jammed between one of the box files and the shelf, and leafed through to the most recently used pages.

"I made some calls. Quarter is a pretty small town. This wouldn't usually be a difficult ask."

Implication: it was on this occasion. Sarah said nothing, waited for her to continue.

"So your neighbor is ..." she glanced down at the pad.

"Rebecca Freel, right? Rebecca and Dominic Freel."

Sarah told her that was correct. She had thought about giving her some of the other names in the notebook too, just in case, but had decided against it.

"Nothing on anyone by those names. So I followed your suggestion. The one thing you knew is that they were headed here, so I called around the hotels. Easy to narrow down because nobody has much reason to stay more than a couple of nights here. Ricky over at the Sunset Motel had a couple of the age you're looking for take a room for two weeks, but their names weren't Rebecca or Dominic ..."

"They might have—"

"Their names were Chai Son and Apsara," she cut in. "They're here from Thailand, seeing the States on honeymoon. I figured that rules them out unless ...?"

"Yeah." Sarah smiled. "Sorry."

Diane continued. "I called my friendly local mailman after that. Terry McCain—Terry is usually the only person I need to ask when I'm looking for somebody. No new mail to people called Freel, but I asked him to keep an eye out for new Rebeccas or Dominics. Nothing yet. So, I called around some of the local realtors. Again, nothing within the timeframe you're looking at. So, just to make sure, I checked cached versions of the local websites going back a few weeks. I found a house over on Sycamore Street that was taken off the website six weeks ago. I hadn't seen that one before, so I called up the agent and asked about it, and got a very confused receptionist. Seems it came off the listings, but she doesn't have a corresponding let in her database. She assumed it was an oversight and said she would get back to me. Ten minutes later, she calls back, apologizing that it really is off the market. The rent is being paid, but weirdly, there's no customer details."

"Nice," Sarah said approvingly.

"I know, right? Curiouser and curiouser. So I said that's great, thanks anyway, hung up, and headed straight over to Sycamore."

She paused again, grinning like the Cheshire cat in the story she had just referenced.

"And?" Sarah prompted.

She said nothing. Walked back to her desk and picked up her handbag. She rummaged in it and pulled out her phone. She tapped on it a couple of times and held the screen up to face Sarah. It showed a woman with short red hair and sunglasses exiting a grey car parked on the street outside a modest suburban home. It was Carol.

"This your girl?"

Sarah grinned. "Very nice work."

"Not too shabby for a small town reporter, huh?"

"Not too bad for any reporter. Diane, I really appreciate this. This is so much better than I could have wished for, thank you."

"Stop it, I had fun. I'm glad I could help."

She slid the notebook with the address toward Sarah, then seemed to change her mind and kept her hand on it. "I have one condition though."

Sarah was wary. This had been almost too good to be true. She braced herself. "Yes?"

"Name a character after me in the next Farrah Fairchild book?"

She smiled. "I think that can be arranged."

31

Carol looked beyond me, as though she was expecting some-body else to be behind me outside the doorway. Then she looked back at me. When she spoke, her voice was calm and controlled. She didn't want the woman outside on the desk to hear her.

"Get the hell out of here."

"It's good to see you, too, Carol. How have you been?"

"I'm not kidding." She spoke calmly and deliberately, but her voice was burning with controlled fury. "What are you doing here?"

I hesitated, unsure of what the least-worst thing to say would be. I felt like a bomb-disposal tech considering which wire to cut to avoid the whole thing blowing up in his face.

"I'm here to warn you about—"

"*Warn* me?"

"Wait a second. All I meant was we're worried that there could be some trouble on the way for you and your hus-band."

Unconsciously, I hesitated a split second before saying that last word. She caught it, her expression becoming pained for a second.

"Well I know you're right about that," she said. "Only trouble isn't on the way. Trouble's standing right in front of me."

I took a step forward into the office and raised my hands in supplication. "Can I ..."

She held a palm up to ward me off. "Stay right there."

I stopped and dropped my hands to my side. "Look, I never got a chance to say I was sorry."

She pursed her lips and the glare she was fixing me with seemed to burn hotter in intensity. She didn't want to talk about the past. Didn't want to talk to me at all. And somewhere deep under the layers of trepidation and remorse, something about that irritated me. My brain counseled diplomacy, but my mouth couldn't help itself.

"But then, you didn't exactly give me the chance, did you?"

She opened her mouth and shook her head, as though she couldn't believe what I had just said. "I thought I was very clear. Did you get my letter?"

"I got it. It was ... concise."

"And yet, here you are. How long did it take you to find me?"

"Carol, it's been six years ..."

"Exactly. Do you know—" she stopped and turned away from me, looking out of the small window. It looked out across a kids' playground. A couple of pre-school age children were climbing around the equipment while their moms chatted to each other.

"I assumed you were dead for a long time," Carol said. "Maybe that was just wishful thinking."

I opened my mouth a couple of times to start to say something; reconsidered both times. It wasn't often I was lost for words. What I had said was true. It had been years. Long enough for both of us to have moved on. But here she was: a little different, a little older ... but in so many ways the same. I had wondered occasionally what it would feel like to see her again, but I hadn't expected it to hit me like an express train.

Don't look for me. Good advice.

She brushed her hand across the bridge of her nose and turned around. "What do you mean 'we'?"

"'We?'" I repeated, momentarily lost.

"'*We're* worried there could be trouble on the way,'" she said. "As in, not just you. We. Who are you here with?"

I lunged at the chance to salvage the conversation like a drowning man striking out for a piece of driftwood. "Sarah, your neighbor from Summerlin. She got in touch with me."

Why the hell hadn't I opened with that? I realized I had made a big mistake coming without Sarah. I could have waited for her, but it hadn't even crossed my mind. Maybe I had just wanted to see Carol by myself first. I had expected it to go a little smoother than this. I don't make a habit of decisions based purely on emotion, and, well, I guess this is why.

"Sarah Blackwell?" for a second the anger vanished from Carol's face. That felt like a minor win. "From Summerlin?"

"She was worried about you. The way you just ... vanished."

She shot me a look that dared me to draw a comparison with the way she had left things with me. I kept my face impassive.

"Wait a minute," she said, sitting down in the chair behind her desk. "How did Sarah Blackwell know about ..." she stopped and sighed. "The notebook."

"The notebook," I said.

She shook her head. "I didn't realize it was missing until we were five hundred miles away. Did you read it?"

"I had to. It was all we had."

She sighed. "Break glass in case of emergency." I thought her tone of voice had warmed a little, as she realized my being here wasn't entirely my fault.

I thought about a couple of different replies. Silence seemed to be safer.

"Where is she?" Carol asked. "Sarah."

"She's here in town."

"Well that was really sweet of her to worry about me, I guess. But I'm fine, really. *We're* fine," she corrected, staring at me pointedly as she said "we." She added a perfunctory smile that was about as convincing as a three-dollar bill.

"In my experience, people don't skip out in the middle of the night when everything's fine."

The smile evaporated. "It's been wonderful to catch up, but I have to go now."

"I know Freel is running from somebody. That's his business. I just don't want you to get in the way."

"And how is that *your* business?"

"How much do you know about the people Freel's running from? We think it has something to with the Ellison heist. He had something to do with it, didn't he?"

"The Ellison—" she stopped, the expression on her face looking like I had just accused her husband of being an alien spy sent to pave the way for invasion. "You're crazy, you know that? Not that it's any of your business, but Dominic is a casino consultant. Some shady people work in that business. A deal went bad, no fault of his, but some of his rivals were upset. He thought it was best if we didn't stick around. It's inconvenient, isn't it, when you have to just leave?"

I ignored that. "Then he was right. The night I arrived in Summerlin, somebody named Trenton Gage showed up at Sarah's house with a gun. He was looking for your law-abiding husband."

She put a hand over her mouth. "Was she . . ."

"She's fine. No thanks to you."

I regretted the words instantly. She didn't say anything.

"I'm sorry, I shouldn't have said that."

"I never thought she would be in any danger."

"And how much danger did you think the two of you were in?"

She hesitated. "Dom was worried about being frozen out of other deals. Worrying about his tires getting slashed. Nothing really dangerous. We thought it would be better to start fresh someplace else. I've gotten good at that."

"I need to talk to him," I said. "Somebody is after him, and they're willing to use lethal force." I looked at her meaningfully. "They don't care who gets in their way. Maybe Freel hasn't told you everything, but ..."

"Not every man keeps secrets."

I didn't have time to argue the point on that one.

"Will you take me to him?"

She closed her eyes and sighed, seeming to come to a decision. I wondered how much Freel had been keeping from her. "I'll talk to him. How long are you in town?"

"As long as it takes."

"There's a restaurant called La Traviata over on South Street. It's actually pretty good, despite the name. Be there at seven tonight and I'll bring him along."

I started to shake my head. "Much as I'd love to shoot the breeze with you both over a pizza, I need to talk to him now."

"Well you're not going to," she said, her voice firmer. "We do this my way, okay? I need to speak to him first."

We stared each other out for a minute. I realized it was her decision. I wasn't going to point a gun at her head. Maybe she had already suspected there was more to Freel's activities than he had told her. Perhaps it would be healthier if he fessed up to her before he did it in front of me. Carol would have time to digest the news in private; it would be less embarrassing. I guessed I owed her that much.

"Okay," I said. I reached into my jacket and took out a card. I wrote my cell number on it and handed it to her. "I know you still have my email, but this'll get me faster."

She looked at the card in my outstretched hand for a long moment; as though accepting it would commit her to a course of action she wasn't sure she wanted to take. Eventually, she took it. She read the name on the front of the card and raised an eyebrow, but said nothing. She slipped the card into her bag.

"Seven o'clock," she said again. "La Traviata, South Street." A statement, not a question.

"We'll find it."

"How could I forget? You're good at finding things."

32

The street was so quiet and so deserted that even in the middle of the afternoon it felt like it was six o'clock on a Sunday morning. Or the first day after the apocalypse, maybe. The rows of pastel-colored two-story houses stretched out behind generous front yards. After driving through the rest of the town, Sycamore Street seemed to be an anomaly. The houses Gage had seen elsewhere were simpler; one-story slump block adobe. These houses looked much newer, shinier, more generous in their proportions. The street had a vague sense of unreality that Gage found appropriate for a reason he could not quite explain. There was no sound but the occasional click of a lawn sprinkler from farther down the street. Nothing moved except the light breeze gently nudging the leaves of the orange trees.

The house at number 18 showed no signs of life, but Gage wanted to watch it for a little while before he made a move.

He turned the engine off and buzzed the driver's window

down. It was like opening the door of an oven. He thought about how well today had gone so far. Perhaps it was the universe balancing out after the unexpected trouble in Summerlin. He had been prepared to get rough with the owner of Norrie's Diner; the place McKinney had mentioned. In the event, it had been much easier than that. The kid on duty had been talkative when he took Gage's order. His nametag had identified him as "Cole." Gage had mentioned to Cole that he was in town to see a friend he had sent letters to care of the diner. Cole said he remembered a letter arriving a week before. The recipient had a deal with the owner. Cole had delivered the letter himself, to an address over on Sycamore. It had been on his way home anyway, so no trouble.

This was one of the best things about small towns, Gage thought. No trouble. Everybody was so friendly and helpful. Not only had he not had to get physical, he had obtained the address he needed for the price of a cup of coffee.

Gage registered movement in the corner of his eye, and saw a well-fed orange tabby emerge lazily from beneath a silver SUV parked fifty yards up the street. The cat strolled unhurriedly across the road in front of him, before disappearing between two of the houses across the road from number 18.

His phone was lying on the passenger seat, plugged into the cigarette lighter to charge. He considered calling Walter to give him an update, and then remembered the brass key in his pocket and decided against it. Instead, he thumbed through recent calls for Courtney's number. As the phone rang, he took out the key for the hundredth time, and turned it over between thumb and forefinger.

"Hello?"

"It's me again. How you doing? Is Jake there?"

"Gage." Courtney's voice had the enthusiasm of someone receiving a call from a pushy double-glazing salesman. "He isn't here right now. He's at kindergarten."

"Right," Gage said. "Kindergarten. When did he start that?"

A car rounded the corner and Gage tuned out Courtney's answer as he watched it pass him by and continue around the corner. Courtney said his name irritatedly when she realized he wasn't listening to her reply.

"Sorry, I missed that."

"What do you want?"

"Nothing that can't wait," Gage said. "It's still okay to come on his birthday, right?"

There was a long silence. "I said so, didn't I?"

"Sure. Okay, just tell him ... tell him I may have an answer to that question."

Courtney replied with a noncommittal grunt and hung up.

Gage examined the brass key in his palm. *The sixty-four-thousand-dollar question.* Maybe a lot more than that. He snapped his fingers over the key in a fist and slipped it back into his pocket. He buzzed the window of the Chrysler up. In the ten minutes he had been watching the house, he had seen only that one car, and no pedestrians. The only indication that this street was occupied at all had been the tabby. He was just about to get out of the car when his phone rang. The incoming call was from the number Walter had provided him with.

He answered, wondering whether they had some new information, or if they were just getting impatient. The one thing he hadn't anticipated was what Walter said next.

"The job's over. We're standing you down."

Gage's eyes narrowed, wondering if he had heard correctly. "What?"

"Don't worry, you can keep your fee, and we'll reimburse you for any expenses you may have incurred. But we won't need you to find Freel anymore."

He had not been expecting this. Did that mean they had located Freel themselves? That seemed unlikely. And Gage was almost positive that this was the house in which Freel and his wife were staying. They couldn't know how close he was, could they? Had somebody else given them a solid lead?

"You want me to stop looking for him?"

"That's correct, yes."

"Any particular reason?"

There was a slight hesitation, and Gage suspected Walter was resisting the urge to tell him "none of your goddamn business." When he spoke again, he was more diplomatic than that.

"We don't need him anymore, is all," Walter said. "The situation has changed. I'm sorry to inconvenience you, but I hope you'll agree the settlement is more than fair. Gage? Are you still there?"

"I'm just thinking."

"What is there to think about? I'm letting you know the job is over, and we're making sure you're compensated. Thank you."

"I'll call you back," Gage said, and hung up before Walter could respond.

What in the hell had *that* been about? Gage looked back at the house. He knew one thing for sure: there was no way he was coming all this way without finding out what made Dominic Freel such a wanted man. The key he had found on McKinney had only reinforced his hunch that there was more to this job than met the eye.

He took out the Ruger he had obtained in Phoenix and

clicked the safety off, after making sure the chamber was empty. He replaced it in his holster, then pulled it clear a couple of times, making sure there were no obstructions. He got out of the car and put his sport coat on over the holster. He walked diagonally across the road to number 18 Sycamore Street. It was a two-story pastel-colored house, like pretty much all of the others. Pleasant enough, and it had probably cost about an eighth of the asking price of the house in Summerlin.

There was a high wooden gate on the left side leading to the backyard. On the right side was a single parking garage. The four front-facing windows of the house all had blinds that were half-shut, as though the occupants wanted to shield themselves from outside glances without drawing attention to themselves by having the blinds fully closed by day. The door was solid wood, painted dark red. There was a doorbell. Gage rang it, waited a minute, rang it again.

There was no sound, no movement from within.

Gage turned around and looked left and then right along the street. No cars, no pedestrians. Even the tabby had found something to occupy himself with.

He walked to the gate, pulled the handle and found it open. He navigated the passageway that led around the side of the house and came out in a simply appointed backyard. There was a small paved patio at the back door, where there were a couple of lawn chairs and a table, followed by a stretch of grass with a sprinkler snaking out into the middle.

Gage tried the handle on the back door just in case, and then took his picks out. A minute later, he was standing in a medium-sized kitchen. Like the backyard, it screamed rental. Everything was neat, clean, functional. There was no hint of a personal touch, nothing that gave any hint of the personalities of the occupants.

He opened the refrigerator and a few of the cupboards and found nothing of note. The trash can in the utility space was stuffed with pizza boxes and Chinese food containers. There was a door that squeaked softly as it opened out to the parking garage, which was empty. The tracks of road dirt on the concrete floor and the lingering scent of gasoline fumes told him that it had been in use recently.

He closed the door and began to check the rest of the house. He moved from room to room quickly, checking the closets and making sure nobody had hidden themselves away when they had heard him ring the doorbell.

He ascended to the upper floor. Two bedrooms and a bathroom. One of the bedrooms looked like it was in use, though as impersonally stocked as a hotel room. He checked the closet, under the bed, the drawers in the bedside table. He moved to the second bedroom, where there was a bed frame and mattress with no sheets, a desk and a laptop. The window beyond the desk faced out on the street outside. It was like looking at a still photograph. He mused that this was the second suburban dwelling he had broken into in the last forty-eight hours. His assignments did not usually lead him to such safe, mundane, middle-class environs.

He opened the laptop and the login screen appeared, requesting a password.

He reached into his pocket and brought out a small canvas case. He unzipped it, selected a tiny USB device and plugged it into the port on the side of the laptop. The login screen disappeared as the laptop rebooted. When it powered up again, it would skip the password request. While he waited for his gadget to do its work, he started to go through the desk drawers. He had finished and was moving to the chest of drawers when he heard the sound of an engine.

The street was so quiet that it was almost a minute before

the gray Toyota appeared in his line of sight. He shrank back from the window and watched it slow and pull into the driveway. The car came to a stop with the engine running, and he heard a smooth hum as the automated door of the garage rolled up.

Quickly, he moved downstairs. He positioned himself on the blind side of the kitchen door and took his gun out as he listened to the car drive carefully into the port and the handbrake ratchet on. A second later, he heard the humming of the motor as the door rolled down again, followed by the clunk of the driver's door opening and closing, and then the squeak of the door from the garage into the kitchen. There was a pause and the sound of someone fumbling with something in the kitchen, and the unmistakable noise of a car key being tossed on a work surface.

The kitchen door opened and Gage saw the back of a man wearing black pants and a light blue shirt. He had dirty blond hair. Gage could see both of his hands, and they were empty. He was headed for the stairs, had his left hand on the newel post ready to turn when Gage spoke.

"Turn around."

The guy practically jumped out of his skin, whirling around and jerking his hand off the post as though it was red-hot.

His expression turned from surprise to anger when he saw Gage and the gun pointed at him. It was Freel, all right. The man in the picture.

"Who the hell are you?"

Gage took a step forward, keeping the gun leveled on Freel's chest.

"Logan McKinney sends his regards."

Freel's brow creased as though Gage had just recited a nonsensical nursery rhyme. He raised his hands and his expression switched to worry. It was an act, entirely transparent. "I don't know what you're talking about. You have the wrong house, buddy."

"You can skip it," Gage said.

"Skip what?"

"I know you're Dominic Freel. I know you're running from some people in Vegas."

"Who's Dominic Fr—?"

"I said skip it." Gage had started out with no opinion of Freel—he was merely a target to be acquired. But now that he had been in the same room as the man for less than thirty seconds, he was already trying his patience. "Your name is Dominic Freel. You left your place in Summerlin, Nevada six weeks ago with your wife. You arrived here a couple of days later. Your former associates are keen to speak to you. Keen enough to pay me to bring you back."

He cocked the gun and the sound sent a visible shiver through Freel, as though Gage had hit a button on a remote control.

"You know this, and I know this. If you want me to put a bullet in your kneecap so you can tell yourself you put up a fight then I'm happy to do that, but ..."

"Okay, okay. I'm Freel. What do you want?"

"I'm supposed to bring you back to Vegas. They didn't specify that you had to be in one piece."

"You don't need to threaten me, all right? I'm cooperating."

"That wasn't a threat."

Freel's hands were still in the air. He moved them down an inch. "Can I ..."

"No."

He hesitated and then said, "Can we talk about this?"

Excellent. This was more like it. Gage kept his face blank, like he had no more interest in Freel than a bug he was about to squash. "What is there to talk about? I have a job; the job is complete. Or it will be, when I take you back."

"What did they tell you? About why I ran?"

Gage watched Freel's eyes. They were the eyes of a man getting ready to bargain his way out of a tight spot. But the terms of the bargain would not be favorable.

"They told me you took something. Something they'd like back."

Freel smiled, seemed to relax. His hands began to creep down again. Gage shook his head and jerked the barrel of his gun up. Freel's smile vanished and his hands shot up again.

"How much are they paying you?"

"I really don't think that's any of your business."

"Well it could be, if you know what I mean."

Gage said nothing.

"How does fifty grand sound?"

Gage exhaled a bored sigh. "It sounds a little far-fetched," Gage said. "Unless you have a suitcase of cash stashed upstairs. Which I already know you don't, by the way."

"I'll get it for you. I just need a couple of days."

Freel tried a nervous smile again. The beads of sweat were shining on his brow. If he was a card player, he wasn't a good one. Gage would have continued toying with him, if time had been on his side, but he wanted to get a move on. He reached into his pocket with his left hand and took out the key. The brass caught the light from the window, casting a golden reflection on the wall behind Freel. His smile evaporated.

"You know what this is," Gage said slowly, "and you know where I got it."

Freel opened his mouth, and then shut it again. The answers to all of his questions were obvious, unfortunately for him. Gage could see in his eyes he had already suspected that something had happened to his partner.

"He called me. When I tried to get ahold of him later, his phone kept ringing out."

"Don't hold your breath on it being answered. Where's the other key? And where's the safe?"

Freel hesitated.

"Don't make me ask twice, Freel."

"The key's up there," he said quickly, pointing toward the stairs.

Gage considered what to do next. Unless he wanted to leave Freel down here alone, they would both have to go upstairs. He gestured with the gun for Freel to take the lead. "Slowly."

He followed him up the stairs and into the second bedroom. When Freel saw the laptop open and the USB device in one of the side ports, he shot a glance back at Gage, but thought better of saying anything.

"Where is it?"

"It's right here," Freel said, moving toward the chest of drawers.

"Stop."

Freel stopped in his tracks, but seemed to be listing toward the chest, as though something within held a magnetic attraction. All of a sudden, Gage was certain that whatever it was, it wasn't a key.

A loud, insistent outburst of noise pierced the silence in the small room. Gage's eyes slipped from Freel's face for a second, looking for the source, his brain taking a second to register it as a cell phone ringing.

Freel flinched and then launched himself across the room toward the chest of drawers. Gage yelled at him to freeze as Freel yanked the top drawer open and pulled out a large wood-handled revolver. He swung his arm around and pointed the gun square at Gage's chest.

33

Sarah bid Diane Marshall farewell, and ten minutes later she was back at the diner on Main Street where they had bought coffees earlier. She pushed open the glass doors and scanned the interior, looking for Blake. The place was either a genuine throwback, or took its retro credentials seriously. It felt to Sarah like an old-time ice cream parlor. Bluesy rock played over the speakers. Sarah didn't recognize the song, but like the rest of the place, it could have been original '60s or could have been last week. The place was busy with teenagers gazing into their phones, which spoiled the ambience a little. After a couple of seconds she located Blake, at the far side of the room in one of the booths. She headed over to him, tapping the folder that contained the pictures Diane had printed against her palm.

Blake was sitting with an untouched bottle of water, his expression inscrutable. His phone lay on the table beside the bottle.

"You know what?" she began. "I may become a ... what was it you called it? Person locator myself. My contact came through, big time: new name, address, even a picture."

Sarah slid into the seat across from him. Her smile faded when she saw the look on Blake's face.

"What is it?"

"I owe you an apology," he said.

"What are you talking about?"

"I already found her."

Once again, she was taken by surprise. She put the folder down on the table, waited for him to continue. Before he could say anything, a wide-eyed waitress materialized with a menu, smiling expectantly. Sarah was mildly surprised that she wasn't on roller skates. She ordered a peanut butter shake and watched her until she had retreated out of earshot before looking back across the table at Blake.

"She works in the library, right across the road." He gestured out of the window. Sarah didn't look away from him. "I wasn't sure she would be there, but ... well, she was."

"What did she say?"

"Aren't you mad that I didn't wait for you? Or call you, even?"

She thought about it for a second. "Mildly irritated, maybe. But no, not mad. Besides, it was worth the trip. I got her address."

Blake smiled. "I don't have that yet."

She narrowed her eyes. "Are you withholding again?"

He shook his head. "Scout's honor."

She sighed. "I get it, you know. You wanted to see her alone first. It's just ... you don't always have to keep the cards so close to your chest. You could stand to loosen up a little, Blake. If that really is your real name." The last part had been a joke, but Blake suddenly looked uncomfortable.

He cleared his throat. "You know, if I had really thought about it, I'd have known it would be better to bring you along. I guess I didn't want to think about it too much."

"Let me guess, it wasn't the happy reunion of your imagination?"

"You could say her reaction was ambivalent."

"Did you tell her why we came looking for her?"

"The edited highlights," Blake replied. "She claims Freel isn't involved in anything shady."

"That she knows of."

"I don't know. She seemed pretty adamant. And from what I remember, she isn't the kind of person who's easily fooled."

"At first, I was adamant that my husband had quit gambling. Several times. Sometimes we believe what we want to believe."

The milkshake arrived, and Blake picked his water up and clinked the bottle against Sarah's glass, taking his first sip.

"Can't argue with that."

"So when do I get to see her?"

"She wants to talk it over with Freel first. She said she'll meet us tonight and bring him along."

Sarah thought it over. "She knows, doesn't she, deep down?"

Blake didn't say anything.

"Okay, so at least we can warn them to be more careful. I mean, if we found them, so could the guy from the other night, right?"

"That's what I'm worried about. I need to talk to Freel, no matter what."

Blake's cell vibrated on the table, the screen signaling an incoming call. He picked it up and glanced at the number, looking up at Sarah as he hit the button to pick up.

"It's her."

34

Dominic Freel lay on his back on the carpet, his lifeless eyes pointing up at the ceiling, the revolver still loosely entangled in the curled fingers of his right hand.

Gage kept the gun trained on Freel's chest as he stepped toward him. Freel had taken three bullets: one in the right shoulder, two around the heart. Gage nudged the revolver out of Freel's unresisting grasp and kicked it across the floor, before dropping to one knee. He put his left hand to Freel's throat, his fingertips searching for a pulse he knew he would never find.

Gage let out a grunt of frustration. This had not been part of the plan. He knew he shouldn't have let Freel lead the way up here, but he had been confident that the man posed no threat to him. That had been correct. There had been no possibility of Freel making it across the room, retrieving the gun and getting a shot off. Gage would have had time to order out for pizza in the time it took him. What he had not anticipated was that Freel would be stupid enough to take such a great risk with such a minuscule chance of success. Gage had waited until the last possible second to stop him. Freel had been no threat to Gage at all, but in the end, he had been a threat to himself.

Freel's mouth was slightly open, as well as his eyes. His features were frozen in an expression of mild surprise.

A three-note chirp broke the silence. The phone again: the source of the interruption that Freel had fatally gambled was enough of a distraction to make his move. Gage patted down Freel's hip pockets, finding a cheap Motorola cell phone in one. He tapped the screen and found Freel had set a PIN lock. It would be a simple matter to break it later on, but for now Gage didn't need to. You could view recent notifications without unlocking it. He swiped his thumb down from the top of the screen and saw one missed call and one text message from the same contact: "Carol."

The wife, he supposed. Gage had forgotten all about her. Perhaps this wouldn't be a complete dead end after all. He could read only the first part of the message, but the preview showed enough:

You home? Coming back, need to t . . .

"*Need to talk,*" was a reasonable bet. He hoped the subject would be helpful to him. He turned Freel's phone on to airplane mode and pocketed it. Dominic Freel would be missing that conversation.

Remembering what he was here for, he grabbed the collar of Freel's shirt and ripped the top three buttons open. Nothing around his neck. He patted the pockets down, worrying that Freel had taken the location of the key—not to mention the lock that it fit—to his grave. Nothing but loose change and the keys for the Toyota. He checked the shoes. No concealed spaces. He rolled the body face down and ran his finger along the inside of Freel's belt. At the small of his back, Gage's fingers contacted something taped to the inside. He pulled it free and grinned as he saw the duplicate of the brass key he had taken from McKinney. Same size, same interlinked Cs logo. Only one difference: a number one instead of a two.

Carol Freel, or whatever her real name was, would be home soon. The town simply wasn't big enough for her to be far away. He considered for a second the best way to welcome the new widow home, and decided it would be important for her to see the consequences of non-cooperation first-hand. He picked up Freel's revolver, emptied it, and put the bullets in his pocket before dropping the gun in the wastebasket. He opened the other drawers to be sure there weren't any other nasty surprises waiting. Satisfied, he walked back out onto the landing and across to the nearest bedroom at the top of the stairs. The office door was wide open, and anyone ascending to the second floor would see Freel's body.

Less than a minute later, he heard the sound of rapid footsteps on the sidewalk outside.

He kept the bedroom door open and flattened his back against the wall, out of sight as he heard a key twist in the lock and the front door open. He felt a frisson of anticipation that he did not altogether welcome. A female voice sounded from the hall downstairs.

"Dom?"

She waited a moment before starting up the stairs.

"Why aren't you answering your phone? We need—"

She stopped mid-sentence, simultaneously with the sound of her footsteps on the stairs stopping. Gage estimated she was on the fourth stair from the top, just into line of sight with the door to the study.

She didn't say anything else, her footsteps quickened as she scaled the last four steps and rushed across the landing. There was no scream, just a sharp intake of breath. He heard a floorboard creak as she knelt down, no doubt checking for a pulse. But she wasn't talking to her husband, wasn't yelling at him to wake up. Perhaps the three holes in his chest had convinced her not to get her hopes up.

Gage stepped out onto the landing as she was getting up and turning back toward the door. She froze as she saw the gun pointed at her, still side on, in the middle of turning. The look in her eyes said she knew the same gun had killed her husband. She didn't try to run. Smart.

"Who are you?"

Her voice was unsteady, but remarkably calm. Her pallor told him she was in shock from the discovery, but she wasn't losing it completely. She wasn't sobbing or fainting or tensing to make an impossible dash down the stairs to the front door. She was keeping it together, because she knew that whatever else was going on, she was in a life or death situation. Gage upgraded her from smart to smart and collected.

Gage didn't reply to her question. He was busy looking her over. She was dressed in jeans and a gray shirt. It didn't look like she was carrying a weapon, but the position she had frozen in meant he could not see her right side or her right hand. He was through taking chances. He didn't want to kill her if he could avoid it.

"Hands where I can see them. Slowly."

She took a breath and slowly straightened so that she was facing him in the doorway to the study. She held both hands out loosely at her sides. They were empty.

"You killed my husband," she said. Her voice was a little louder than it had been, as though the enormity of the fact had only just hit her.

"I'm sorry about that," he said. "He didn't give me much of a choice. Believe me, I'm as upset about it as you are."

"He's dead."

She was kind of laboring the point, now. Perhaps he had been hasty. Perhaps this was just the delayed reaction. If she was about to dissolve into a hysterical mess, she was no good to him. He needed her lucid.

"He is dead," Gage agreed. "All I wanted to do was talk to him, and he drew down on me."

She said nothing, but took a step back. She looked shaky on her feet.

For some reason, Gage thought of another time he had held a gun on someone and tried to speak soothingly to them. Nearly two decades before, he had confronted a strung-out junkie who had taken four people hostage in a liquor store in a small town near Victoria, killing one before Gage and his partner showed up. Even now, years later, he could remember vivid details. The sick, greenish skin tone of the junkie. The dark red blood pooling underneath the dead clerk. The green light from the neon Busch sign in the window glinting off the shards of shattered liquor bottles.

"I love the cheese," he had kept saying over and over. The nonsensical phrase sounding more and more urgent as he struggled to make Gage understand him. In the end, he had put the gun to his own head. Gage had considered just letting him pull the trigger for a second, before adjusting his aim and putting a bullet in the junkie's hand.

He didn't want to have to shoot Freel's wife, too.

"Same rules now," he said. "With you and me. All I want to do is talk."

Her eyes focused. She seemed to take it in. She tilted her head in the direction of the desk and swivel chair, on the opposite side of the room from the body of her husband. "Can I ... can I sit down?"

"Fine, slowly."

She backed over to the chair and sat down, no sudden moves. Gage lowered the gun slightly. Easing a little of the tension off would help, he hoped.

"How did you get into my house?"

Again, her voice was unnaturally loud. It was almost as though she was speaking to ...

Finally, Gage realized what was happening. He raised his gun again and hardened his voice. "Give me your phone."

She hesitated. "I left it in the car."

Gage took a step forward and saw a raise in her right hip pocket. The side he hadn't been able to see when she was turning to leave the room. "Give me the phone." He pointed the gun at her head now.

She looked at him for a second and then reached into her hip pocket. Slowly, she withdrew it. When it was out of her pocket he roughly grabbed it with his free hand and glanced at the display.

As he had guessed—almost too late—there was a call in progress. She must have dialed the number as she was examining the body, then slipped it into her pocket when she saw Gage.

He raised the phone to his ear, not taking his eyes off Freel's wife, who he had now upgraded to tricksy bitch. She said nothing, but her blue eyes burned with defiance.

"Who is this?" he said.

There was a pause. An open line, he could hear traffic noise in the background and an echo. A car in motion. And then a man's voice. Clear and deliberate.

"Somebody who will find you, and make you sorry."

35

We crossed an intersection just after the light had turned red, narrowly missing a white van that was a little too quick off the mark on the other traffic stream. Sarah sucked air through her teeth as she corrected her evasive steer and brought us back into the lane. I barely heard the blare of the van's horn. I was too focused on the voice at the other end of the phone.

"Be very careful who you threaten," the voice said calmly. "I already killed one person today. I may decide to make it two."

"If you—" I began, but whoever was speaking on Carol's phone had already hung up.

I took the phone from my ear, cursing as I looked at the screen. The end-of-call log told me it had been four minutes, twenty-two seconds since my phone had rung in the diner. Four minutes, twenty-two seconds since I had picked it up and heard silence on the other end. I was just about to hang up when I heard a low mumble. A man's voice, some distance from the speaker and muffled, saying something about *hands*, and *slowly*. And then a clearer voice. Carol's voice. Words that sent a chill through me.

"You killed my husband."

How far were we from the house now? How close had four minutes and change gotten us?

Sarah risked taking her eyes off the road and saw that I had taken the phone from my ear. "What happened?"

I had managed to convey to her what was happening while keeping a hand over the receiver and listening. She had known what to do, had headed straight for the car and got in, punching the address Diane Marshall had given her into the GPS as I held the phone to my ear and jumped in the passenger side. We hadn't even discussed that we were heading to Carol's house, it was simply the only place we knew to go. Carol herself had confirmed it a couple of minutes later—"How did you get into my house"—but in doing so had tipped her hand to the man who was threatening her. And I was pretty sure I knew exactly who that man had been.

"Blake!" Sarah prompted, snapping me out of my train of thought.

"Just get us there," I said. "How far?"

Barely an hour before I had been thinking about what a small town this was. At this moment it felt roughly the size of Tokyo.

Sarah glanced at the map on the GPS screen. "Half a mile."

"Look out," I yelled.

Sarah looked up and yanked the wheel hard right, just avoiding a taxi that had pulled out of a side street without looking. The evasion left us diagonal across the road, facing oncoming traffic. Sarah slammed on the brakes, and a dirty green pickup braked inches from hitting us. Another horn sounded as Sarah backed up, straightened, and slammed the car into drive, wheels spinning as she let the clutch in.

She covered the rest of the distance in under a minute, barely reducing speed as she took the final turn onto Sycamore.

"Drop me here, then move up the street." I looked ahead, scanning the street for safe spots. "Park behind that panel van."

Sarah nodded. I had the door open and was out of the car as soon as she slammed to a halt two doors from the address Diane had given her. It was on a quiet street lined with new-looking two-story houses. Sarah floored the gas as soon as I was out and moved herself and the car away from the front of the house.

I kept my gun by my side, ready to bring it up quickly as I surveyed the house. It had been at least three minutes since the call had ended. I was pretty sure that we would find no one in there, no one alive, anyway. The red front door was half-open. I kept my eyes on the windows, looking for movement. I weaved my way toward the door to present a moving target.

More than three minutes from the moment Carol's

clandestine call to me had been discovered. Enough for the man on the other end of the phone call to make his escape. Trenton Gage had found his way to Quarter a lot quicker than I had bargained for.

I held the gun up and nudged the front door the rest of the way open with my foot. The door swung back, revealing a hallway and a staircase. I moved through the doorway and cleared the ground floor in seconds, moving from room to room with increasing urgency.

I climbed the stairs and as my head drew level with the top floor I saw a doorway, and within, the lower half of a man's body, lying on the carpet. I forced myself to go slow, listen for the small giveaway noises of someone lying in wait, but my gut told me there was nobody up here.

Nobody but me and Dominic Freel.

Gage had spoken the truth. He had killed somebody today.

I recognized the face of the dead man from the picture Sarah had emailed me three days before. Whatever Dominic Freel had done in Vegas had finally caught up with him, and caught up with Carol too. I cursed myself for letting her go an hour before.

I surveyed the rest of the room. There were no breakages, no overturned furniture. No evidence of a struggle at all. The intruder had either surprised Freel, or he hadn't had a chance to fight back. I found an unloaded Smith & Wesson revolver in the trash, and wondered if it had belonged to Freel. There was a laptop on the desk, the screen lit up and a notification window on the screen. It showed a progress bar lit up in green and the words "download complete." There was a USB device plugged into the side. I had seen gadgets like it before: Gage must have used it to break the password on the laptop and download the contents. But it looked as though he had forgotten to retrieve the device in all the excitement. Carol's purse was lying by the body. I picked it up and looked through but found nothing but fifty dollars in cash and a set of house keys.

I thought about the evidence in front of me and tried to piece things together. The empty revolver, the laptop, Carol happening on the scene. A sequence of events suggested itself. The intruder had come in here looking for Freel, or information that Freel had. Freel was armed, and Gage had had to kill him. That meant he had been forced to improvise by kidnapping Carol. Who had only been there because she had wanted to talk to Freel following our conversation.

"Blake?"

Sarah's voice drifted up from downstairs. I went back out on the landing and called down to her.

"I thought you were going to stay in the car."

"I didn't hear any shots, so I figured it would be okay."

"Freel's up here, he's dead. You might not want to come up."

Sarah didn't respond right away. I heard her footsteps on the hall carpet and then she rounded the corner and started to come up the stairs. "I've seen dead bodies before."

I stepped out of her way. When she came out of the bedroom again, she had a sad look on her face.

"Are you okay?"

She seemed to consider the question. "I didn't know him well. I didn't know him at all, really." She turned to me. "Do you think it was him?"

We both knew who she was talking about.

"I think so."

"And he has Carol, now."

I nodded. Finding her gone was only the second-worst outcome, but still . . .

"Why do you think he took her?"

"Only one reason it could be. He didn't get what he wanted from Freel."

I thought back to the phone call. It had been hard to hear exactly what Gage was saying, presumably because the phone was concealed on Carol's person, or underneath something, but I thought he had said something about wanting to talk. He had been sent after Freel, but I had a hunch that killing him had not been part of the plan. I crossed to the window and looked out at the nondescript suburban street. I thought about what had brought them here, what they were running from, and I knew where we had to go next.

36

Gage relaxed a little when he had put a few streets between the house and himself. He slowed down, knowing that this would not be a good time to be stopped by a traffic cop. Traffic cops like to check the trunk when they're doing a routine stop.

He followed the signs leading to the highway and picked up speed again when he hit the open road. After ten miles, he saw a sign indicating an exit onto a minor road ahead. He took it. The ground dropped away into a shallow valley, and when he was fully out of sight of the main road, Gage pulled the car to a stop on the dirt shoulder. He got out, walked up the dirt verge on the side of the road and took a look around. The highway stretched off to the north, and was free of traffic. The roughly surfaced road he was on wound its way to the distant hills on the horizon, the heat shimmer distorting the view. The sky was a hazy blue, the air silent and still. It was hot, hotter than Vegas had been. The only other man-made thing he could see was a line of telegraph poles crossing the road a mile away.

He picked his way back down and walked around to the trunk. He took his gun out before putting the key in the lock and turning it. The trunk lid popped up and Freel's wife looked up at him, holding a forearm over her eyes to shield them from the glare of the sun.

"Sorry about the bumps," Gage said. "Can't have been comfortable."

She didn't say anything.

"Come on out."

She made no move, so Gage stepped back and jerked his head to hurry her along. He kept the gun on her as she climbed out. She leaned back against the bumper, brushing a lock of red hair out of her face. Now that he had the opportunity to have a good look at close quarters, he could see it was a dye job. Done well, natural-looking, but fake as her swooning victim routine earlier on. He wondered what her real color was. The red suited her, certainly. She glanced around, taking in their surroundings quickly, not wanting to take her eye off the gun

He sighed. "My name's Gage. How about you and me start over?"

She said nothing, just stared back at him.

"Tricky move with the phone, by the way. Who was your friend?"

"Not a friend," she said. "Just somebody I used to know."

Gage let that one go for now.

"Anyway, before we were so rudely interrupted, I was explaining that I wanted to ask you a few questions."

"I told you, I can't help you."

Gage's tone hardened. "That would be a shame. For both of us."

In truth, he would take no pleasure in harming this woman. She had caused him some inconvenience, but he couldn't really blame her for that. If she couldn't help him, though, or wouldn't, then she would become one more problem that would have to be dealt with.

She stared back at him, coolly appraising his words. He knew she was smart enough to understand that this was no idle threat. The dead man in her house was evidence of that.

"Look, I know my husband was involved in some things he didn't tell me about."

Progress. She had stopped pretending this was a case of mistaken identity, at least. She had known, deep down, even if she didn't know the details. The wives always did.

"It was easier for you not to ask the questions, right? You didn't want to know too much about where the money was coming from. Nice house, new kitchen, new car every three years ... you're happy. Am I right?"

A flash of irritation crossed her face. The reaction gave Gage some satisfaction. He thought what he was suggesting was largely true, but he had deliberately couched it in those terms to get under her skin. To make her rail against being cast as the poor, dumb little kept wife. He hoped it would encourage her to be more forthcoming, to prove that she was more than a blind eye, a closed mouth and a nice kitchen. Sometimes you had to let the subject trap herself.

"Why are you ..." she stopped and realized she was using the wrong tense. "Why were you looking for my husband?"

"This isn't a two-way conversation, Mrs. Freel."

She grimaced.

"You don't like being called that? You're right. First

names are friendlier." He searched his memory for the name he had seen on Freel's phone. "Carol? It is Carol, isn't it."

She ignored the question and asked her own a second time. Ballsy.

"Why were you looking for him? I just want to know. Maybe it will help me to think of something."

Gage narrowed his eyes. He was wary of anything that came out of this woman's mouth. Likely this was just a time-wasting exercise. But so what if it was? It couldn't benefit her. He had frisked her before throwing her into the trunk. She had no other phones or devices. Nothing that could help her friend, whoever he was, track her down.

"I think you know. Or maybe you think it's normal to disappear from your house overnight, the way you did back in Vegas."

"Dom said it would be best."

"'Dom said it would be best,'" Gage repeated, making sure to inject just the right note of condescension.

She didn't rise to the bait. "He was concerned about some business associates. That they might be turning nasty."

"So you just went along with it."

She shrugged. "We move around a lot. What's one more move?"

Gage watched her with interest. Either she was astonishingly naive, or just ruthlessly pragmatic. "Dom was right," he said after a minute. "And that's why I'm here. His business associates brought me in. If your husband hadn't tried to take me on, I wouldn't have had to bother you at all. You would have come home to an empty house, and Freel could have gotten back in touch with you when it was over."

She looked down, avoiding his gaze. "Did he say anything? Before he ..."

"He didn't get the chance."

He reached into his pocket and took the matching brass keys out, holding them in his palm so she could see them. One and two. If she recognized the keys, or understood what they were, she gave nothing away.

"What are those for?"

"They're for a dual-lock safe," Gage said. "I took one from your husband, one from a man named McKinney. The only thing I don't have is the safe. Where is it?"

"I don't know."

Gage replaced the keys in his pocket and brought his gun back up to point at her. He didn't say anything, just turned his head from side to side. If she really didn't know anything, it would be better to deal with her here and now. There was nobody around. The ridge provided cover. In the distance, they could hear the noise of a big rig passing on the highway. It might be hours or days before somebody else came down this quiet little road.

"Okay, maybe I have something that could help," Carol said. Her voice wavered slightly, as though she was finally realizing he wasn't bluffing.

Gage waited, still holding the gun on her.

"We took a road trip down here before we left Summerlin for good," she said. "Dom said he wanted to get out of town for a few days. We stayed in Phoenix the first night. Dom met a friend ... Logan, I think his name was. He suggested visiting this old town in the middle of nowhere. The three of us headed out there the next day."

"What was the name of the town?"

She shook her head. "I don't remember the name."

"Try."

"It wasn't a real town."

Gage sighed. "A make-believe town, huh? This doesn't sound all that helpful."

"Wait, no. I didn't mean it wasn't real. It was abandoned. A ghost town, one of those old mining places."

"And, presumably, you can find your way back there."

She hesitated, looked at the trunk. She didn't want to get back in. Reluctantly, she nodded.

"We had packed a picnic. We ate and then we explored the place a little. Dom and his friend went back to the car at one point. There was an old building I wanted to sketch. It's kind of a hobby, I guess. I like to—"

"Fascinating, get to the point."

"I remember there was a case in the trunk when we left Vegas. Hard plastic, like a briefcase, but smaller. I remember because I had never seen it before. Logan got into his car and went back to Phoenix, and we went on ahead. When we got to our hotel, the case was gone."

Gage said nothing, waited for her to continue.

"I think, maybe, whatever you're looking for could be there."

"That's what it sounds like, from your story."

"You don't believe me?"

"I'd have to be an idiot not to be suspicious."

"If I take you there, show you where we went, will you let me go?"

Gage kept his eyes on her, not lowering the gun. He wondered how long he had to find the safe. He would have to call Walter in a few hours. He and his friends would not be pleased when they discovered that Freel was dead, particularly after they had told him to stand down. But perhaps that didn't matter anymore.

He gestured at the car with his free hand. "Get in."

She glanced briefly at the trunk, not wanting to take her eyes off his gun.

"How will I . . .?"

He shook his head impatiently. "You're driving."

She went around to the driver's side of the Chrysler and got in. Gage reached around to the back of his belt and unclipped his handcuffs. He snapped one cuff over the steering wheel, and the other over Carol's left hand. He walked around the car and got in the passenger side, keeping his gun on her in his right hand. In his left, he dangled the car key. She reached for it and he pulled it just out of her grasp.

"You're going to turn and drive back up to the road, and then you're going to take a left and head north. You're going to keep it to sixty, max. You're going to ask my permission before you deviate in any way from the road. You're not going to try anything stupid. Your husband was stupid. What do you weigh?"

She looked confused. "What?"

"I'm guessing about a hundred and twenty, if that," he guessed. "So don't get any ideas. I'm not going to have any trouble moving your body out of the way and taking over the wheel, if I have to. If you swerve off the road, I'll shoot you and grab the wheel. If you try to signal another driver, I'll shoot you and grab the wheel. If you ..."

"Okay, I get it."

"Do you?"

Carol sighed and stared ahead out of the dusty windshield. "Look, I'm not going to try anything stupid. I want this over as much as you do. If I take you to this place, you let me go, all right?"

Gage didn't say anything for a minute. Carol didn't break eye contact.

"All right?" she repeated.

He dropped the key into her palm.

"Drive," Gage said.

37

"Where is he taking her?"

Blake had his mouth open to answer Sarah's question when they heard a loud banging on the door downstairs. Sarah's eyes met Blake's. Neither of them moved. A few seconds later, the knock on the door was repeated.

"Hello? Who's in there?" A woman's voice. Insistent, suspicious.

The knocking continued. Blake edged over to the window and looked down onto the front. The porch roof covered the door, so it was impossible for him to see who was there.

"I'll go," Sarah said. "It doesn't sound like she's going to give up."

She walked out of the room and down the stairs. The door was solid wood, with a peephole in the center. She took a look through the fisheye lens and saw a distorted image of a thin woman in her fifties with gray-blonde hair and a look of impatience on her face.

Sarah tried to banish the image of Freel's body from her mind and composed herself before opening the door.

"Hi, can I help you?"

"Who are you?"

Sarah affected a look of confusion. "I'm Jane. I'm Carol's sister?" She held her hand out. The woman ignored it.

"I live across the road. I saw a woman leaving with a man in a hurry. Looked like he was manhandling her. They didn't even stop to shut the door. And then I saw you and your friend arriving in a hurry." She pursed her lips, waiting for an explanation.

"Oh, right," Sarah said. "Nothing's wrong if that's what

you were worried about, she just stepped out to the store."

The suspicion stayed on her face. Sarah decided on a change of tack.

"Are you a friend of Carol's, Miss ...?"

"Mrs. Phillips. I'm on the neighborhood watch."

Sarah put on her most dazzling smile. "That's wonderful you thought to come over and check everything was okay. I'm so glad Carol has such considerate neighbors."

Mrs. Phillips softened a little. "Well, just as long as everything's all right."

"Everything's fine. I'll ask Carol to stop by your house later to thank you."

Sarah closed the door and went upstairs again. Blake was examining the laptop.

"Nicely done," he said without looking back at her.

"I just hope she doesn't have a good memory for faces. Unless you're planning on calling this in."

"Too late for it to do any good."

Sarah gave Freel's body a wide berth, but she couldn't help glancing down at him.

"Should we put something over his face?"

"No," Blake said quickly. "And don't touch anything."

"Right, of course," she said, remembering that this was a homicide scene, and any traces they left would have to be explained. She tried to think if she had touched anything. She was pretty sure only the door handle and the banister, which she would wipe down on the way out. Blake was examining the laptop on the desk, which was switched on. He appeared to be breaking his own rule, and then Sarah realized he wasn't planning on leaving the laptop behind.

"If Gage was here to kill Freel, why take Carol?"

"I don't think he did want to kill Freel," Blake said.

"What's on the laptop?"

"It looks like he used a USB hacker to break into it. The bonus for us is we're in without a password."

"Worth a look, but we better get out of here. I don't want to risk Mrs. Phillips coming back."

Sarah crossed over to the window, keeping Freel's body as far from her as possible. She was looking out at a world that was carrying on as though a man hadn't just died. She wrapped her arms around herself as if she were cold, although it was over eighty degrees.

"They could be anywhere," she said. "We don't know which way they went; we don't even know what kind of car he was driving."

"Maybe we don't need to know," Blake said. "The way I see it, we only have one shot—assume they're headed back to Corinth."

38

At first, Gage kept the gun just below chest level. Where it could not be seen from outside of the car, but where Carol couldn't help but be aware of it pointing at her stomach. She turned the car in the road and headed back toward the highway. Gage was pleased to note that she was following his advice to the letter. No sudden moves, no erratic driving. Not too fast, not too slow. Considering her situation, she was a model of calm. She could be taking her driving test.

He remembered that he had forgotten to retrieve the USB device he had used to crack Freel's laptop, and cursed softly under his breath. If Carol heard him, she didn't acknowledge it. Too late to worry about it now. A few miles out,

Gage tensed as they saw flashing red lights approaching from the road ahead. He heard Carol take a sharp breath and he moved the gun an inch closer.

"Easy now," he said, eyes fixed on the police car approaching in the opposite lane.

Carol swallowed and kept both hands on the wheel. The blue and white vehicle flew past them, the Doppler effect distorting the siren as it passed.

Carol didn't say anything, but she glanced down at the gun. Gage smiled and relaxed a little. He rested it on his lap, ready to raise it again if he needed.

"Very good."

Almost an hour passed without either of them exchanging a word. Gage was grateful for the silence. It gave him time to think. If Carol was on the level about the ghost town and the case, this trip might be more than worthwhile. Whatever McKinney and Freel had been hiding had to be there. Gage didn't know exactly what to expect, but he knew it had been valuable enough to have cost them both their lives. Drugs or cash, most likely, and hopefully the latter. If this worked out, perhaps he would even turn Carol loose as a reward.

Even if the trip turned out to be a bust—if they couldn't find the safe opened by the dual keys, or if what it contained was worthless, or if it never existed in the first place—then he would be no worse off than he had been after he had pulled the trigger on Freel.

If that happened, he would check in with the men in Vegas, explain the situation, and offer them Carol instead. Maybe he would still do okay out of the deal, salvage the rest of his fee at least. After all, even if she knew nothing, they didn't know that.

He watched her as she drove. The highway was wide and

straight, which meant her eyes had very rarely strayed from looking ahead. There were fine beads of perspiration on her brow and on the back of her neck; from the heat, he guessed, not from nerves. He wondered about the men in Vegas. Would they torture her for information? He found himself hoping not. Understandably, the woman had been hostile toward him ever since they met, and was only grudgingly cooperating with him now. But despite himself, he found himself warming to her. He admired the way she had been able to process the shock of Freel's death and function well enough to prolong her own survival.

For some reason, that made him think of the voice on the other end of Carol's phone call. Not a friend, just "somebody she used to know." He wondered if this someone had been close to the house. If so, he would have arrived on the scene and found Freel's body by now, and the police would likely have been called. It would take time to identify the body and his identity might not be made public right away. He had no idea what connections the men in Vegas had, but it was likely there was some time to play with. The Vegas trio were in the dark at the moment, and Gage might need to exploit that uncertainty.

He glanced back at Carol. Her eyes were focused on the road, her expression calm.

"You don't seem very upset," he said.

She turned her head to look at him, then looked back at the road.

"We have to make conversation too?" she said coldly.

Gage smiled. He really hoped he wouldn't have to turn her over to the men in Vegas.

"I mean, I've never been married," he said. "But I've met a few widows. You seem to be taking it pretty well, is all I'm saying."

"If it disappoints you, we can pull over and I'll break down into a sobbing mess," Carol said. She glanced at him and then back at the road. "You get off on that kind of thing, huh?"

"Not in the slightest," he said. "Your composure is appreciated. This is much less hassle for me. Killing your husband was nothing personal, like I said."

"You can stop apologizing."

"It wasn't an apology," he said, tightening the grip on the gun. A little smart mouth was endearing, but he didn't want her forgetting who was in charge.

She glanced down at the gun and straightened in her seat.

"So when were you going to leave him?" Gage asked.

"Who says I was?"

"You can't have liked him much. A woman comes home and finds three bullets in her husband, doesn't shed a single tear? You either hated his guts or you are the coldest goddamn broad I ever met."

She looked across at him. "Maybe it's both."

"Maybe it's both," he repeated.

39

Central Arizona had a lot to recommend it, as far as Gage was concerned: wide open spaces, no pollution, very few people. Blanket cell phone coverage was not, however, one of its primary attractions. Gage's phone had lost its weak signal a few miles after leaving Quarter, and had picked up a signal only sporadically since. He doubted whether the single bar that occasionally appeared would be enough to connect a call, anyway. The sky was darkening as they saw a sign for gas, and a couple of minutes later, Gage told Carol to pull off the highway into the small filling station.

There were four pumps under a canopy and a small convenience store. Gage was pleased to see a payphone attached to the wall outside the store. He told Carol to park up next to the pumps.

"I need to make a call," he said. "Keep both hands on the wheel."

Carol said nothing, but moved both hands up so they were on top of the steering wheel.

He turned in his seat and surveyed the forecourt. No other cars. An attendant sitting by the register inside reading a magazine.

He looked out at the road. They had passed other cars every few minutes or so, but right now it was deserted.

Gage leaned over to take the keys from the ignition, got out and crossed to the payphone.

He took his cell out and thumbed through it to get the number, before dialing it in to the payphone.

Two rings and a pickup. A cautious, suspicious voice that Gage recognized as belonging to David, the younger, more irritable member of the trio who had met him in the bar. "Hello?"

"This is Gage."

A pause.

"We've been waiting to hear from you."

There was a hint of irritation in the voice, but nothing more than that. So they didn't know Freel was dead. If anything had been reported on the news yet, they hadn't put two and two together. Why would they? Quarter was a long way from Vegas, and Freel would likely have been using another assumed name.

"I've been out of range," he said. "This is the first opportunity I've had to call you. Put Walter on."

"Walter isn't here right now," David responded sharply. "Talk to me. He said there was some sort of confusion. He told you we didn't need you anymore."

"Tell Walter there was no confusion. I've thought about it and I'm willing to accept. I'll call him back later tonight to arrange the balance of my payment."

"Where are you?"

"I'll tell you tonight."

"Fine. We'll call you at ten."

"Don't bother. I'm out of range, remember? I'll call you. Eleven o'clock." Ten would have been fine, but Gage wanted to make a point.

"Where are you?" he asked again.

"Speak soon," Gage said, and hung up.

David would be wondering why the hell he had bothered checking in at all. But the call had given Gage the information he needed. He still had time to see if Carol's story about the ghost town tied up with the twin safe keys.

Gage had kept his eyes on Carol while he had been talking. She hadn't moved her hands. She had stared back at him at first before looking away, in the direction of the road.

He pointed to the store to indicate he was going inside, then pointed at his eyes.

He opened the door and stepped inside. The layout of the store and the windows meant he would be able to keep Carol in his line of sight for the whole time until he had to face the attendant. If Carol tried to signal the attendant, it would be obvious. She would be signing his death warrant. He didn't think he needed to tell her that. He bought a couple of bottles of water and some snacks and paid for a tank of gas. He glanced back at Carol, who was staring at the road now.

The attendant, a short, bespectacled kid of no more than twenty, processed the transaction without giving Gage a second glance and looked back down at whatever he was reading. It was an oversized book, lots of text. Something academic. A college boy minding his own business and biding his time until he could get out of his shitty nowhere job and whichever shitty nowhere town from which he commuted to it. Good for him.

Gage pocketed the change and was pushing open the door when he heard the sound of an approaching vehicle. He turned his head in the direction of the road and saw the blue and white Arizona Highway Patrol car pull off the road, angling toward the pump adjacent to his own car. His eyes flashed to Carol, who was looking back at him. Her expression gave nothing away, as usual. He hesitated for a second and walked over to his car, passing in front of the police car as it pulled into the space. There were two officers inside: a black cop driving and a white cop in the passenger seat, who examined him from behind mirrored sunglasses. Gage reached for the pump and started filling up, angling his body so that it blocked the view of Carol with her left hand cuffed to the wheel.

The cop in the passenger seat got out and fixed his hat on his head. He was short, maybe five-seven, but very wide, with a thick mustache that was beginning to go gray at the edges. He looked at Gage again as he passed by in the direction of the store. Gage held his gaze, offering a friendly smile.

"Evening."

The cop gave an almost imperceptible nod, glanced at the car and continued on his way. Gage looked back at the police car and saw the driver watching him, before looking away. Gage glanced at the gallons clocking up on the meter.

He watched the windows of the store out of the corner of his eye. The cop had selected a couple of bottles of soda and was headed for the register. He looked down at Carol. Her blue eyes looked back at him, blankly. They were impossible to read. The horn was less than two inches below the thumb of her right hand.

"Hands down," he said. Under his breath, but loud enough for her to hear through the open window.

She seemed to consider it for a moment. She did that a lot, he had noticed: it was as though every time he gave her an order, she had to decide whether to obey. She dropped her right hand from the wheel and lowered her left, but the handcuff caught on the spoke of the wheel, preventing her from dropping the cuffed hand below view.

The cop in the store was paying. The one behind the wheel was leaning an arm on the window sill, staring out at the road.

Gage switched hands so that he was holding the pump with his left hand, leaving his right free. The pump clicked off as the tank filled. Out of the corner of his eye he saw Carol flinch at the abrupt silence.

The cop in the store was coming back now. His angle of approach said he was headed for Gage's car, rather than his own.

Gage moved smoothly, twisting the cap back on the gas tank with his left hand, his muscles tensing for the moment when the cop spotted Carol's handcuffs. He hadn't seen them yet, or if he had, he was playing it cool. The soda bottles were in his left hand; the necks dangling between three beefy fingers. His right hand hovered by his holster. He was closing the distance, looking at Gage. Fifteen feet, ten now. Gage turned around and fixed a "can I help you?" smile on his face. The cop's eyes stayed on him, which was good, but he knew it was fleeting. In the next couple of seconds, he would take a closer look at the car and the driver. He wouldn't be able to help it: human nature, to say nothing of years of training and experience. The cop's mouth was opening to address him when they both heard it.

Another engine. Louder this time, no intention of pulling into the gas station. Gage kept his eyes on the cop as the other man's attention shot straight to the source of the noise. A cherry-red Mazda MX-5 flashed by, headed north. Gage guessed the driver was doing better than ninety.

The next sound was immediate: the patrol car's engine growling to life, followed by the howl of the siren starting up. The cop with the mirrored shades ran to the passenger side as the patrol car maneuvered around the forecourt. The driver paused long enough for his partner to yank the door open and get in. The cop car peeled out of the station and was gone, leaving the sound of ascending gears and the siren fading gradually in the distance.

Gage stood there until the sounds had died away to nothing. The attendant had come outside to see what the commotion was about. He stared down the road and then looked at Gage, giving him a "how about that?" look. Gage ignored him and got back into the car, handing Carol the keys.

"That was lucky," he said, forgetting for a second that they were not co-conspirators.

"I suppose that depends on your point of view," Carol said mildly as she put the keys back in and started the engine.

Gage said nothing, just watched her as she pulled onto the road. A little rebelliousness was a likeable quality, he mused, but sometimes a person can push things a little too far.

40

In contrast to our easy conversations on the way down, there was a tense silence for most of the return trip north toward Corinth. Both of us understood we were on the back foot. We had had the chance to keep Carol safe and had let it slip through our fingers. Or to be more accurate, I had. I had known she was in danger ever since talking to Sarah that first night. Everything that had happened since—Gage breaking into Sarah's house, the revelation that the police were looking for Freel in connection with a high stakes robbery—had only emphasized that danger. I had been stupid. I had screwed up the chance to keep Carol safe for a second time. I just had to pray I would get one last chance.

Every car we passed on the road, we glanced at the faces inside. I knew Sarah would be a lot more use than me in identifying Trenton Gage, given that she had seen him up close, but she didn't see anyone who fit the bill. It wasn't the kind of face you forget, she assured me.

Corinth was the only lead we had, so it had been a simple decision to head back there. Even so, part of me worried that it was possible we were going in the wrong direction, putting more miles between us and Carol.

We had brought Freel's laptop with us, and Sarah had spent some time going through the files on the hard drive. There hadn't been a whole lot there, certainly nothing that told us anything new about why someone would want to find or kill Freel. The laptop was either very new, or had been professionally wiped recently. Between the two of us, Sarah and I knew all the places to look for hidden files on a computer, and none of them yielded any results. The browser history might be worth looking at, and any emails we could access of course, but we would need to wait until we could connect to the internet to check that.

There was still so much we didn't know. Whatever the explanation was for the actions of Freel and the men pursuing him, I knew it had something to do with the Ellison heist. Did he know where the rest of the take was? That seemed like a strong possibility. Or perhaps he was a witness to something he shouldn't have seen. The way I was feeling, I would have gladly killed Freel myself if Gage hadn't beaten me to it. Somehow he was involved in the Ellison job. It didn't matter whether he was the master planner or a hired hand: because of him, Carol's life was in danger.

With Freel dead, Carol was left alone as the only potential lead. She had claimed not to know about Freel's activities—was that the whole truth? Maybe she would know enough about her husband's activities to be useful to her captor. I found myself hoping so, remembering the body on the floor of the bedroom. From what little I knew of him, Trenton Gage did not strike me as a man who cared to leave loose ends.

That was one of the reasons why I had suggested Sarah stay in Iron City, while I approached Corinth myself. I had half-expected her to argue the point, to demand to come, but she understood what we would be walking into, and that she would be a distraction at best, a liability at worst.

The sun was kissing the western horizon when we reached Iron City. Sarah had called ahead and booked two rooms in the same motel we had stayed in the night before. I hoped I would be around to use mine.

Sarah got out and shivered in the cool air. She pulled her leather jacket on and regarded me with the nervous expression of a student about to go into a tough exam.

"You'll be careful?" she asked. It sounded like she was trying to reassure herself, rather than warn me.

In answer, I reached under my jacket, took my gun out and placed it on the passenger seat.

"I'll call you after I ..." After what? I didn't know what was going to happen. I didn't want to think about it too much. "After," I finished.

"I'll see you soon, Blake," she said and swung the door shut. She turned and walked for the motel entrance without looking back. I pulled out of the lot and onto the road.

Less than ten minutes later I took the turn onto the badly surfaced road indicated by the worn sign. Only a few more miles to Corinth. I put my foot down, gripped the wheel, and kept my eyes on the horizon.

41

"This is it?"

Gage's question was rhetorical, and Carol's silence indicated she knew it. He had checked the map from the gas station after Carol had given him enough information for them to identify the town. Corinth was the only destination on this road. He knew the road terminated on the eastern edge of town, leaving nothing but desert.

The dark husks of the buildings loomed in the headlights. There had been no streetlights, no lit windows to home in on, so they found themselves on top of the town almost before they knew it.

"Dom was a sucker for places like this," Carol said. For the first time since he had met her, she sounded unguarded.

A note of sadness had crept into her voice. A second later she remembered why they were here and turned her face away. When she spoke again her voice was back to normal.

"There are towns like this all over the state," she said. "Boomtowns. They appeared out of nowhere when a mine was sunk, blew up like crazy over a few decades, and now they're left here to rot."

Gage reached into his pockets and produced the twin keys, showing them to Carol in the palm of his hand. She regarded them for the second time, showing no sign that they meant anything to her. She looked up from the keys and met his gaze, waiting for him to say something. Had this all been a waste of time? A wild goose chase?

"These unlock a safe. It's here, isn't it?" The sudden impatience in his own voice surprised him. "Where?"

Carol glanced from side to side, examining the patch of street lit by their headlights, and shook her head. "I don't know."

"Bullshit. You know, all right."

"It was daylight when we were here, it looks different. Maybe we can find it."

Gage held her gaze for a long moment. She stared back, unblinking. Gage reached into his pocket and withdrew the key for the handcuffs. He leaned over and hesitated for a second.

"If you try to run ..."

"You'll shoot me. I'm very clear about that, you don't have to keep saying it. Besides ..." she looked from side to side at the empty town and the black desert night beyond. "Where would I run?"

A good point. Gage relented and put the key in the cuffs. He unlocked them and Carol sighed, letting her left hand drop into her lap and massaging her wrist with her other hand.

"Get out, we don't have all night." Gage heard the under-current of anger in his voice and knew it was displacement. He wasn't angry at her; he was angry because he would have to kill her soon.

They got out of the Chrysler and Carol stood by the driver's door as Gage circled around and opened the trunk. He took out a powerful flashlight and clicked it on, bathing the immediate surroundings in a white light. Immediately, he saw fresh tire tracks, underneath the wheels of their own vehicle. Not a big car; probably a sedan. Somebody else had been here recently.

He played the beam over the nearest buildings, and then farther down the main street, before looking at Carol expect-antly.

"We just looked around for a while," she said, then pointed at a large building fifty yards away. It was bigger than the other structures. "We went inside that one, I think. There's no door."

Gage directed the beam on the ground ahead of them, creating a path of light, and gestured for Carol to take the lead.

As they approached the building, Gage could see it must have been the hub of the community: a town hall. As Carol had said, there was no door. The space in the wall was big enough for two entrance doors, but all that remained was the hinges on either side.

Gage stopped. Carol took three steps before she realized he wasn't following and turned around.

"What's in there?"

"Nothing much."

Gage handed her the flashlight. She hesitated, then took it. He raised his gun and pointed it at the doorway, indicat-ing that she should lead the way.

"No surprises in there, are there?"

She shook her head. Nothing to hide. But Gage remembered the trick with the phone, and the look on her face when the police car rolled into the gas station. He kept a couple of paces behind her as she walked into the darkness.

Carol was standing in the middle of an open space. She played the beam of the flashlight around, catching the remains of the old building in the light. A stage, some broken chairs lying around.

"We had a picnic in here," she said. "Dom and his friend went to look around. I went outside to sketch the building, and when I came back, they were coming down from up there."

She moved the beam of the flashlight upwards to take in a metal spiral staircase leading to a platform halfway up the wall. There was a door at the far end of the platform.

Gage said nothing, regarding the platform and the closed door. It seemed like more details were coming back to Carol, just as her recollection of the town's location had as they got closer. She hadn't said any of this back in Quarter. Which meant something was up there, all right.

Carol took a step toward the spiral staircase. "If you want, I could go up there and check ..."

"Not so fast."

Gage closed the distance between them and took the flashlight from her. He held it loosely in his left hand while keeping the gun on her. "We'll both go. You can lead the way."

Carol turned and walked unhurriedly to the foot of the staircase. Gage followed, pausing to shine the flashlight around again. He was uneasy about this. They were in the middle of nowhere, he had a gun, she was unarmed. So why did it feel like he wasn't fully in control of the situation?

Carol took the first three stairs, and then Gage noticed she stepped over the fourth. He paused as she continued to climb and then stepped onto the third step. Briefly, he moved the beam of the flashlight down to see that the join between the fourth step and the central column was almost rusted through. Keeping all his weight on his left foot, he pushed his right foot down firmly on the fourth step. It buckled and sagged downward with a creak.

At once, he heard Carol's footsteps quicken above him. He looked up as he hopped up to the fifth step to see Carol racing to the top of the spiral and stepping onto the platform. He closed the distance quickly, gaining the platform just as Carol reached the door.

He took careful aim and put a bullet in the wall a couple of inches from where her hand was reaching for the handle. She cried out and flinched back from the door. Gage closed the distance between them and grabbed her roughly by the wrist.

She started to protest. "I was just trying to—"

"Enough bullshit."

She shut up and stared back at him. It wasn't just defiance he saw in her eyes now. It wasn't fear, either. She was pissed off; as though he was inconveniencing her, not just threatening her life.

Gage jerked his head back at the staircase. "You knew that was rusted through. That means you've been up here before."

She said nothing.

Gage pushed her back against the guard rail of the platform, hard. Her eyes widened in surprise and for an instant, he wondered if the rail might be rusted through too. But she slammed against it and it held her weight.

There was an old rusted padlock on the door. Gage

examined it, took a step back and trained the Ruger on it. He watched Carol as he pulled the trigger. She flinched, and he heard the remains of the padlock smash to the floor. He pushed the door open and it creaked open. Gage grabbed Carol's arm again and yanked her around, pushing her toward the door while jamming the gun into the small of her back. A voice at the back of his head told him to squeeze the trigger and be done with it. He could search the place himself. It was starting to feel like killing Carol would be safer.

He calmed the urge. He was in control, no one else.

Carol stood in the doorway. It was pitch-black inside, not even lit by moonlight through a window. He directed the flashlight beam past her and it lit up what looked like an office. A heavy wooden desk, some shelves, a pile of cardboard boxes. A doorway on the far wall, bricked up. If he had the correct sense of the building's dimensions, this was an exterior wall, so it had probably been a fire exit.

Gage nudged Carol to step inside with the barrel of the gun and then swung the beam around to see if he had missed anything. On the right-hand side of the room, the wall was damaged. There was a gaping hole in the brickwork. Peering through, he could dimly make out that the void behind dropped all the way down to ground level. Perhaps this had been Carol's plan, to escape that way. A few feet to the right of the hole there was a wall safe, the door slightly open. The plaster around it had been chipped away and some bricks had been removed. It looked as though the owners had tried to rip it out when they abandoned the building, or some optimistic looter had tried to take it at some point over the past few decades. Either way, whoever had made the attempt had given up.

But this wasn't the safe he was looking for. This one had

a combination lock, no keyholes. It had been here decades before the safe the shiny new keys in his pocket fit would have been constructed. Aside from the heavy desk and the shelves and the safe, the room was empty.

Gage looked at Carol.

"Open it."

She walked over and gripped the edge of the safe door with both hands, pulling toward herself. It resisted for a second, and then creaked the rest of the way open. Gage stepped forward and directed the flashlight beam inside.

It was empty.

"Maybe they hid the case somewhere else," Carol said quickly.

"There never was any case, was there?"

Carol looked at him, then at the gun.

Gage raised the gun again. "Not that it matters, but I'm sorry about this."

His finger was already tightening on the trigger when she spoke.

"Stop."

She didn't shout the word. It wasn't a plea. Just a calm instruction. Gage relaxed his finger just for a second, feeling the trigger slide back into place.

Carol raised her hands and took a step back, toward the bricked-up doorway.

Gage didn't move. "Show me. Slowly."

Carol reached a hand out slowly and touched her fingertips to the bricks. Gage stepped forward and directed the beam of the flashlight on the doorway. Up close, he could see that something looked out of place. This was recent work. Old bricks, new mortar. An effort had been made to dirty up the mortar between the bricks, but it was obvious when you looked close.

Carol looked at the pile of boxes next to the desk, saying nothing. Gage stepped back and lifted a couple of the boxes. On the floor underneath them was a sledgehammer, also new.

"I'll let you do the honors," Carol said.

Gage hesitated, then handed her the flashlight.

"You didn't come up here, huh? I have to admit you were convincing."

He holstered his gun and picked up the sledgehammer. He looked from the head of the hammer to Carol, and decided he didn't need to say anything. She stepped back from the wall and gave him room. Gage gripped the shaft with both hands, weighed it in his hands and swung. The bricks at the impact point smashed and gave way easily. Although the work was new, the bricks themselves weren't. They were as old as the building. It only took him four swings to demolish the makeshift wall.

Gage wiped sweat from his brow and tossed the sledge-hammer back in the corner. He took the flashlight from Carol and shone it through the newly opened doorway. There was a small chamber that led to a fire door with a pushbar. On the floor, coated with dust and brick fragments, was a small, new-looking black safe with two keyholes.

He took the keys from his pocket and handed them to her. "Open it."

For once, she didn't hesitate, and even before he saw the contents of the safe, he understood that it was because there were no calculations left for her to make, no cards left to play.

She climbed over the remaining bricks at the bottom of the doorway and crouched down at the safe. She fit each key into its respective lock. She turned the one on the right first, and then the one on the left. A catch popped and the door swung smoothly open on its hinges.

Gage stepped forward and directed the beam inside. There was a canvas backpack inside. Carol pulled it out and unzipped it. She took out a small black case, just as she had described. It was a few inches thick, height and width about the size of a magazine.

She flicked back two catches and opened it on its hinges and there it was: shining and sparkling and refracting the light from the flashlight into a thousand tiny reflections on the walls. The biggest pile of diamonds Gage had ever seen.

42

A couple of minutes before I reached the edge of Corinth, I cut the headlights. There was still a little light in the sky, so I could see well enough to make it the rest of the way. I slowed right down as I made it to the edge of town. If Carol *had* brought Gage here, I had a pretty good idea of where they would be going. I thought whatever this was about was behind that locked door in the town hall.

A second later, I came in view of the bend in the main street. There was a car parked right outside the old town hall building; a gray Chrysler.

I pulled to the side of the road and cut the engine, hoping that I was far enough away that the sound of my approach had gone unnoticed.

I reached beneath my jacket and drew the Beretta free from its holster. I advanced toward the town hall, keeping as close to the buildings on the north side of the street as their most recent coat of paint. We had been right: Corinth was important. The only question was, would Gage have any use for Carol after she had brought him here? I held my breath as I got closer to the Chrysler, bracing myself for what I might see inside. Unwanted images flashed before me like premonitions. Carol's head resting on the dashboard, her blood coating the inside of the windshield.

The car was empty. No body, no blood. I stopped and listened. I heard nothing but the desert wind whispering between the abandoned buildings.

I climbed the stone steps outside the town hall and edged close to the bare doorway. I looked into the main hall. It was almost full dark outside. Inside, it was already as black as a cave.

But on the other side of the main hall, twenty feet above the ground, I saw an illuminated rectangle. The sealed door on the platform was open. And there was someone up there.

43

"Is that what I think it is?" Gage heard the unguarded excitement in his own voice and grimaced as the hint of a smirk on Carol's lips told him she had heard it too.

"Unless you think it's bubble wrap, then yes."

It wasn't bubble wrap. Gage was no expert, but the diamonds looked very real to him. Loose white diamonds, cut and polished. There had to be fifty or sixty of them, each one worth tens of thousands of dollars. No wonder the men in Vegas had been keen to talk to Freel.

"This is why they wanted him," he said, almost to himself.

"So they really didn't tell you. Dangerous to give the help too much information, huh?"

Gage looked back at her, too caught up in the revelation of the diamonds to issue a rebuke. It took him a couple of seconds to put it together. McKinney and Freel had been doing time for armed robbery. Robbery and diamonds and Las Vegas and the timeframe added up to only one thing.

"This is from the Ellison heist, isn't it? Freel and McKinney. They were the ones who got away."

She opened her mouth to say something, and then they heard it.

The wings of the birds out in the main hall beating as something, or someone, disturbed them.

Gage turned back to the door and stepped out on the platform, just in time to see the silhouette of a man in the dim twilight cast through the open door, before he vanished into the shadows. He tracked the movement and fired three times into the shadows by the door.

Gage ducked back into the room and turned his head to tell Carol not to move an inch.

Something hard slammed into the side of his head as he turned, a blinding flash of light exploded behind his eyes. He fell to the floor, barely keeping hold of the gun as the flashlight dropped from his fingers and bounced across the floor.

He started to get up and immediately was felled by another blow to the head, this one from the toe of Carol's boot. He jammed his eyes shut to blink away the star burst and slurred a curse as he felt Carol's hand dig into his pocket and come out with the keys to the Chrysler. He felt her hand close around his on top of the gun and managed to tighten his grip. She struggled for a second and then let it go.

He urged his muscles to start working and move him off the floor. He could hear footsteps, both up here and downstairs. He heard a creak, became conscious of the room lightening slightly as Carol used the pushbar to open the exterior door beyond the vestibule with the safe. As the door slammed shut again, he heard footsteps on the metal spiral staircase out in the hall and willed himself to move from the ground. He got to one knee, shaking the stars out of his vision and saw what Carol had hit him with. She had struck him with enough force to break the old brick in two. The age and condition of the brick was probably the only reason he was still conscious. He was just glad he hadn't left the sledgehammer too close by.

There was no time to dwell on that. His ears ringing, he got to his feet as he heard the sound of footsteps outside on the platform. He moved toward the exterior door and pushed at the bar. It didn't budge. She had jammed it with something. He forgot about it and moved back to the interior door.

He swung around the doorframe and fired, just as the man on the platform fired back at him.

44

As soon as I saw movement, I fired. Gage's shot went wide, mine punched into the wood of the doorframe. I stopped midway along the platform, hugging the wall to make the angle from the doorway impossible. But that cut both ways, of course.

I listened. I could hear breathing.

"Carol?" I yelled. "Carol, it's me, are you there?"

There was no answer for a moment, and then the voice I didn't want to hear.

227

"You're a little late. I just killed the bitch."

A tightness seized my chest. But something in Gage's tone gave me hope. There was a pure, insulted rage beneath the words. As though he desperately wanted this to be the truth, but it wasn't.

"Carol, are you in there?"

A pause, and then I heard movement. I tensed for another round of gunfire from the door and then realized he was moving away from me. Quickly, I walked the length of the platform, keeping my gun on the doorway. I reached the doorframe, took a breath, and pivoted around. The room was empty. On the other side I saw an old fire door with a pushbar, closed tight. For an instant I guessed Gage had made his escape, before I realized there would have been no way to get the door open and closed in the time it had taken me to get to the door.

I looked in the right place, almost too late. He was behind the door. I lunged backward out of the room just in time, hearing bullets thud into the wall at the spot I had just been. I kept low and scrambled back behind the wall again. And then I realized it didn't provide as much cover as I had assumed. Two bullets punched holes through the wall by my head, sending me tumbling back along the platform. When I was far enough along, I stopped and returned the favor. I fired a couple of shots into the wall, knowing that from this angle I was about as likely to hit my assailant as I was to win the lottery.

There was a lull. I knew he was still in there, because I hadn't heard any movement or the sound of the door being rattled again. At least I had managed to determine that he had been lying: Carol wasn't in that room, dead or alive.

"Where is she?" I called out.

There was no answer. Had I hit him? No way, I couldn't

be that lucky. I waited another minute. And then from outside, I heard the sound of a car start up. The engine noise told me it wasn't mine, but the gray Chrysler I had seen on my way in. Carol: it had to be.

As the engine noise died away, I heard another sound from within the room, a quiet, scraping noise. Not like the sound of a door opening; more like two rocks being rubbed together. I crept along the platform until I was next to the doorway once again. I tensed and then glanced around it, just in time to see the upper body of Trenton Gage dangling through a large hole in the wall on the far side of the room. He was a big guy, and had obviously spent the last couple of minutes removing enough bricks so that he could squeeze backwards through the gap. His gun rested on the edge of the bricks. Our eyes locked, and he reached for the gun, cursing as he fumbled it. As it dropped to the floor inside the room, he let go with his other hand, dropping back through the gap. I heard a thud and a grunt of pain a second later. I moved to the hole and looked down, seeing only darkness. I rushed back out onto the platform and down the spiral stairs.

I stopped and listened when I reached the ground floor. I heard a whisper of movement behind me and turned to see him rush me from the shadows. I got my gun up and trained on the spot between his eyes. He stopped in his tracks, five feet from me.

Gage had stopped in a sliver of dull twilight from one of the windows, giving me my first good look at him. He was a big man, wide at the shoulders. He had a fully shaved head and bushy eyebrows. There was an abrasion on the left side of his head, and blood was glistening on the side of his face. On his right cheek was the white crescent-shaped scar Sarah had described. He wore a black shirt, rolled up at the sleeves. He had an empty holster clipped to his belt.

Slowly, he raised his hands. His eyes were fixed on mine.

"Where's Carol?" I asked calmly.

Carefully, he reached a fingertip to the side of his bald head and wiped away blood. He examined the bloody fingertip and looked back at me. "That's a good question. I think I'd like to know the answer more than you."

So she was okay. Better than okay, she had obviously gotten the drop on this goon.

"Trenton Gage, right?"

He looked surprised for a moment. "I'm impressed. I guess my reputation precedes me. We've met before. The woman's house in Summerlin."

His accent was difficult to place. Maybe Canadian.

"Who sent you?" I asked.

"Who says anyone did?"

"You're not a local: not to here or Vegas. And from what I've seen so far, you seem like outside help. Somebody who was brought into this, not somebody with a dog in the fight."

"You have a name?" he asked.

"Blake. I'm a friend of Carol's."

He smiled knowingly. "But not a friend of Freel's."

I didn't respond to that. Now that the bullets had stopped flying and things had calmed down a little, I became conscious that all of a sudden, I had a prisoner by accident. And I didn't have the first idea of what to do with him.

"Where did she go?"

"You asked that already. And I told you I have no idea, other than wherever she is she's getting farther away with the merchandise while the two of us keep yapping."

The merchandise? Could that mean ...? I shelved the thought and asked another question quickly, not wanting to let Gage know I was still in the dark about exactly why Corinth had recently become such a visitor magnet.

"You killed Freel. Were you going to kill her, too?"

A lightbulb went on behind his eyes as he confirmed a suspicion. "You don't know," he said with satisfaction.

"Don't know what?" I said with a little more irritation than I had intended.

"You're just here for her," he said, breaking into a grin. "Boy, you have some surprises coming."

Surprises? I knew it would be pointless to ask him to elaborate and besides, I didn't want to give him the satisfaction of confirming he knew more than I did. I glanced back at the door, wondering how I was going to get him out of here, and what I would do with him if I did. One thing at a time.

"Come on," I said, jerking my head in the direction of the entrance to indicate he should go first.

He started to walk. And then I made my first mistake: letting him get within arm's length of me.

Gage moved like a snake, knocking my hand up and charging me. My gun clattered to the floor. I ducked a swing from the left and blocked one from the right. If I had learned one thing the other night, it was that I was no physical match for Gage. I might have speed and agility on my side, but those were only advantages so long as I kept my distance. I slammed my fist into the middle of his stomach. He barely flinched. I stepped back and came up against a cracked tile wall as he advanced forward, those big hands reaching for me. Then they were around my throat and he was lifting me off the ground. I gagged and scrabbled at his hands, then gave up and slammed the blade of my hand down on his collarbone. He grunted and his grip released just enough that I was able to struggle free. I staggered backwards and looked across the hall toward the main doorway. Too far. He would be on top of me before I reached it. And then I remembered I had one other advantage: advance knowledge of the terrain.

I turned and ran. Not toward the door, but in the direction of the stage. I heard Gage's footsteps behind me. I let him gain, knowing the timing had to be perfect. I kept my eyes on the floor and saw the gaping hole Sarah had fallen through. I launched myself forward, jumping the gap and landing on the other side. I heard a surprised cry from behind me followed by a crash as two hundred and fifty pounds of asshole slammed into the floor of the basement. I stepped back toward the hole and looked down. I could make out Gage lying spread-eagled. No way to tell if he was dead or just unconscious. The memory of those hands around my throat made my mind up that I wasn't going to stick around to find out.

I went back to where he had knocked the gun out of my hands and retrieved it, then made my way to the doorway, forcing myself to tread carefully. As I reached the doorway, I got an answer to my question. A yell of pure rage erupting up from the basement.

"Blake—you're a fucking dead man!"

I didn't answer. Even if I had been able to think of a witty retort, my throat was too sore from the choking. When I got to the doorway there was no sign of the Chrysler, as I had expected. Carol was long gone, for better or worse.

I ran back along Main Street to my car, unlocked it, and got in. As I started up the engine and turned the headlights on, I kept my eyes on the town hall, half-expecting Gage to come stumbling out after me.

I turned in the road and drove out of the dead town, putting my foot down as I reached the open road heading back to the highway. I hoped it would take Gage a while to find a way out of the basement and retrieve his gun. When he did, he would still be twenty miles from anywhere. Good enough, for now.

But as Corinth shrank and then vanished in my rearview mirror, I started to think he wasn't my problem anymore. Carol was. The big man's words came back to me as the sign for Iron City flashed by.

Boy, you have some surprises coming.

45

Sarah lay on the small motel room bed, trying to think about anything but what might be happening twenty miles away in Corinth.

For the hundredth time or so, she reached for her phone. No calls, no messages.

She had barely had time to draw breath from the moment she and Blake had arrived in Quarter until checking into this room. First the meeting with Diane Marshall, then the revelation that Carol was indeed in town, and that Blake had spoken to her. From there it had been a rollercoaster: the frantic drive to Carol's place, the discovery of Freel's body, Blake's decision to go back to Corinth alone.

On a practical level, she understood that that had been the only course of action that made sense. Trenton Gage, or whoever had killed Freel and kidnapped Carol, was armed and dangerous. She knew that her insisting on coming along would have done no good. And yet ... she felt so useless waiting on the sidelines, doing nothing.

Not quite nothing. She remembered the laptop. She had changed the display settings to make sure the screen never locked, as she wasn't sure if Gage's little USB gadget would work twice. They had already gone through the file space, but now that she could connect to the hotel's wifi, she would be able to see if Freel had left any sort of internet trace.

A few minutes on, the laptop seemed to be a busted flush. There were two separate browsers installed on the machine: one was never used by the looks of it; the other was set up to erase the history each time it was closed. If Freel or Carol had visited any sites that might give them an idea of exactly what was going on, there was no easy way to find them. Sarah had been briefly elated to find that there was a free Outlook.com email account that was logged in. Then her spirits had sunk when she found the inbox empty, and nothing in sent messages.

But then she had clicked on deleted items and found three messages, all from earlier in the day. The folder would empty automatically after a few days, or when it was manually purged, but Freel evidently hadn't gotten around to doing that. And the fact that there were both received and sent items deleted indicated he had wanted to remove them.

The first message had been sent from this account today, in the early hours of the morning, 2:47 a.m. It was addressed to another free webmail account with the name "Vegas Office."

We may need to accelerate the timescale. As in, next couple of days?

"Vegas Office," whoever that was, had taken his or her time to respond. Probably he or she was asleep when the original message arrived. A reply had appeared at 8:02 a.m.

Not easy, but I'll see what I can do. Come to the new place, noon on Friday. Not empty-handed.

FD

What did FD stand for? Somebody's initials, most likely, or maybe some sort of code.

Freel had obviously been waiting by the keyboard. His reply was sent at 8:04:

See you then.

And that was all there was. No address for the meet, no real hint of what they were discussing. If they were talking about this Friday, that was tomorrow. All she could say for sure was that Dominic Freel wasn't meeting anybody at noon tomorrow.

She got up and paced the floor of the tiny room. The window faced west. The flat landscape extended uninterrupted for miles until it met a line of black hills beneath the deep blue night sky. She knew the town of Corinth was out there. She looked back over at the bed where her phone lay. Its screen remained stubbornly dark.

She groaned out loud. She wasn't a big drinker, but suddenly she craved something to smooth off the edge off her anxiety. If nothing else, it would be something to occupy her for a while. Anything was better than staying in this room, bouncing off the walls waiting for a call from Blake. And now that she thought about it, she wouldn't put it past Blake to forget to call her even if there was an important development. That stunt earlier on, going to see Carol alone, had been typical of him.

She was halfway down the stairs to reception when her phone buzzed again. She took it from her pocket, hoping to see Blake's number. But it wasn't him. She had saved Detective Costigane's number yesterday when he called, and it was his name that showed on the screen. She let it ring out. She wasn't sure she wanted to take that call right now.

When the call alert disappeared from her screen, she opened the internet browser on her phone and typed the words "Quarter" and "Arizona" into news, hoping there would be nothing of note.

But there it was: *Quarter, Az. Man Killed in Home Invasion.*

Just a brief paragraph, sketchy on the details other than to say police had been called to a home in the town where they discovered the body of a yet-unidentified male appearing to be in his early forties. No further details had been released so far, but police were warning residents to be vigilant.

As Sarah had been reading the brief article, the icon at the top of her screen for a new voicemail had lit up. She was surer than ever that she didn't want to take Detective Costigane's call now.

She held on to the phone while she descended the rest of the stairs. She walked across reception, smiling in acknowledgment as the guy on the desk bid her a good evening, and entered the small bar. There were a couple of other people sitting alone. She ordered a Jim Beam and took a seat at a table near the window. She took a sip and felt a shiver as the liquor burned her lips, then her tongue, then down her throat, before sending a pleasant warmth back upwards again.

The voicemail was brief, terse, and to the point.

"Ms. Blackwell, this is Detective Costigane again. Please call me as soon as you get this."

That was it: no thank you, no goodbye, no apology for disturbing her.

She thought about ordering another bourbon before calling back, but then steeled herself. She considered several different approaches as the phone rang. Should she sound sleepy? Should she be in a good mood, blissfully unaware of the news Costigane was about to break? No, that would be ridiculous. Cops don't tend to be calling to give you good news, so anything other than trepidation would sound suspicious. Which was just as well, as it was the only mood she could convincingly pull off at that moment.

"I'm afraid I have some bad news," Costigane said when he answered.

Her mouth felt dry and she swallowed before responding. "Go ahead."

"Dominic Freel was found murdered this evening."

"Dominic ... you mean?"

"Yes Ms. Blackwell, your former neighbor."

"Oh my God, where did ... what happened?"

"We're not sure of all the details right now. He was shot and killed in a small town down in Arizona. The name of the place is Quarter. Does that ring any bells with you?"

Had she imagined it, or had Costigane injected a meaningful pause there after he had given her the name of the town? Did he know something?

"No, not at all," Sarah said, pleasantly surprised at how naturally the lie came out. "Is Rebecca okay? His wife, I mean."

"We don't know where his wife has gone," Costigane said. The question was implicit.

"I haven't heard anything from her at all. Oh my God, this is awful. Do you think it could be related to what happened at my house?"

"We can't rule anything out, which is why I need you to come in and speak to us. Where are you right now?"

"I'm still out of town," she said, then quickly added, "L.A. I don't know how I could help, though, I've told you everything I know. I mean, like I said, I barely spoke to Dominic."

There was a long pause, as though Costigane was making his mind up about what he was going to say next.

"Do you have access to email on your phone?"

"Of course."

"I'm going to send you a picture that I want you to look

at. But first I have to tell you something that has to remain absolutely confidential."

"Understood."

"I've been working on the robbery of the Ellison Jewelry Company a few months back; you might have heard about it on the news. Mr. Freel's name came up a few times with reference to the case."

Sarah was careful in her reply. Costigane knew she was a journalist, and presumably he was assuming she was a person of reasonable intelligence. "You're saying he may have been involved in the Ellison heist. You think that's why he was murdered?" Costigane didn't reply, and she knew he was waiting for her to ask more questions. She asked the question that she would have asked, if this had really been new information. "You don't just think he was a witness, do you?"

"That would be correct. We think he was involved. How long did you work for the *Tribune*, Sarah?"

"About ten years."

"You worked the crime beat?"

"Sure."

"Then you know how it goes. There are loose ends in any investigation. When we get a promising suspect and we can build a good case against him, some of those loose ends get ... swept under the carpet."

"What kind of loose ends are you talking about, Detective?"

"Well that's the thing. I never gave this particular loose end too much thought before. And then you started asking about your neighbor, and someone realized that the guy who lived next door to you was Freel. One thing led to another and I got ahold of the picture you shared with Detective Stansfield in Missing Persons."

"The one with Dominic Freel at the barbecue?"

"Yeah. Only it wasn't Freel who got my attention. What did you say his wife's name was again?"

All of a sudden, Sarah felt the hairs on the back of her arms stand up.

"Rebecca," she said.

But as Sarah well knew, that wasn't Carol's only name.

46

I had given up hope of catching up with Carol long before I reached the intersection with the highway. She had ten minutes' head start, and a binary choice of direction that would multiply into several additional choices by the time she reached the next town, whether she was headed south to Iron City or north to the next place. I decided to go back for Sarah, and the two of us could decide what to do next.

My phone was on the passenger seat of the Ford, and I glanced at it occasionally, impatient for a single bar to appear on the reception. It's funny how quickly we've become accustomed to being contactable anytime, anywhere. It felt like I'd traveled back in time two or three decades. By the time my phone registered a sign of life, I was almost back to Iron City. I pulled off the road and got out of the car. It was full night now, the stars impossibly clear in a sky that seemed too big.

I called Sarah's number. She picked it up on the first ring.

"She's gone," I said simply.

"What do you mean gone? Gage still has her?"

"No. Carol jumped him and got away."

Got away *with* something, too, I was betting. The something that Trenton Gage was interested in. Now that I had time to reflect on the previous hour, I could recall what I had seen in the little room in the derelict building. It was like a still picture in my mind's eye. A doorway partially bricked up, broken through by the sledgehammer that lay on the floor nearby. A new safe in the old wall; its door open, its contents gone.

That was why they had gone to Corinth, to hide the Ellison diamonds.

"How far away are you?" From the urgency in her voice, I could tell Sarah had news of her own.

I looked down the road ahead. I could make out the lights of the gas station on the edge of Iron City, no more than a mile away. "Not far."

"Then hang up now and get over here. There's something you need to see."

Five minutes later, we were in Sarah's room at the hotel. She handed me her tablet and for the second time in a few days, I found myself looking at a picture and wondering how much trouble it meant.

The framing and low picture quality told me it had come from a store surveillance camera of some kind. Probably one of those cheap units that captures ten frames a second rather than full motion video. It showed a woman turned slightly away from the camera wearing dark glasses. She was wearing a coat and carrying a small bag. The color was oversaturated, so on the evidence here, the woman's hair could have been either brown or red. I was betting on red.

"I take it this is who I think it is?"

"I'm pretty sure it is, yes."

I stared a little longer at the image. The background was hazy; looked like a sidewalk somewhere. That was about as specific as it was going to get, in terms of pinpointing a location. I turned my eyes from the screen to look at Sarah, waiting for her to elaborate.

"You remember the cop who called earlier?"

"Costigane, the guy investigating the Ellison job."

"He called me again tonight. He knows Freel is dead, they found the body a couple of hours ago. He pretty much ordered me back home. I had to agree to meet him tomorrow evening at six in Vegas. Anyway, before that, he started asking me some more questions about Freel. He told me about the investigation into the Ellison heist. How they were looking at Freel, and there were a lot of loose ends."

"There always are."

"That's what he said. But one of the early lines of inquiry was this woman."

I motioned for her to go on. I had a bad feeling about what was coming.

"When they looked back at the security tapes, they found the same woman hanging around the store on three separate occasions. She never goes in; she never buys anything. After they found Rayner Deakins and recovered most of the take, the investigation was deprioritized, so this was one of the loose ends that never got followed up."

That was enough. I didn't need Sarah to continue. Everything began to click into place neatly, and I started to wonder why this hadn't occurred to me before.

"Blake, I know this sounds crazy, but ..."

"It doesn't sound crazy at all," I said. I looked back at the image on the screen. The woman in the dark glasses was just close enough to the crappy quality security camera so that you could see her expression. It was entirely calm, composed. Unreadable.

"Then you think she could have been involved? As in, not just because of Freel?"

"She still is involved," I said.

47

Gage had hurt his right arm in the fall, and everything below the elbow felt numb with occasional bursts of pins and needles. Not a break, but a trapped nerve, maybe. His fall had been broken by some empty wooden packing crates. The damage would have been far worse if he had hit the stone floor of the basement directly. The reduced function in his arm meant that it took Gage a while to break through the sealed basement door. By the time he got back up to ground level, Carol's friend Blake was long gone.

He touched the rapidly-swelling bruise on the side of his head and winced. Despite the sudden reversal of his fortunes, he thought the trip hadn't been a total loss. Now he knew exactly why Walter and his men had wanted to track down Freel, and he knew this job was more than worth his while. Earlier on, after he had killed Freel, he had harbored thoughts of cutting his losses and moving on. The revelation of what had been in the safe had made him very glad he had stayed the course. From what he remembered of the coverage of the Ellison heist, much of the take had been recovered, but what was missing was valued in millions. Enough for a new start. Enough for a lot of new starts. He understood now why McKinney, and Freel, and then Carol had risked so much to keep the secret. A sixty-four-thousand-dollar question, and then some.

And Carol had outdone her late husband and his friend. Not only had she stayed alive, she had used Gage to retrieve the diamonds. He had underestimated her, that was for sure, but she had required a good deal of luck. Had it not been for the intervention of the guy who called himself Blake, she would never have gotten the drop on him. Who the hell was he? A friend, according to him; merely somebody she used to know according to her. Whoever he was, he didn't know about the diamonds. He had given that away—he was only interested in finding Carol. Gage didn't know why. Maybe she had stolen something from him, too. And then he remembered the concern in his voice inside the old building. The threat he had made over the phone. Ex-boyfriend perhaps. The jealous type.

Gage touched a finger to the cut at the side of his head. The bleeding had stopped, and his arm was working okay through the numbness, but right now he needed painkillers and some rest. Both would have to wait a while. He made his way to the edge of town, stepped onto the broken asphalt of the highway, and started walking.

48

Like an idiot, I hadn't even considered the possibility Carol had been lying to me not just to protect Freel, but herself as well. She didn't just know or suspect something about Freel and the heist, she knew it all. She knew exactly where the diamonds were stashed, and somehow she had suckered Trenton Gage into taking her right to them. Helped along the way by yours truly.

I thought back to the first time I had laid eyes on Carol Langford, in the lobby of a midtown skyscraper, en route to a meeting with her boss. She had been harassed and abrupt, but I had immediately liked her. Sure, there was an immediate physical attraction, but it was more than that. I had instantly liked her as a person. She had been ... good. As simple and as complicated as that. I tried to reconcile this with the woman who I now realized had ripped off a corporate jeweler, shrugged off the murders of her partner and husband, and then sucker-punched a cold-eyed killer who looked like he was a missing part of Mount Rushmore. I didn't know whether to feel shocked or impressed.

I could tell Sarah was going through the same process, as she stared at the picture of Carol from the security footage.

"Here's what I think happened," I said. "Carol and Freel were involved in the heist, that's pretty obvious. That's why those men came after them. Not because Freel was a witness, but because Carol and Freel were part of the gang, and they ripped off part of the take. The rest of it has been recovered. The only thing left is two million dollars' worth of loose diamonds, which we can be pretty sure is what they stashed in Corinth."

Sarah didn't say anything for a while. She shook her head.

"I can't believe that. Maybe it's ..."

"A coincidence?"

She grimaced. "No, not a coincidence. Maybe she didn't know about Freel's involvement. Or what if Costigane is wrong about Freel, or was trying to railroad him? What if he witnessed something to do with the job and the people involved knew about it? That would explain why they ran, why this guy was looking for them."

"But it wouldn't explain why they were quite so keen to track them down. The single suspect the police found is

244

dead, and the trail has gone cold on the rest of the diamonds. Why pay a professional to stir up trouble? You would just as likely force them into going to the cops." It was my turn to shake my head. "No, Freel and Carol took the diamonds. It explains why they came here, why they stopped in Corinth. And it fits with what Gage said: Carol took something. Something he was interested in."

"It just ... it doesn't fit with the Carol I know. Knew."

After a moment, I said quietly: "You mean the Rebecca you knew?"

"That's not the point," she said sharply. But I thought it was exactly the point.

Neither of us spoke for a while. I understood her reaction. But at the same time I knew that if it hadn't been for my personal connection with Carol, I would have started thinking along these lines much earlier.

"Okay, so it's a theory," she admitted after a moment. "If you're right, maybe they realized somebody was closing in on them back in Summerlin and that's why they left." She puffed her cheeks up and blew out in bemusement. "I guess you never really know what's going on next door, huh?"

"This is why I don't like to have neighbors," I said. "Sarah, we have to find her. She's in deep and unless we can get her out of this ..."

I didn't finish. I didn't need to.

"Okay," Sarah said after a minute. "For the sake of argument let's say you're right. Carol—or *Rebecca*, or Lara freaking Croft, or whatever her name really is—is some kind of master criminal, and now she's on the run with a couple of million bucks' worth of diamonds. In that case, you're right, we need to find her and talk to her. But where would she go now?"

I got up and paced the room while I considered Sarah's

question. I was relieved to be focusing on an area where I was more comfortable: working out where someone in a certain situation might go under a given set of circumstances is my bread and butter.

"Well, that's what makes things interesting. If she has the diamonds, she's going to be easier for us to find."

"How do you mean?"

"Before, we had no real idea why she was running, or what kind of resources she had."

"Exactly. Now she has unlimited resources. She'll be impossible to find."

"No, her resources are very limited indeed right now."

"Two million bucks? I should be so limited."

I grinned. "You think so? When was the last time you tried to buy a house with a bag of diamonds? Or a plane ticket. Or a Big Mac."

She slapped a palm off her head. I sympathized. We were both playing catch-up here. "She needs to sell the diamonds quickly."

"That's right," I said. "She needs a fence, and not just any fence. A professional operation, big enough to deal with the volume and experienced enough to be comfortable with the risk. But Gage showing up wasn't exactly plan A, even though they anticipated the possibility. They hid the take from Ellison in Corinth so it would be safe. I'm guessing they knew there was a real danger someone would track them down."

Sarah was nodding. "So they hid the diamonds, then took the place down in Quarter. They probably thought they could wait until the heat was off, until they felt safe, and then go back for them. But that's all changed now. Carol isn't going to be able to get top dollar for them anymore. She just needs to move them for the best price she can get."

She paused and then shook her head at the absurdity of it. I knew what she was thinking. She had known Carol for months, spoken to her every day, and had never once suspected what was going on.

She shook her head. "It's too risky. She'll go to ground again, wait until things settle down."

"No," I said. "She won't want to risk hiding them again."

"Why not?"

"Two reasons. First, Gage is on her trail, and he won't give up while he knows she has the diamonds. He'll find her again. I know that from spending five minutes with him, and she had a lot longer in his company, so she knows it too. Either she gives him what he wants, or she offloads the reason he's looking for her and gets clear. The second reason is more psychological. She came very close to losing it all tonight. She'll take less than they're worth rather than risking losing them again. She knows the longer she hangs on to them, the thinner her luck wears. Like Freel—his luck wore out yesterday."

Sarah's mouth dropped open and I realized she knew something I didn't.

"She doesn't want to be left empty-handed," she said, as though to herself.

"What?"

In answer, she got up and retrieved the laptop we had taken from Freel's house. "I completely forgot about it after Costigane called, but I found something else, and it makes a lot more sense now."

Thirty seconds later, Sarah was scrolling through the emails she had recovered earlier in the day. She opened the message she was looking for and turned the laptop to me so I could read it.

Come to the new place, noon on Friday. Not empty-handed.
FD

"They were setting up an exchange. This must be the guy who's buying the diamonds," Sarah said. "It's just a pity we don't have a name or an address. Freel obviously would have known where 'the new place' was."

"I can't do anything about a name," I said, "but maybe we could do something about the other thing."

"How do you mean?"

"If they were very careful, this won't work. But if people were careful all the time, I would be out of a job."

I had made use of this little trick before. The information you see in the common-or-garden email communication is just the tip of the iceberg. Every email contains a header with details of the routing of the message and the original IP address. The email from "Vegas Office" was no exception. The metadata quickly told me that the email had indeed originated in Las Vegas, and gave me the ISP the sender used.

I opened another browser window to access a tracing widget, and copied and pasted the relevant lines of code from the email, holding my breath. A second later, I was looking at an address.

122 Wilston Street, Las Vegas.

When I searched for the location, it showed a building in downtown Vegas home to a list of small businesses. On the third floor was a business called "FDC Partners." There were no details anywhere about what FDC partners did.

Sarah and I exchanged a glance.

"What do you think?" she said.

"Something obviously spooked Freel last night and he set this meeting up. It all comes down to whether Carol knew about the meeting. If she did, we have a pretty good idea of where she's going to be at noon tomorrow. If she didn't, we still have to assume she needs to cash in, and maybe this is the guy she'll contact. Either way, she's going back to Vegas."

"You don't think that would be too risky? The people she and Freel double-crossed are probably back there. To say nothing of the police."

"That could be an advantage. They won't expect her to come back."

"But still, it's like walking into the lion's den."

"I've had to catch up quick, just like you," I said. "I think the woman who we're discussing wouldn't shy away from a little risk. And to tell you the truth, I don't think the woman I knew six years ago would, either."

"It's a high stakes gamble for her. And for us, betting everything on her going back there. If you're wrong, we may lose our chance forever."

"You're right. It is a gamble. But if we're going to gamble, I guess we picked the right town."

49

"So how do we find her?" Sarah asked. "I mean, even if you're right about where's she's going, Las Vegas isn't exactly the kind of place where somebody new in town is going to stick out, you know?"

Blake had opened up the map they had bought at Grady's Rest Stop again, and had spread it across the floor. He was crouched down, gazing at the territory around them. "You're right," he said. "And we don't have a lot of time. So that means we put Vegas to one side for a minute, and start with the one thing we absolutely know for sure."

"Oh good," Sarah said drily. "There's something 'we' know for sure now?"

He looked up. "Your other friend in the police, not Detective Costigane. You think he'll do us another favor?"

Sarah folded her arms. "Kubler? What did you have in mind?"

Blake got to his feet and looked around the room for something, stopping when his eyes alighted on a small notepad and pen on the bedside table. He grabbed the pen and sat on the edge of the bed. His hand hovered over the paper, clutching the pen. He closed his eyes tight.

"What are you ..."

She stopped talking when she realized Blake was concentrating hard on something. He reminded her of some hokey old black-and-white movie she had seen last month, the expression on the face of a medium summoning an ethereal presence at a séance. Was that what he was doing?

And then his eyes opened and the pen hit the paper. He wrote something on the notepad with careful deliberation. When he was done, he ripped off the top sheet and handed it to her, and she saw that it was a license plate.

"This is Gage's car," he said. "The Chrysler, the one she took."

Sarah looked at the plate number doubtfully. She rubbed the bridge of her nose, suddenly realizing how tired she was. "Blake, even if we knew where to tell them to look, Kubler isn't going to start stopping cars on our say-so."

"He doesn't need to," Blake said. "Just ask him if it's in the system. I think she'll get rid of Gage's car as quickly as she can. Or maybe we'll be lucky and she runs a red light or gets stopped for speeding."

She thought it over. "Worth a shot, you're right."

A minute later, she was speaking to Kubler again. She apologized for the evening call. Kubler told her she was lucky that he was a night owl.

"This is about your friend?"

"That's right. I wondered if you could do me just one last favor."

She laid it out for him, pre-empting his concerns by telling him she only needed to know if the plate had popped up in the system recently. Kubler told her he would see what he could do.

When she hung up, Blake was on his feet, bouncing the car keys in his right hand. "Ready for the return trip?"

Sarah picked up the tablet. "I have a better idea. I checked departures from Phoenix and there's a red-eye out of Sky Harbor we can just make if we leave right now."

She was watching his expression as she spoke, and he looked just as uncomfortable about the suggestion as she had expected.

"Or, you could drop me there and give me a head start while you drive four hundred miles through the night for no good reason."

Blake had a pained expression. "Would you believe I have a crippling fear of flying?"

"Do I want to know?"

"You really don't, trust me."

Sarah rolled her eyes. She was dealing with enough insane revelations about people she thought she knew today without digging deeper into Carter Blake's reluctance to go near an airport.

"Just get me to Sky Harbor, Blake."

50

Gage reached the intersection of the Corinth road with the highway just under three hours after he had set out. The sign at the intersection told him the nearest town was a place called Iron City, and it was still another ten miles distant. There was nothing else to do but keep walking, so Gage kept walking.

At least he was on a main road now, and there was an outside chance of picking up a ride. Three northbound cars passed him during the following twenty minutes. Two of them blew by without a second glance. The third, a tiny blue Corvette, slowed as it approached him, and then immediately sped up when the young-looking brunette woman driving got a good look at him.

After another half hour or so, he crossed the invisible barrier between the wilderness and civilization and his cell phone erupted to life in his coat pocket. He ignored the first couple of buzzes, but the notifications kept coming. He reached for the phone and looked at the screen. Texts, voicemails, missed calls.

He didn't need to look at the content to know that the three men in Vegas were not happy.

Mildly curious, he thumbed through the record as he walked. Six missed calls, starting before ten, with the gaps between getting shorter each time. Messages from the same number, repeating the same terse instruction: *call when you get this*.

He knew that meant Freel's body had been found and identified. As he looked at the screen, the message disappeared and was replaced by the same number calling again. He ignored it and put it back in his pocket. He was confused by the fact they seemed so eager to talk to him. Did they think they could persuade him to unkill Freel or something? He would contact them when he was good and ready.

Gage kept walking. In contrast to the day the air was bitterly cold, but the exercise kept him warm. The sky was clear, the stars bright and countless above him. The hills in the distance created a black, fluctuating horizon against the stars. He heard an avian cry as some nocturnal predator swooped on its prey out in the desert. Just over an hour after the driver of the blue Corvette had thought better of stopping, the headlights of a Toyota pickup appeared, headed the same way he was going. Gage slowed his pace and watched as the pickup slowed.

It pulled to a stop a little ahead of him. Gage kept walking. The window rolled down and he heard a voice from within.

"Where you headed?"

The driver was an older guy, looked like he might be grateful for some company to keep him awake. As he spoke, his voice trailed off a little as he saw the blood on Gage's head and the condition of his clothes. Perhaps poor eyesight had led him to stop where the others had passed by.

"Are you okay, mister?" the tone concerned, and not for Gage.

Gage smiled and tried to look non-threatening. "Can you get me to the nearest town? Anywhere I can get a car."

The driver seemed to be physically shrinking into his seat. He shook his head slowly. "I'm sorry, mister, I don't think I can help you."

Gage sighed. "I really wish you hadn't said that."

He raised his gun and shot the old man in the head.

An hour and a half later, after dragging the old man's body

fifty yards off the highway and leaving him for the morning buzzards, he stopped at a gas station in Holbrook. He filled up the tank and took advantage of the restrooms. He stripped to the waist and scrubbed the dirt and blood off his arms and his head. His arm was still hurting, but his fingers all worked and he could move the arm in all directions with a little pain. It was manageable. He could book himself a hotshot physio or something, once he got the diamonds back.

He bought a microwave burrito from the store and went back out to the car, eating it on the way. He got behind the wheel and opened the glovebox, hoping the old man had aspirin or something. No aspirin, but there was a hip-flask two-thirds full. Gage popped the cap and sniffed it. Bourbon. He took a gulp, hoping it would help the dull pain in his arm, and looked at his phone. Up to eighteen missed calls now. That told him they were more than just pissed. It told him they needed him. The phone rang for a nineteenth time as he watched. He let it ring while he thought it over, taking another sip.

Start with Walter's call yesterday in Quarter. Walter had stood him down for a reason. That could only be that they had found another way to get to Freel. Something that was an absolute sure thing, otherwise they wouldn't have called Gage off. Did they have someone else in Quarter already? Could Blake be working for them too? He didn't think so. Blake was only interested in finding Carol, he was convinced of that.

Anyway, a few hours on from Walter's last call, and Freel shows up dead. All of a sudden they needed to talk to him in a hurry. Again, there was a good reason for that, and this one was much clearer. With Freel taking his secrets to the grave, their only hope was that he had passed some of them on to Gage.

He thought it over for another minute as he finished the contents of the flask. It would take some careful maneuvering, but if luck was on his side, he might just be able to use Walter and his men to lead him right to the diamonds.

He called the number back.

The call was answered on the first ring. There was no preamble, no pleasantries.

"What happened in Arizona?" Walter's voice, this time. Not too busy to speak anymore.

Gage took his time responding. He could feel the tension on the other end of the line, and it amused him. "I guess you know what happened in Arizona."

"I told you the job was over. We didn't need him anymore."

"Well, it just seemed a shame to go all that way for nothing."

Walter's voice lost its composure. "We told you we wanted him alive. You were supposed to fucking call us."

"I remember that. Unfortunately, Freel forced the issue. He didn't give me a choice."

Gage didn't say anything else. He sure as hell wasn't going to apologize for defending himself, but he wanted to see what their next move would be. He was under no illusions that they still wanted to pay him the balance of his fee, so why did they want to talk to him so badly? There was only one reason.

"Did you talk to him before it happened?"

"Some words were exchanged," Gage admitted.

There was a longer pause. "Did he . . . did he say anything?"

"Like what?"

"Anything. It could be important."

Gage paused, as if to consider. "He did say one thing that interested me."

"Yes?" the voice betrayed desperation. Gage enjoyed toying with the man for another second.

"He said he would make it worth my while, if I let him go."

"And ...?"

"And that's it. He pulled a gun on me, I had to put him down or get shot myself."

"So it was you who killed him."

"You worked that out all by yourself, huh?"

Walter was too preoccupied to respond to that. "And you have no idea what he was talking about. How he was going to pay you off."

Gage took his time. The bourbon had already dulled the ache from his arm, and created a pleasing haze in his head, but nothing to stop him from thinking clearly. He had to play this just the right way. Say he knew nothing, and he would never hear from them again. Admit everything he knew, and they might decide he was another problem to be solved.

"I have no idea, no."

An exasperated sigh on the other end of the line. Before Walter could say anything else, Gage spoke again.

"But I think maybe his wife might."

51

Sarah made the gate with five minutes to spare. She boarded, navigated down the aisle and found her seat at the middle of the plane. There was a big, stocky guy in a business suit squeezed into the window seat, and spreading over into Sarah's. She nudged him aside and he grunted and moved over as she strapped herself in. As she was about to turn her phone off, it rang. Costigane's number again. She thought about ignoring it again, but decided to pick up.

The gruff voice got straight to the point, as usual. No pleasantries, no apologies for the lateness of the hour.

"I'm just checking in to see if you had heard anything from Carol."

"No, not at all. I told you I'll call as soon as I hear anything."

Costigane grunted. "I'm starting to be a little concerned about your safety. If the people involved in this think you may know something ...You're sure you can't be back here any earlier than tomorrow evening?"

"I'll come straight there as soon as I get back into town, I promise."

There was a long pause. "All right, Sarah. I suppose that will have to do. We'll see you at six o'clock tomorrow. And if you should hear anything ..."

"If I hear anything I'll let you know right away."

"Thank you. Have a good trip back from San Francisco."

"Los Angeles. I'm in L.A., remember?"

"Of course."

Sarah hung up and stared at the phone as though it was conspiring against her. Every time she spoke to Costigane, she couldn't shake the feeling he knew a lot more than he was letting on. But perhaps that was just the usual cop sleight of hand. Most likely he only suspected she knew something, and wanted to intimidate her into blurting it out. She hoped she didn't have to speak to him until their meeting at six o'clock. By six o'clock, all being well, this would all be resolved. She didn't know whether they could persuade Carol to cut her losses and run, but with any luck they would get the chance to try.

A kid in the seat in front, maybe five or six years old and up way past his bedtime, had turned around and was staring at her through the gap. She smiled at him. He stared back at her until his mother pulled him back around and told him to sit straight.

She was grateful that they would only be in the air about an hour. The cabin crew began running through the standard spiel, including the part about "the unlikely event we are forced to land on water," which would be unlikely indeed over the desert. Sarah used the last few moments before the instruction to switch off cell phones and devices to download a series of news articles to her tablet. They were all on the one subject: the Ellison heist.

She looked up and gazed past the snoring businessman to watch takeoff, and then she settled back in her seat to read the articles. Within minutes, she was so absorbed she barely noticed the snoring anymore.

The heist had been professionally executed. It had clearly been planned in advance by people who knew what they were doing. Taking advantage of the priorities of policing in the twenty-first century, a bomb threat had been called in to

a casino across town. With that section of the city on lock-
down, the real attack had taken place fourteen blocks south.
Three masked men had entered the Ellison Jewelry Company
and immediately taken control of the building. An inside man
on the security detail—Rayner Deakins—locked the other
two guards up while the four men looted the displays and the
vault, completing their work in under four minutes.

The three men plus the guard went outside and got into a
black SUV driven by a fifth person. They were clear of the
scene a full minute before the first police arrived. No shots
fired, not a scratch on any of the customers.

For four days it looked like the perfect crime. The national
media reported on it with barely concealed admiration.
Nobody had been seriously hurt in the operation, so there
was a certain Robin Hood cachet to the Ellison raiders. They
had vanished with over twenty million in jewelry. The pun-
dits speculated that it wouldn't all be plain sailing for them:
much of the merchandise was identifiable and traceable
to that store. There were some loose stones, but that only
represented a tenth of the haul. So they would have to deal
with a specialist to extract the raw materials, wait until the
heat died down, or smuggle them overseas.

Sarah's background let her read between the lines of the
story with ease. She could translate the euphemisms the
police had tossed out at the briefing, make educated guesses
at the gaps in what was being reported. Her reporter's nose
told her the police really did have a live line of inquiry in
those early days. Although the focus was on the brazen
criminals getting away without a trace, she could see that it
was a different story on the inside. It was easy to tell when
an investigation was stalling, and she didn't get that impression from the quotes from the investigating officers over
those first three days.

And then on the fourth day, the investigation bore fruit. Following a tip-off, Deakins was tracked down and killed in an exchange of gunfire with police at a house in Boulder City, twenty-five miles southeast of Vegas. They found the bulk of the haul at the house, concealed beneath the floorboards. Still missing were the loose diamonds, about two million dollars' worth. And now Sarah knew exactly what had happened to those stones. As Blake had said, in contrast to the identifiable jewelry, the stones would be the easiest part of the haul to fence. Such a large haul could not be disposed of for maximum return anytime soon, which was no doubt why Freel and Carol had been sitting tight in Summerlin. She thought about their pleasant three-bedroom house on a quiet cul-de-sac, and knew that they had been smart. It just wasn't the kind of place you would go to look for a fugitive. But somebody had found out enough to look there, and it hadn't been the police.

She looked up as the seatbelt lights went on with the familiar chime, and the cabin crew started advancing down the aisle, gently reprimanding people to close their devices and return tables to the upright position for landing. The other passengers craned toward the windows to get a glimpse of the neon sprawl below. Sarah looked down at the clusters of multi-colored towers and the brightly-lit boulevards. From up here, the city looked like a garish pinball machine. She sat back in her seat, closing her eyes as she felt the aircraft start to descend to Las Vegas.

All that time. All the time she and the woman she had known as Rebecca had been waving to each other, chatting over coffee, discussing the mundanities of life. Considering taking in a show, where to try for lunch, the new Netflix show that had started. All that time, her neighbor had been sitting on top of a secret. A big one. And Sarah had never once suspected. Had anything about the period been real? Or had Sarah just been one more part of a convincing cover? Window dressing for the life of Rebecca and Dominic Smith: two people who didn't really exist. She wondered if they were even married. She remembered she had forgotten to ask Blake if he knew Carol's real last name.

On wheels down, Sarah reached for her phone and switched it back on. There was a message from Greg Kubler: *Call me.*

The kid staring through the gap in the seats in front scowled.

"You're not 'sposed to have your phone on."

She frowned. "You're not 'sposed to be out of your seatbelt either, kid."

He mirrored her frown and his head disappeared from the gap.

Five minutes later, Sarah walked briskly down the stairs into the warm Vegas night. When she stepped onto the tarmac, she called Kubler.

"Looks like your lucky day."

"You could have fooled me," she said, though she felt a charge of anticipation.

"The Chrysler was found abandoned in Flagstaff an hour ago."

Sarah paused as she entered the terminal, oriented herself, and headed for the taxi stand. A notification chimed in her ear. It could wait until she had finished speaking to Kubler.

"Flagstaff, an hour ago," she repeated, trying to work out if the time fit. She thought that it did.

"Sarah?" Kubler's question reminded her she hadn't said anything for a few moments.

"Sorry, yeah, got it. Any other details? How did they know it was abandoned?"

"I took a little shortcut, I'm afraid."

"I forgive you," she deadpanned.

"We ran the plate and it came up as a Hertz rental. I called them and they used their tracking gizmo to find it for us, then I made a call to the Flagstaff PD and they sent a uniform to have a look. It was right where Hertz said it would be. The doors were unlocked, keys in the ignition. I called Hertz back, and they said it was rented in Phoenix. In the name . . ."

Kubler stopped and Sarah knew why.

"Trenton Gage," she finished.

"You asked me about that name the other day."

"I did, and I promise I'll fill you in as soon as I can."

"Be careful, Sarah."

"I owe you one, thank you."

She called Blake as soon as she had hung up, and related what Kubler had told her to Blake. He sounded like he was taking notes.

"So she dumped it in Flagstaff," Sarah said. "Makes sense. Like you said, she wouldn't want to risk going all the way in a hot car. But how's she going to get to Vegas? She can't fly, not with the diamonds."

"Best way would be to take a bus," Blake said. "But I don't think she did that."

Sarah shook her head. "Bus would be too slow, and it's late. I don't even think there's a direct route; you'd have to go via Phoenix, maybe even L.A."

"Too slow," Blake agreed. "And if she wants to meet this guy at noon tomorrow, she can't just get a room in Flagstaff. I think she would want to get another car instead."

"And how do we track that down?"

"Leave it with me," Blake said. "I'll see you in a few hours."

She started to put her phone back in her pocket and then remembered about the notification she had heard and looked at the screen again. It was a missed call, from Costigane.

She stared at the number for a while. He knew something, all right—why else would he keep pestering her? Now she knew how a Columbo villain must feel. She was really skirting the line now, putting herself at risk. Maybe she should forget about trying to shield Carol from the law: she had made her own bed. As she was making her mind up, the phone rang again. Costigane's number.

"Hello?"

"I thought you were going to call me as soon as you got back into town."

Sarah's blood froze and she turned around slowly, eyeing the crowd at arrivals.

"I don't know what you mean?"

"Getting warmer, Sarah. A little to your left."

Her eyes moved to that position and she saw him, standing by the exit, holding the phone up like a signal and staring right at her. Costigane was taller than she had pictured him. In his mid-fifties with graying hair, wearing a sport coat over a light blue shirt with a dark blue tie, loosened slightly. His eyes were all business.

52

Sarah cut the call off and waited for Costigane to come to her. The gimlet-eyed cop weaved through the onward flow of passengers and stopped a couple of steps in front of her.

"Why did you lie to me about where you were?"

Sarah looked down at the phone in her hand and realized the true reason for his calling earlier in the night. He had used cell phone data to triangulate her position. He had known she was at Sky Harbor in Phoenix, not in Los Angeles. From there it would have been simplicity itself to work out which flight she was taking and when it arrived in Las Vegas. Didn't you need a warrant for that kind of thing? Would Costigane have been able to show just cause? Perhaps, perhaps not. Either way, she wasn't about to make an official complaint right now.

She shook her head, pissed at herself as much as him. "Why did you do that?"

"Because this is serious. There's one dead man already, and if you're sheltering a suspect ..."

"I'm not," Sarah said. "Listen, I know Ca ... I know Rebecca didn't kill her husband, but I think she's in danger."

Costigane paused long enough to absorb this. "I think you need to tell me what you know."

A mild panic seized Sarah. If she let Costigane take her downtown, she would lose her chance to find Carol. Her only other option was to give Carol up; explain about the diamonds and the meeting with the fence. But that would mean she would be arrested. Cleared of murder, perhaps, but possession of stolen goods from a high yield heist wouldn't exactly carry an insignificant sentence. Blake was still hours away. She had no one to turn to, nowhere to go. Unless ...

"Okay," she said. "But let me make a call, first?"

"To Rebecca?"

"To my mother. I need to tell her I'm going to be late."

Costigane looked around, eyeing the potential exits, and sighed. "Okay, but be quick."

Sarah turned away from him and dialed information. She kept her voice low and asked for the number of the airport.

"McCarran International, how may I help you?"

Sarah kept her voice low. "Can you transfer me to airport security please?"

The operator asked her to wait a second. There was a click and a male voice answered.

"Security."

"Hi, I'm in your arrivals area right now and there's a man threatening me. He won't let me leave. Is there any chance ..."

"What does he look like, ma'am? Where are you exactly?"

Sarah gave the man Costigane's description and location and told them to hurry. When they hung up, she kept the phone to her ear and kept talking. From out of the corner of her eye she saw Costigane grow impatient and approach her.

"I know, mom, but I promise I won't ... No, it's absolutely nothing to be worried about."

"Time's up. Come on," Costigane said, jerking a thumb in the direction of the exit.

Sarah mouthed, "One second," smiling apologetically. She could see two burly guards in short-sleeve shirts and chinos approaching them now. They would be here in another ten seconds. She turned and took a step away from Costigane.

Just as she had hoped, he put a hand on her shoulder.

"Come *on.*" It couldn't have been better timed for Sarah.

She raised her voice and cried out, "Don't hurt me!"

The two guards saw the physical contact, the edge of frustration in the man's voice and the fear in the woman's, and acted immediately. The bigger of the two grabbed Costigane's wrist and lifted it firmly from Sarah's shoulder.

"Excuse me, sir, is there a problem here?"

As Costigane turned around to see who was there, Sarah moved. It all depended on how long it took them to verify Costigane's credentials. She heard him say he was a cop, she heard the first one say, "Sure you are."

Costigane turned back and saw that she was already half-way to the exit.

"Stop right there," he yelled, and started after her. The bigger of the two guards grabbed his shoulder.

Sarah didn't look back. She bolted for the exit. She ignored the taxi stand at arrivals, crossed over to the multi-level parking structure, and descended down the stairwell to the basement, where she knew the secondary taxi stand was. By now the security men would have checked Costigane's badge, and all three of them would be coming after her. This was probably going to involve some unpleasant explanations, but she could worry about that later, once they had found Carol.

She got in the back of the taxi and told him to drive. She couldn't go home now, so she would have to find somewhere to lie low until the morning. She almost forgot about her phone. She took it out and switched it off. Blake would just have to catch up with her tomorrow at noon on Wilston Street, like everyone else.

53

I drove through the night, knowing Carol was ahead of me, but knowing there was nothing I could do about narrowing down her location until morning. From Phoenix it was a straight route north and west on US-93. I guessed Sarah would be tucked up in bed by now.

If Carol was aiming to get to Vegas tonight, she would be almost there by this time. If she was keeping the noon rendezvous, she couldn't afford to wait around. I had a few ideas to find out where she had gone, but nothing I could do at this time of night.

I stopped for gas at a place that was the first sign of life on the highway I had seen for about an hour. I bought two cups of coffee and took a break from sitting behind the wheel. I splayed the map over the hood of the Ford. To give Sarah a head start, we had gone via Phoenix. Carol wouldn't have had to make that detour. She would simply have taken the most direct route to Vegas, which would take her through Flagstaff and Holbrook, and a few other small towns. The gas station had slow and expensive wifi. I paid for a half hour and looked up some numbers: hotels and pawnbrokers and used car lots on the direct route. In fifteen minutes, I was back on the road with a list of phone numbers, feeling about as refreshed as I was going to get.

I hoped we could find Carol and talk to her. I hoped we could do it before someone else did.

54

The clock on the dash told Gage it was 2:19 a.m. as he reached the outskirts of Flagstaff. After Gage had baited the hook with Freel's wife, Walter had given him an address in Las Vegas and a time to be there. He had plenty of time to make the rendezvous. The old man's pickup truck looked battered on the outside, but it was running fine. It had almost a full tank of gas now, too, so Gage wouldn't have to stop for a while.

The buzz from the bourbon had long since worn off, and there had been no other forms of pain relief in the glove box. Rooting around in there, Gage found a photograph of the old guy with two young boys he assumed were his grandkids. They would probably miss him, grow up wondering why he had been taken from them. Too bad, that was life. That made him think about Jake, and if Courtney would even tell the kid if something happen to Gage. And that made him think about Carol's little nest egg. Two million in diamonds. That was retail value, of course, but he knew a fence in San Antonio who could give him a good return. Good enough to start planning for the future, maybe even putting down some roots.

The area on his face where Carol had hit him with the brick stung. He touched a finger to it. She had suckered him. She had been convincing with the kept-in-the-dark wife act, all right. He wondered what she would have done if Blake hadn't shown up and distracted him at a crucial moment. He doubted she had anything specific planned, other than being ready to take advantage of any distraction that arose. He couldn't help admire her a little.

It wouldn't stop him from killing her when he found her.

Step one was to talk to Walter, and that meant going all the way back to Las Vegas. That was okay. Gage had a funny feeling that Carol would be headed to Sin City too.

55

LAS VEGAS
FRIDAY, 02:35

Sarah told the driver to drop her a couple of miles from the airport, just in case someone had seen her and taken down the license plate of the taxi. She wasn't sure how much trouble she would be in for running from the police, but she just had to hope she could find Carol before Costigane did, or worse, before Gage did. She walked a couple of blocks and hailed another taxi telling him to drop off at the edge of the Strip. She went into a burger joint and sat at the back, with a view of the door. She ate slowly and nursed a bottomless coffee until the place closed and she ventured back out on the street.

Sarah hadn't been out in the city at this time of night for years. She recalled the last time with an effort. Date night with Edward, their fifth anniversary. Dinner and a luxury room at the Bellagio. Edward had lingered a little too long on the tables at the casino downstairs, of course, but that aside it had been a fun evening.

She had always liked the lights of the Strip, even though she affected a native's cool disdain for the garish display of neon. Tonight, they seemed *too* bright. The millions of flashing lights in all directions assaulted her senses, made her wonder what the glare was hiding. She kept her eyes on the street as she tried to stay close to the knots of people still walking the sidewalks in search of booze and further good times. Every time a police car passed she hunched her shoulders and put her head down. One of them seemed to linger longer. She didn't dare look to see if it was her they were staring at. Eventually, it moved off and she sighed in relief, raising her eyes once again.

She couldn't go back home, that was obvious. Not tonight. Maybe tomorrow, once they had found Carol. Then, having seen this through, she could go to Detective Costigane, try to explain, and accept the consequences. She wasn't certain she had committed any crime, but she assumed tricking and running from a police detective was frowned upon at the least. She sighed. *You sure made my week interesting, neighbor.*

She remembered the names in the notebook. How many places had Carol lived? How many times had she left in the middle of the night? The notebook dated back long before the Ellison heist, probably long before Carol had met Freel. She had been running for years. Sarah shivered at that thought, though the night was warm. How had she coped? Sarah had felt like a fugitive for a matter of hours, ever since she had switched taxis a mile from the airport and the reality of her situation dawned on her. Years of this would be impossible to bear. What did that do to a person?

Easy, she realized. It would make them look for an escape route. Even one that meant risking your life.

She took a turn off the Strip and ventured down a side street; the contrast jarring. When the lights are this bright, it only means the shadows are deeper.

Fewer pedestrians here. The next neon she saw was a vacancy sign outside a dingy-looking hotel.

A huge, bald man in a sweat-stained white shirt was on the desk. He looked up as she entered. It wasn't the Bellagio.

"Evening."

"I'd like a room, please."

The bald man didn't change his expression. "Fifty."

Sarah reached automatically for her credit card, before remembering that wouldn't fly. She had used almost all of her cash on cab fares and dinner. The bald man was waiting expectantly.

"I forgot my purse, but perhaps I could leave something as collateral? I can pay you back tomorrow."

His eyes moved to the Cartier watch on her wrist. She hesitated. The only other thing of value she had was her cell phone, and she couldn't risk that being switched on. She sighed, slipped the watch off, and slid it across the desk, knowing it was the last time she would see it. *Time flies*, no use wasting any of it on regret.

The bald guy took it, looking like he couldn't believe his luck. He picked up a pen and held it poised over the registration book.

"Name?"

"Lara Croft," she said coldly.

"Whatever you say, ma'am."

56

Wilston Street, the address of Freel's contact, was deserted when I got to it just after eight o'clock in the morning. It would be hours before Carol showed up, if she was going to. I parked a few blocks away and got out, pacing up and down to work some of the aches out of my limbs. I spent a minute doing that and breathing fresh air, and then I checked my phone again. No new messages. I tried Sarah first, because she hadn't called since she had landed. Her phone appeared to be switched off. I could call her back later, after I tried some of the other numbers on the list I had made.

The news that Carol had dumped the Chrysler in Flagstaff had been promising, because it indicated her direction of travel was north, as we had guessed. As I had told Sarah, I thought it was unlikely that Carol would stick around in Flagstaff after getting rid of Gage's car—she would want to keep the noon rendezvous in Vegas. Either way, if my initial hunch didn't pan out, I could start calling hotels within reach of the location the car had been found. They wouldn't give out personal information about a guest at the drop of a hat, of course, but there are always ways around that.

Pawnbrokers first, because, as I'd pointed out to Sarah, buying a car or a bus ticket with a diamond tends to attract attention. Carol's purse was back at the house in Quarter, so she had whatever change was in her pockets and the diamonds. She was in a hurry, and people in a hurry are more predictable. There were four pawn shops in Flagstaff, three of which were open to midnight. I struck out on the first two. The third picked up on the first ring.

"Dunlop's, how may I help you?"

I launched into my story, which I had honed carefully over the previous two calls.

"Hi, I wonder if you can help me," I began. "My name's Thomas, Roy Thomas."

"Okay ..." a little wariness in the voice. The same tone that had greeted this opener the first two times. I guess when you're in this line of work, you start to become a little wary of requests for help.

"This is, uh ..." I hesitated. Just long enough to sell it, not long enough for him to interject. "This is a little embarrassing. I just found out that my wife may have hocked some of her jewelry."

"Okay." The wariness was gone now. The guy on the other end of the phone already had a good idea of where this was going, and that it was nothing to worry about. Just a standard business transaction. But, out of good manners, he let me tell it my own way.

"I got laid off last month," I said, injecting just the right note of embarrassment into my voice. "She was worried about money I guess, I mean we both were, and she thought this would help with the bills."

"Sure."

"Anyway, the good news is I got a new job yesterday, and things are looking up."

"Well that's good to hear."

"Thank you. So, as you'll have guessed already, I'm trying to track it down so I can buy it back."

"Not a problem, as long as this was in the last thirty days. What was your wife's—"

"That's the thing," I said. "She doesn't know that I know.

So I don't know which store she went to. She may even have used another name."

The guy made a sensitive noise, to show that he understood such a scenario was theoretically possible.

I told him that she would have come in last night, and started to describe her. I stopped myself just before I told him Carol had blonde hair, realizing that I was describing her as she had been six years ago. I had got about halfway through the description before he cut in.

"Sure, she was in last night."

"She was?"

"If it's the same lady, yes. She sold us a couple of diamonds, said they came from a pair of earrings ..." he tailed off as he consulted some kind of log. I didn't hear keys tapping, so maybe it was an old-fashioned ledger. When he spoke again I could tell from the tentative tone that he was about to quote me double the usual commission. "You're looking at four and a half grand, all in."

Which meant he hadn't paid Carol a dime over three and a half, I estimated. I thanked him for his help and told him I would try to drop by in the next couple of days.

"One last thing."

"Shoot."

"This is kind of a long shot but—you say she was in around eleven?"

"That'd be about right."

"You don't have any used car dealerships open that late around there, do you?" I had already checked. There weren't, but it never hurts to ask.

"Is this about the Civic?"

"The what?"

"She asked the same question as you, Mr. Thomas. And I told her no, and why did she ask? She said she needed a car quickly. I told her that was too bad, but Martin's opens at eight, and she ..."

"She asked if she could buy your car? A Honda Civic?"

"Oh, she told you about that?"

57

LAS VEGAS
FRIDAY, 10:21

The address Walter had given Gage was just within the Vegas city limits, on the boundary with the Strip. He had decided it was safer to hold on to the old man's battered pickup, on balance. His body wouldn't be found for a while, and stealing another car would likely draw more attention. He parked it a block away and approached on foot, keeping his eyes open for any surprises. For a second he wondered if he had taken down the street number wrong, because there wasn't a building there. Or at least, there wasn't yet.

It was a construction site: rising ten stories up from the street, a stack of concrete floors supported by visible steel beams. The site was closed off by wooden construction hoarding branded with the name of the company. Beck Concepts Ltd. When he saw the sentry at the entrance, he knew he had the right place. Sentry was the right word, not security guard. Instead of the hard hat and hi-vis jacket Gage would have expected, this guy was clad in a cheap gray suit with a noticeable bump under the left lapel. He was bald, a little overweight, and was staring straight at Gage from across the road.

He looked both ways, waited for a gap in the traffic, and crossed over. The sentry's gaze hardened at his approach.

"You Gage?"

"I'm here to see Walter. I hope he's on time."

The sentry glanced up at the structure above them, and then looked back at Gage.

"I'll take you up. They're waiting for you."

He turned and unlocked the door in the hoarding that surrounded the site. He walked in and held the door open for Gage, then led him to the stairwell, ignoring the service elevator. Gage followed as he walked briskly up the stairs, surprisingly nimble on his feet for a large man. There was another big guy in another cheap gray suit waiting for them on the sixth floor. Gage thought back to his first meeting with Walter, David and Grant in the bar a few days back. Grant's general look and demeanor had given him away as a cop immediately. Just as Grant had been unable to mask his background, neither could this pair. Only these two certainly weren't cops.

The second guy had more hair and was a lot thinner than his friend. Neither spoke. The one with hair took a step toward Gage, deliberately getting into his personal space. He reached into Gage's jacket and opened it, frisked the pockets, then got on one knee and patted down his legs. As his jacket stretched tight over his back, Gage could see he was armed too.

The guy got to his feet and straightened his tie. There had been nothing to find, because Gage had expected this welcome. The guard jerked his head to the left.

Gage stared him out for a second and then looked away. He walked in the indicated direction, following the corridor until it opened out onto the main floor. The space was unadorned apart from the support pillars; just a floor of rough concrete stretching out to where the building was wide open to the sky, waiting for plate-glass windows to be installed at some point in the future.

He heard his name being called and turned to see two figures on the opposite side of the floor, at the edge of the drop on the opposite side. Walter and David were waiting there. As he approached he saw that this side overlooked a space in the core of the building. The six-story drop bottomed out in a pit that would be a courtyard when the building was finished. The courtyard was obscured from outside by the bulk of the building. Nothing that went on up here would be seen by anyone passing by. Heavy industrial noises drifted up from below: the scream of angle grinders and the churn of cement mixers. He could see why they had chosen this spot for the meeting.

Walter and David were wearing matching "this better be good" expressions. Gage wondered if they'd practiced those while they were waiting. It was cute.

Gage walked past them and right up to the edge of the drop. Six stories, straight down. "Nice place, this yours, David?"

He saw David's sneer out of the corner of his eye. At least he was smart enough to know when he was being condescended to.

"Mine," Walter said. "One of my projects."

"A man of many projects," Gage said, turning to face them at last. "Where's Grant?"

Walter ignored the question and countered with one of his own. "What did you mean, about Freel's wife?"

Gage stepped back from the edge and looked at them. "Why didn't you tell me about the Ellison diamonds?"

David turned his eyes to Walter and started to open his mouth. Walter silenced him with a motion of his hand. He stared at Gage for a moment, as though carefully considering what he was going to say next.

"What do you know about that?"

"What do I know about it? I know it's the reason you really wanted Freel. So I'll ask again, why didn't you give me the whole story?"

He exchanged a glance with David. "It wasn't relevant."

"Wasn't relevant? Maybe if you had found it relevant, he would still be alive and I wouldn't have almost gotten killed."

There had been zero chance of that, of course, but they didn't need to know that.

"We told you to back off."

"But I didn't. So here we are. Why did you do that, by the way? It didn't seem to make a whole lot of sense, after hiring me to do the job."

Walter sighed, as though he saw no reason to waste time arguing about it. "So what's your proposal? You know about the diamonds, which means either Freel told you about them, or his wife did. They tell you where they hid them?"

Gage stared at him for a long moment. "My price went up. I want what we agreed, plus another two hundred grand."

"Your price went up?" David repeated, speaking for the first time. His voice was straining to contain his incredulity. "You fucked up. We're not paying you a cent."

Walter nodded agreement. "He's right. That's outrageous. And we already told you we don't need you."

Gage shook his head sadly, as though he was disappointed they had chosen to waste more time. "Except that I'm here, talking to you. Which means something changed and you do need me. I'm guessing the thing that changed is Freel's pulse rate. You thought you had him, now you don't. You can bore me with the story behind that, or we can talk about our new arrangement."

Walter considered this for a second. "Okay, you're correct. We want Freel's wife. If you can help us find her, we'll keep our end of the original deal."

Gage took a step back and looked down at the courtyard again. Six floors, straight down. No guardrail, no scaffolding. Nothing between them and the ground but fresh air.

"Like I said: you didn't give me the full picture, so that deal is null and void. I think my new terms are more than reasonable."

They were, in fact, more reasonable than Gage had any intention of being. As soon as he found Carol and the diamonds, the last thing he would be doing would be handing them over to these guys. He stepped away from the edge and looked Walter in the eye.

"You have nothing to lose. Freel's gone, and one way or another, his wife won't be far behind him. I'm your last chance to keep anything from the Ellison job. If I don't find her, we'll call it even. But if I do—and I will—I want to be compensated."

Gage thought he caught the mildest twitch at the edge of Walter's mouth. As though he were about to smile, and then stopped himself. He glanced at David, whose eyebrows were bunched together, his lips pursed.

"What would you need?" Walter asked, his voice the model of reasonableness once more.

"I think they were waiting until things had cooled off, then they were going to cash in. There can't be that many people out here who could move that kind of merchandise. I figured you would know who was on that list of names. I'll do the rest."

Walter took a moment to think it over. In the corner of Gage's eye, he saw a smug look cross David's face, as though there was an inside joke.

"That makes sense," Walter agreed.

He took a pen and a small notebook out from his jacket. He scribbled a list of names down and tore the sheet off, extending his hand to offer it to Gage. Gage could see from where he was that it was a short list. And he was pretty sure the name he needed wasn't on it.

From the moment he had stepped onto the sixth floor, he had made sure to keep one eye on the demeanor of the two flunkies while his conversation with their boss unfolded. As soon as he had begun talking to Walter, they had taken a step back. Don't mind us, pretend we're not here. They had stuck close together, which was good. For Gage, not for them.

He reached out and took the list from Walter's outstretched hand. At that moment, he sensed a change in the atmosphere on the floor. Out of the corner of his eye, he saw the thin one with hair move his shoulders a little, as though to adjust the position of his jacket over the gun.

When Walter finally gave his signal, Gage was way ahead of him.

"Thank you for coming in," Walter said. "This has been a big help." Then he looked beyond Gage, at the two men, and nodded.

Gage spun around and saw the thin one was already reaching his right hand inside his jacket. The fat boy was a little slower on the uptake. His hand was just beginning to move in the direction of his jacket and the gun beneath.

Gage grabbed the thin one's wrist as he tried to pull the gun free, pinning his hand beneath his jacket. He couldn't get his hand free to defend himself without letting go of the gun. As he was running through this dilemma in his head while recovering from his surprise at Gage's reaction speed, Gage took both options off the table and smashed his forehead into his nose, hard.

The guy yelped and staggered backwards, blood spilling from his nose. Gage let go of his wrist and grabbed the handle of his gun instead, feeling the familiar contours of a .45 in his hand. His thumb moved to the safety as he pulled it free from the holster, and found it was off already. Unless this guy was a real idiot, he had most likely left the chamber empty. Two trigger pulls to get off the first shot. Faster than fiddling with the safety.

While these thoughts were crossing his mind, he was turning to the second guy: the heavier, balder one in the set. Already slower than his comrade on the uptake, he had hesitated a fatal second to watch as Gage downed his colleague. Gage saw the realization that this mistake was about to cost him his life as he scrambled to pull his own gun out. Gage leveled the gun and pulled the trigger twice in rapid succession. A click, followed immediately by an explosion. A red circle appeared in the fat boy's forehead and he toppled backwards, the gun falling from his dead grip. Gage swung the gun around, expecting an attack from the first guy, but he was still on the floor.

Gage turned and saw that Walter and David were still reacting. Walter froze and then slowly began to raise his hands. David hesitated, and his right hand moved toward his own jacket. Gage brought the gun over to cover him and shook his head.

"I wouldn't."

David hesitated again, and then dropped his hands. His face displayed a mixture of shock, anger, and fear.

Gage shot him twice in the chest. David's mouth opened and he took a step back, then pitched backwards off the edge. A heavy thud followed a second or two later.

Walter flinched at the sound and spoke quietly, his voice barely carrying over the industrial sounds. "Don't kill me."

Gage paused and looked around at his handiwork in the last twenty seconds. The thin flunkey on the ground, clutching his broken nose and trying to get to his feet. The fat one, face down dead on the concrete. David in a broken heap six floors below.

Gage put two bullets in the thin man's head.

"No promises," he said quietly as he approached Walter.

Walter seemed to come to a realization that it was fight or flight. Denied of the latter, he launched himself at Gage. Gage had plenty of time to fire again, but instead, stepped forward and batted Walter's arms away with ease. He dropped his gun and gripped Walter's lapel, moving the older man closer toward the edge of the drop.

"Why did you call me off?"

"Don't kill me!"

"I didn't come all the way up here for the aerobic exercise. Tell me why you called me off."

Gage jerked him backwards toward the drop but held on. Walter started talking quickly.

"We got to the guy they were going to sell to weeks ago. It's why they ran from the house in Summerlin. They didn't have a buyer, and we think they were just going to wait it out. But after you got to McKinney, Freel must have realized what happened. He got spooked, he contacted a fence named Kailani, here in Vegas. Only Freel was careless. He didn't know Kailani does some work for me. Kailani asked me what to do, I told him to set up a meeting. We didn't need you anymore, after all this, the dumb son-of-a-bitch was going to come straight to us."

Gage searched Walter's eyes. He was telling the truth now. He lowered his voice to a menacing whisper.

"Look down."

Walter hesitated, looked down at the void. Nobody to see them, nobody to overhear his screams. Exactly what he had had planned for Gage. He looked back at Gage, his eyes pleading.

"Now," Gage said. "Tell me the address."

58

LAS VEGAS
FRIDAY, 10:45

With nothing better to do for the moment, I bought coffee and a couple of donuts: enough caffeine and sugar to keep me awake for a while. I spent some time cruising the streets on the south side of the city, looking for Honda Civics. As morning rush hour built, the task became impossible, so I parked up again and looked at the blank screen of my phone. I hadn't heard anything from Sarah at all, and I was worried now. I knew she would have been tired, but there was a little over an hour left before the rendezvous time, and there hadn't been so much as a text. Perhaps she had decided things had gotten a little too crazy, and gone back home to forget any of this ever happened. I wouldn't have blamed her, but I didn't believe that theory in a million years.

When my phone finally did ring at ten forty-five, I grabbed it and checked the screen, hoping to see Sarah's cell number. But it was a landline. A Las Vegas area code.

The caller was male. He asked for me by one of the names I had used when calling hotels earlier.

"This is Matt at the Howard Johnson over on Tropicana?"

My disappointment that the call was not from Sarah turned to cautious optimism.

After I had extracted the color and license plate of the pawnshop clerk's Honda Civic from him, I had called around some of the hotels on the east side of Vegas, figuring Carol would need somewhere to lay low until the meet. There are about a billion hotel rooms in Las Vegas, of course, but I narrowed the search down to places that were cheap and unobtrusive. The direction of her approach meant it was only logical she would pick one on the east side, rather than going all the way across town. I had included a few hotels deeper into town but adjacent to freeway exits, just because I had the time. It was a long shot, but as much as anything else it had been a way to occupy my mind as I waited and worried about Carol, and now Sarah.

I used the same line every time: saying my wife had checked in somewhere in that area, had lost her phone, and she had forgotten to tell me the address of the hotel. She was driving a green Honda Civic, and I knew the license plate.

The polite, well-spoken voice on the other end continued. "It was just to let you know that you were right, this is where your wife checked in."

I felt a jolt and grinned. Sometimes long shots pay off. If I could get to Carol before she tried to meet with the fence, it would make things easier. I asked Matt for the full address.

"One more thing," I said as he was about to hang up. "Would you mind not mentioning my call to my wife? I'm going to surprise her."

There was a pause. "Oh, I'm afraid we already contacted your wife."

I winced. "You did?"

"That's right, I called her just before I called you, just to make sure . . ."

Just to make sure you were legit, was what I assumed he was too polite to say out loud.

I started making calculations. From my memory of looking up the numbers, that hotel was in the southwest corner of the map, close to an exit off the 15. It would take me at least ten or twenty minutes to get there. Carol would be long gone by then. I started the engine and swung out into the traffic. I kept my voice steady.

"Has she gone yet?"

The desk guy's voice sounded puzzled. "No, sir, she says she'll see you when you get here. Room 27."

I didn't say anything.

"Sir?"

"That's great, thank you, Matt."

I hung up. When I stopped at the next set of lights, I called Sarah. I got voicemail again, just like the last dozen times. Where the hell was she?

59

LAS VEGAS
FRIDAY, 11:12

Sarah had waited in her room until checkout, and, with no money for a cab fare, had risked walking to Wilston Street. She was early, but as she approached the building where "FDC" was based, she kept her eyes peeled for Carol.

One-twenty-two Wilston was a mid-twentieth-century four-story building tucked between two smaller, more modern structures. She approached it on the opposite sidewalk, slowing down and regarding the exterior from behind her sunglasses. FDC's office was on the third floor, going by the number. She scanned the floor, trying to work out which one it was. On the left side of the building as she looked at it, there were two separate businesses, going by the signs. One was a print shop, announced by colorful window decals. The next was a tailor, more measured in its publicity with a neat logo on half-shut roller blinds. The two pairs of windows on the right side were unadorned. It would be one of those.

She paused under the shade of an awning and took her phone out, wondering if she could risk turning it on to call Blake. No. Before she could even make the call, it would light up her location for Costigane like one of the neon signs this city was so famous for. She lifted her eyes from her phone and looked back across the road at the building. The four windows on the right side of the third floor. There was no sign of life. The meeting place was up there, tantalizingly close. She looked at her watch. If Carol was going to keep the meeting, she would be here within the hour.

Sarah juggled the phone in her hand. Looked up and down the street. Came to a decision.

"Hell with it," she said out loud.

The building's air conditioning was either broken or very inefficient. It was hotter inside than out. A radio was on in one of the units on the first floor, playing pop music with an insistent Latin beat. The music faded as Sarah ascended to the second floor landing. A man in a suit emerged from the door on the right, looked her over, and hurried past. She wondered if he worked here, or was a customer. She knew buildings like this were good bases for people in illicit lines of work. Lots of people coming and going; mixture of long-established businesses and flash-in-the-pan outfits. Nobody paid anybody else much attention.

The third floor landing had the same layout. Two doors opposite one another and a window. This one was open. This side of the building was in shade, and she lingered by the window to take in some fresh air.

The door on the left had signs for the print shop and the tailor; the one on the right had two stickers: one, which looked old and yellowed, was for a milliner; the second simply had "FDC Partners." Nice and anonymous. Not a laundromat or a restaurant or anything that would give the authorities reason to launch a fishing expedition if they were so inclined. Just some partners. Probably finance-related. Quite boring, really. Nothing to see here.

Sarah knocked twice and waited.

She heard movement from within and an old man appeared at the door. He was in his sixties, of Asian or Polynesian appearance, maybe one of the many Hawaiians who had settled in this town. He wore chinos and a mustard-colored shirt that had damp patches under the armpits. He looked at Sarah's face, and then widened his focus to regard the rest of her. She could tell he was looking for something she didn't have: she guessed a big bag of diamonds. His face gave nothing away, but Sarah noted that he had a hand on the door to stop it swinging fully open.

"Can I help you?"

"I'm a friend of Dominic's."

The old guy just stared back at her for a moment, and Sarah started to wonder if she had made a mistake, gotten the wrong place. But the name was on the door, the same as the email. And then she saw something in his eyes that made her realize she hadn't knocked on the wrong door. But nevertheless, she had made a mistake.

Her mouth was open, about to say something when it hit her. There was a reason the old man was holding the door that way, and it was beyond a desire to be security conscious. He blinked at her, trying to signal something.

"My mistake," Carol said, hearing the off-guard phoniness in her own voice. "I was looking for the ..."

All of a sudden her mind had gone blank. She was wracking her brains for what she was looking for when the old man shuddered and then his eyes rolled upwards. He disappeared inside the room as though there was a rope attached to his back. The imposing figure of Trenton Gage replaced him in the doorway.

Sarah turned and ran for the stairs. She was too late. She felt fingers as strong as steel cable grip her upper arm and pull her roughly backwards. She staggered back and collided with the wall. Gage was on her in a second, his arm under her throat, a bloody knife an inch from her neck. Out of the corner of her eye she saw the old man lying face down on the floor, blood seeping from the wound in his back.

Gage's cold gray eyes regarded her. She saw recognition in them and knew that he remembered her from the house. From two floors down, she heard the muffled beat of the pop song on the radio, and wondered if anyone would hear her if she screamed as he killed her.

"Not who I was expecting," he said at last. "But you'll do."

60

The Howard Johnson on East Tropicana Avenue was a two-story building with a wide parking lot out front bordered by tall palms. It didn't take me long to find the car. At the back of the lot, hunching between two larger vehicles, was the green Honda Civic formerly owned by the Flagstaff pawn-shop clerk. I parked in an empty space a couple down from the Civic and cut the engine.

I hesitated a second before I got out of the car. Unless she had changed her mind, Carol was inside that building. It couldn't be anyone else, could it? I looked up at the row of anonymous windows on the top floor.

In reception, there was a young Asian guy in a dark green shirt behind the desk. Matt, I presumed. He gave me an appraising look.

"Can I help you, sir?"

"We spoke over the phone a few minutes ago. My friend is checked in here. Room 27, I think."

He smiled in recognition. "Of course, sir. She's waiting for you." He leaned over the desk to indicate the way. "Take the stairs, turn right at the top."

I thanked him and followed his directions up the single flight of stairs. At the top was a long carpeted corridor interspersed by numbered doors. I counted along the doors. I knocked lightly on 27 and then, when I didn't get an answer, I tried the handle. It swung open.

The room was small and unremarkable: exactly what you would expect from a budget hotel. Queen bed, minibar, vertical blinds on the window.

She was sitting in a faux-leather armchair by the window.

She had obviously had time to buy clothes and freshen up since Corinth. She wore a sky-blue summer dress with white sandals. A pair of sunglasses was perched above her forehead, pushing her red hair back. Her blue eyes were fixed on mine.

"What kept you?"

"I'm fine, thank you," I said.

"'Blake.' That's the name you're going with now, huh?"

"For a while now," I said. "Carter Blake."

Carol continued to stare at me, and then looked away. "I figured you would be all right. After all, I thought you were dead before. But that just doesn't seem to be something you do."

"Stop. I'm getting all choked up here."

"I told you I didn't need your help."

"I know about the Ellison job. You're in over your head."

"In fact I told you more than that. I told you to stay the hell away from me."

I said nothing. Thanks to the ever-helpful Matt on the desk, Carol had had at least twenty minutes' notice that I was on my way. She could have been miles away by now. But she wasn't.

"You're wondering why I let you find me this time, right?"

"It crossed my mind."

She stood up and reached down on the far side of the bed, she lifted a small backpack onto the bed. She unzipped it and took out a black case about the size and width of a phone book, and opened it on its hinges. Two million dollars twinkled out at me from within. I glanced at it and then back at her.

"Is that why you're here?" she snapped. "You want your cut?"

I shook my head in frustration. "What happened to you?"

"What happened to me? *You* happened to me. You."

"I never got a chance to talk to you. To explain everything."

She shook her head and started to smile, as though I had cracked a joke. The look in her eyes showed anything but amusement. She closed the case and put it back into the backpack, ready to take with her to her rendezvous on Wilston Street.

"You want to know what happened to me? I had to learn how to survive. Do you know what it was like? Running all the time, trying to find the cheapest motel in every new town. Working shitty jobs for tips. Hitching rides with God-knows-who. Looking over my shoulder every day wondering if today was the day someone was going to find me."

She stopped to take a breath and looked out of the window.

"I didn't even know who I was running from. I knew who had gotten me into it ..." she snorted. "Actually that's not even true. I didn't know you. I never knew you, 'Blake.'"

I tried not to let the wince show on the outside. I stepped away from the door and sat down on the bed. Carol paused for a second and then lifted the strap of the backpack over her shoulder and walked past me to the door.

"I never thought any of that would happen," I said.

"I had to leave everybody behind. And the worst thing? The worst thing was that no matter how much I hated you, I actually *missed* you. I thought about you for months. Even though you destroyed my life, even though for all I knew you killed the senator yourself, I couldn't stop thinking about you. I thought we had something, and you just ..."

"We did," I said. "And I never stopped thinking about you."

She stopped, her right hand on the door handle. She didn't turn around. Waited for me to continue.

"Carlson came to me. He wanted to blow the lid on Winterlong, but he needed proof. Proof I could get him."

I waited for her to turn the handle and walk out of the door again. She didn't move. And then she relaxed her grip on the handle, still not turning to face me.

"You know about Winterlong," I continued. "I read the notebook, I know you put two and two together. I wondered if you would, last year. If you were still out there, if you would hear about it and know it was over."

"It's never over," she said softly.

I thought about how I could tell her everything now that I couldn't say back then. About the job, about Senator Carlson, about Afghanistan. I thought about telling her what I had done since then, where I had been, who I had become. But it wouldn't make a damn bit of difference. Because she was right. What's done is done. But it's never over.

"Carol, I'm sorry."

She turned back to face me finally. She made no move to drop the bag. Her eyes were a little red, but she wasn't crying.

"Dom was a little like you, you know that? I didn't see it at first, otherwise I would have run a mile. He seemed normal, down to earth. It was an act. A good one. By the time I found out what he was really like, about his past, it was too late. And I thought, what the hell? I spent the last few years surviving, I'm good at it. Why not?"

I turned away from her and moved to the window, looking out at the cars passing on the street below. Without thinking too much about it, I realized I had assumed Carol's marriage was fake; somehow part of the setup. Now I knew it had been real, at least to begin with, I wasn't sure how I felt.

I cleared my throat. "How did he get involved with the Ellison job?"

She sighed. "He was just a hire. Somebody else planned everything out and needed personnel."

"Who?"

"I don't know, I never met him. The offer came through one of Dom's friends. A guy named McKinney he did time with. I knew Dom well enough to know something was going on, and I made him tell me everything. He and McKinney, drove out to meet this guy in a big house down in Clark County. Dom said the place was empty, like it was between owners. There was another guy there too: that was Deakins. A minute after they arrived a car pulled up outside and two men came into the house. The man in charge said his name was Walter, and that he specialized in this kind of thing. Putting together the plan and getting somebody else to run it ... like a franchise, he said. Dom thought it sounded like a great idea. It didn't take me long to work out something wasn't right."

"Like what?" I prompted, then added, "Apart from the obvious."

She shrugged. "It sounded too good to be true. Dom had a lot of good points, but he was no master criminal. He was small-time, they all were. McKinney and Deakins too."

"So why were they chosen?"

"That's exactly why they were chosen. They were supposed to be the fall guys. A job like that, they pull out all the stops to find the perpetrators. Their job wasn't just to do the dirty work, it was to get caught afterwards."

I thought back to what I had read about the case. The shootout in Boulder City a few days after the heist. An anonymous tip-off. "They were being set up," I said.

She nodded. "But to do that, I knew that they had to make sure the job went through all right first. And the plan itself was solid. We talked about it. At first I wanted to bail, get the hell out of there and let them find some other idiots to take the fall ... but it was a good plan. And we were talking millions. Between us, we came up with a plan."

"A heist on the heist."

"You could say that. We talked to Dom's friend McKinney, too. We made an agreement. We made an agreement. They knew what they were doing on the job itself, I worked out what we would do afterwards. Logistics."

I couldn't help but smile. That had always been one of her talents. I could put together the rest of it myself. The three of them made sure the diamonds were spirited away before the bust. An arrangement to hide the take until the heat was off: one safe, two keys, a secure remote location hundreds of miles away where no one would think to look. And then it was just a waiting game. Lying low, hiding from their pursuers in plain sight. It had all gone perfectly until ...

"Why did you leave Summerlin?"

"Our original buyer disappeared on us. We don't know exactly what happened to him, but, well, you can guess."

"You think the men who hired Freel got to him."

"We didn't know what to do after that. We talked to McKinney and the three of us decided we had to find a way to cash in. It was only a matter of time before they found us, too."

She was right. It had taken them a while, but they had found the house. I didn't know how all of the pieces fit together yet, but it had set in motion a train of events that left Freel dead, and Carol and me in this hotel room. And out there, somewhere, Trenton Gage. I didn't know what kind of man this "Walter" was, but his employee gave me concern enough. Perhaps it wasn't too late, though.

"You don't need to run anymore."

"You're right," Carol said. "I'm sick of running, sick of

surviving. After today, I'll never need to run again. You remember what you told me once? Names are like hotel rooms. I'm checking out of Carol, I can leave all of this behind."

"Not like this. If you walk out of that door, sooner or later you're going to find yourself with your back to the wall, staring down the barrel of a gun. Or you can forget about this, leave those diamonds in this room and get out of here with a real chance at a new start."

She shook her head. "You wanted to know why I waited for you? To say goodbye. I figured maybe it would take if I gave you the message in person this time."

I had nothing left to say. Carol turned the door handle, and at the same second, my phone buzzed for an incoming call. I looked down at the screen.

"Who is it?" Carol asked, holding the door half-open.

"It's Sarah."

61

But it wasn't Sarah calling. It was Gage.

"We can't keep meeting like this, Blake."

I swallowed and tried to keep the anger I was feeling out of my voice. "Put Sarah on the line."

"Why not? If it'll make things go faster."

A pause as the phone was moved from his ear and then I heard Sarah's voice.

"I'm sorry, Blake."

"Don't be," I said calmly. "Did he hurt you?"

"I'm okay. I went to Wilston Street and he had already ... the fence is dead."

"This is going to be fine. Put Gage back on the line."

Gage wasted no time on pleasantries. "You know what I want, and I know you can find her."

My eyes darted to Carol, still standing in the doorway. "I don't know where she is. Even if I did, I'm not giving you Carol."

Carol's expression had been puzzled, but now her mouth dropped open as she began to realize what had happened.

"That's a pity," Gage said. "For your friend here, I mean."

"I wasn't finished. You're right, I can find her, and I can get you the diamonds. But I need a guarantee Sarah won't be harmed." I watched Carol as I spoke. She didn't move, didn't react to what I had said at all.

"You're not in a position to be demanding guarantees, my friend." He thought it over. "Okay, I'm not an unreasonable guy. If you can get the diamonds, we can all live with that. You want her to come out of this okay, the best thing you can do is make sure I have what I want by two o'clock."

My watch said eleven thirty-two. "That's not enough time."

"You're being modest," Gage said dismissively. "It's plenty. Your friend here says you're good at finding people, and from what I've seen so far, as one professional to another, I'm impressed."

He wasn't so bad himself, I thought, but there was no way in hell I was going to tell him that.

"I'll call this number again in a couple of hours and give you the location," he continued. "If I don't see you, unarmed, with the diamonds at two o'clock, I'll kill Ms. Blackwell here and review my options. Two sharp. I take timekeeping very seriously."

I believed him. There didn't seem to be anything else to say.

"Blake, are you still there?"

"No," I said. "I'm too busy finding your goddamn diamonds."

He laughed out loud. "That's the spirit. I'll talk to you in two hours. Make sure you answer, otherwise ..."

I hung up on him, feeling the smallest scintilla of satisfaction in the minor act of rebellion. It would be the last one I would get: Gage was running the show now.

Carol looked down at the bag, and then looked at me.

"He has Sarah," she said. A statement, not a question. There was nothing I could tell her that she hadn't gotten from hearing my side of the conversation.

I nodded.

"I guess we don't have much of a choice, do we?"

"We don't."

"Can we trust him? To let Sarah go, I mean?"

"Maybe, maybe not. But I do know that we can trust him to kill her if he doesn't get what he wants. As to whether he'll play nice if we give him what he wants? I hope that he'll take the line of least resistance. No reason for him to make things messier than they have to be."

Carol looked down at the bag containing the diamonds and shook her head. For a split second I wondered if she was thinking about refusing to go along with the trade. The sheer frustration in her next word told me she hadn't changed that much.

"*Fuck.*" She let out a long sigh.

Two million dollars. Even with the hefty commission the fence would take, it was certainly enough for the new start she needed. I couldn't help but sympathize a little. I almost wanted to say sorry.

"You're putting a lot of faith in him acting reasonably," she said after a minute.

"That's where you're wrong," I said. "I try not to put faith in anything, without good reason."

"How could I forget. Okay, Blake. What's the plan?"

62

Gage smiled as the phone went dead and looked across at Sarah Blackwell. She was sitting in a chair in the corner of the room, her hands cuffed together in her lap. He would have to be careful when getting her out of here. And that had to be his next move. If Sarah knew about this place, then Blake knew about it too.

"Good news," he said. "Blake is cooperating."

Sarah's expression didn't change. "How do you know he can find Carol? What makes you think she'll give him the diamonds?"

Gage glanced down at the old man's body on the floor. "If he can't, I guess we'll have to think of something else to try. Let's just hope your old neighbor liked you."

Her brow furrowed as he switched her phone off and dropped it to the ground. As he lifted his foot up to stamp down on it, she called out.

"Wait!"

He paused, mid-stamp, and left the heel hovering over the screen. He cocked a questioning eyebrow at her.

"Won't you need it? So Blake can get back in touch, I mean."

"That's a good point," he said. Then he brought his heel down hard, splintering the screen and smashing the inner workings of the phone against the tiled floor. "But no."

Gage had high hopes that Blake would find Carol, if he hadn't already. He was confident of it. Now he needed a location. Somewhere quiet and private. Somewhere with more than one exit.

He turned and walked over to the window. He looked out at the city. It wasn't late enough in the day for it to actually look like itself. Vegas was like an empty theatre, still hours from showtime. The city sprawled before him, all of those thousands of miles of neon tubing waiting patiently for the sun to dip below the hills.

And just like that, it came to him. He had the perfect place to meet Blake.

There was an old sweater hanging over the back of the swivel chair at the desk. He picked it up and tossed it to Sarah. "Cover your hands, we're going outside."

Sarah stood up carefully and made an effort at concealing her bound hands beneath the sweater. Whether because the task was difficult or because she wasn't motivated to obey, the sweater kept slipping off. He picked it up from the floor and wrapped it around her hands. As he stepped back from her, her eyes found the old man's corpse on the floor again. He had noticed she had avoided looking at it before. Her eyes rolled in her head and she staggered on her feet, pitching forward. Gage caught her and pushed her gently back down in the chair. He slapped her lightly across the cheek.

"No time for a snooze, let's go."

Sarah opened her eyes and took a deep breath. She got to her feet again, avoiding looking at the corpse, and leaned on him as they walked toward the door. He was glad he hadn't parked too far from the building.

63

Sarah thought her faint had been reasonably convincing, all things considered. To tell the truth, between the heat and the second dead body she'd seen in as many days, it hadn't required a lot of acting talent. The aim was simple: to waste a little more time. She kept playing woozy, dragged her feet as Gage escorted her back down to the sidewalk, but whenever she got too slow he would grip her arm tighter and force her to up the pace. In all, she probably managed to delay an extra couple of minutes.

The whole way down she was listening for sirens, hoping against hope that she had managed to buy enough time. Gage had used her phone as a way of letting Blake know he really had her. What he couldn't know was that Detective Costigane had already tracked her location once using that phone, and that he would no doubt be informed when it was switched on again. Sarah was reasonably well versed in cell technology from her days at the *Tribune*, but her knowledge was a couple of years out of date. She knew a phone would check in with the nearest cell tower as soon as it was switched on, whether a call was made or not. She just had to hope that Costigane's people were on the ball. In barely an hour, she had gone from obsessively hoping the police wouldn't find her, to praying they would. She knew it was an incredibly slim chance. It had been ten minutes or so since Gage had made the call—could that possibly be enough time?

They emerged onto the heat of the sidewalk. Still no sirens. Gage steered her toward a beat-up pickup truck parked at the side of the road.

"Don't do anything stupid," he said under his breath. He

didn't have to worry. The few pedestrians nearby barely glanced at them as they walked straight ahead, focused on their own business. Gage opened the passenger side and told Sarah to get in. She hesitated, scanning the street. She saw no police cars, heard no distant sirens. Goddamn it. She had been banking on him taking the phone with him.

Gage grew impatient and put one hand on her shoulder, the other on her head, and pushed her inside, slamming the door. As he circled around to the driver's side, Sarah saw a gray sedan turn the corner at speed and then immediately slow down as it approached the building. She allowed herself to hope for a second. But then the car slowed further and stopped, fifty yards from where they were parked. Gage glanced in the direction of the car and then checked his mirror as he turned the key in the ignition. Sarah's heart sank. There had been just too little time. By the time Costigane made it here, all he would find would be a dead body and a destroyed cell phone.

Gage made a turn in the street and headed west. After he had made a couple of turns, he seemed to relax. He fiddled with the air conditioning, coaxing a weak stream of cool air from the vents.

"Don't worry," he said. "It's cooler where we're going."

64

With no idea of where we were going to end up, Carol and I decided that the best place to wait was somewhere that would give us the maximum number of options. We took both cars and drove three miles south from the hotel, parking in a vacant lot on Las Vegas Boulevard across from Town Square Park. Right by the cloverleaf where two major routes intersected: the 15 and the 215. Traffic permitting, this position gave us a lot of options.

Carol got out of the Civic and sat with me in my car while we waited. There were no awkward silences. The current situation gave us more than enough to keep us occupied. But neither of us talked about what had happened six years ago. The closest we came to that was when I handed Carol my gun and asked if she was confident to use it.

She turned the Beretta 92FS over in her hands, checked the load, made sure the chamber was clear, clicked the safety off and then on again. "I've learned a lot over the past few years. You'd be surprised."

I didn't doubt that, but said nothing in response.

"Why did she get herself into this?" Carol said after a minute.

"She was worried about you," I said. I had told her about Sarah's concerns when they had disappeared, and how they had crystallized when she saw the men breaking into their house later on. When I mentioned that the note had made her curious from the beginning, Carol rolled her eyes.

"That was Dom. He told me about it later. He knew we were friendly and thought leaving the note meant Sarah wouldn't worry."

"Bad idea. It just made her more curious."

"Yeah, well he was full of bad ideas. I seem to be able to pick 'em, huh?"

Gage kept us waiting a little longer than he had promised. As the minutes counted down, I kept the phone on the dashboard, resisting the urge to call Sarah. I knew it wouldn't do any good: he would have dumped her phone right after the call. The next call would come from a burner.

At one thirty-eight, I was proved correct. The screen of my phone lit up with a call from a private number. Carol and I exchanged a glance and I put it on speaker. Gage's voice filled the interior of the car. I listened for anything in the background that might give a clue to his whereabouts, but could hear nothing. I guessed wherever he was, it wasn't outside.

"I hope I'm not going to be disappointed," he said.

I glanced into the back seat to reassure myself the bag was still there.

"It's your lucky day, assuming you've kept your end of the deal."

"Don't worry about that, Blake. She's just fine."

"Let me speak to her."

"She's not with me right now, you're going to have to take my word for it."

"That's not good enough."

"It's going to have to be."

As he raised his voice, the quality of the sound changed slightly. Was that an echo? It sounded like he was in an enclosed space, like a concrete stairwell.

He kept talking. "Do you remember payphones, Blake?"

My confusion lasted a second before I realized what he was talking about. "Where?"

"They still have one at the 7-Eleven on Wyoming and Commerce. Can you get there in twenty minutes?"

"I'm not sure," I said. "I'm not from around here."

"Do your best."

The line went dead. Twenty minutes. And if we couldn't make it in that time? What then?

No use dwelling on it. I looked at Carol and repeated the address. She had the map of Vegas splayed on her lap and traced her finger to the coordinates. "Wyoming and Commerce ... It's all the way downtown."

"Can we make it?"

She looked doubtful. "It's going to be tight."

I didn't waste time debating it.

"Go. I'll follow."

Carol took the gun and got out. She jumped in the green Civic, turned the key in the ignition, and peeled out of the vacant lot. I pulled out into traffic behind her. We reached the cloverleaf and turned onto the 15, headed north. I was grateful the evening rush hadn't kicked in yet. As it was I almost lost her a couple of times as she weaved in and out of traffic. I kept glancing at the clock. Carol took exit 40 with five minutes left. We got delayed for almost a minute at an intersection as a big rig took its time negotiating the turn. The minute felt like a decade. Carol ignored the light turning to red and moved ahead. I followed to a chorus of horns from oncoming traffic. Two blocks later, she hit her hazard lights briefly, and then signaled left. I looked over at the left side of the road and saw the payphone at the 7-Eleven on the corner. Carol continued ahead without pausing, as we had arranged. I assumed Gage was going to send us from payphone to payphone. We had no idea how many links there would be in this daisy chain, and I didn't want to risk him spotting Carol.

I pulled in. My watch said less than a minute before the deadline. I hoped he hadn't jumped the gun. I watched the receiver, waiting for it to ring. And then my own phone rang again.

"Hello?"

"Not bad," Gage said.

"I thought you were calling on the payphone?"

He laughed. "Who uses payphones anymore?"

"I almost didn't make it," I said, hearing the anger in my voice and not caring. "You're going to have to give me more time for the next one."

"Easy there. Okay, the next stop is in Palm Springs ..."

For a second I contemplated whether he was joking. For another second I thought about my response, and decided on a robust one.

"Don't fuck me around, Gage, I've got what you want."

"All right. You have it with you, I take it? Is it in the trunk?"

"Back seat. In a backpack."

"Good. When you hang up, I want you to walk back to your car and take the pack out."

That caught me by surprise. I started to turn around slowly, watching the windows of the stores and the people on the sidewalks. I listened to the background noise again. He was on a cell phone, and this time it sounded like he was outside. I could hear traffic noise.

"Why do you want me to take it out here?"

"Don't play dumb, Blake. You know exactly why. Once you've taken the pack out, I want you to take your jacket off and put it in the car. Then I want you to pull your shirt up and turn around so I can see you're not hiding any surprises. Both legs, too."

"Okay," I said. "Then what?"

A horn sounded as a truck driver took issue with the bus in front of him stopping at a yellow. I heard the sound reproduced on Gage's end, from farther off. If he noticed, his voice gave nothing away.

"You're on foot from here on in. Keep your phone switched on."

The background noise on the other end disappeared as he terminated the call. I kept my phone in my hand. I was careful to carry out the next move without looking obvious. As I turned and walked back toward the car, I thumbed into recent calls, found Carol's number and hit loudspeaker, so I could talk to her without holding the phone to my ear. Wherever Gage was, he was close and he could see me.

She answered immediately. "What's happening?"

Moving my lips as little as possible, I talked as loud as I could without making it obvious I was speaking to someone. I hoped Gage didn't have a set of binoculars.

"He's around here," I said. "He's going to call me in a minute. Mute your phone, stay on the line and listen, okay?"

"Be careful," she said after a second's hesitation. The concern was genuine. I tried not to let myself be distracted by the fact that felt good.

I tucked the phone into my pocket, being careful not to cut the call off, then I unlocked the car, pulled the backpack out and dumped it on the sidewalk. I followed Gage's instructions to the letter, shrugging my jacket off and pulling my shirt out. I turned a slow three hundred and sixty degrees with my stomach and back exposed, earning a curious glance or two from passers-by. Then I knelt down and raised one pant leg, then the other, to demonstrate there was no backup piece strapped to my ankle. After that, I rose up again, dropped my hands and stood expectantly.

Ten seconds later, I heard the soft beep from my phone I had been waiting for. Not a ring, because the call with Carol was still in progress. A call waiting notification. I took the phone out and saw the incoming call from a withheld number. I tapped into conference call, putting both calls on the line.

"You're doing well, Blake. How hard was she to find?"

"I've had tougher jobs," I said.

"And did you have to get rough with her? I bet she didn't want to part with those stones easy. I have a bruise on my head the size of a watermelon to remind me of that."

"Let's just say she isn't too happy with either of us," I said.

"I bet she isn't."

"Let's get this over with."

Gage told me to turn around. I did as instructed. I was now facing the road. Pedestrians passed on the opposite side of this street, dallying beneath awnings where they could to take shelter from the sun. I glanced at the screen to confirm both calls were still live. I wondered where Carol was, hoping that she stayed out of Gage's field of vision.

"Okay," Gage's voice continued. "You see the Thai place on the other side of the road?"

I scanned the line of storefronts and quickly found the place he was talking about.

"Thai Kitchen?"

"That's the one. There's an alley right next to it."

"I see it."

"Use it."

I waited for a gap in the traffic and crossed the road, wishing I had a map or could use my phone to check out the path ahead. I knew Carol would look for an alternative route, rather than attracting attention to herself by passing through the bottleneck. When I reached the other side, I paused a second at the mouth of the alley. It was narrow, the buildings high on both sides. It looked like it widened out after sixty yards or so. Nowhere to run, once I was in that space.

I took a deep breath and walked forward.

65

Hope for the best, plan for the worst. I was hoping that my assessment of Gage was correct: a pragmatist who would hold up his end of the bargain. Not because he was a stand-up guy, but because he knew not doing so would be an unnecessary risk. He could either take precautions and make sure he walked away with the diamonds, or he could complicate the issue by harming Sarah or me and risking a reprisal. It was a simple cost / benefit equation. There would be no possibility of additional benefit in that scenario, and every possibility of additional cost.

A simple exchange. The diamonds for Sarah. Gage wouldn't care too much about the method by which I had relieved Carol of the diamonds, but he would assume she hadn't relinquished them willingly. It wouldn't occur to him that Carol was still in the equation.

I advanced down the alley, moving as slowly as I dared to give Carol time to go around the long way. Maybe I was wrong. Maybe Gage had what he thought was a foolproof way to kill me and take the diamonds.

"Talk to me, Blake."

He couldn't see me now. He was relying on me to tell him where I was in the alley.

"Still here," I said.

"Just keep going."

I slowed a little more as I reached the far end of the alley. As I advanced I could see it opened out into a vacant space between the buildings. There were a couple of cars parked and a line of storage units and the rear of what looked like some kind of warehouse. Was that where he was holding

Sarah? It would make sense. Inside, out of sight.

"Keep walking, straight ahead."

I hesitated, surveying the space between the alley and the buildings on the other side, wondering how I could let Carol know where I was headed.

"The warehouse?" I asked. "The one with the red roof?"

"I said keep walking."

There was an edge of irritation in his voice. I didn't want to do anything to risk tipping him off that we weren't the only two people on the line. I kept it simple and concentrated on putting one foot in front of the other. The empty lot was sheltered from the noise of the traffic. My footsteps on the rough concrete echoed off the buildings around.

I slowed as I reached the opposite side of the lot, gazing from side to side. Where was Carol? Between my hesitation at the end of the alley and the measured speed with which I had crossed the lot, she should have had enough time to circle the block and approach from the opposite direction.

"Stop right there," Gage said.

I said nothing, waiting for instruction like a rookie actor waiting for the director to give his orders. There were three units close to me, all with steel shutters rolled down and a door on one side.

"Walk to the far end, right-hand side."

Did that mean he was behind the door on the far right? I looked at the three identical units with their three identical steel shutters and their three identical blue doors, looking for a distinguishing feature that I could mention out loud for Carol's benefit. It was like one of those old game shows, which door held the prize? I walked to the end of the row. There was a ten-foot-high chain link fence bridging the gap between the factory and the next building. I examined the door. It was locked, but fresh paintwork and a new padlock told me this unit was in use.

"Climb the fence."

I looked away from the door and took a closer look at the chain link fence. On the other side of it was a stretch of cracked concrete, with some hardy weeds poking through. After that, there was what looked like some kind of drainage ditch, and then another fence and the road beyond.

Out of the corner of my eye I caught a flicker of movement. Being careful not to look directly at the corner of the lot, I turned my eyes to look. A slight movement in the shadows. Someone was there. Carol had found a way around.

"Blake ..."

"Climb the fence, got it," I said.

"Don't flake out on me now," he said.

I was carrying the backpack by one strap over my right shoulder. I took a second to loop the second strap over my other shoulder and grabbed the fence. I climbed up and over, grateful there was no barbed wire at the top.

I waited for instruction, and when there was none, walked to the edge of the drainage culvert. It was much deeper than it had looked from behind the fence: a sloped concrete incline that descended around ten feet. The channel emerged from beneath the warehouse on one side where there was a steel grill, and then went back underground about ten yards later, into a large open tunnel about ten feet by eight.

"Get some shade," Gage said.

I took a long look at the eight-by-ten entrance to the tunnel. Tunnels, to be exact. I knew this was part of Las Vegas's underground drainage system. I had read an article about it a couple of years back after the system flooded during a big storm. I didn't relish going down there in the dark. I comforted myself with the knowledge that Gage couldn't shoot me until he had confirmed I had the diamonds.

"Okay," I said out loud. To myself, as much as Carol. "Looks like I'm going down there."

"I don't need a running commentary, just get on with it."

I took a deep breath and stepped over the edge, running down the slope fast enough to stop myself from falling. I stepped across the shade line and felt the temperature drop immediately. It was still warm in here, just not as warm as it was outside. A deeper, more animal part of my brain told me it was the coldest I had been in more than a year.

The wide opening meant that there was enough light to see by for the time being. I stepped forward cautiously, blinking my eyes to adjust them to the dark. I stepped around an old refrigerator that somebody had dragged in and left ten feet from the entrance. I wondered how deep Gage would lead me into the labyrinth, and couldn't help but appreciate the ingenuity of his chosen drop point. Absolutely no way it could be surveilled, and tracking devices would be useless. But he had been talking to me the whole time, which meant he couldn't be...

As if in confirmation of that thought, from behind me I heard the crack of shoes landing on concrete from a height. I turned around. Trenton Gage was standing in the tunnel entrance. A perfectly black shape against the sunlight streaming into the gap. There was a gun in his right hand.

"Where is she?" I said.

The black silhouette moved as Gage pointed the gun lower, at the bag in my hands.

"You first."

I hesitated again. This was it. As soon as I opened the bag, he would know I had what he wanted. And then I would find out just how committed to the concept of a deal Trenton Gage really was.

66

"Let me speak to her now, or I walk right out of here."

My demand echoed softly against the walls of the tunnel. Gage took his time answering. "I don't believe you'll do that, Blake."

"We had a deal," I said, hoping Carol was on the way.

I couldn't see the look on his face against the sun, but I knew he was smiling.

He called out, his voice louder now. "Tell your friend he can relax, Sarah."

There was a pause, and then I heard a voice from deeper along the tunnel.

"Blake? Is it you?"

Reluctant to turn my back on a killer with a gun, I kept my eyes on Gage and called out.

"Are you okay? Where are you?"

"I'm fine. I don't think I'm too far in. There's a smaller tunnel on your left-hand side."

"Satisfied?" Gage asked.

"Not yet," I said. I raised my voice to address Sarah again. "Can you walk toward the sound of my voice?"

Gage seemed to consider it, before nodding. "Come on out, it's fine."

I heard nothing at first, and then the soft sound of footsteps, slowly getting louder. I didn't turn around. A moment later, I felt arms around my neck. I looked down and saw they were cuffed together. Gently I ducked under the hands and turned around to face Sarah. She looked okay, all things considered, just grateful to see somebody who wasn't Gage.

"Are you okay?"

"I'm fine. I'm so sorry. It was so stupid to go there alone, I just ..."

"It wasn't your fault. Besides," I said, turning back to Gage. "We're all done here, right?" I said.

Gage had advanced so he was just five yards from me. His gun didn't move. I knelt down. I unzipped the pack and took out the case. When I opened it on its hinges, the light from the tunnel mouth caught the pile of diamonds and cast stars on the walls of the tunnel like a disco ball. I placed the case on the ground gently, like I was leaving an offering at an altar.

Gage closed the rest of the distance. He kept the gun on me, and crouched down next to the case. He took a long look at the contents, then nodded approvingly.

"Pleasure doing business with you," he said. He put the case back into the pack and zipped it closed again. He paused before standing up. The gun didn't waver. "Just out of curiosity, what did you do with Carol?"

I didn't answer, because I was too distracted by a faint metallic scuffing noise. Like the sound a chain link fence makes when someone is scaling it, trying not to make too much noise. A second later, another silhouette appeared behind Gage. This figure had a gun in its hand, too.

Gage saw something in my eyes and reacted with the speed of a panther, turning around and training his gun on the new arrival. My first thought was it was Carol, and that she had decided to risk our lives to get the diamonds back.

When I realized the silhouette belonged to a man, I knew the trouble we were in was a whole lot deeper.

67

"Police, everybody drop their weapons."

Gage made no move to obey. I raised my hands to show I was unarmed. The man stepped inside the tunnel. The face was silhouetted, but the sunlight at his back picked out gray hair, the wide frame of a man about six feet tall wearing a sport coat. The body language certainly said cop.

"It's okay, Blake, I think it's Costigane." Sarah's voice was uncertain, but hopeful.

It took me a second to remember the name. Costigane as in *Detective* Costigane, as in the cop who had been looking for Freel. But how in the hell had he found us down here, at this exact moment?

"Gun down, now," he yelled, addressing Gage. Gage had a funny look on his face. His gun was still pointed at Detective Costigane, and he showed no inclination to lower it.

"How did you find me?" he asked.

"You," Costigane said, addressing me. "Kick the bag over here."

"There are no weapons in it," I said.

"He knows that," Gage said calmly. "He knows exactly what's in that bag."

Sarah spoke quickly, a tremor in her voice. "He tracked my phone to the airport. When Gage used it to call you, he must have ..."

If Costigane heard Sarah, he ignored her. "Gun down now, or I blow your fucking brains out. Three of us against one of you."

There was an edge to Costigane's voice. I knew what

he was doing: hinting that I should rush Gage to take his gun out of play. My mind was already calculating the risk, blocking out potential moves. But something held me back from acting; I was curious about what Gage had said.

"Costigane," Gage repeated, not moving an inch. "That's not the name you gave when you hired me."

"Shut your mouth and put down the gun," Costigane yelled.

"It's good to see you again, Grant. I missed you at Walter's little meeting."

I looked from Costigane to Gage. They knew each other? Everything was moving and changing a little too quickly for my liking.

"He's one of the guys who hired me to find Freel," Gage said quietly. "You help him and he'll put a bullet in your head next. He wants what's in the bag."

"Don't let him bluff you," Costigane said. "My name is Detective Ray Costigane. Ask your friend. I'm a police officer."

"And crooked as a pretzel. We have a deal, Blake. I'll let you both walk out of here, this guy will put you in the ground."

Sarah was looking from one man to the other, uncertainty creeping into her eyes.

"Where's your backup?" Sarah asked. "That was you in the gray car back at Wilston Street, right? You had to have followed us from there. Why wait until now to come down here?"

Costigane ignored her and looked back at Gage, perhaps realizing he had made a mistake by not firing as soon as he had Gage in his sights. Police training dies hard, I guess, even if you're not exactly a shining example of the profession.

"Put the gun down, you son of a bitch!"

I held my breath. This situation was about three seconds from one of them pulling a trigger, and I was too far from either one of them to do anything but get shot. My eyes met Sarah's. She knew it too.

The click of the Beretta being cocked echoed through the wide concrete tube. No one moved. Gage and Costigane tensed, but kept their eyes on each other. Carol broke the silence after a second.

"I think both of you should put your guns down."

I smiled. Carol had negotiated the fence with far greater stealth than Costigane. I hadn't even heard her approach.

She circled around toward me and Sarah, keeping both of the men within range. She stopped within a couple of feet of the bag. I could sense her fighting the urge to look down at the prize that had slipped from her grasp once already.

"I'm a cop," Costigane said from between gritted teeth. He knew the situation was spiraling out of his control, and he was not enjoying the experience. "Both of you put your fucking guns down."

Gage's eyes flicked to Carol. In that second, Costigane's gun exploded. Things seemed to slow down. Gage grunted in pain and returned fire. I saw Sarah dive for the ground and cover her head with her cuffed hands. Costigane fell back behind the old refrigerator as Carol cursed and dived toward the wall. She needn't have bothered. Gage was firing in one direction: at Costigane. He had been hit, but he was fit enough to fire six shots at Costigane's position.

I kept my head down. There was a lull and I heard a scuff and then quick footsteps. I saw Carol running into the darkness, holding the bag. "No," I shouted, "they'll kill you!"

As if to reinforce the point, Costigane looked from behind the refrigerator and fired three shots after Carol, forgetting about Gage. Gage hadn't forgotten about him. He fired back at Costigane, but the wound had obviously messed up his aim. Both shots went wide: one into the back of the refrigerator, one smacked into the wall of the tunnel. Costigane ducked behind cover again as Gage moved backwards down the tunnel, firing another couple of cover shots over our heads as he headed after Carol.

I knew Gage would have explored the territory in advance: he would know this section of the tunnel system. If he caught up with Carol, she would be no match for him. But I had my own problems to deal with first.

Costigane got to his feet cautiously and approached me. Sarah was still hunched over at the far side of the tunnel. I could see her moving, so I knew she was okay. He seemed to have forgotten all about her, or maybe he just remembered her hands were cuffed. Costigane was out of breath. He was pointing his gun at me, his badge held up in his other hand.

"Why the hell didn't you help me, asshole? I had him."

I kept my hands up and didn't respond, thinking about what Gage had said, and more importantly what Sarah had said, and how it matched up with his actions since arriving on the scene. He put his badge back into his pocket and reached to his belt for a set of handcuffs.

"You're under arrest. But first we're going after your friends."

He kept the gun on me and stepped closer, the cuffs in his left hand. He held the cuffs up and waved them at my hands. Slowly I lowered them, brought them together in the correct pose, wrists up. When Costigane glanced down at them, I winked at Sarah, hoping she would get the message.

"Oh my God, look out!" she yelled.

It was utterly convincing, and so loud in the confined space that Costigane could not ignore it. His head turned for a split second, and that was enough.

I flipped my hands from the cuffs position and cupped them around his gun hand, forcing it upwards as he pulled the trigger. The gun discharged, deafeningly at close quarters, but the bullet passed harmlessly over my head and into the ceiling. Costigane tried to wrestle the gun back using his other hand, but he hadn't had time to drop the cuffs, and they got in the way. I changed my grip, yanked the gun out of his hand with my left and slammed a short, jabbing right into the middle of his face. I felt his nose break like balsa wood. He swung his now-empty right hand around, turning it into a fist. The swing was wild, a reaction to the sudden pain. I batted it aside with my left forearm. I slammed the butt of the gun into the underside of his jaw. He staggered backwards from the impact, his eyes rolling up in his head. He looked like he needed a little more encouragement, so I hit him again, hard in the middle of his face. His knees buckled and he dropped face first into the trickle of water running down the center of the tunnel. The set of handcuffs rattled off the concrete as it bounced loose from the fingers of his left hand.

I shook the ache out of my fingers and knelt down next to him. Every atom of my being wanted to charge down the tunnel after Carol and Gage, but I knew I couldn't take the chance of Costigane recovering and following me. I could still hear footsteps from deeper into the tunnels, hushed chatter. Only it sounded like more than two people. Our little fracas seemed to have attracted some attention.

I grabbed Costigane's wrists and brought them together around his back, snapping the cuffs on over them. Sarah came over to us, slightly unsteady on her feet, as though she was walking away from a car crash.

There was a key ring on Costigane's belt with a handcuff key on it. I ripped it free of his belt loop and fitted it into the slot on Sarah's cuffs, grateful Gage hadn't used a non-standard set. I twisted the key and the lock clicked open.

"That looked ... painful," Sarah said.

I flexed my fingers again. Nothing felt broken. "I'm fine."

"I wasn't talking about you."

68

Gage tucked the gun into his belt and gripped his bloody shoulder for a moment; the additional pain brought out blossoms of stars in his vision. He had chosen the location well. Unlike everyone else, he knew where all the exits were.

As he had anticipated, Carol had taken the wider tunnel. He knew she was just ahead around the turn. She was moving quietly, but she couldn't do anything about her quickened breathing. He had had some time to enhance his knowledge of the tunnels while he waited for Blake. Carol's luck seemed to be holding. She had chosen well; was headed for the nearest of three potential exits he had identified. But that meant in another couple of seconds, her hands would be occupied. He stopped and listened. From farther back, he heard the sounds of a struggle, and then a gunshot. Costigane taking care of Blake, or vice versa, he guessed. It didn't matter, he had too much of a head start on them. It was just him and Carol. He heard other sounds too: people moving around, disturbed by the noises. Low, scared whispers. *The community*, as Kevin had called them on Gage's first trip to the underworld.

Finally, closer to him, he heard the sound he had been waiting for. The soft clapping noise of palms wrapping around steel rungs, and an answering tap as feet joined them on the lower rungs.

Gage stepped around the corner and through the circular mouth of the tunnel into the wider shaft. Rungs bolted to the wall led up into a narrow shaft in the tunnel ceiling. He cleared his throat and stepped forward. A small amount of light was coming in through the gaps around the hatch at the top of the shaft. Carol was about fifteen feet up the ladder, her gun tucked into the back of her belt, and both of her hands gripping the rungs. The backpack hung around her shoulders. She stopped and looked back and down to see him training the gun at the small of her back. He couldn't see her expression, only a slight slump in her posture as she realized she had made a critical mistake.

"Nice try."

Carol let out a sigh and started to descend.

Gage told her to stop, and to remove the gun with her left hand and drop it. She did so, and it dropped straight down and clattered to the floor. The sound of the metal on concrete echoed in the shaft. Gage picked it up and put it in his pocket. She climbed down the rest of the rungs and dropped the pack. The two of them stared at each other for a moment, both of them understanding that this was it; it was over.

"Where are Sarah and Blake?"

"Dealing with Grant. Costigane, whatever his goddamn name is."

"Who is he, anyway?"

"A dirty cop. One of Walter's men. A pain in the ass for all of us."

"Walter hired you too, then," she said. "How much is he paying you?"

Despite the pain in his shoulder, he smiled. "Not enough for me to give him these back."

Gage picked the bag up with his left hand, keeping the gun on Carol. He realized he couldn't leave her down here. Not alive, anyway. Climbing that ladder was going to be a big ask with a shot shoulder, and he knew better than to turn his back on this woman.

Carol sighed. "I don't suppose we can make a deal."

Gage stepped forward. He felt a tug of sadness as he shook his head.

He raised his gun and pointed it at the center of Carol's forehead. Her eyes widened as she realized that this, finally, was the end of the road.

69

The key clicked home and Sarah's cuffs sprang open. "Are you okay?" I asked. My own words sounded like they were coming from far away, after the loud gunfire in a confined space.

"Yeah," she replied, her voice only a little shaky. "You?"

I gave myself another look over, just to make sure. "No new perforations, thank you."

She smiled, and then her face changed in the dim light from the phone as something occurred to her. "Where's Carol?"

Before I could answer, three more shots rang out from deeper in the tunnels. I froze. Gage had found her.

70

Gage was already squeezing the trigger when something took the breath out of his lungs.

Someone moving fast had slammed him against the side of the tunnel wall. Not someone, more than one someone. Three guys at least. No, five or six. More. He struggled, pushed two bodies back hard, and then more swarmed him.

"Take him down!"

He heard yelled curses, fingers around his hand and on his gun. He turned the gun and fired, the muzzle flash lighting up hands and eyes and teeth. He wanted to tell them to keep back, explain to them that this was no damsel in distress, and none of their damn business. But it was too late for that, because he had already killed one of them.

Still more figures joined the fray. The stench of unwashed skin and moldy clothing and cheap wine filled his nostrils. He tried to pull the trigger again and felt the gun being pulled from his grasp. Fingers clutched at his shoulder, digging into the wound and making him scream out in pain. Other hands gripped at the backpack and tugged it. He gripped it harder and harder as the blows rained down on him. It felt like being at the bottom of a football scrum. And then the world lit up again once, twice. He saw dirty faces, yellow teeth. Before he felt the pain in his abdomen, he realized his own gun had been used against him. As he felt the burning pain in his chest, he heard a rip as the canvas of the backpack gave way, and then a sound like a hundred windows breaking.

71

The acoustics of the tunnels made it impossible to get a read on how far away the gunshots were. I started down the tunnel in the direction of the noise and stopped when I saw Sarah was following me.

I opened my mouth to warn her, but she got in first.

"Let me guess: 'too dangerous.' Are you kidding me? Like staying put down here is safe?"

She had a point. I activated the flashlight app on my phone and lit up our immediate surroundings. I handed the phone to Sarah.

I led the way, gripping Costigane's gun as we approached each corner. A minute or two after the gunshots, Sarah flinched as we heard a sudden, sharp clang, as though someone had dropped a heavy piece of metal. The sound came from ahead of us. We were going in the right direction. I heard approaching footsteps and a shape emerged from the darkness into the beam of our flashlight. The figure froze as he saw my gun and I saw it wasn't Carol or Gage.

It was an old homeless man, dressed in a ripped Houston Rockets basketball jersey and a wool hat. He had a straggly beard and was cupping something in his hands.

"Don't shoot, man. I'm a Christian."

"I'm not going to hurt you," I said. "Anybody back there?"

"I'm a good Christian," he repeated. "Don't want no trouble." He blinked twice and took a nervous step forward, clutching his burden to his chest. I waved him on his way. With a look of intense relief, he stepped out of the flashlight beam and disappeared back into the comfort of the darkness.

A minute after that, we came upon a fork in the tunnel. The main shaft continued ahead, and a smaller, circular tunnel led off into even greater darkness. I heard more movement all around us, and wondered if all of the denizens of the tunnel were as harmless as the good Christian we had encountered.

"What do you think?" Sarah whispered.

She cast the beam of the flashlight around inside the smaller tunnel. It extended for twenty feet before curving off to the left. I stepped into the tunnel and moved along about ten feet. I was approaching the bend when I heard it.

A quiet, rasping noise. You could almost have mistaken it for someone sleeping, snoring softly.

I exchanged a glance with Sarah. She motioned for me to go ahead, not arguing about waiting this time. I saw that the tunnel extended another forty feet or so before terminating. I could see a little farther than the field of the flashlight's beam should have allowed me to. I turned the light off and the passage around us was plunged into black again. I could still see a very faint light at the far end. A way out? I felt Sarah's fingers grip my upper arm.

"Be careful," she whispered, so softly that I barely heard it.

I gripped the gun and held my breath, following the curve around until it straightened out. As my eyes readjusted, I could make out the circular opening at the far end of the tunnel: a shape of slightly less-dark darkness. The raspy snoring sound was closer. I forced myself to go slow, to keep my footsteps as soft as possible on the molded concrete. I tried not to think about exactly what, or who, was ahead of me. Instead, I was thinking about reading *Tom Sawyer* as a kid. About Injun Joe, sealed up in the caves, found dead among the remains of the candles he had eaten. That detail about the candles had stayed with me. Maybe that was why I had never liked being underground.

I felt a chill as I saw a body lying face down ahead of me. Slight build, with long hair. As I got closer I realized it was a man. Another homeless man, by the looks of his hair and clothing. I reached the mouth of the tunnel and saw another body slumped against one wall in the murky light. I held my position, made my eyes work to discern if there was anyone else in the space at the end of the tunnel.

It was like trying to teach my eyes how to see again, translating the vaguest sensory input into a sense of the space in front of me. It was the bottom of a shaft, about fifteen feet square. Irregularities in the far wall arranged themselves into a meaningful pattern after a few seconds: steel rungs bolted into the concrete. A ladder. The floor was clear apart from the body. I turned my gaze upwards and saw the rungs led up the shaft, which was thirty or forty feet high. It got lighter toward the top. I stepped fully into the space and saw a razor-thin square of bright light at the top of the shaft; the source of the faint illumination down here. A closed hatch, or manhole. Someone had opened and closed it recently, explaining the clang we had heard a little while after the gunshots.

Steeling myself, I turned my attention to the body on the ground. I knew I was alone now, so there was no harm in turning the flashlight on once more.

To my surprise, I felt no sense of relief when I saw that the figure on the ground was Trenton Gage. The shoulder wound he had taken earlier had bled profusely, covering the sleeve of his shirt. There were more wounds to go with it in his chest. I swept the beam around and saw the ripped tattered remains of the canvas backpack and the diamond case smashed open on the floor, and knew at once what the

Christian had been carrying. I wondered where the rest had gone. I saw the gun lying by Gage's outstretched hand.

As I knelt down to pick up the gun, Gage spoke.

"Looking ... fr your ... girlfriend?"

He was still alive, just. And having great difficulty getting the words out.

I crouched down on one knee and looked into his half-shut eyes.

"She's not my girlfriend."

I shifted my gaze down and examined the bullet wounds in his chest. He had lost a lot of blood. He wasn't leaving this place.

"Not ... good ..." Gage rasped. His chest was rising and falling with what looked like an immense effort. It would flutter up and down quickly, and then stay still for moments, as though he was holding his breath.

I shook my head, agreeing with his assessment.

I glanced upwards, estimating that it would take me at least a couple of minutes to scale the ladder. Carol had a big head start.

"Where's she going?" I wasn't really sure why I asked.

Gage's lips pulled into a half-smile. He winced, as though it caused him additional pain. I could see pink foam at the corners of his mouth.

"That's ... sixty-four-thous'n ... quesshun."

His eyes took on a look of sadness as he said that, as though he were mourning for someone else. He moved his head slightly so he could look down at the gun. I tensed, ready to kick it out of his reach, and then relaxed when I saw he was just contemplating it like an artefact from some long-ago life.

"Can't ... complain," he said, and then coughed weakly. "That's ... way it ... goes."

I heard an intake of breath from behind me and looked back to see Sarah. I had forgotten all about her. She had a hand over her mouth as she surveyed the scene.

"Is he?"

I turned back to Gage again and saw that he was. He had died in the time it took me to look back at Sarah. His eyes were still open, but the rasping noise had stopped, finally.

I was still holding on to Costigane's gun. I tucked it into my belt. The square of illumination burned away, forty feet above us. Sarah looked down at Gage's body, and then at me, and then up at the square of light.

I let her go first and followed when she had scaled the first half-dozen rungs. My arms were aching by the time Sarah reached the top. With a pained grunt, she managed to push the manhole cover open, letting the sunlight flood down on us.

72

We emerged at a strip of derelict land adjacent to a freeway overpass. Sarah climbed up the verge for a better view, oriented herself by the Stratosphere Tower and worked out that using surface roads, we were about a mile and a half from the place where we had entered the tunnels. By the time we made it back there, Costigane had gone. There was a bloodstain on the floor where he had lain, and intermittent drops heading back outside. No way he had scaled the fence with both hands behind his back, so he must have managed to signal someone for help. He was still a cop, of course.

We found no trace of Carol's car, and the cell phone she

had been using was switched off. I knew she would have dumped it somewhere as soon as she left the tunnels.

Sarah called her cop friend Kubler and he sent a car to pick us up. It took us to the headquarters of the Las Vegas Metropolitan Police Department on South MLK Boulevard. Sarah hadn't been exaggerating about him being high up in the department. He held the rank of Undersheriff, which was one below the big cheese. I became even more appreciative of what he had done for us so far, and how effectively he had kept his contributions to our search quiet.

Sarah told Kubler about what had happened in the five days since she had found Carol's notebook. We told him almost everything: her neighbors' connection to the Ellison heist, Walter and his men, Gage, Costigane, the diamonds. There was no point keeping much of it back. We didn't know where Carol had gone, and by the looks of things, the Ellison diamonds had been equitably distributed among Las Vegas's homeless population.

Kubler didn't take as much convincing as I had expected. He made a couple of calls to some of his people, and nobody told him they were too busy right now. Costigane proved easy to find. It turned out he had managed to get out of the tunnel before collapsing with a concussion by the fence. A public-spirited passer-by called an ambulance and made sure he got to Desert Springs Hospital, where he was under sedation when his colleagues arrived to arrest him. By the time he regained consciousness, they had enough evidence from his apartment and his personal cell phone to raise some very serious questions about his conduct over the past few weeks, and his investigation of the Ellison heist. It looked like the man Carol had mentioned, the one who had planned the operation, had reached out to Costigane as the lead investigator on the case and convinced this gamekeeper to turn poacher. It was an ignominious end to a solid thirty-year career. I thought about all of the people who had been consumed by a kind of insanity when it came to the diamonds.

As for the diamonds themselves, the CSI team processing the tunnels and the bodies of Gage and the unidentified homeless man found only two of the stones from the case. There was no trace of the rest. Or of the woman who had lived at 32 West Pine Avenue under the name Rebecca Smith. When Kubler asked what we knew about her, we told him some of the names she had used, but that we couldn't be sure if any of them were real. Sarah exchanged a meaningful glance at me as Kubler looked away.

By the time the police told Sarah it was okay to go home, it was late evening. I drove her the ten miles back to Summerlin. We passed most of the journey in silence. We had come a long way together over the past three days, but it seemed like we had wound up with more questions than we started out with. Sarah suggested we stop and get coffee at a place on the outskirts of Summerlin. I pulled into the parking lot and we went inside, took a booth and ordered.

"I bet you wish I had never sent that damn email," Sarah said. "Seems like nothing good came of it."

"Who can say?" I said. I had been wondering about that myself. Maybe we had saved Carol's life a couple of times, allowed her to get away. On the other hand, maybe she wouldn't have needed us to save her.

"Well at least I know one thing. I know Carol will be okay." She said it like it was a grim joke. She gazed out at the parking lot. The landscape was flat, and the stars were shining brightly in the clear sky above the Spring Mountains. "I was so worried about her. Now ... part of me is mad at her, part of me is relieved. I don't know what to feel right now."

I didn't have anything to add to that, so I just sipped my coffee. It was hot and strong, just what I needed. My stomach rumbled appreciatively as the liquid hit it, and I realized this was the first food or drink that had passed my lips in hours besides the water I had drunk at the police station.

Sarah added some milk to her own coffee and gave it a little stir with the spoon, studying the whorl of milk as it spun around in the cup like a miniature galaxy. She raised her eyes to look at me. "How about you?"

"What about me?"

"Are you okay? I know you wanted to find her, make sure she was safe. I guess this wasn't what you were expecting either."

"Always assume trouble," I said. "Maybe I should try listening to my own advice."

She smiled. "Was it worth it? Finding her at last?"

I thought about it and realized that Sarah was proceeding from a false assumption. We hadn't found her. We had tracked down a person who looked like the one Sarah knew as a neighbor, the person I had loved six years ago, and yet we had both found somebody else.

"I don't know," I said at last. "I think ..." I stopped and tried to form the thought into words. "I think some people you can't find."

She thought about that for a second, and then looked away from me, in the direction of the window in the wall dividing the restaurant from the kitchen. A few plates were awaiting an available waiter under the heat lamps.

"The steaks are good here," she said. "You want to have dinner?"

I was grateful for the change of subject. I put the big questions of love and loss and human nature out of my mind and turned my attention toward the here and now and two of the rare things in the world that were knowable and constant: good food and good company.

"Why not?"

EPILOGUE

TWO MONTHS LATER
TRONCONES, MEXICO

The woman with short blonde hair who now called herself Alexandra Loomis smiled at the receptionist as she passed through the tiled foyer of the Casa Negra hotel.

She walked along the beach, savoring the warmth of the sun on her face and staring out at the kids playing on the beach, and the blue expanse of the Pacific beyond. She liked to be close to the water. Perhaps it was all that time she had spent in the last few years so far away from the ocean. She had hated Vegas and its suburbs. Arizona too. The arid desert climate had always made her feel hemmed in. By contrast, the deep blue sea seemed to represent the possibilities of an uncharted future.

She thought occasionally of the people she had left behind. After the initial adrenaline of her escape from Las Vegas had subsided, she had found she missed Dom more than she expected to. He had been a crook and a loser, and he had been more than capable of being a jerk at times, but he had really loved her. His fate had been of his own making, but she felt a little responsibility regardless. She could have talked him out of the Ellison job. She was good at talking people in or out of things. When the time came to commit, she had wanted to do it as much as he had.

Sarah, she still felt guilty about. Sarah had been the one bright spot of that difficult period in Summerlin, during which she had made the decision to gamble the relatively safe life she had built up for herself on a new start. She might have gone insane biding her time in that boring little house, waiting for the other shoe to drop, without her daily conversations with Sarah. She wondered if Sarah believed that it had all been an act; just a way to blend in and keep tabs on the neighborhood gossip. She hoped not.

The other person who occupied her thoughts lately was no stranger to them. She had spent so long being angry with him, and when they had finally met again, she had felt ... differently. She was sure he felt differently about her, too. Although she knew she had the means to contact him, to break the glass, she had not done so. She wondered where he was now, what he was doing.

She took her usual table in the café she visited every Friday morning. It had an unobstructed view of the beach and the ocean. Felipe, the manager, spotted her and smiled. He held up one finger to say "one minute."

She sat down and saw that somebody had left a copy of today's newspaper on the table. Something of a novelty, these days. She glanced at the headline story, something about a double murder in Lázaro Cárdenas, the big city along the coast. Related to the drug wars, by the looks of things, as most outbreaks of violence were down here. She raised an eyebrow when she saw that the victims had been two American men. She scanned the story. Her Spanish was improving, but it still took her a while to process the words. And then she felt a jolt as a familiar name passed before her eyes. Disgraced former Las Vegas police detective Raymond

Costigane and another man named Walter Donald Beck, who was a Nevada businessman strongly rumored to have ties to the underworld.

She felt a shiver and looked around. Nothing had changed in her immediate surroundings. The Australian family in the corner was still bickering good-naturedly over what to order for breakfast. Actually, it was closer to lunchtime, which would make it *Almuerzo*. The kids on the beach were happily building sand castles.

"The usual?"

She looked up at the smiling face of Felipe, who had appeared at the table.

"What?"

"Huevos Rancheros, toast, orange juice, right?"

Her brow creased. "Actually, all of a sudden I don't feel so hungry, I think I'll—"

She had turned her eyes toward the door and stopped as she saw someone new had entered. The man was wearing jeans and a white cotton shirt with the sleeves loosely rolled up. His green eyes were concealed behind sunglasses, but she knew he was looking straight at her. She stared back at him, and Felipe followed her gaze.

"Friend of yours?"

She broke the stare and looked back at Felipe. "On second thoughts, just bring us two black coffees. Thank you."

He took another look at the man, nodded, and moved away.

Carter Blake crossed the floor and took the chair opposite her. He removed his glasses.

They just looked at each other in silence for a minute. She reached for the newspaper and slapped it down on the table, turning it around so that he could read the headline.

"What do you know about this?"

Blake's eyes didn't move from hers. He didn't even glance at the newspaper.

"Some nasty business with the cartels, from what I hear. Seems like somebody got the idea these two were down here trying to muscle in on the Sinaloa's action."

"And how did they get that idea, I wonder?"

"Beats me. I don't think Mr. Costigane and his friend will be missed, do you?"

She shook her head, allowing herself a little smile. "I suppose I should thank you."

Blake looked innocent. "For what?"

The coffee arrived and she tried to ignore the fact that it felt good to see him. Her relationship with him six and a half years ago had turned her life upside down. She had left everything and everybody she knew behind. She had hidden herself away in the darkest corners of the country, always looking over her shoulder, until hiding became as natural as breathing. That chance meeting in New York City had set her on the path to where she was today. She wasn't entirely sure how she felt about that.

"I know you didn't just come here for my benefit," she said. "You couldn't help yourself. You don't like to lose."

"I have no idea what you're talking about," Blake said. "I decided it had been too long since I had taken a vacation south of the border. Got here today and by coincidence, I see an old friend. Small world, isn't it?"

"Sometimes a little too small," she agreed. "I wouldn't have let Costigane get near me, you know that. You know I can take care of myself."

He took a sip of his coffee. "I thought so. But better safe than sorry. Costigane jumped bail and disappeared. I thought it would be worthwhile having a look for him, but now he's dead I don't think you'll have anything to worry about. Assuming you're careful."

"I'm always careful," she said.

Blake stared at her and then nodded. "Good."

"So are you in town long? On this ... vacation?"

"Not long. I'm leaving this afternoon, in fact."

"I'm sorry," she said after a minute.

"What for?"

"For what happened in Vegas. I know I left you and Sarah in danger, and nothing I can say will make up for that."

"It wasn't all your fault."

"Maybe. Like it wasn't all your fault back in New York. God, I was so angry with you for years."

"And now?"

"Not as angry."

Blake smiled. "This isn't exactly how I thought it would go, if I ever saw you again."

"That makes two of us."

Something about him had changed since New York, and it wasn't just his name. It wasn't a good or a bad thing, it just was. All of a sudden, she was put in mind of that Ancient Greek aphorism, about how no man steps into the same river twice. Perhaps no one ever meets the same person twice, either.

They sat in comfortable silence for a minute, and her thoughts turned to her next destination. Blake was probably right: with Costigane and his partner dead, there was no one alive who knew where the rest of the Ellison diamonds had wound up. But it wouldn't do to be complacent. Her next move had to be far from here. That was okay, though. The diamonds she had emerged from the tunnels with had eventually netted her a nice return from the fence in Juarez. Not two million dollars, but enough to buy a lot of possibilities in places like this. She could make those plans later. For now, there was just the two of them, and the ocean, and another morning of clear blue skies and white sandy beaches.

"How long do you have before you have to go?"

Blake seemed to consider the question carefully. "A little while."

She reached her hand across the table. "Carter Blake, right?"

He took her hand. "Right."

"Alexandra Loomis, nice to meet you. Would you like to take a walk on the beach?"

Blake turned from her and looked out at the expanse of sand and the Pacific beyond. When he turned around again, there was a trace of amusement in his green eyes.

"I'd like that."

Dear Reader,

I'm really excited to share my latest book with you. If you're not familiar with Carter Blake, then this is a great place to start. I've so enjoyed building his character and seeing it develop over the series. He's come a long way from his days working for Winterlong (my last book, *The Time to Kill*, will give you an idea of what I mean by that ...) and he's taking a break from his career as man-hunter. But the break doesn't last long. When he recognises that the woman he once loved is in danger, there's no question about what he will do – he has to go after her.

In the book, you'll see Blake trying to find someone who doesn't want to be found, discovering that there's more to the case than meets the eye. So far, so familiar. But while, in the past, Blake has been a coldly efficient professional, doing what he does and not getting too invested in his targets, in this book, he's emotionally involved, big time. The mystery in *Don't Look For Me* isn't a whodunit. It's the characters themselves – Blake learns more than he bargained for about his former love, Carol, and even about himself. I had a lot of fun taking Blake way out of his comfort zone and putting him in some situations he's ill-equipped to handle.

If you're new to Carter Blake, I hope you go back and read the earlier novels – they are all out in paperback now. You can read each book as a standalone, but there are little rewards and Easter eggs for regular visitors to the series. And I'd love to hear when you find these. Or just what you thought of the books. If you want to get in touch you can go via my website, or tweet me @MasonCrossBooks. Or you could sign up for my Readers Club (http://masoncross.net/readers-club) and hear straightaway when a new Carter Blake book hits the shelves, as well as getting access to exclusives and competitions. You can opt out at any time, and I promise not to send you endless amounts of spam. You'll only hear from me when I have something interesting to say.

Thanks for reading. Carter Blake will be back soon, and I hope you will too.

Mason Cross

Carter Blake will return in

MASON CROSS

PRESUMED DEAD

SO WHY ARE THEY
CONVINCED
SHE'S STILL ALIVE?

THEN

Adeline Connor was the Devil Mountain Killer's final victim.
After she was gunned down, the murderer disappeared and the
killing spree ended.

NOW

Carter Blake has been hired to do what he does best: to find
someone. But this time he's hunting a dead girl – Adeline
Connor's brother is convinced she's still alive.

But this town doesn't want an outsider digging up old business.
And as Blake gets deeper into the case, it starts to become clear
that the murders didn't just stop fifteen years ago.

The killer is on the hunt again.

Enjoy an early extract from this incredible thriller now.

APRIL 6, 2004

It was raining again, but not like it had rained on the night she had last seen her father.

This was merely a moderate downpour. Nothing that would flood the low part of the south road, or make the river burst its banks; both of which had happened over the winter. She sat in the easy chair by the window and watched as the rain fell through the branches of the big oak tree and splashed in the puddles in the yard. From the living room window, she could see all the way down the hill. She saw the lights of the car two minutes before it got close enough to be sure that it was a sheriff's department vehicle.

She heard the creak of a floorboard and turned to see her mother standing in the doorway. She was staring out of the window as the blue-and-white patrol car reached their house and stopped. Her hand was pressed against her chest, her eyes wide.

Her mother didn't look at her. She turned back to the window, in time to see the sheriff and one of his men get out, fitting their hats on and hunching over in their black rain-coats. They approached the door with expressions darker than the late afternoon sky. Time seemed to be suspended in the gap between the car doors closing and the inevitable ring of the doorbell.

Her mother's voice was almost inaudible. She had known this was coming for five months. She was resigned to it now. It didn't make it any easier to hear.

"They found him."

Thursday

1

CARTER BLAKE

After the service, most of the mourners moved on to the gathering at Betty's house. I hung back, watching as the crowd shuffled away from her graveside. I found a spot by a tall pine tree that was far enough from any of the knots of people hugging or smoking that I wouldn't get drawn into a conversation. A white-haired man in a rumpled black suit who looked to be in his early eighties squinted at me over the rims of his glasses. He stared at me for a few seconds before shaking his head and moving on. I didn't know him, but maybe he had seen me around in the old days.

I bowed my head, which made me fit in just fine in the circumstances, and everyone else filed past without comment. I recognized a few faces: all of them older and sadder. Nobody I felt like talking to, in particular. And then I saw a familiar face. Karen Day's mother, Lauren. She looked in good health.

I hadn't been back to Ravenwood in more than twenty years. I hadn't thought much about the place in almost as long. Only one thing could have brought me back, and unfortunately that one thing had happened. I didn't intend to linger: just stay long enough to pay my respects. But it was a crisp and cloudless late November day, and I felt an unexpected urge to hang around a little longer. Perhaps it was the funeral, perhaps it was being back in a place I had put down roots, once upon a time.

I was parked a couple of streets down from the church, and I took a circuitous route back to the car, partly to avoid the crowds, partly because it would take me past the house where I used to live.

Forty-two Hemlock Road was still there, though I knew Betty had long since moved to the small apartment where she died. The house had weathered the years well. The lawn was neatly kept, the paint job looked fresh. A shiny red kids' bicycle was lying on its side at the line where the grass met the sidewalk, its owner clearly having no cause to worry about passing thieves. There was a love seat hanging from the lilac tree out in the front yard – a new addition. When I looked closer, I could just make out a frayed, gray loop of rope curled around the thickest branch, from the tire swing I had hung there a lifetime ago. I wondered if I was the only one of Betty's kids to come back for the funeral. It had been pure chance I had happened to read about her passing. I guessed the rest of them were out there somewhere. I had never formed any lasting friendships with any of the others she fostered. The only person I ever occasionally thought about from my Ravenwood days was Karen Day – the lost girl.

I took a last look at the house and headed back down the hill toward Main Street. I was passing Dino's Diner, reaching into my pockets for the car keys when I heard a name being called. A name I hadn't gone by in twenty years.

I turned and saw Karen Day's mother, standing in the doorway of Dino's, holding the door open. Lauren Day had to be in her mid-sixties by now, but was wearing it well. Her brown hair showed only a few streaks of gray. She was slim and had a narrow face, only a few lines around her green eyes. She was dressed for the occasion. Dark pants, black shoes and a white blouse. No coat, so I guessed she had come out of the diner just to see me. I turned and retraced my steps. I hesitated over the appropriate greeting then she pulled me in for a hug, kissing me lightly on the cheek.

"I thought that was you," she said. "Are you staying in town?"

I shook my head. "Just here for the funeral."

"It was a lovely service," she said. "People always say that, though, don't they?"

She was still holding the door open. "Do you have time to get a coffee?"

I hesitated, but made my mind up when I saw the hope in her eyes. What harm could it do?

We went inside and sat down in a booth by the window and I ordered a black coffee. Lauren already had a full cup of Earl Grey in front of her.

"It was good of you to come. We tried to get in touch with all of the kids, but ..."

"Hard to find some people," I said. "I saw the obituary in the *Times*."

It had been the first time I had picked up a physical newspaper in months. The previous customer had left it on the table at one of my regular breakfast places.

She smiled. "Betty wouldn't have minded. It was enough for her to know she had made some kind of difference."

"Dino isn't around anymore, huh?" I observed as my coffee was delivered by a teenager with a buzzcut and a preoccupied expression. Dino – a short, rotund guy with not much hair and even less regard for service with a smile. The diner was open seven days a week, seven a.m. till nine p.m., and if he took a day off, I never knew about it.

She shook her head. "Heart attack. Ten years ago, maybe."

I wasn't surprised. "You look well," I said.

She waved away the compliment. "You're seeing me at my most presentable, dear. Weddings and funerals. So, what do you do now? Somebody said you had joined the military?"

"That was a long time ago," I said. "I work for myself now."

"Doing what?"

"Consultancy. The work varies."

"My, that's awfully vague."

I smiled. "I look for people. Usually they're the sort of people who don't want to be found. How about you?"

She took a breath and hesitated a second. "Actually, I look for people too. I've been doing what I do for a lot of years. I started it up after what happened to Karen, figured I would get the ball rolling, but it's just grown and grown."

Karen Day had been in the year above me in high school. She was tall, and had her mother's brown hair and eyes. We were friends, but not close friends. Then again, none of my friends had been all that close.

She had gone missing on the night of May 25, 1995. She had been working at the Esso station on the edge of town and left at eleven, after closing up. Nobody ever saw her alive again. Over the course of that long, hot summer, we searched for her. There were six hundred acres of woods separating Ravenwood from the next town. At first, we had teams of volunteers out there, all of us reassuring each other she would be found safe and well. The whole town searched for weeks. Gradually, it set in that if we found anything it would be a body. Little by little, the volunteers found other commitments, until there were only a few of us. The first big storm of the fall brought her back. The coroner speculated that her killer had trapped her body under water, and that was how her corpse ended up on the riverbank. She had been dead for months, probably since the night she disappeared. Her killer was never found.

"It's called the Missing Foundation," Lauren continued. "We have staff now, a half-dozen offices across the country. We work with families of people who go missing. We eventually found Karen, but not every family is so fortunate."

Fortunate. Some would think that an odd choice of words. I didn't.

"It sounds like important work."

She nodded. "I really think so."

We looked down at our drinks in silence for a few moments. I thought about Karen. How the whole town had gone from concern to foreboding to despair. I had gone through a different cycle. Building frustration that I couldn't find her, rage when we learned her fate. I had never really forgotten those feelings. I couldn't help but admire Lauren Day. She had channeled her own grief and sense of helplessness into something worthwhile, something that touched other lives.

"Are you able to help everyone?"

She considered. "Nothing can fill the hole in these families' lives. Nothing. But in some way, we can usually help. There's this one man I've been in contact with who—"

She hesitated. I motioned for her to go on.

"Obviously, confidentiality is important, but I don't have to tell you his name. Some of our clients, we have a relationship that lasts years. This man is one of those. His sister was taken many years ago."

"Taken?"

"They never found her body, but she was one of several people who disappeared in the same area at the same time."

She didn't have to say any more. There are at least a couple of dozen serial killers operating in the United States at any given time, according to the experts. Some of them are never caught, some of their victims are never found. I have more knowledge about this subject than I would like.

"Something happened recently that was curious," she said.

I met her eyes, realizing that perhaps there was a reason she was relating this particular story about this particular client. Maybe on some level, it was the reason we were having this conversation. She needed to talk to somebody about this case.

"You have to understand," she continued, "denial is incredibly common among these families, especially in the early days. This man never really got over his sister's disappearance, but I always thought that intellectually he knew she was never coming home. Head and heart pull you in different ways, don't they?"

"What happened?"

Lauren Day looked out at the street for a long moment.

"His sister is dead. The authorities are sure of it, and deep down I believe he had accepted it too. But then something happened."

"What?"

"He says he saw his sister. Alive."

2

CARTER BLAKE

What do you know about the Devil Mountain Killer?

Lauren Day's question came back to me that evening as I turned my key in the door of the fortieth floor apartment in Battery Park City that was my home for the moment.

I switched the coffee machine on in the kitchen, took my jacket and shoes off and sat down on the couch, looking out at the view of the Hudson that was one of the main reasons I hadn't felt the urge to move on just yet.

She was good: I didn't realize I was being recruited until it was too late. Maybe she had been doing the work she was doing so long that she could identify the right skills in someone she needed to do a job.

I had told Lauren I knew the name, but not much more than that. She gave me the potted history. The Devil Mountain Killer was the moniker given to the unidentified person or persons responsible for a series of murders and disapperances in northeast Georgia fifteen years ago. A rural, sparsely populated area, not far from the course of the Appalachian Trail.

The killer had claimed at least nine victims, with more suspected, between August 2002 and October 2003. The murders attributed to him shared the same M.O.: killed by gunshots to the head from a .38 caliber pistol. The same .38 caliber pistol. The gender balance was almost even: five men and four women. There was no evidence of ante-mortem beatings or torture, no evidence of sexual assault. These were more like dispassionate executions: a double tap to the head. As far as the investigators could work out, the killings had always taken place out in the woods. Lonely stretches of highway, remote trails. The victims were hikers or hunters or drivers passing through, who must have stopped for the wrong person. The bodies were found concealed in rivers and shallow graves in the vicinity of Devil Mountain, hence the media-friendly name.

The killer was never caught. Too often, they aren't. The killings just ceased with as little explanation as they had started. People did what they always do when there's a loose end: they speculated about what had happened. Some thought he had moved on to a new hunting ground, or gone to jail for another crime, others assumed that he had killed himself. The authorities worked along the same assumptions, looking closely at anyone from the area who fell into one of those categories. There were no similar killing sprees in nearby states that matched the pattern. They found candidates for the jail or suicide explanations: one man serving time for a stabbing in a bar fight, another for holding up a liquor store, and another who had hanged himself in the first week of November of that year. The lack of evidence left behind by the killer meant that there was frustratingly little information to work with to definitively rule any of the three in or out. Both of the imprisoned men denied involvement, and the one who killed himself hadn't left a note.

Over the years, the media and the police moved on to fresher cases. It was still technically a live investigation, but the FBI had enough active murderers to catch without expending resources on the ones who were retired or dead.

On the way home, I had stopped to buy a book on the case called *Devil Mountain: State of Fear*, by a guy called William P. Heaney, along with a Rand McNally state map of Georgia. In the middle of the book were a series of pictures showing some of the locations where bodies had been discovered. There were photographs of some of the lead investigators on the case, a couple of the suspects, and family snaps of some of the victims. I was looking at one of these.

The man Lauren Day wanted me to talk to was named David Connor, and the girl in the photograph was his sister, Adeline.

The photograph in the book showed a seventeen-year-old girl. She was pictured sitting on the hood of a red car. She wore cut-off jean shorts and a T-shirt the color of claret. She had black hair and brown eyes, and wore a thin chain around her neck with a small gold crucifix attached. Adeline Connor's wasn't one of the eight bodies that had been recovered, but the cops were sure enough of her death that she had been written up as the final official victim of the Devil Mountain Killer.

Sometimes, the bodies of victims are found years or decades later. Often, they're never recovered. What doesn't happen is them showing up alive and well. Chances were good that David Connor had seen someone who looked like his sister and had been blinded by wishful thinking. Chances were also good that any attempt to find her would be a waste of time, and worse, would reopen old wounds.

I thought about it for a long time before I picked up my phone and dialed the number Lauren Day had given me, looking at the picture of Adeline Connor as the phone rang.

"Hello?" The voice was that of a relatively young man, but with a smoker's huskiness. The tone was wary. Someone who wasn't used to his phone ringing.

"Is this David Connor?"

"Who's asking?"

"Lauren Day asked me to give you a call. My name's Carter Blake."

Don't miss out on the rest of this explosive page-turner – available to order now.

ACKNOWLEDGEMENTS

The list of people who help me write a novel seems to grow with each new one I complete. First of all, thanks to my wife Laura, and the kids Ava, Scarlett and Max (the boy with many names) for both inspiring me and putting up with me as I wrestle these things into shape.

Huge thanks to my outgoing editor Jemima Forrester for helping me get this book started, and to my brand new editor Francesca Pathak for getting me across the finish line. Thanks also due to Jon Wood and Bethan Jones for helping to make the transition smooth, and their great ideas and enthusiasm for the next one. All of the fine people at Orion in fact, particularly Angela McMahon, Lauren Woosey, Laura Swainbank, Virginia Woolstencroft and Marissa Hussey.

My wonderful literary agent Luigi Bonomi, Alison Bonomi and all at LBA for generally being fantastic and always going the extra mile. A big thank you to Richard and Judy, and the team at WHSmith for the boost.

My early readers Laura Morrison, Mary Hays, James Stansfield and Eve Short. Susi Holliday for some last-minute assistance. Claiborne Hancock, Iris Blasi and everyone at Pegasus in the United States. All of my crime writer buddies, too numerous to name here but you know who you are; we have the coolest workplace in the world – see you at the bar.

All of the booksellers, bloggers, librarians and most importantly, readers – I hope you like this one, and yes, I'm working on the next Blake book already.